S0-ARB-835

For Heaven's Eyes Only

"Green continues to deliver enjoyable, fast-paced, and fun entertainment. This one is not to be missed." —SFRevu

"A thoroughly entertaining book, packed full of the usual blood and thunder which has signified the series so far. It's a perfect popcorn book, unapologetically in-your-face and quintessentially Simon R. Green in execution."
—The Green Man Review

"Clever world building, madcap characters, cheeky one-liners, and a James Bond feel make this series stand out, and a surprise ending will have readers eagerly anticipating the next Eddie Drood adventure." —Publishers Weekly

From Hell with Love

"Gripping, fast-paced, emotionally intense . . . [a] deft combination of urban fantasy adventure, sharp-edged sarcasm, and treachery upon treachery." —Publishers Weekly

"Heroes and villains strut their stuff across a worldwide stage, and the end result is something so entertaining, it's almost a guilty pleasure. The cliff-hanger pretty much guarantees readers will be back for the next in the series, but I'd come back anyway just to see what the heck happens next."
—SFRevu

"From Hell with Love is both an intelligently written novel that advances the story of the characters while telling a ripping good yarn." —The Green Man Review

The Spy Who Haunted Me

"As usual, the narrative moves at a fast clip and the sarcasm flows freely. Another action-packed melding of spy story and fantasy, featuring suave sleuthing, magical powers, and a generous dash of dry wit." —Kirkus Reviews

"Eddie gets to the bottom of things with style and a particularly cynical sense of humor. Series spinner Green's Drood books are fun, funny, and action-packed, and Eddie is one of his most entertaining creations." —Booklist

"No one delivers a story quite like [Green]. . . . I thoroughly enjoyed *The Spy Who Haunted Me*, and I'll cheerfully recommend it to anyone who wants some wide-screen, no-holds-barred, big ideas and snappy execution thereof, urban fantasy adventure." —The Green Man Review

Daemons Are Forever

"Green loves the wide-screen splash of cinematic battles against zombie hordes, and genuine traces of tragedy and nobility underlie the nonstop punning banter and pop-culture references, lending surprising nuance to this merry metaphysical romp." —*Publishers Weekly*

"A rapid-fire paranormal suspense . . . a surprisingly moving tale of self-sacrifice and hope in the midst of chaos and loss. This excellent follow-up to *The Man with the Golden Torc* will have readers applauding the reluctant hero and anxiously awaiting his further adventures." —Monsters and Critics

The Man with the Golden Torc

"Packed with enough humor, action, and plot twists to satisfy fans who prefer their adventure shaken, not stirred. . . . Readers who recognize the pun on Ian Fleming's James Bond title will find the secret agent in question has more up his sleeve than a fancy car and some high-tech gadgets." —*Publishers Weekly*

"Take some James Bond, and throw in some of Green's own Nightside, and mix liberally with the epic over-the-top action of his Deathstalker novels, and you're somewhere in the right neighborhood for describing *The Man with the Golden Torc*. It has everything one comes to expect from Green's work: distinctive characters, stylized ultraviolence, more mad ideas per page than most writers get in a lifetime, and a wild roller-coaster plot that doesn't let up."—The Green Man Review

Casino Infernale

A Secret Histories Novel

Simon R. Green

A ROC BOOK

ROC
Published by the Penguin Group
Penguin Group (USA) LLC, 375 Hudson Street,
New York, New York 10014

USA | Canada | UK | Ireland | Australia | New Zealand | India | South Africa | China
penguin.com
A Penguin Random House Company

Published by Roc, an imprint of New American Library, a division of Penguin
Group (USA) LLC. Previously published in a Roc hardcover edition.

First Roc Mass Market Printing, June 2014

 REGISTERED TRADEMARK—MARCA REGISTRADA

ISBN 978-0-451-41430-4

Printed in the United States of America
10 9 8 7 6 5 4 3 2 1

The name's Bond. Shaman Bond. The very secret agent.

They all know my name, in the back streets of London, in the shadowy places where shadowy people do all the things the everyday world isn't supposed to lust after. Shaman Bond is a face on the scene—a character, a chancer, always au fait with the very latest in sin and diversion. Always up for a little deviltry, with a taste for the illegal and the unnatural. Shaman Bond can turn up anywhere, and no one will ever be surprised. Because his type are ten a penny in the hidden life, the secret world. Not a bad man, necessarily, but always around when the bad stuff is kicking off. Sometimes he does good things, when he thinks no one's noticing. Sometimes he'll help out in a con or a sting, especially if they're designed to show the real Bad Guys the error of their ways. But really, he's just . . . around. A part of the scene. He hangs out at all the right places, with all the wrong people, smiling his crocodile smile.

The name is Eddie Drood, and only the older members of my family call me Edwin.

My family exists to stand between Humanity and all the hidden horrors that threaten it. We fight the monsters so you don't have to know they really exist. We've been doing it for centuries, and I've been trained to the work since I was a child. I'm a Drood field agent, searching out the nastier secrets of the clandestine world, and doing whatever it takes to keep the lid on. To keep the everyday world safe. I'm an agent, not an assassin. Though I have killed more than my fair share in my time. They all needed killing, but in the early hours of the morning, when the dawn seems farthest away . . . that doesn't help. When I'm out working in the field, my name is Shaman Bond. A pleasant and personable mask for me to hide behind. So people will tell him all the things Eddie Drood needs to know.

He's a nice enough guy. Just a shame he isn't real. Merely a cover story. So why do I feel so much realer being him than I do when I have to be me?

When I'm with my family, I'm Eddie Drood. When I'm out in the world, I'm Shaman Bond. But now that I've left my family because they told me one lie too many, and gone to work for the Department of the Uncanny, who am I now?

Who am I, really?

CHAPTER ONE

They Break Horses, Don't They?

'd go to the end of the world for you. I suppose we've all said that, or something like it, to the one we love. Only I really did do that, once. I should have known that the end of the world is where the lies run out, and the truth returns. And while the truth may satisfy, it's never going to be as comforting as a treasured lie.

Scotland has almost eight hundred offshore islands, though fewer than a hundred are populated. Trammell Island is the most northern, way out past the Orkneys and the Shetlands, just a jutting rock set in dark and deathly cold waters, where no one goes any more. Or at least, no one with any sense. Not a big island; you could walk round the perimeter in less than an hour. Trammell Island has a beach, a cliff face, and an ugly stone hill with a single building at its summit. Monkton Manse. The house at the end of the world. Originally a monastery many centuries ago; then a rich man's holiday home; now nothing more than a deserted property, an abandoned folly. Empty and silent, holding within dust and shadows and bad memories, and one last terrible secret.

Trammell Island: a long way from anywhere, and soon to be the end of more than one person's world.

I stood at the very top of the cliff face, as close to the edge as I could get. Dry, cracked earth crumbled and fell away under my weight, dribbling streams of dirt down the sheer rocky face and into the crashing waters far below. I looked down at the heavy swelling waves as they pounded the narrow pebbled beach and broke against the outcropping rocks. Night-dark waters, cold enough to kill anyone unfortunate enough to end up in them, they threw great clouds of frothing spume into the air as the waves fell back, frustrated, from the inhospitable shore.

A cold wind blew savagely in from the north, bitter enough to have come all the way from the North Pole. Which wasn't that far off, truth be told. I hunched my shoulders inside my heavy, padded greatcoat, thrust my gloved hands deep into my pockets, and wished I'd worn a hat like everyone suggested. I hate hats. Never found one I looked good in. I shuddered despite myself as the cold sank into my bones and Molly Metcalf thrust an arm through mine and snuggled up against me. She was wearing a long sheepskin coat with stylishly fringed sleeves, and a bobbly woollen hat pulled down over her ears. She looked like a traveller on her way to protest against something fashionably despicable.

It's hard to know what to wear when you're visiting the island at the end of the world.

Molly looked down at the bleak, empty shore and the raging waters, and smiled brightly at me.

"You take me to the nicest places, Eddie."

"Easy on the name," I said. "As far as everyone we're going to meet here is concerned, I'm just Shaman Bond. General bad boy about town. No one we'll be meeting would be at all happy to meet a Drood."

"Not many are," said Molly. "Your family might protect the world, but no one ever said the world would thank you for it. Especially given some of the tactics you use. Hey, speaking of names, I looked up Trammell in the dictionary before we left London. It's an old Scottish name for a burial shroud. Very fitting."

"So it is," I said. "More importantly, it also means an impediment to function, or a shackle for a horse."

"Smugness is very unattractive in a man," said Molly.

"Always go for the complete *Oxford English Dictionary*," I said. "Never settle for the lesser."

"You've got a dictionary built into your armour, haven't you?" said Molly accusingly.

"Look at those gulls," I said. "The only birds that will come out this far, pursuing the fishing boats. And even they've got more sense than to come anywhere near Trammell Island. Just black smudges on a grey sky . . . with the saddest cries in the world. There are those who say that seagulls cry for the sins of Humanity. And that if we ever get our act together, they'll be able to stop crying."

"You're in a mood," said Molly. "Don't you dare try to out-gloom me. I'm the only one here entitled to indulge in deep dark existential brooding. This is my past we're visiting."

"Never look back," I said wisely. "All you'll ever see are lost opportunities creeping up on you with bad intent."

"You don't have a sentimental bone in your body, do you?" said Molly.

"If I did, I'd have it surgically removed. Sentiment just gets in the way of seeing things clearly."

"Sometimes . . . that can be a good thing."

I looked at Molly, but she'd already let go my arm and turned away from the cliff edge to look steadily at the single great building at the top of the hill. Monkton Manse. An ugly building, with an ugly past. Once upon a time it was a monastery, founded by a heretic offshoot of the monks of Saint Columba. Long abandoned now, left to fall into ruin and decay. In the 1920s it was rebuilt and refurbished to resemble an old English country manor house complete with pointed gables, a slanting grey-tiled roof, protruding leaded-glass windows in a mock Tudor frontage, and a really big oaken front door. Large and solid and blocky, grim and forbidding; built to withstand Time and the bitter elements. Even though no one had lived in Monkton Manse since the late twenties, it still looked ready for visitors. In a dark and threatening sort of way.

Monkton Manse looked like it should be on the front cover of some old paperback Gothic romance, with just the one light showing in a window.

"Looks to me like the setting for some old Agatha Christie murder mystery," said Molly.

"You know I've always preferred Ngaio Marsh," I said. "She cheats less in the denouement."

"This house was the last meeting place for the old White Horse Faction," said Molly. "My parents' old group. Supernatural terrorists, or ecological freedom fighters, depending on who you listen to. I was here with them ten years ago, when they planned their last great adventure. Before your family had them all killed."

"And so, you went to war with my family," I said. "Now here we are together, you and I. Who would have thought . . ."

"The house doesn't look at all how I remember it," said Molly, frowning. "I thought it would look . . . brighter. Happier."

"Given the house's downright disturbing history, that was never on the cards," I said. "I have to ask, Molly: Given that the old White Horse Faction had their roots in English countryside Leveller traditions . . . what the hell were they doing all the way out here?"

"My parents chose this location," Molly said sternly, "because it was as far from England as they could get. Because it was one of the few places in this world where they could be sure they were free from spying eyes, very definitely including the Droods. This whole Island lies inside a natural, or perhaps more properly unnatural, mystical null. No one can see in. Trammell Island is invisible to crystal balls, remote viewing, and spy satellites. Not at all easy to get to, but worth the effort. The perfect place to plot the overthrow of all the sanctimonious, two-faced, hypocritical Powers That Be."

"We're talking about my family again, aren't we?" I said. "The Droods are like the dentist: a necessary evil. Because all the other options are worse."

"Eddie," said Molly. "Sorry, I mean Shaman. . . . Why are you still holding the Merlin Glass in your hand? Are you anticipating a hurried exit?"

I looked down. She was right. I still had the looking glass in my hand. I honestly hadn't realised. Not much to look at, at first glance. Just a simple hand mirror with a silver frame and handle. A gift to my family from the old Arthurian sorcerer himself, Merlin Satanspawn. The Glass could show you anything, anywhere, and then take you there through a dimensional short cut. It could do other things, too; some of them very disturbing.

"Is that the original Merlin Glass?" said Molly. "Or is it the one we found in the Other Hall—the other-dimensional duplicate that replaced Drood Hall for a time?"

"Other people don't have conversations like this," I said. I hefted the Merlin Glass in my hand. "The original mirror was broken during our attack on the Satanic Conspirators hiding out in Schloss Shreck, in the Timeless Moment. The Armourer did his best to repair the Glass, but even his skills are no match for that old devil Merlin. So, my uncle Jack got out the second Merlin Glass, from the Other Hall, so he could compare the two. He put the mirrors down on his work-bench, side by side, and they just . . . slid together and merged into one. So I guess this is both. And no, I don't know why I'm holding on to it. Except . . . that I really don't like this island."

Molly sniffed loudly. "We could have come here through the dimensional gate in my wild woods."

"We don't want anyone else knowing that way exists," I said firmly. "You're only safe in those woods because no one else knows how to get into them. And I need there to be somewhere I can be sure you're safe when I'm not around.

"I can look after myself," said Molly. "But you are a sweetie for saying it."

"Boyfriend brownie points?"

"Well, a tick in the plus column, at least," said Molly. She looked past the great hulking house. "There's an old fairy circle, out behind the Manse. A Fae Gate. The elves used to use it as a stepping-off point on their way to places beyond this world. I don't think anyone knows why. Elves don't talk to humans if they can help it."

"You must show it to me, after we've completed our mission here," I said. "It might explain how all the old Columbian monks came to disappear, so suddenly and completely."

"You always were big on doing your homework before a mission," said Molly. "Go on; lecture me. You know you love it. But keep it concise, or I'll heckle you and throw things."

I took a moment to stuff the Merlin Glass into my pocket. I keep a pocket dimension there, for storing weapons and dangerous objects, and things I don't want other people to detect.

"There are a lot of stories about what the heretic monks of Saint Columba got up to here, in their monastery on Trammell Island," I said. "Most of them not suitable for everyday company, or those of a nervous disposition. They established their monastery here precisely because the Island existed in a mystical null zone, and they didn't want anyone to see what they were doing."

"You know, of course," said Molly. "Droods know everything."

"Not this time," I said. "The monks just vanished, overnight. A supply boat turned up one morning to find the monastery completely deserted. No monks, no signs of a struggle or violence of any kind. Just the monastery, standing silent and empty with its front door wide open. The monks had no boat of their own, no known way off the Island. A single severed human hand was found, in the hallway, with one finger pointing at the open front door. Not a drop of blood anywhere. Interestingly enough, nothing inside the monastery had been disturbed, but every single book in the monastery's extensive and infamous library . . . was missing. Nothing left but empty shelves. So we never did find out what they were up to here . . . but given how things turned out, I doubt it was anything pleasant."

"The monks could have left through the Fae Gate," said Molly, "if they thought their enemies were closing in on them."

"Some of my ancestors explored that possibility," I said. "They were quite positive no one had activated the Gate in years. Trammell Island has a long history of dark secrets, and sudden disappearances. People came here to do things they didn't want the rest of the world to know about."

"I escaped through the Fae Gate," said Molly. "It opened onto the wild woods, and then closed again, so I could be safe."

"What?" I said. "Escaped? Escaped from what, Molly?"

"I don't know," she said, frowning. She looked suddenly confused, disoriented. "I don't remember. And I didn't even realise there was anything to remember, until just now."

She shuddered heavily, and not from the cold. Her eyes were fey and distant, her mouth pulled into a tight grimace.

"The others will be here soon," I said. Just to be saying something.

"Let's get inside the house," said Molly. "I don't like it out here. This whole island gives me the creeps."

We headed towards Monkton Manse, Molly clinging tightly to my arm again. I was disturbed, because it wasn't like Molly to be scared of anyone or anything. More usually, it was the other way round. The huge manor house loomed over us as we approached—dark and foreboding. Evening was falling fast on Trammell Island, and there were no lights on anywhere in the house. The dark windows seemed to study us like so many thoughtful eyes, planning and plotting. At least there weren't any gargoyles. I've never liked gargoyles. We stopped before the massive oak door, which was, of course, very firmly closed and locked.

"I suppose you know all about the house, as well?" said Molly, trying to keep her voice light.

"Of course," I said. "And no—there isn't a key under the flowerpot. Why don't you do a quick search for security spells, and hidden defences, while I regale you with the horrible history of Monkton Manse?"

"Way ahead of you," said Molly, rubbing her chin with a single gloved knuckle as she concentrated.

"Monkton Manse was built on the ruins of the abandoned monastery building, in 1924," I said. "Hence the name. By the first and last Lord of Trammell; otherwise known as Herbert Gregory Walliams. War profiteer, quite obscenely rich, and an utterly appalling person by all accounts. He bought Trammell Island so he could set it up as his very own independent kingdom, with him as its self-appointed lord, so he wouldn't have to pay taxes. They were still fighting that one out in the courts when he died."

"Suddenly and violently and horribly, I trust?" said Molly. "And no, I'm not picking up any defences, of any kind."

"Once again, it's hard to be sure what happened to him," I said. "He held huge parties here, in his big new home away from home. Celebrations for the rich and famous, the idle and the eccentric, and celebrities of all kinds. There were quite a lot of all of those, back in the Roaring Twenties. Desperate to show they were still having a good time, even as the world closed in on them. Sex and drugs and really hot jazz—often for days or even weeks on end. There were scandals and atrocities, murders and suicides, and abominations of all kinds. It was all building up to a really nasty exposé, involving big names from politics and business as well as high and low society . . . when once again, it all went suddenly very quiet. A boatful of policemen and journalists, and certain other interested parties, arrived at the Island to discover everyone in Monkton Manse was dead. There were signs to suggest it all happened quite recently, over one very long night. They used guns and knives and blunt instruments, and finished the slaughter with their bare hands. There were signs some of the killers had paused to feast on the flesh of the victims before continuing their bloody business. The authorities found the first and last Lord of Trammell scattered all over the house; bits and pieces of him in every room."

"I can't find a single defence, protection, or booby trap anywhere," said Molly. "Which is . . . odd. So, why did they all kill each other?"

"No one knows," I said. "Again, my ancestors investigated very thoroughly, and found nothing. Not a single answer, not even the smallest clue. I suppose it is possible the jaded partygoers went a little too far in their dabbling with the black arts . . . ventured into areas best left alone, and attracted the attention of . . . Something. Perhaps the same Something that came for the missing monks . . .

"Monkton Manse was emptied out, cleaned up, and then sealed. Left to rot and fall apart, far and far from the civilised world. Trammell Island was declared off-limits, to everyone." I looked at Molly. "And this is the place your parents brought you to? How old were you then?"

"Fifteen," said Molly. "And don't you dare judge them. It's not like they had much of a choice. It's not easy finding places in this world that the Droods can't see into. But . . . I don't remember this as a bad place. I don't remember anything but happy times here."

"In this house?" I said.

We studied the closed, locked door. "You've got a key, haven't you?" said Molly.

"Of a sort," I said.

I subvocalised the activating Words, and Drood armour slipped out of the golden collar around my neck, and ran down my right arm to form a golden glove around my hand. I pressed one gleaming finger against the heavy brass lock, and golden filaments extended from my fingertip, filling the lock and forming into just the right key. I turned the key in the lock, pulled my armour back into my torc, and pushed the door open. It swung slowly inwards, revealing a dark, shadowed hallway. The hinges groaned loudly.

"How very traditional," said Molly.

"Be fair," I said. "No one's oiled those hinges in years. You have to make allowances."

"No, I don't," said Molly. "In fact, I am famous for not making allowances. However . . . that is a very dark hallway."

I peered into the gloom. It was hard to make out anything much. "I haven't been inside yet, and already I don't like this place," I said steadily. "It feels . . . unpleasant."

"Given that this island is still hidden from the eyes of the world by its mystical null, and thus the perfect place to hide from prying eyes, I'm surprised no one else has made use of it," said Molly.

"People have tried, down the years," I said. "No one ever stays. Trammell Island has always had a really bad reputation, and I can understand why. This house is supposed to be haunted, you know."

"Who by?" said Molly.

"Take your pick," I said. "The missing monks, any number of dead partygoers, all the bits and pieces of the first and last Lord of Trammell . . ." I paused for a moment, before looking at Molly. "I have to ask—did the old White Horse Faction do . . . something bad here?"

"I don't know," said Molly. "I don't remember! But I do think that whatever happened here . . . the echoes still remain. I didn't realise how much I'd forgotten about my time here. . . ."

"Could this memory loss be connected to the death of your parents?" I said carefully. "Emotional trauma, perhaps?"

"I don't see why," Molly said immediately. "It's not like I was there, when it happened. No . . . no. This is the last place I remember being really happy. I was so happy here, with my parents."

"Aren't you happy with me?" I asked.

She shot me a quick smile. "You know I am. Stop fishing for compliments. This . . . was different."

"You had a happy childhood," I said. "I'm glad one of us did."

"It didn't last," said Molly. "Your family killed my family."

"You know I had nothing to do with that."

"Yes. I know. My love . . ."

She took hold of my hand, and held it tight. And together we walked through the open doorway, and into the long dark hall of Monkton Manse.

We didn't go far. We stopped just inside the door, and waited for our eyes to adjust to the gloom. Neither of us liked the feel of the place. The long hallway stretched away before us, its ending lost in dust-swirled air and shadows deep as the night. The silence had a heavy, oppressive quality. I called out to announce our presence, just in case, and the brooding presence of the place seemed to just swallow up my voice. There were no echoes, and nobody answered me. My vision quickly adjusted, and dim shadowy figures lining the length of the hall were revealed as suits of medieval armour. Set standing at irregular intervals, in unnatural, inhuman stances. Someone had daubed unpleasant mystical symbols on the dully gleaming steel in what looked very much like old dried blood. The steel helmets were all missing, replaced with sculpted heads of giant insects and alien monstrosities.

Dust and cobwebs were everywhere, like an attic no one had visited in years. Some light fell in muddy streams through the smeared windows, but it made little progress into the stubborn shadows. I could smell damp on the air, and musk, and mushrooms. I decided very firmly that I wasn't going to touch anything. I moved slowly forward, down the hall, with Molly moving quietly beside me. It felt like moving into enemy territory, with the threat of imminent attack from any number of unseen hiding places. Except, there was nobody home. I could tell. Just the house watching our every movement like a cat with a mouse.

Rows of portraits lined both walls, painted in any number of styles; mostly head-and-shoulder portraits of the famous names who'd visited Monkton Manse, back in the twenties. None of them were smiling. And in many of them, the paint seemed to have . . . slipped, or melted, so that the famous faces seemed strange and monstrous. Perhaps that was how they'd looked after one too many parties in this awful place. There's no hell so savage as the one we make for ourselves.

"This isn't how I remembered the house," said Molly. Her voice sounded small, and lost. "I remember it as being full of light, and life, and laughter. I don't remember any of this."

"You want me to take you out of here?" I said.

"Hell with that!" she said immediately. "I never ran from a fight in my life, and I'm not about to start now. Though whether it's a fight with this house, or my memories . . . this is weird, Shaman. I don't remember *anything* of this."

We pressed on. The portraits changed, to show all the pretty people doing things of an increasingly nasty nature . . . including sex with things that weren't in any way people. After a while I stopped looking. You can't keep on being shocked; it wears you out. I couldn't shake off a vague but definite feeling of being watched by nearby, unseen eyes. Molly stopped abruptly, and I stopped with her. She looked up at the heavy brass chandeliers overhead, still stuffed with the stumps of old candles. She snapped her fingers smartly, and all the candle stubs burst alight at once, shedding a comforting butter-yellow light down the length of the hallway. The light pressed back the shadows, but couldn't dispel them. Or do much to improve the general uncomfortable atmosphere.

Molly cried out suddenly, and pointed a shaking hand at a mirror mounted on the left-hand wall. I moved quickly forward to stand between her and whatever had alarmed her, and it was a measure of how unnerved she was that she let me do it. I glared about me, but couldn't see anything immediately threatening. I looked at Molly, and she pointed again at the mirror on the wall. I strode over to stand before it, Molly sticking close to my side. I was becoming increasingly worried about Molly. This wasn't like her. I studied the mirror carefully, ready to smash it to bits if necessary and to hell with the seven years bad luck, but nothing looked back at us except our own reflections.

It doesn't matter whether I'm being Eddie Drood or Shaman Bond, I always look like an ordinary, everyday kind of guy. Just another face in the crowd—no one you'd look at twice. Average height, average weight, the kind of nondescript features you'd forget in a moment. Best kind of look for a secret agent. It takes a lot of training, and a lot of practice, to look this forgettable, like no one in particular.

Molly looked like a china doll with big bosoms, bobbed black hair, dark eyes in a sharply defined face, and a rosebud mouth red as sin itself. Normally, Molly took pride in appearing arrogant and assured enough to stare Medusa in the eye, and ask who the hell the Gorgon thought she was looking at. Molly Metcalf was a fighter and a brawler, ready to take on the whole damned world at a moment's notice. Only . . . not here, not in this place that wasn't at all what she remembered. Her face was pale and her eyes were wide, and in the mirror's reflection she looked like a frightened little girl. I didn't like that.

What had really happened to Molly here, all those years ago?

"What is it?" I said quietly. "What did you see in the mirror?"

"A face," she said, forcing the words out. "A great white face. Not human. Looking at me."

"Nothing there now but us," I said, carefully. "It's not like you to be . . . jumpy, Molly."

"No," she said. "It isn't." She stood up a little straighter, gathering some of her old arrogance around her like familiar armour. "Eddie . . . yes, I know, I should say Shaman, but there's no one else here, I can tell. . . . Can you see ghosts, through your armoured mask?"

"Sure," I said. "I can See pretty much anything when I'm in my armour. If there's anything to be seen. You think there's ghosts here?"

"There's something here," Molly said flatly. "Do me a favour. Armour up and take a good look around. Tell me what this place looks like when it's caught with its underwear down."

I called my armour out of my torc again, and it slipped over me from head to toe in a moment, like a second skin. I could see myself in the mirror, looking like an old-fashioned knight in armour, gleaming gold and glorious. My face mask was blank and featureless, not even any eyeholes; the better to scare the crap out of my enemies. But from inside, I could See everything. I always feel stronger, faster, sharper, when I'm in my armour. I can hear a mouse fart, or the wind change direction, and I can see infrared and ultraviolet. I can also See all kinds of things that are fortunately hidden from the everyday people of the everyday world. If people could See what they really share this world with, they'd shit themselves.

But when I looked carefully up and down the hallway, I couldn't See a single thing out of the ordinary. No ghostly figures, no stone tape memories repeating old actions in sealed loops, like an insect caught in amber. Nothing moved in the shadows or walked through the walls, and all I could hear were the slow shifting sounds of an old house settling itself. I armoured down, looked at Molly, and shook my head helplessly.

"For a place where so many really bad things have happened, it's actually very quiet here," I said. "I still don't care for the feel of the place, but I think that's more down to atmosphere, history, and rising damp, than to anything supernatural."

"Then why is this house affecting me so badly?" said

Molly. "All I have are good memories of my time here before. I actually looked forward to coming back here again!"

"I think we need to phone home," I said. "Check in with the man in charge; see if perhaps there's something he didn't get around to telling us about Monkton Manse."

I moved over to a nearby side table, reached into my pocket, and retrieved my computer laptop from my pocket dimension. I keep all kinds of useful items there. I wiped a thick coating of dust from the tabletop with my coat sleeve, and then set down the laptop and fired it up. I sent my armour back down my arm again, and delicate golden filaments surged into the laptop. Which is a bit like introducing nitrous oxide into the engine of a family car. The laptop danced about for a moment, like I'd goosed it when it wasn't looking, and then settled down, its screen glowing bright. I tapped in the necessary start-up commands with two fingers. One of these days I'm going to have to learn to type properly.

"You really think you can reach anyone with that?" said Molly. "In the middle of a mystical null zone?"

"I'd bet Drood armour against any kind of null zone, any day," I said cheerfully. "The whole point of strange matter is that it trumps magic and science. . . . There! We have contact!"

A pleasant, smiling face appeared on the screen, nodding politely to Molly and me. It wasn't real; just a simulacrum set in place to take messages. The face looked just human enough to be subtly disturbing when it started to speak. The mouth movements were too stylised, and the eyes were just dead.

"Hello. You have reached the Department of the Uncanny. Please state your name, and the office you wish to be connected with."

"This is Eddie Drood, on Trammell Island," I said. "Put me through to the Regent."

"Please wait. Please be patient. Your call is important to us."

The face continued to smile, while the eyes remained lifeless. Orchestrated versions of old Britpop classics played remorselessly in the background.

"This is what happens when you go to work for the Establishment," I said. "Every chance they get, they do their best to bland you to death."

"Are you still happy you did the right thing in leaving the Droods for the Department?" said Molly.

"Yes," I said. "My family lied to me one time too often. Not least about the Regent of Shadows. They should have told me my grandfather was still alive. Hell, they should have told me my parents were still alive! I'm not sure how much trust I put in the Regent, or the Department, they're both too close to the Government for my liking . . . but I need to put some space between my family and me. And how could I turn down a chance to work with my parents, and my grandfather?"

"Very good," said Molly. "Now try saying all that like you mean it."

I had to laugh. "Let us look on this . . . as an extended vacation. Getting away from it all in favour of cases that actually mean something to us. Are you happy to be working alongside me, Molly?"

"I go where you go," said Molly. "Forever and a day, sweetie."

I smiled, but didn't say anything. I knew Molly came with me because the Regent promised her the truth at last about what really happened to her parents all those years ago. She'd always believed her parents were killed by a Drood field agent in a shoot-out with the White Horse Faction. A dangerous supernatural terrorist organisation. The Regent promised her the name of her parents' killer. But I of all people knew better than to believe the official version of any event. No matter whose official version it is. Facts could be slippery things in the secret agent business. Especially where my family's concerned. But how could I stand between anything that mattered so much to my Molly? I needed to be there with her when she finally learned the truth, whatever that turned out to be. And do my best to put the pieces back together again afterwards.

Molly had spent years at war with the Droods and everything they stood for. Fighting them on every level, opposing them with a fierce and unrelenting rage. Until she and I ended up on the same side, working to reform the Droods from within. And we became an item—much to our mutual surprise. I'd done everything I could to convince Molly that my family was a force for good in the world, mostly; but it was hard going. My family has more hidden sides and secret motives than a barrel full of Hollywood lawyers.

The two of us had only just accepted the Regent's invitation to come work with him at the Department of the Uncanny, when he hit us with our first official mission. He wanted us to infiltrate the newly reformed White Horse Faction. As Shaman Bond and Molly Metcalf. The Faction would gladly accept Molly, because of her parents' importance to the old Faction. And they'd accept Shaman, because the whole point of him was that he could turn up anywhere. Molly and I went along because the Regent promised us there were answers to be found, within this new White Horse Faction, as to who actually killed Molly's mother and father.

The false face on the laptop disappeared abruptly, replaced by an image of the Regent of Shadows himself. An elderly man in a scruffy suit with leather patches on the elbows, sitting comfortably behind his desk in his office. He had iron grey hair, a neatly clipped military moustache, a charming smile, and piercing blue eyes. He seemed affable enough, but you had to meet his steady gaze for only a moment to see the iron backbone in the man. He nodded easily to Molly and me. If he was at all concerned about sending Molly to investigate a group that her parents had once believed in and died for . . . he didn't show it.

"We're on Trammell Island," I said. "Inside Monkton Manse. Spooky bloody place. No sign of anyone else yet. Are you sure this new White Horse Faction is a real threat? I know the old group were supernatural terrorists, back in the day; hard-core protectors of Mother Earth and all that . . . but all the information I could dig up on this new version suggest they're really just a bunch of non-violent New Age hippie tree-hugger types."

"Well, that's what you're there to confirm, isn't it?" said the Regent, in his usual calm and untroubled voice. "Just work your way in, old boy, and see what's what." He looked at Molly. "I promise you, my dear; the true nature of your parents' death can be found among these people." He looked back at me. "This new iteration of the White Horse Faction may present themselves as a less threatening alternative to the bad old ways, but we need to know the truth. Talk to them. Get them to open up to you. I have to say, my boy, that I have my suspicions.

"Reports have reached this Department that this new generation of the Faction have reached out to the one surviving member of the old group. A certain Hadrian Coll, also known as Trickster Man. A most untrustworthy fellow, with a long history of moving from one dangerous group to another, stirring up trouble, persuading them into violent and destructive acts, and then moving on. Always managing to disappear just before the ordure hits the fan."

"I remember Hadrian," said Molly, frowning. "He was a close friend of my parents, and a tutor to me. He wasn't like that! He was a freedom fighter, a constant defender of noble causes. He was a good man!"

But her frown deepened even as she was speaking, as though she was troubled by conflicting, newly surfacing, memories.

"Yes, well," said the Regent, entirely unmoved, "that was then; this is now. The current leadership of this new White Horse Faction are on their way to Monkton Manse to debate their future, and the nature of future tactics. I am concerned that they've invited this Hadrian Coll, this Trickster Man, to be a part of their debate. Whatever happens on Trammell Island, hidden from the eyes of the world, will decide what direction the next generation will take. It's up to you . . . to help guide them in the right direction. You are authorised to take whatever action may

be necessary to deal with the Faction in general, and
Hadrian Coll in particular." He looked steadily at Molly.
"Coll was a very violent man, back in the day. And he was
very definitely present when your parents died."

"Of course he was there," said Molly. "He was their
friend. He wouldn't abandon them."

"He claims to have reformed," said the Regent. "That
he's no longer the man he used to be. And, that he doesn't
want the White Horse Faction to be what it used to be.
Which is all very nice and as it should be. But, has he really
embraced non-violence? Or is he still the dangerous Trickster Man, ready to say whatever it takes to have influence
over the next generation of Faction leaders?"

"I'll find out," said Molly. "He wouldn't lie to me."

"Someone's coming," I said. "Talk to you later, Grandfather."

I shut down the laptop, whipped out the golden filaments, and made both my armour and the laptop disappear. I turned quickly to face the open front door, Molly
standing stiffly at my side. I wanted to put a hand to the
collar at my throat. The golden torc isn't normally visible
to the everyday eye. Normally, you have to possess the
Sight, or at the very least be the Seventh Son of a Seventh
Son (exceedingly rare in these days of family planning),
just to be able to detect the torc's presence. But Monkton
Manse didn't feel like a normal place, with normal conditions. If they found out I was a Drood . . . this whole situation would deteriorate faster than an argument about who
didn't have a starter in a row over a restaurant bill.

And I needed this to go well, for Molly's sake. So she
could get to the truth, at last, and put it behind her.

Footsteps approached the open door from outside, and
then suddenly there they were. The three leaders of the
next generation of the new White Horse Faction, standing
together in the doorway, staring blankly at Molly and me.

They stood very still, clearly under the impression that
they'd been the first to arrive on the Island. Certainly not

expecting anyone to have got to the house ahead of them. They appeared alarmed, then suspicious, and finally distinctly annoyed. They looked Molly and me over, taking their time. I gave them my best confident, charming, and in no way dangerous smile, and Molly . . . did her best. It wasn't that she lacked in people skills; it was mostly that she just couldn't be bothered. The three next-generation leaders glanced at each other, exchanged a quick flurry of smiles, raised eyebrows and shrugs, and then turned back to present Molly and me with a united front. Doing their best to look as though they were in charge, and full of authority. But their lack of experience was against them; neither of them had progressed very far into their twenties, and there was no overlooking the way they stood very close together, for mutual support.

The young woman suddenly stepped forward. "Hi," she said, just a bit ungraciously. "I'm Stephanie Troy. I know who both of you are, of course. We're happy to have you here with us on this auspicious occasion. The rebirth and regeneration of the White Horse Faction! It's an honour to meet you, Molly Metcalf."

Troy barely gave me a second look, but then, that was how it should be. Shaman Bond has a history with most supernatural organisations, usually as a supplier of information, but no reputation at all for getting personally involved in dangerous action. Unlike the infamous Molly Metcalf . . .

Stephanie Troy was tall and fashionably slender, and positively blazed with nervous energy. She had short-cropped honey blonde hair, flashing eyes, and a tightly pursed mouth. She wore a smart grey suit with sensible shoes, minimal makeup, and no jewellery. I was pretty sure she would consider such things distracting, and frivolous. This was a woman who had given herself to a cause, and everything and everyone else would always come second to that.

She darted forward and grabbed Molly firmly by the hand. Molly suffered her hand to be shook, and nodded amiably enough.

"Hi!" I said. "I'm Shaman Bond! Happy to be here; glad to help out."

"I know who you are," said Troy, reluctantly releasing Molly's hand. "Your reputation precedes you." She didn't make that sound like a good thing. And she didn't offer to shake my hand.

"I'm Phil Adams," said the shortest member of the next generation. He stepped forward, shyly and deferentially, and made a point of shaking my hand as well as Molly's.

He was barely medium height, far more than medium weight, with a constant little smile and an evasive gaze, wearing a baggy shapeless jersey over grubby blue jeans that looked like they'd been through several wars. His heavy boots were held together with two different-coloured sets of shoelaces, along with a certain amount of knotted string. He wore his long mousey-coloured hair in untidy dreadlocks, and sported a stubbly and not particularly successful beard. He had a calm, easy manner, but didn't seem to want to look directly at anyone. I'd seen his kind before. More at home with animals than people, he loved Nature so much there wasn't a lot left in him for people. He would almost certainly turn out to be the heart and soul of the group, but he'd always leave it to the other two to do the talking.

The last one to come forward announced himself loudly as Joe Morrison. He was a big one, broad-shouldered and barrel-chested, wearing a hooded jacket of indeterminate colour over designer jeans and cowboy boots. Given the way he moved, and the way he held himself, I got the feeling he was probably ex-military. Or at the very least, ex-bouncer. He looked like he would have enjoyed saying *No trainers!* and *Your name's not on the list.* He was dark and not particularly handsome, and gave every indication of knowing and not giving a damn. He nodded to Molly, clearly pleased to see her, but just as clearly not as impressed by her reputation as the others. He glanced at me, and sniffed loudly.

"I did my research, once I knew you two would be

here," he said. "Everyone knows Molly Metcalf is the real deal, but I couldn't get anyone to agree on what you are, Shaman. Have you ever believed in anything, I mean really believed, in your whole crooked life?"

"I believe in getting paid," I said easily. "And Molly is paying me really good money to watch her back, while she's here. What do you believe in, Joe Morrison?"

"I believe in protecting Nature, and Mother Earth," said Morrison. In a way that suggested that hadn't always been the case. There's nothing more fervent and more dogmatic than a recent convert.

For a while, we all just stood there in the hallway, and looked each other over. These three may be the next-generation leaders of the White Horse Faction, but Molly and I were the only ones with real reputations. We'd actually done things. In the end, Troy nodded briskly to Molly, and favoured her with a brief smile.

"We're really glad you've come back to the White Horse Faction, Molly. Your parents left a hell of a legacy. We admire their commitment, and revere their contributions, even though we have chosen to follow a different path. I'm sure we'll have lots to discuss. What we decide here, in this place, will change the world."

And then she looked at me. I smiled calmly back at her.

"I know," I said. "I'm just a dilettante in all this, and I'll never be a true believer. But as long as Molly is putting money in my pocket, you can depend on me."

"To do what?" said Troy, bluntly. "What can you bring to the cause?"

"I can open doors for you," I said. "I know people. I can make connections, get you whatever you need. For a very reasonable percentage, of course."

"Parasite," said Morrison. He gave Molly a hard look. "What's he doing here? Is he your . . . significant other, these days?"

"Hardly," I said smoothly. "Dear Molly's just the boss lady. I am here . . . because this is a bad place. Which you'd know, if you'd done your research."

"I wouldn't have thought the infamous Molly Metcalf would need a bodyguard," Adams said quietly, tugging reflectively at a dreadlock. "And didn't I hear you were stepping out with a Drood these days, Molly?"

"A rogue Drood," said Molly. "And I didn't bring him, because if I had . . . you wouldn't have dared turn up. My Eddie has left his very scary family, but I knew you wouldn't be comfortable in his presence. That's why I hired Shaman. We're old colleagues."

Troy was already shaking her head. "Our invitation was just for you. We are here to decide the final direction of the White Horse Faction—and the future of the whole world."

"Just the three of you?" I said, innocently.

"We represent hundreds of supporters," Adams said quietly. "Hundreds of cells, with thousands of fellow travellers, spread out across every country in the world. All of them dedicated to give their all in defence of Mother Earth. We will dictate policy, and our armies will carry it out."

"Armies?" said Molly. "I thought it was all about nonviolence, these days."

"We have to use language the rest of the world will understand," said Morrison. "We're at war with all those who would pollute our waters and poison the air. Just because we don't believe in violence, doesn't mean we'll shy away from open confrontation. We have to save the world while there's still time."

"And this meeting will decide how we're going to do it," said Troy.

"Occupy!" said Morrison, smiling for the first time. "Stand in the way. Place ourselves between the bad guys and their evil ways. Make it impossible for them to screw up our poor planet any more."

"In a totally non-threatening, non-violent way, of course," said Adams.

I didn't smile. I approved of their sentiments, and admired their courage, but in my experience, the nail that sticks up most is the first to get hammered down.

"Who knows?" said Troy, smiling frostily in my direction. "When you've seen all the evidence, and heard all the arguments, perhaps we'll convert you, Shaman."

"Non-violence is an excellent idea," I said. "I just wish it worked more often. Is everyone in your new White Horse Faction equally dedicated to turning the other cheek? Only, a little bird did tell me a certain Hadrian Coll will be joining us. . . ."

The three next-generation leaders looked at each other quickly, and that glance was all I needed to see how they felt about Hadrian Coll, also known as Trickster Man. Troy looked excited, Adams looked disapproving, and Morrison looked conflicted, like he thought they were all making a big mistake.

"He's . . . on his way," said Troy. She made an effort to appear upbeat. "You mustn't be put off by his past reputation. He's changed. It's only because he's heard how much we've changed the organisation, and its methods, that he's agreed to come out from deep cover, to talk with us here."

"He was a warrior, in defence of Mother Earth," said Adams. "It took great courage for him to admit the old ways didn't work."

"He still needs to understand that he's not in charge any more," said Morrison.

"He was a good friend to my parents," said Molly. "And a tutor to me. He helped make me everything I am today."

All three of the next generation looked seriously uncomfortable, as they considered all the very definitely violent and destructive things the infamous Molly Metcalf had done in her time. They might revere her parents, and be impressed by her accomplishments, but none of them wanted anything to do with her idea of tactics. I could see in their faces they were all wondering whether they'd done the right thing in inviting her, after all.

"Well, it's good to know I haven't been forgotten," said a new, cheerful voice. We all looked round sharply, and there he was in the open doorway, grinning easily at all of us. Hadrian Coll himself; the Trickster Man. The only surviving member of the original White Horse Faction.

He stood tall and proud, loud and cocky, hard worn and showing his middle age, but still possessed of a certain shop-soiled charisma. He looked like a retired business-man, dressed for a walking holiday, all casual and slouch-ing. But you had to look at him for only a few moments to see that was just a mask, with the real and very dangerous persona peering out from behind it. Then, he looked a lot more like a mercenary soldier, dressed for a walking holi-day. He had thinning white hair, bushy black eyebrows, and a heavy broken nose protruding from a blocky, hard-lined face. He smiled easily enough, but it never reached his eyes.

I'd seen his sort before drinking happily at the end of the bar, just waiting for trouble to break out, so he could join in and get his hands bloody. He'd never start anything, but you could always be sure he'd be the last one standing. And he wouldn't care at all how many bystanders got hurt in the process. Now here he was, claiming to have retired and reformed. Ready to do non-violent penance for his bloody past.

I wanted to believe it. Wanted to believe Molly's old tutor wasn't what the Drood files said he was. But I didn't.

Troy and Adams and Morrison just stood there, mouths open and wide-eyed, dazzled by the glare of Coll's reputa-tion. His legend. Molly squealed with delight, and ran for-ward to hug Coll fiercely. He wrapped his great arms around her and lifted her off her feet, so he could swing her around in a circle. They both laughed loudly, as he hugged her to him like a friendly old bear. He finally put her down and let her go, and turned to grin at all of us, one arm still draped companionably over Molly's shoulders. Like she belonged to him. Molly's face was flushed, and her eyes were shining. Coll nodded easily to the next gen-eration.

"So, you're my replacements. Good to see you all! Great to be here! Seems I've been away too long; the world's grown even worse, while I turned my back. Well, no more of that! I have returned and all my knowledge and experience is at your disposal. My way didn't work; I can only hope that yours will. Molly, my sweet, do the introductions, there's a dear girl."

He was probably the only one present who could have got away with calling her that. Molly ran through the names quickly, and Coll strode forward to shake each of the next generation firmly by the hand. He gave them all the same big smile, and lots of eye contact, and they all smiled and simpered, like a dazzled fan meeting their favourite movie star. They fell all over each other to say how proud they were to meet him, and how delighted they were he'd agreed to come out of retirement to be their spiritual mentor and advisor. Coll nodded easily to each of them. And then, finally, Molly introduced him to me.

I gave Coll my best harmless smile, playing the chancer con man act to the hilt; but I couldn't tell whether he bought it or not. He crushed my hand in his, clapped me hard on the shoulder, and loudly said any friend of Molly was a friend of his.

"Shaman Bond! I know the name, of course," he said. "You've been around, haven't you? I've pitched up at every trouble spot there is in the last few years, and as often as not, your name was there before me. Never anything big, but always there, hanging around on the edge of the scene. A good man to know, they say, when you need a helping hand."

"For a reasonable price," I said.

He laughed. "Your reputation precedes you!"

"That was going to be my line," I said.

"Ah," he said sadly. "I'm not the man I was. And mostly, I'd have to say that is a good thing."

He turned abruptly, to face the next generation again and give them his full attention. "It's been a long trip, getting here. Took a lot out of me. I could use a nice sit-down, and a spot of something to eat. I'm old now. I get tired. I have Nam flashbacks."

"You were in Vietnam?" said Morrison.

"No," said Coll. "That's what makes the flashbacks so

worrying . . ." He laughed again, a great roar of joyous sound, and everyone joined in. The next generation looked at him like he was the Second Coming. Molly looked at him adoringly. And I smiled until my cheeks ached.

Troy and Adams and Morrison led the way down the hall, chattering loudly, trying to make a big fuss of Coll, though he would have none of it. He was just there to advise and support them, he insisted. They were the important ones. Molly wandered after him, smiling just a bit foolishly, while I brought up the rear, thinking my own thoughts. I just couldn't see it. This amiable old bear of a man wasn't the tricksy, dangerous man I'd discovered in my research. Hadrian Coll had killed a lot of people, for any number of causes. He planted bombs in public places, arranged magical booby traps for important people, undermined whole governments for any number of organisations. And was never, ever, around when it came time to pay the butcher's bill. Of course, the records covered only what he did, not why he did it. And I had enough blood on my own golden hands to know that appearances aren't everything.

But, no one had seen hide nor hair of Hadrian Coll, the legendary Trickster Man, for almost ten years. No one knew where he'd been, or what he'd been doing. Why would he reappear now, to support a White Horse Faction that was nothing like the group he used to belong to? Did he feel the need to do penance, for the monster he used to be?

Or was he just here . . . because Molly was here?

We left the hallway and entered a huge dining room. Molly snapped her fingers and once again the candle stubs in the overhead chandeliers blazed into friendly yellow light. The next generation looked startled, and then applauded lightly. Coll grinned at Molly.

"You always did show such promise, Molly, my sweet," he said. "It's been so many years since I last saw you . . . look at you! My little girl is all grown up!"

"I need to talk to you, Hadrian," said Molly. "About my mother and my father. And what really happened to them."

"Of course you do," said Coll. For the first time he sounded properly serious. "Don't you remember . . . how they died?"

"I thought I did," said Molly. "I thought I knew what happened . . . until I came here, and realised I only really remembered bits and pieces."

"That's probably for the best," said Coll.

"No, it isn't!" said Molly, so loudly that everyone winced, and backed away from her. Molly fixed Hadrian with a cold hard gaze. "I need to know! I need to know everything that happened."

"We'll talk later," said Coll. "I promise. But I have business with these good people, and I owe them my full attention. Afterwards, we'll sit down together, you and I, and I'll tell you everything."

He smiled fondly at Molly, and after a moment she smiled back. I couldn't help but feel that he was putting it on, but Molly just smiled and nodded, and hugged him quickly.

"I am so proud of you," Coll said quietly. "So proud of everything you've achieved, and what you've made of yourself. You've far surpassed your old tutor. . . ." He looked suddenly at me. "Why do you need a bodyguard, Molly? And why him?"

"Because even the infamous wild witch of the woods needs someone to watch her back, on occasion," I said. "And like you said, Hadrian, I've been around. I'm not easily fooled, or distracted, and I'm really hard to surprise."

Coll nodded, and then turned the full force of his charisma on the patiently waiting next generation. "Ten years! I can't believe it's been that long since I last set foot in this monstrous old house. Later on, I'll have to give you the grand tour; fill you in on all the old stories. I have so many memories of this place . . . and the original White Horse Faction. The long nights we spent here, talking and talking into the early hours, plotting and planning . . . we would change the world, we said."

"We still can," said Troy, her voice entirely serious. She

may be impressed by Coll, but he was still nothing compared to her devotion to the cause. "You must tell us everything about the old times, and the old organisation. If only so we can avoid making their mistakes."

"We want to hear everything," said Morrison.

"And so you shall, my friends!" said Coll. "But first, food and drink! Something for the inner man, hmm?"

He looked meaningfully at Stephanie Troy. Anyone else, she would have told to go to hell. That just because she was a woman, she wasn't there to cook and make the tea and wait on the men. But this was Hadrian Coll, so she just nodded quietly.

"I'm sure I can manage something. Our advance agents are supposed to have left some food in the kitchens, tins and things. . . ."

"Excellent!" said Coll, rubbing his large hands together.

"You do that," I said. "I think I'll go for a little walk, down on the beach. Get some fresh air in my lungs. Care to accompany me, Molly?"

She tore her gaze away from Coll, looked at me for a long moment, and then nodded quickly.

"Of course," she said. "Fresh air. Just the thing."

"Don't take too long," said Troy. "A meal will be ready soon."

"Don't be late," said Coll. "Or we'll start without you."

Molly and I smiled meaninglessly all round, and then I took her by the arm and led her away. No one seemed too disappointed to see us go. The next generation wanted Hadrian Coll all to themselves. I wasn't sure yet what Coll wanted. I led Molly out of Monkton Manse, chatting cheerfully to her all of the way, of this and that, until the front door slammed shut behind us.

Once we were outside Molly pulled her arm free of mine, and strode on ahead on her own. I let her go. She strode back to the cliff edge, and then set off down some very steep stone steps, cut into the cliff face itself. She hurried ahead of me, not waiting for me to catch up. I pressed my shoulder hard against the cliff face, to keep from straying too close to the edge, and the long drop. The gusting, bitterly cold wind hit me hard, ruffling my hair and plucking at my clothes. The steps just seemed to fall away forever, and by the time I finally reached the bottom and stepped off onto the beach, my legs were aching fiercely.

Molly stood with her back to me, farther down the beach, just short of the incoming tide, looking out at the great crashing waves. I took my time, stretching my back and stamping my feet to ease the kinks out of my leg muscles. Finally, I moved forward to join Molly. She didn't say anything. I looked around me. Not a stretch of sand anywhere on Trammell Island beach; just dark pebbles, for as far as the eye could see, interrupted here and there with great swatches of ugly green and brown seaweed, washed up by the heavy tides as they pounded up and down the beach. Not a living thing to be seen anywhere—no crabs, or lobsters. Not even a gull in the sky overhead. The overcast sky was darkening from evening into night, but there was still enough light to see there was nothing much to see.

I picked up a pebble, hefted it thoughtfully, and then sent it flying out across the uneven surface of the waters. It bounced several times, before sinking. After a moment Molly bent down, picked up a pebble of her own, and threw it out across the sea. Her pebble bounced a lot farther than mine. For a while we just stood there, throwing pebbles with all our strength, trying to outdo each other. Neither of us could manage much in the way of distance; the huge waves just snatched at the pebbles and dragged them under. The tide was coming in. I stooped down for another pebble, and a length of seaweed curled suddenly around my hand and clamped down, painfully tight. I had to use both hands to break the seaweed's grip, and throw it aside. It was tough and springy, and unnaturally strong.

"There are those who say you can use seaweed to tell the weather," said Molly.

"Oh yes?" I said. "Like, if it's wet, it must be raining?"

"Something like that," said Molly. "Tell me, Shaman—what are we doing here?"

"Here on the beach, or here on the Island?" I said, carefully.

"You don't like Hadrian, do you?"

"I don't trust him," I said. "But then, I don't trust any of the next generation, either. We're here to do a job, Molly."

"Hadrian was my first tutor. He taught me so much. My parents admired him. I think he was the closest friend they ever had."

"A lot of people trusted him, in a lot of organisations, most of which aren't around any longer. He was a very dangerous man, Molly. He still has a bad reputation in many parts of the world."

"So do I," said Molly.

"You always believed in your cause," I said. "Hadrian Coll, aka Trickster Man, let us not forget . . . claimed to believe in a great many causes down the years. But somehow he was never there when the authorities closed in to round up the groups and make them pay for their crimes. I'm . . . not convinced by him. He has the feel of a professional politician. The kind who'll say anything, do anything, that will advance his cause. Whatever that might turn out to be. I don't trust this man, Molly, and I don't think you should either."

"No one ever did," said Molly, surprisingly. "Not even my mother and father. But there was no one like him for getting things done. No one like him for stirring things up, for starting a fire in people's hearts, and then aiming them at a target and encouraging them to do what needed doing. When Hadrian was around, people stopped talking and theorising, and started practising what they preached. That was what Coll always brought to the party: how to commit yourself to direct action. Even back then, in the original White Horse Faction, a group with a solid history of direct action . . . there were always people ready to talk any subject to death. To avoid committing themselves to getting their hands dirty. Or bloody. Coll put an end to that. Coll got things done."

"Good things?" I asked. She didn't answer.

We stared out across the beach at the dark and disturbed sea, and after a while Molly slipped her arm through mine. Where it belonged.

"You said . . . Monkton Manse isn't the way you remembered it," I said slowly. "Is Hadrian Coll . . . how you remembered him?"

"That's the problem," said Molly. "He's exactly the way I remember him. As though he hasn't changed at all. How can that be possible, after ten years? There's a part of me that wonders if he's just playing a part."

"For your sake?" I said. "Or the next generation's?"

"They seem straight-forward enough," said Molly. "If . . . inexperienced in the real world. I'm not sure they're ready to deal with someone like Hadrian Coll. Trickster Man."

"Good thing we're here, then. Isn't it?" I said.

And then we both looked round sharply. From somewhere farther down the beach, stretching far and far away before us, a horse was running. I could hear the sound of its hooves, pounding along the pebbles. The sound was quite clear and distinct, rising above the crashing of the waves. And from the way Molly stood tensed beside me, I knew she heard it too. But no matter how hard I looked, straining my eyes against the distance and the lowering light, I couldn't see a horse anywhere. The beach just stretched away into the distance, open and empty.

"There's nothing there," said Molly. "But I can hear it, clear as day. What the hell would a horse be doing here?"

I murmured my activating Words, and pulled my armour out of my torc to cover my face. The golden mask settled easily into place, and I used its expanded Sight to zoom in on the end of the beach. But no matter where I looked, there was no sign of any horse. Just the sound of one, endlessly running. And then, quite suddenly, it stopped. Gone, between one moment and the next. I dismissed the golden mask and looked at Molly.

"I couldn't See a damned thing. And look at the beach.

A real horse, running on this beach, would have kicked up pebbles everywhere. I can't see any sign of a disturbance."

"A ghost horse?" said Molly. "How likely is that? And what would a ghost horse be doing here? A lot of people may have died on this island, but no animals, as far as I know."

"Maybe it came through the Fae Gate," I said. "The living and the dead can travel the elven ways."

"No," said Molly, frowning. "If I'm remembering right . . . there's never been any animal life on Trammell Island. Not even rabbits, or rats . . . animals just die here. Even birds won't land, or so I'm told. Who told me that? Why can't I remember?" She stopped, frowning so hard it must have hurt her forehead. She looked distracted, almost frightened. "This means something, Eddie. It means something to me, something important that I just can't remember! Like a word on the tip of your tongue. A horse . . . There's something significant about that. Something that matters."

I waited, but she had nothing more to say.

"If you say so," I said, finally.

"There are gaps in my memory," Molly said flatly. "Though I never knew that, until I came back here. I'm remembering things I never remembered before, important things, that I'd forgotten I ever knew. But there are still great gaps in my memory of my time here before. How could I have forgotten so much? And not even noticed?"

"Because someone didn't want you to remember," I said. "And perhaps that someone was you, Molly. You didn't want to know. If something really bad did happen here, maybe something to do with the death of your parents . . ."

"I need to know," said Molly, coldly. "I need to know everything."

She shuddered suddenly. I took her in my arms and held her, but it didn't help.

Some time later, we made our way back to Monkton Manse. All the windows were lit now, blazing with bright electric light, and the whole place felt more comfortable, and inviting. It looked inhabited again, the kind of place where people might actually live. It even felt comfortably warm in the hallway as we came in out of the bitter cold, and slammed the heavy door shut behind us. We rubbed our hands together, and stamped our feet, and finally took off our coats and hung them up.

"Coll must have got the old generator working again," said Molly.

"They've blown out your candles," I observed. "I think I preferred the candlelight. Less harsh."

"You old romantic," said Molly. And then she frowned. "I don't think this place was ever romantic. Or even happy . . ."

"But . . . you had good times here?" I said.

"Maybe," said Molly.

We made our way through the winding corridors and hallways of Monkton Manse to the main dining hall, where a meal of sorts was waiting for us. We joined the others, all sitting around one end of the long mahogany dining table, eating cold cuts of tinned meat, along with a couple of bottles of half-way decent wine. The food had been neatly arranged on the very best china plates, along with gleaming stylised cutlery. Presumably courtesy of the first and last Lord of Trammell.

We all huddled together for comfort at our end of the table, which stretched away into the massive dining hall. It had clearly been originally intended to seat thirty or maybe even forty people at one sitting. The hall had an oppressively high ceiling, and gleaming wood-panelled walls. No portraits or paintings here, or decorations of any kind. This was a setting for the serious business of food and drink.

We kept our voices low as we talked, and tried not to look around, half intimidated by the sheer scale and opulence of the dining hall. Doing our best to ignore all the extra empty space, and pretend it wasn't there. Hadrian Coll wasn't bothered. His great voice boomed out endlessly, telling one story after another as he attacked his food and drink with great enthusiasm. I did my best to seem a little overwhelmed, because Shaman Bond would be, but this was actually a bit more than even Eddie Drood was used to at Drood Hall. This dining hall had been deliberately designed to be too big for people, to put them in their place in the presence of the Lord of Trammell.

I really didn't like the shadows at the end of the dining hall. There were too many of them, too deep and too dark. And I am not the sort who is usually bothered by shadows.

Coll did most of the talking, often with his mouth full, dominating the conversation by the simple expedient of never letting anyone else get a word in edge-ways. The next generation were overawed enough to let him get away with that, and Molly seemed genuinely interested in everything he had to say. Perhaps because she was checking it all against her memories. Looking for contradictions, and loopholes. I watched everyone else, as they listened to Coll.

"It was a different time then," he said grandly, refilling his wine-glass with a flourish. "All those years ago . . . the big businesses and the corrupt politicians held all the big cards. And they owned the law. So all we had left to work with was violence, to force change for the better. And yes, that meant playing their game, but when it's the only game in town . . . We were at war with vested interests, who were never going to be persuaded to change things by reason or logic. Not if it meant giving up power and money. Arguments got you nowhere, persuasion didn't work, so all that left was hitting them where it hurt. It was all we had.

"Now, things have changed. The Internet means that arguments and philosophies can shoot around the world in minutes, backed up by hard evidence. Information wants everyone to be free. If I've learned anything from my time with so many groups and organisations, it's that you can't get people to listen by shouting at them. You have to gang up on them, and drown out their lies with the truth."

He stopped abruptly, to look at Molly. She'd hardly touched her food or her wine, which wasn't like her, and now she was leaning forward, scowling, and rubbing at her forehead as though bothered by some intrusive new pain. Or memory.

"Are you all right, Molly?" said Coll. "Is something bothering you?"

"I remember being here, before," said Molly. Her voice sounded odd, strangely detached. "At this table. With the old White Horse Faction. Everyone was here, including my parents. And you, Hadrian. I can see them all, as clearly as I see you . . . sitting around this table. Talking, planning . . . something big. I'm here, excited to be included in their plans. I see my mother and my father, smiling at me. They don't look that much older than I am now. Oh, God . . . it's been such a long time, since I saw them smile at me . . . but now everyone's talking at once, raising their voices, shouting at each other. Something's changed. My parents aren't smiling any more. No. No! They're gone. . . . They're all gone."

She raised her head, to look sharply at Coll. "What were they planning here, Hadrian? It was something much bigger, and far more dangerous, than they were usually involved in. Why did my parents look so sad then, at the end? And why did you look so worried?"

"This isn't what you really want to talk about," said Coll. "You want to know how your parents died. All right, you've waited long enough. Look at this."

He produced something from his pocket, and held it up for all of us to see: a single brightly glowing jewel. Smooth and polished as a pearl, shining fiercely with some intense inner light. Almost too bright to look at directly. Like staring into the sun. Coll rolled the thing back and forth between his fingers, splashing unnatural light around the length of the dining hall. Enjoying the way he was holding everyone's attention.

"This . . . is a memory crystal. Supersaturated with condensed information. Future technology, of course . . . fell off the back of a Timeslip, in the Nightside. It contains a complete recording of what happened here, in this room, at the very last meeting of the original White Horse Faction. The night everybody died."

"What?" Molly sat bolt upright, glaring at him. "My

parents died here? In Monkton Manse? Why didn't I remember that?"

"Because you were here when it happened," said Coll. "Now hush. And watch."

He murmured some activating words over the memory crystal, and just like that a vision appeared, floating on the air before us. A deep and distinct image from the Past, showing exactly what happened, in this dining hall, ten years earlier.

Some twenty-odd people sat around the long table, talking heatedly with each other. We couldn't hear their voices, couldn't hear what they were saying, but none of them looked happy. Hadrian Coll was there, looking a lot more than ten years younger. He wasn't talking. Just sat there, watching the others. Beside him sat a man and a woman I immediately recognised as Molly's parents. A good-looking pair, strong and noble, arguing with passion and intensity. And sitting beside them a teenage Molly Metcalf. Obviously upset by all the raised voices and arguments. She looked so young, so vulnerable. Unmarked by all the harsh pain and anger to come, that would scar her so deeply. I wanted to reach out to her, to hold her and protect her; to save her from what I knew was coming. But I couldn't.

All I could do was watch.

Everyone at the table looked round, startled, as the door at the far end of the dining hall slammed open, to reveal a dark and shadowy figure. And before anyone at the table could properly react, the shadowy figure produced a gun and opened fire. Those nearest him died first, blood flying from gaping wounds and shattered heads. Bodies crashed to the floor. People started to their feet, reaching for weapons or magical protections, but bullets found them first. They all died, one after another; the entire White Horse Faction wiped out, in just a few moments.

Molly's mother and father were among the last to die. Jake Metcalf put himself between his wife and his daughter and the bullets of the shadowy gunman, trying to push his wife away from the line of fire. A row of bullets stitched across his chest, throwing him backwards into his wife's arms. And then a bullet hit her, in the side of the head, blasting half her face away. The blood splashed across Molly's face as she stood there at the table, horrified. She screamed and screamed, silently, like she would never stop.

The last few remaining members of the White Horse Faction opened up on the shadowy gunman with everything they had. Energy guns, enhanced weapons, shaped curses and pointing bones. But none of it had any effect. The shadowy man stood his ground in the doorway, and nothing touched him. Molly turned and ran for the door nearest her. By the time she reached it, everyone else who'd been sitting at the table was dead.

The vision snapped off, and Coll put the memory crystal down on the table. Molly was on her feet, staring down the long table at the far door, where the gunman had been. Her eyes were wide, wild, lost. I was on my feet beside her, but she didn't even know I was there. The next generation stared at Coll as though seeing him for the first time, and not liking what they saw. He sat calmly in his chair, giving all his attention to the wine in his glass. I glared at him.

"You didn't have to show her everything at once! You didn't have to throw her in the deep end like that, you bastard!"

Coll shrugged, entirely unmoved by the anger in my voice, or Molly's condition.

"Watch your mouth, Shaman. I gave her what she wanted. Sometimes you have to just rip the scab right off. Less painful, that way."

I leaned in close to Molly, careful not to touch her, just yet. "Is that . . . how it was, Molly? Is that how it really was? Do you remember now?"

"Yes," said Molly. "My mum and dad died right here, in this room, right in front of me. I only remembered flashes before, and it never occurred to me to look too closely. People told me it happened somewhere else, so often, that I believed them. And forgot all this . . . I was so sure it was a Drood who killed them, like everyone said . . ." She turned her head slowly to look at Coll. "Why was the killer just a shadow, when everything else was so clear?"

"Because you're not ready to see who it was, just yet," said Coll. "And because I feel the need . . . to keep a little something in reserve. In case I need something to bargain with."

"This, all of this, is why I became the wild witch," said Molly. "Why I made so many deals, with so many Courts, for power. So I'd never be helpless again."

"And to avenge your parents," I said. I looked at Coll, and he stirred uncomfortably in his chair, at something he saw in my face. "That shadowy figure," I said. "He definitely wasn't wearing Drood armour, despite his . . . untouchability. So he wasn't a Drood. You've known that, all these years, but you never said anything to Molly. Why?"

Molly looked at me. "You thought the killer was a Drood . . ."

"Because that's what it says in the Drood files," I said.

"What?" said Troy. "How would you know something like that?"

"Because I'm Shaman Bond!" I snapped. "I get around, everyone knows that. I know things I'm not supposed to know. Take it from me: the original White Horse Faction was quite definitely wiped out on the orders of the Droods, supposedly to prevent them from doing something quite extraordinarily dangerous. I always believed it was a Drood field agent who did the job; but now it's starting to look like the Droods contracted out for the hit. I have to wonder why . . ."

"Talk to me, Hadrian," said Molly, and she didn't sound like an old friend, any more. "Explain to me what happened here. What did you talk the Faction into? What did you get my parents involved in that was so bad they all had to be murdered on Drood orders?"

"And why weren't you killed, along with all the others?" I said.

Coll looked at Molly and me, and then at Troy and Adams and Morrison, and saw he didn't have a single ally in the room any more. He smiled.

"Well. I see it's finally time . . . to tell the tale. The

truth, the whole truth, and everything in between. I suppose I'm the only one left now who knows everything. Very well. The truth is that the Drood's agent got here too late. The bad thing had already happened. The White Horse Faction had already carried out their greatest mission, and their most terrible failure. We performed a great magical Working, and it all went horribly wrong. That's why we ran all the way back here, to Trammell Island and Monkton Manse; not to plot and plan but to hide away from prying eyes . . . and from the awful thing we'd let loose in the world.

"The Faction discovered, while looking for something else entirely—and isn't that always the way—that a nuclear power plant down in the south-west of England had been constructed over an ancient Celtic barrow mound. A very magical, and significant, burial mound. The owners and builders of the power plant were horrified when the mound was discovered during the early stages of construction. They knew bringing in architects and historians would bring construction to a halt, costing them millions. They might even be required to stop building and move the plant somewhere else, and God alone knew how much that would cost them! So the owners just paid everyone off, and kept building. The nuclear power plant went online, on time, and the truth never came out.

"Except—someone wrote it all down. A complete record. Just in case it ever came back to bite them on the arse. And someone who supported the White Horse Faction got hold of this document, and passed it on. The Faction investigated, and found this particular barrow mound was built to contain Something so powerful it had to be put down into the earth and left there, to sleep the sleep of ages. And that's when the Faction all came up with this great idea.

"We would wake the Sleeper, raise it up and take control of it through a great Working. We would use the Sleeper's power to blow up the nuclear power plant, and then channel all that released energy into a second, even greater

Working. One that would rewrite Reality itself, according to our needs and wishes, to remake England and the world in our preferred image.

"It seemed so perfect: to use the hated power of the enemy to create a new and magical world that would have no need and no use for nuclear power plants."

"What the hell made you think you could control something that powerful?" I said.

"More blind luck," said Coll. "We'd managed to get our hands on all kinds of useful Objects of Power, courtesy of various fellow-travellers and well-wishers ... who didn't have the balls to use the things themselves. And one new item in particular made the whole scheme seem possible. Or so we thought. We really did think we could bring this off; it's important that you understand that. We thought we were saving the world. But we had no idea just how powerful the Sleeper under the mound was. We didn't know what we were dealing with ...

"We had the Red King's Ruby, you see. And we thought that with that, we could do anything." He saw the look of horror in my face, and the blank incomprehension in everyone else, so he sighed heavily, and paused to explain himself. "The Red King's Ruby is a magical artefact that originally existed only in dreams. A purely conceptual item, and therefore unlimited in its power. Someone found a way to bring it forward, out of dreams and into reality. Once it was made manifest, and material, it was supposed to be powerful enough to give its wielder control over everything. How could we resist?"

"Who gave you the Ruby?" said Molly. Her voice was very cold.

"The Most Evil Man In The World: Crow Lee. He didn't tell us how he got his hands on it, and we didn't ask. We didn't even have to pay him for it! His only requirement was that we use it. I think ... he was scared to try it out himself. He wanted someone else to do it for him, first. And I believe it amused him to think of something like the Red King's Ruby in hands like ours. I did wonder, afterwards, whether he knew what we were planning . . . and knew that it would never work."

"Something so powerful that even Crow Lee never dared use it," I said. "Didn't that tell you something?"

"I talked them into it," said Coll. "That was my job. And this is where we get to the part of the story you know nothing about, Molly. The part that not even your parents suspected. I was a spy. A double agent, working for the Droods. It was my job to infiltrate dangerous underground groups, find out their plans and secrets, and pass that information back to the Droods. So they could decide what to do. That was why I kept moving, from one group to another. And, because the other part of my job was to act as an agent provocateur. Encourage these groups to act before they were ready, to perform violent acts that would discredit them in the eyes of the world, and sink them hip-deep in trouble. I, of course, was always long gone by then. That's how I acquired my other name: Trickster Man. Though no one ever suspected the truth. I was . . . very good at my job."

"Why?" said Troy. And in that one word was all the shock and betrayal of a disappointed child. "Why would you do such a thing?"

"For the money, of course! And because I'm a Drood bastard," said Hadrian Coll. "Illegitimate child of James Drood, the legendary Grey Fox. He did put it about, you know. There's a lot of us Grey Bastards out and about in the world, all of us desperate to ingratiate ourselves with the mighty Drood family. In the hope of earning a place among them. Of being invited home, to Drood Hall. Maybe even presented with a torc . . . Any of us would have done anything, for that.

"I was sent into the White Horse Faction to do my usual number on them . . . but a funny thing happened. The more I listened to them, the more I found I agreed with them. Your mother and father were good people, Molly. I became a convert to their cause. I was the one who heard about the Red King's Ruby, and used my Drood connections to put the White Horse Faction in touch with Crow Lee. So in a way, everything that happened afterwards was my fault. But I swear to you . . . I had no idea then what the Faction wanted it for. What they intended to do with it.

"Once it was all explained to me, I was horrified. I knew it would never work. I tried to talk them out of it, but for once my famous powers of persuasion failed me. They'd suffered too many defeats, endured too many set-backs. They were desperate for one big win that would settle everything. And put an end to a war they were so tired of. I could see it all going horribly wrong in so many ways . . . so I turned them in, to the Droods. I told them everything the White Horse Faction were planning, and they said they'd send a field agent to stop them. I was so relieved. I thought the agent would just walk in and take the Ruby away from them before anyone could get hurt.

"But the Droods took too long making up their minds. By the time their chosen agent arrived, it was too late. We'd already awoken the Sleeper under the mound.

"Do I really need to tell you how badly we'd misunderstood the situation? The Sleeper . . . wasn't what we thought it was. I had to go along. They would have suspected the truth, otherwise. I was right there with them, on the hill overlooking the nuclear power plant. In the bright summer sunshine; still trying to talk them into setting up stronger safeguards . . . but they wouldn't listen. They used the Red King's Ruby to make contact with what had lain sleeping under the barrow for so many centuries. Used the Ruby's power, to turn their dream into reality."

"Hold it," I said. "Let me get this straight. You were close enough to see a nuclear power plant you were planning to blow up?"

"I know!" said Coll. "We were young, we were stupid, and intoxicated with the possibilities for our cause. And we truly believed the Ruby would protect us. Perhaps fortunately, things never got that far. When the Sleeper awoke, and burst forth from its barrow mound, we saw at once that it wasn't at all what we'd expected. It wasn't some ancient

Celtic chief, or magician, or some powerful remnant of Times Past. No. It was a Horse. A great White Horse. It came ghosting up through the nuclear power plant without even touching it, invisible to their scientific mindsets, growing larger and larger. Filling the sky. We only saw it because we were connected through the Red King's Ruby. The White Horse was huge, massive, overwhelming to merely human senses. A brilliant, dazzling white too terrible to look at directly. The embodiment of all horses, and the power they gave the Celts over their enemies.

"That's why there are carvings of white horses on hills and cliffs all over England. Because our ancestors worshipped the White Horse. What we'd awoken, and called forth, was a living god. Not the god of horses, but the idea of a Horse, worshipped as a god. Worshipped by so many, and for so long, that the sheer concentrated belief was enough to create what they believed in. We never had a hope in hell of controlling such a thing. An idea, with the power of a god. Once it was out and free again, it shrugged us off like we were nothing. After so long asleep, imprisoned under the barrow mound by priests who'd grown afraid of what they worshipped, all it wanted to do was run free.

"Scared out of our minds by what we'd unleashed, we tried so hard to rein it in, to break the White Horse to our will, and control it. But the Red King's Ruby just faded away, driven out of reality and back into the world of dreams by the sheer power of the living god. Because the Ruby was only ever a dream of a thing, made solid by its dreamer's faith . . . and it was no match for the certainty of a living idea. We'd brought other things with us, other Objects of Power, I'd insisted on that . . . but none of it did any good. Just the backlash was enough to weaken us all, rob us of our strength and certainty. So we ran away.

"We used a preprogrammed teleport spell to transport us back here, to Trammell Island. Our oldest and most secret bolt-hole, where no one could see us. We thought we'd be safe here."

"You ran away?" I said, so angry I could hardly speak.

"Leaving the White Horse to run free? You didn't even try to warn anyone?"

"There was nothing we could do!" said Coll.

"You could have told the Droods!" I said. "You were their agent. They've handled worse things than living gods in their time!"

"I wasn't thinking clearly, all right!" said Coll. "None of us were. We were all in shock. Some of us thought we should try to control it again, later. Some just wanted to hide, somewhere the White Horse could never find us. We would have found some way to warn the world, I'm sure, but that was when the Drood's chosen agent turned up. Because I'd already told the Droods about Trammell Island. They might not be able to see in, but they could still get in. And you all saw . . . what their agent did."

Coll held up his memory crystal again, and the vision of yesterday returned. We all watched as the shadowy figure stepped forward into the light, looking calmly and dispassionately around him at the dead bodies sprawled across and around the long dining table. There was no mistaking that old man, with his iron grey hair and military moustache. The Regent of Shadows. My grandfather Arthur Drood. The man Molly and I now worked for.

"Of course," said Molly, in a dangerously calm and far-away voice. "That's why none of their weapons could touch him. Even though he didn't wear the golden torc. The Regent had Kayleigh's Eye—that ancient amulet. Nothing can touch him while he's wearing it."

"I don't understand," said Adams. The beginnings of anger were stirring in his soft voice. "Who . . . who is that?"

"That is the Regent of Shadows," I said. "A rogue Drood, who left the family to set up his own organisation. These days, he runs the Department of the Uncanny. Presumably . . . the Droods learned what the White Horse Faction had done, and decided they were too dangerous to be allowed to continue. They were to be an object lesson; *pour discourager les autres*. And they sent the Regent, as an independent contractor, so they could have deniability. Just in case it ever came back to bite them on the arse. Perhaps the Drood Matriarch wanted other underground groups to see this . . . slaughter, as the cost of endangering the world. Martha always was ready to do the hard, necessary thing."

"Yes," said Coll. "Only I was left alive to spread the word . . . of the consequences of defying the Droods."

He turned the memory crystal in his hand, and the vision continued. We all watched the Regent of Shadows move steadily through the dining hall, making sure everyone was dead. And then he left the room, and Monkton Manse, in pursuit of the fleeing teenage Molly Metcalf. It broke my heart to see her, running blindly across the black rocks, her face still stained with the blood of her murdered mother. The Regent emerged from the rear of the house just in time to see Molly run through the Fae Gate and disappear. He stopped, and shrugged, and went back inside.

But the vision continued, following Molly through the dimensional gate and into the wild woods . . . where she finally collapsed, to lie on a grassy bank, weeping for all she had lost, surrounded by tall trees. Animals and spirits of the wild woods slowly emerged from among the trees and the bushes, to protect and comfort her. A huge brown bear slowly turned his great shaggy head to look right at us, as though he could see us, watching him. He lunged forward, and the vision disappeared.

Coll made his memory crystal disappear. "I survived, because I turned and ran the moment I saw the Regent of Shadows in the doorway. A Drood field agent would have been under orders to let me go, but seeing the Regent changed everything. The warning and slapped wrist I expected had been replaced by a hired killer. The Regent of Shadows did have something of a reputation for such work, back then."

"I never knew that," I said. "But then, the Droods got up to a lot of things that I never knew about."

Coll shrugged. "No reason why you should. Even the infamous Shaman Bond can't be expected to know everything. I'm told the Regent has . . . mellowed, in recent years. Getting old will do that to you."

"How did you escape, Hadrian?" said Molly.

"I fled through the Fae Gate, long before you reached it," said Coll. "I know; I should have taken you with me. Made sure you were safe. But what can I say; I panicked. I was convinced the Droods wanted me dead, because I'd taken part in the Working. So I disappeared through the Fae Gate and just kept on going—jumping in and out of a dozen more dimensional portals, across the world. Until I was sure I'd muddied my trail sufficiently. I finally went to ground in Shanghai, crawled into a hole, and pulled it in after me. I didn't come out again until I'd arranged for a new identity and a new face. And then I moved on . . . from city to city, country to country, always moving so no one could find me, or track me down." He smiled briefly at Molly. "This is the first time I've looked like me in ten years. All for you, Molly." He turned to Troy and Adams and Morrison. "I thought the world had forgotten all about me until you came and found me and invited me here. And I saw a chance to redeem myself, at last. By helping create a new White Horse Faction, completely different from the old."

Molly looked at me. She didn't say anything, but now we both knew why the Regent had sent us here, on this mission. To learn the truth about Molly's parents, and their execution, that he couldn't bring himself to tell us, face to face. Coll said the Regent had changed, but he also said the Regent of Shadows had a reputation for bloody work. And I had to wonder: what else was there my newly found grandfather had done that he couldn't bring himself to tell me?

Just what kind of a man was I working for now?

For a long while, no one said anything. We all just sat there round one end of the stupidly long dining table. Lost in our thoughts, looking at each other for some clue as to what we should say, or feel. Coll ate everything on his plate, poured himself another glass of wine, and seemed content for someone else to start the ball rolling again. For someone who'd supposedly experienced so much guilt and remorse over his previous sins, he didn't seem particularly upset. In the end, Stephanie Troy broke the silence, speaking quietly, with great dignity and utter certainty.

"We . . . would never do anything like that. What the old Faction tried to do with the White Horse was utterly unacceptable. The crushing of a free spirit . . . no. We would never do that. We are different."

"That's why we're here," said Adams, in his soft and calm voice. "To plan a new, non-violent way of bringing about lasting change."

"Damn right," said Morrison. "You can't defeat the enemy by becoming the enemy."

"Fine words," said Hadrian Coll.

And then the next generation of the White Horse Faction turned as one to look meaningfully at Molly. She stared right back at them.

"What?"

"Your reputation precedes you," said Troy. "Your violent reputation."

"We've heard all the stories," said Adams. "And while we admire your . . . passion, there's no room in our organisation for anyone who still believes in the kind of violent confrontation that fills your . . . exploits."

"They say you once made all the portraits inside Number 10 Downing Street come alive, to attack the then prime minister," said Morrison. "And that you briefly gave the American Pentagon a new sixth side, full of horrors."

"No," said Molly. "The Pentagon has always had a secret sixth side. I just fixed it so everyone could see it, for a while. Not that it made any difference. Most people didn't understand the significance of what they were seeing. Next time, I'll put up some explanatory signs. Maybe something in neon . . ."

"Mischief is one thing," said Troy. "Mass murder is another. You blew up an entire private members club in the West End of London. Killed everyone inside. Do you deny it?"

"Hell no," said Molly. "I'm proud of it. That particular club was a brothel, where men of wealth and privilege could go to do appalling things to underage children. I got the kids out, before I killed everyone else. Do it again, in a moment."

"I have always been so proud of you, Molly," said Coll.

She didn't look at him. She didn't look at me, either. Which was probably just as well, because I was thinking of a whole bunch of other things she'd done that I knew for a fact were a hell of a lot more extreme than anything the next generation had mentioned. Usually with good reason, but probably not one the avowedly non-violent next generation could accept. They were looking steadily at Molly in a way that suggested they were still sitting in judgement of her, and hadn't made up their minds yet.

"The word is, that you've calmed down a lot since you hooked up with your Drood," said Troy. "Now you've got in bed with the enemy."

Everyone winced at that, just a bit. Trust a woman to fight dirty.

"I got involved with one particular Drood," Molly said calmly. "My Eddie. I have never been a part of his family. I didn't bring Eddie here with me because I knew you wouldn't approve of him. That's why I shelled out good money to hire Shaman Bond, to watch my back."

"Now you finally know the truth," I said carefully, "about what really happened to your parents. . . . What do you want to do next, Molly? Do you want to kill the Regent?"

"Yes," said Molly. "But, I have to think about it."

She didn't say, *Because he's your grandfather. So it's complicated.* She didn't say any of that out loud, but I could see it in her eyes.

Phil Adams rose to his feet. "I'm really not comfortable with the atmosphere in this room. I'm going to get another bottle of wine. I hope to experience a more positive atmosphere, when I return."

He left quickly. Obviously thinking he was making a point of principle. And not just running away from questions he couldn't cope with. Troy and Morrison looked at each other knowingly.

"He's never been comfortable with clashing emotions," said Troy. "Always wants everyone to be nice, just because they're on the same side."

"Don't give me those negative vibes, Moriarty!" said Morrison.

We all managed some kind of smile, at that. Troy and Morrison talked with Coll some more, ignoring Molly and me. Coll was full of apologies and justifications for his past, and how much he wanted to make up for his sins, by helping them build a new White Horse Faction. Troy wanted to believe him. I wasn't so sure about Morrison. Molly and I sat side by side, and didn't even look at each other. We both had a lot to think about. It took all of us a while to realise that Phil Adams hadn't returned.

"Oh, bloody hell," said Morrison. "He's not sulking again, is he?"

"He's probably hovering outside in the corridor," said Troy. "Refusing to come back in until we're all being happy bunnies together."

"Get your arse in here, Phil!" Morrison said loudly. "This is as positive as it's going to get!"

There was no response. Morrison got up and went to look out the door. Adams wasn't there. Troy went to join Morrison, and they both called Adams several more times. There was no reply. Coll got to his feet.

"I think we should go look for him. This isn't a good place to be on your own."

"Why?" said Troy. "What do you mean?"

"Don't you know about this house?" I said. "Didn't you research the awful history of Monkton Manse before you came here?"

"No," said Morrison. "We chose it because it was the last meeting place of the original White Horse Faction. And because the Island's in a null."

"You should have checked," said Coll.

I rose to my feet, and Molly immediately rose to her

feet to stand beside me. "Trust me," I said. "This is a bad place. Really bad things happened here . . . long before the Faction massacre. I think we need to find Adams quickly, before someone or something else does."

Molly led the way out of the dining hall, since she knew the house best, and we all followed her through a twisting maze of hallways and side corridors. Some of the lights had gone out, leaving whole areas nothing but darkness and shadow. I told myself it was just old bulbs failing, but I wasn't sure I believed me. We called out Adams' name, at regular intervals. He never replied. Eventually, we split into two groups, to cover more ground. Coll went off with Troy and Morrison, while Molly and I stayed together. We went back and forth, and up and down, checking every door and room we passed, until finally, we found him.

Phil Adams lay at the bottom of a flight of stairs. From the way his head was twisted around, it was clear his neck was broken. There was a lot of blood around the body. At first, I thought he must have fallen. Maybe even been pushed. But once I turned him over, I saw that he was covered in bloody hoof-marks. His flesh was torn and his bones were broken and his face was a bloody mess. He looked like he'd been trampled to death, by some great horse.

Or Horse.

I checked for a pulse anyway, because you have to. He was still warm, but he was very definitely dead. Whatever had attacked him had done a real job on him. It felt like every bone in his body was broken. Stephanie Troy turned up while I was still checking out Adams. She'd got separated from the others. She couldn't even look at the body. She turned away, saw Morrison coming down the corridor, and ran to him to press her face into his shoulder. He held her to him, patting her back automatically, and then he looked past her at the dead body, and his face went white . . . with what looked a lot more like anger than shock. He held Troy tightly, murmuring comforting words, unable to take his eyes off the body. Coll turned up last, saw what had happened to Adams, and swore briefly. I straightened up, stepped away from the body, and glared at Coll.

"What the hell were you thinking, letting those two go off on their own? You know this house! You know better."

"It wasn't his fault," said Troy, finally letting go of Morrison. She looked at Coll and Molly and me, but she still couldn't bear to look at the body. "There were just so many doors and exits and corridors that doubled back on themselves, we got separated. What . . . happened to Phil?"

"Looks to me like he's been trampled to death," said Coll. I was glad he said that, so I wouldn't have to. Morrison glared at Coll.

"Are you insane? Trampled? How could anything have trampled Phil to death, without any of us hearing it?"

"Are we talking about a horse?" said Troy, just a bit shrilly. "You think a horse got in here and did that?"

"Shaman and I heard a horse, earlier," said Molly. "We heard it running along the beach, but we couldn't see it anywhere."

Coll looked at her sharply. He looked like he wanted to say something, but didn't. Of us all, he seemed the most shaken. I looked at him steadily.

"You know what's going on here, don't you?"

"It's the White Horse," said Coll. He looked older, his face grey and slack and sick. "The Horse from under the mound. It's here."

"It shouldn't have been him," said Troy. "Not Phil. He was always the gentlest of us all."

She turned abruptly and ran down the corridor, heading in the direction of the front door. Morrison hurried after her. I didn't want to leave the body, but I didn't want Troy off on her own, either. So we all went after her. She managed a remarkable turn of speed, and we were all seriously out of breath when we finally caught up with her. She was standing in the entrance hallway, staring at the closed front door with wide, spooked eyes. Morrison got to her first, and grabbed her by the shoulder. She didn't look round. He spoke sharply to her, but she couldn't tear her eyes away from the closed door. Molly and I stood together, leaning on each other as we got our breath back. Coll brought up the rear, hacking and coughing noisily. Troy paid no attention to any of us.

And then we heard it. From somewhere outside, beyond the closed door, came the clear and distinct sound of approaching hooves. Slow and steady and deliberate, and much heavier than they should have been. Troy whimpered out loud, one hand pressed against her mouth. Morrison put both hands on her shoulders, and pulled her backwards, away from the door. Coll looked at the closed door like a man looking at his death.

"I could go and open the door," I said quietly to Molly. "See what's really out there."

"Really not a good idea," said Molly, just as quietly. "First, you can't use your usual . . . protection, in present company. And second, we didn't see anything on the beach. What makes you think you'll see anything here?"

"No one is to open that door!" said Coll. "Monkton Manse has its own protections! I don't think it can get through the door."

"Are you crazy?" said Morrison. "It's already got in here once, to kill Phil! We need to get out of here! Out of this house, and off this cursed island!"

"Best idea I've heard so far," I said.

I turned away and got out my Merlin Glass. But when I tried to activate it, nothing happened. The hand mirror remained just a mirror.

"Okay," I said quietly to Molly. "That's . . . unusual. I didn't think there was anything here powerful enough to block the Glass."

"If there really is a living god out there . . ." said Molly.

"I don't know," I said. "I'm not convinced. This doesn't feel right. I think we're missing something. . . ."

"It's the Horse," said Coll. "It's found me."

"Shut up!" screamed Troy. "If you brought it here, then this is all your fault!"

"Easy, Steph," said Morrison. "The enemy's out there, not in here."

"Maybe we should head for the back door," I said. "The Fae Gate could get us all off the island."

"You really think we can get to the Gate before the White Horse catches us?" said Coll.

"Come on," I said. "It's just a horse! How dangerous can it be?"

"You saw what it did to Phil," said Morrison. "I served two tours in Afghanistan, and I never saw anything that brutal." He glared at Coll. "You should have told us. We'd never have brought you here if we'd known. . . . Why don't you go open that door? Go outside! You're the one it wants!"

"Take it easy," I said quickly. "If that really is a living god out there, the last thing we want to do is present it with a human sacrifice. So, let's take a little time and think this through. Figure out exactly what we're dealing with. No more stories, Hadrian; give us the facts. What exactly are we facing here?"

"It's a living god," said Coll, spreading his hands in a helpless gesture. "An idea given shape and form and power, by those who worshipped it for so long."

"Listen!" said Troy. "It's stopped . . ."

We all listened. There were no more noises from beyond the closed front door.

"Is it gone, do you think?" said Troy.

"Either that, or it's standing really still," I said. "Want to go open the door and take a look?"

"What is the matter with you?" said Coll. "Why are you so eager to let the bloody thing in?"

"Sorry," I said. "Danger makes me flippant."

"If it's there, I can hit it," said Molly. "I ain't afraid of no Horse."

"You would be," said Coll, "if you'd seen it."

Morrison turned suddenly, and ran back down the hallway. Troy called out after him, miserably, but he just kept going. Didn't even look back. I started to go after him.

"No!" Molly said immediately. "In situations like this, it's always a bad idea to go rushing off on your own. It's so much easier to pick off someone when they're on their own."

"But we have to find him!" said Troy.

"He could be anywhere, by now," said Coll. "But you're right, we can't leave him to the mercy of the White Horse. Or the house . . . so, we split into two groups again, and this time we stick together. Troy, stay close to me. Molly, don't let Shaman out of your sight. Whoever catches up with Morrison first shouts out and stays put. Molly, follow the house perimeter, see if you can get a glimpse of whatever's outside."

He led Troy off down the hallway. She stuck so close to him she was practically hiding in his coat pocket. Molly and I looked at each other, shrugged pretty much simultaneously, and set off.

Monkton Manse was a really big house. It took a long time for us to work our way round the perimeter, staring cautiously out of each window in turn. Darkness had fallen, and the light from the house didn't penetrate far into the shadows outside. It seemed to me that a really big White Horse ought to show up clearly, but I couldn't see anything. We checked every room we passed, just in case the Horse had sneaked in, somehow, but there was no sign of it anywhere. I'd never felt comfortable in Monkton Manse, and now I was starting to jump at every moving shadow or sudden noise. If we really were under siege from a living god, I wanted my armour. But I couldn't call on it without betraying my true identity. I wasn't sure that really mattered any more, but I was reluctant to throw aside my mission until I was sure there really was a living Horse god on the prowl around Monkton Manse.

The dead body had been real enough, but anyone can fake horse sounds. It bothered me that I hadn't seen anything.

"If it is the White Horse, can you take it down with your armour?" said Molly, casually.

"Oh, sure," I said. "I'd bet the strange matter in my armour against anything with four legs and hooves. Maybe we could offer it some sugar lumps."

"A concept, made manifest, and then buried for centuries because its own priests grew frightened of what they'd created," said Molly. "What do you want to bet, Shaman, that when the Horse woke up, it woke up angry?"

"But how powerful can it be after being asleep for so long?" I said. "That must have weakened it."

"Unless," said Molly, "it's been quietly rebuilding its strength, all this time. I'm more concerned with its state of mind. Finally released from its prison, after so many years, and immediately someone tries to break it to their will, to make it their slave. . . ."

I looked at her steadily. "You were there, at the meeting, after they called it up. How much of that do you remember, now?"

"Still only bits and pieces." Molly scowled fiercely. "I'm pretty sure I wasn't there at the Working. My parents would never have allowed that . . . I can't believe I forgot so much!"

"You were in shock," I said. "You didn't want to remember."

"My past isn't what I thought it was," said Molly. "I'm not what I thought I was."

"Yes, you are," I said firmly. "You're the wild witch, the laughter in the woods, kicking arse in the name of the good and the true. And I wouldn't have you any other way."

And then we both looked round sharply as we heard a scream. It sounded like a man, facing something truly horrible, and then the sound broke off, and stopped. Molly and I were already off and running. It didn't take us long to find Joe Morrison, lying dead on the rucked-up, bloody carpeting. Torn and broken, his ruined flesh was stamped with hoof-marks. There was no sign of Troy or Coll anywhere. I checked the body, shook my head at Molly, and then studied the surroundings carefully.

"Odd," I said. "I don't see any hoof-marks in the carpeting, the whole length of this corridor. Or in the spilled blood around the body. Nothing to show anything else was ever here."

"Apart from the very thoroughly trampled body," said Molly.

"Well, apart from that, yes," I said. "I suppose . . . if the White Horse is a supernatural creature, it wouldn't have to make impressions on its surroundings if it didn't want to."

"Try the Merlin Glass again," said Molly. "I really don't like this place."

"You could always teleport us out of here yourself," I pointed out.

She shook her head quickly. "I already tried. This whole island is set inside a mystical null, remember? I can't get my bearings. . . . The only way off Trammell Island that doesn't involve a boat or a hell of a long swim are the established dimensional doors, like the Fae Gate. The Merlin Glass was powerful enough to get us in; I'm hoping it can get us out."

I shrugged, and tried the Glass again. I murmured the activating Words, and the image in the looking glass changed immediately to reveal the Horse's huge white head, filling the Glass. It shone out of the mirror like a spotlight, supernaturally bright. The long bony face glared at me, and then surged forward, as though trying to reach out through the Glass. The crimson eyes were wide and wild, and full of a terrible old knowledge. Great blocky teeth showed in its snarling mouth. Molly cried out. I shut down the Glass, shouting the words at the mirror, and the image disappeared. The hand mirror was just a mirror again. I put it away, in my pocket dimension.

"It was coming through," said Molly. She sounded shaken. "And it felt . . . so much *bigger* than any living thing has any right to be."

"Okay," I said. My voice didn't sound quite as steady as

I would have liked, but I pressed on. "We are facing a very determined living god. It's already killed two people, for reasons that aren't clear yet. What does it want with us?"

"Not us, Eddie," said Molly. "With me. It wants me, because I was part of the group that tried to tame it, and break it to their will."

"But you weren't a part of the Working! You didn't know anything about it until it was all over!"

"I don't think the White Horse cares," said Molly. "You saw it, in the Glass. Did that look like a rational Being to you? No, it saw me. It's marked me. And soon it will come for me. . . ."

"Well, tough," I said. "It can't have you. You're mine."

She smiled at me, and put a hand on my chest. "Am I?"

"Forever and a day," I said, putting my hand over hers. "I know you've been through a lot, Molly, but you have to get a grip on yourself. It's just a horse."

"Yes," she said. "It is. And I have faced far worse, in my time." She seemed to straighten up, and her gaze sharpened. "Time to get back in the saddle . . ."

"Come on," I said. "Let's track the bloody thing down. I've got my armour, and you've got your magics; we can do this. Bloody horse isn't going to know what's hit it."

"Damn right," said Molly. "Been a while since I've punched out a living god." And then she stopped, and frowned. "But I can't help feeling . . . that just maybe the White Horse is the innocent party in all this. It didn't ask to be buried, called forth, and used."

"It's killing people," I said flatly. "And that crosses the line. My family exists to keep things like living gods from killing people."

There was another scream. It sounded like a woman, this time. Horrified, hysterical, and once again cut off, abruptly. Molly and I ran through the narrow corridors, to find the next body lying crumpled in a doorway. Stephanie Troy, who only ever wanted to do good and protect people, had been trampled to a bloody pulp. Broken bones protruded in splinters through the torn flesh, and one side of her face had been completely smashed in, a single great hoof-mark obliterating half her features. Her one remaining eye stared helplessly out, at the world that had betrayed her.

I knelt down beside her, but didn't try for a pulse this time. I couldn't see the point. They were all gone now; three good-natured and good-intentioned young people, who would have been the next-generation leaders of the White Horse Faction. They had such great dreams; I should have taken them more seriously.

"I let them down," I said to Molly. "I was right here, and I couldn't even keep them alive."

"Don't blame yourself," said Molly. "Blame the mission. We weren't briefed for any of this. There's no way we could have anticipated . . . what's happened here. There's nothing you could have done for any of them. We got here too late."

"We've been too late all along," I said angrily. "Always one step behind, while something else has been leading us around by the nose. I'm starting to get a bad feeling about this, Molly. I don't think we understand what's really going on here."

I subvocalised my activating Words, and my armour spilled out of the torc to cover my face in a golden mask. And through the expanded senses of my mask, I studied every detail of Stephanie Troy's corpse. Every wound, every impact, every impression of a great hoof. I zoomed in on every detail, using the mask like a magnifying glass and a microscope; checking and collating and comparing every last little bit of evidence.

Until quite suddenly, I spotted something interesting. All the hoof-prints were exactly the same. Same shape, same depth, same details. If this body had been trampled by a Horse, I would have expected four different and quite distinct hoof-prints. It might be a living god, but it was still a quadruped. Instead, there was the same single hoof-mark, over and over again. I called up several of the imprints on the inside of my mask, and superimposed them, one on top of the other . . . and they were all exactly alike. I dismissed my mask, stood up, and quietly explained my findings to Molly.

"The White Horse wouldn't take the trouble to trample its victims to death one hoof at a time," I said.

"So it's not the Horse that's been killing people," said Molly.

"No," I said. "Whatever else is going on with the White Horse, I don't think it gives a damn about the next generation of the White Horse Faction. I think . . . we have ourselves a very human murderer, in Monkton Manse. And unless someone else has been hiding here all along, which doesn't seem likely . . . we know who the killer is."

"Hadrian Coll was my parents' best friend," said Molly. "It can't be him. He taught me how to be a free agent!"

"He was a double agent, working for my family," I said. "He betrayed people to the Droods, over and over again. He never was who you thought he was."

"That was the job, all right," said Coll.

We looked quickly round, and there he was, standing in a doorway, half hidden in shadows, smiling at us. I had no idea how long he'd been there. He looked entirely relaxed, even calm. Didn't even glance at Troy's body. He nodded to me. "I should have known you'd be the one to find me out, Drood."

"How long have you known?" I said.

"From the moment I met you. Your torc is well hidden, but I am half Drood, after all. I inherited the Sight from your uncle James, the legendary Grey Fox. Who was always quick enough to father a child, but never wanted to hang around to see how they turned out. I take it you are his nephew, the equally legendary Eddie Drood? Molly's fellow. What happened to the real Shaman Bond?"

"I took his place," I said smoothly. "He doesn't even know I'm here, using his name. But even with the Sight, you shouldn't . . ."

Coll shrugged, almost angrily. "You can't spend as long on the run as I have, with learning to See all kinds of things that you're not supposed to be able to." He looked at Molly. "You, with a Drood. Never thought I'd see the day. . . ."

"You don't know me," said Molly. "You don't know any-hing about me. How could you, when you kept so much rom me? How could you do this, Hadrian? How could you ust murder these people, after they went to all the trouble f tracking you down, to give you a second chance?"

"It's all about survival," said Coll, entirely unmoved. "I never asked for their help, or their second chance. And I certainly never wanted to be found. Bloody fools. Survival always comes first, Molly. I taught you that."

He stepped forward, out of the shadows of the doorway, into the light. Like the Regent had, so many years before. Coll carried a huge wooden club, with a steel hoof attached to the heavy end. The hoof, and much of the club, was soaked with blood and hair and gore. Thick crimson drops fell steadily from the club's end to the carpet. A terrible, brutal weapon.

"I arrived on the Island first," said Coll, smugly. "Long before you two, never mind the Faction. I watched you from the Manse, while I decided how to play this. It gave me quite a turn to see you, Molly, all grown up. I almost gave it up then . . . almost. Survival has no room in it for sentiment, or pity. I'd brought this nasty little toy with me, carefully designed to confuse the issue. I hid it here, in the house. I still hoped I wouldn't have to use it . . . if the White Horse didn't show up. But it did. I knew it would. The new Faction leaders had to die, in a sufficiently brutal manner that no one would even try to reassemble the White Horse Faction again."

"But . . . why?" said Molly. "Why did they have to die? What did they do that was so much of a threat to you, that you had to bludgeon them to death?"

"They found me," said Coll. "And I didn't want to be found. Couldn't afford to be found. It's the Horse, you see. It's been chasing me, all these years. Because I'm the last survivor of the Working that called the White Horse forth, and then tried to control it. Because I'm the only one who might be able to put it down, and put it back under its barrow mound again. That's why I disappeared so thoroughly, ten years ago. Why I've been on the run ever since. Always on the run, never able to stop and rest for long, running from one bolt-hole to another, so it could never find me. Until those three young fools tracked me down.

"I still don't know how they managed it. Someone must have talked. Someone always talks, eventually. But Troy and Adams and Morrison found me, and knocked on my door . . . when even the Droods didn't know where I was."

"My family stopped looking for you years ago," I said. "You were never that important to us."

Coll flinched, and then laughed. Briefly, and perhaps a little bitterly. "Oh, but I was important. . . . When the White Horse finally finds me, and has its revenge upon me, it will turn its hatred on all Humanity. For burying it under that mound for centuries. For the sin of not worshipping it any more. I've kept the world alive, all these years, by keeping the Horse's attention fixed on me!"

"You do fancy yourself, don't you?" I said. "It's just a horse! My family will deal with it. We've dealt with worse."

Coll laughed again, and shook his head stubbornly. He'd been the hero of his own story far too long to give it up now. Even with a murder weapon in his hand, dripping blood and brains from people who had wanted so badly to be his friend.

"I had to kill them," he said, patiently. "Because if they could find me, then the White Horse could use them to find me. It wasn't difficult. All I had to do was wait for one to go off on their own, and then just pick them off, one at a time. They never saw it coming. . . . Now I can just disappear again. Escape to somewhere else, become someone else . . . after I've killed you two. Sorry, Molly. I don't have any choice. No witnesses left behind . . . so no one will ever know what happened here. Just a few more dead bodies, in a house with a bad reputation. One more mystery, in mad old Monkton Manse."

"You'd kill me, Hadrian?" said Molly stepping forward. "You'd really kill me?"

"That's close enough, Molly," said Hadrian. "Glad to see you haven't forgotten what I taught you. I am still fond of you, and very proud of what you've made of yourself

ou're . . . important to me; but not more important than
e. It's always all about survival."

"You betrayed my parents to the Droods," said Molly,
nd her voice was cold, so cold. "They were your friends!"

"I've had many friends, in many groups," said Coll.
And left them all behind when I moved on. That was the
b. I was only ever in it for the money. After all, you can't
ope to survive, and protect yourself properly, without
oney. So that always has to come first." He turned his
mpty eyes on me. "The Droods promised me they'd take
e in. Make me one of them, part of the family. I'd have
een safe, as one of the family. Like my father. But they
ept putting me off, saying, 'just one more mission' . . . un-
l I finally realised they never had any intention of making
od on their promises. Not while I could still be useful to
em. So really, this is all your fault, Drood."

"You actually think you can take me, Hadrian?" I said.
Your club with a bit of metal on it, against my strange-
atter armour?"

"Oh, this is so much more than just a club," Coll said
arnestly. "I've invested a lot of really nasty magics in this
ld wood, soaked it in vicious aptitudes and powerful
ualities, down the long years. . . ."

"Powerful enough to stand against my magics?" said
Molly. And just like that, she no longer sounded like the
irl who idealised her old tutor. She sounded calm and cold
nd very dangerous. Her old self again.

Coll didn't look impressed. He held the club out before
im. "You have no idea of what you're dealing with."

"Right," I said.

I stepped forward to distract him, and when he turned
e club in my direction, Molly stepped briskly forward and
icked Coll square in the groin. His face squeezed up, and all
e breath went out of him. I hit him hard in the arm muscle
ith my fist, and his hand leapt open, dropping the club.
ame over.

And that was when we all stopped abruptly, and turned
ur heads, to look around. Suddenly, we were back in the

entrance hallway again. Even though we'd left it far behind, ages ago. We were half-way across the house, standing before the closed front door. Because something had called us there. And once again, we heard the sound of hooves approaching, outside. Coll forced his eyes open, past the tears streaming down his cheeks. He stared at the door with horrid fascination.

"No . . ." he said, almost pleadingly, like a child. "It can't do that . . . it can't!"

"It's found you," I said. "It's not too late, Hadrian. I suppose my family does owe you a debt. Come with me, agree to accept what punishment and penance my family decides on . . . and I'll stand between you and the Horse. Because I think there are still some things you're hiding from Molly that she needs to know."

But he wasn't listening to me. All his attention was fixed on the closed front door, and the terrible purposeful sounds outside. Drawing steadily closer. The noises were very loud, very heavy, very close now.

"You can't take me!" Coll screamed defiantly at the door. "You'll never have me!"

"I told you it was here," I said. "Molly and I heard it down on the beach. Funny that it didn't try to attack us . . ."

"It's found me again," said Coll. His eyes were bright, almost fey. "It always finds me. . . ."

"You're not the man I knew," said Molly.

Coll turned abruptly to face me. "You've got a deal, Drood. Everything I know, every dirty deal and trick I've been involved with, everything I know about the Regent of Shadows, and everything I haven't told you about Molly's parents. Just—protect me! That's your job, isn't it, Drood?"

I looked at Molly. "He's right. It is. But this isn't about me. It's about you. What do you need, Molly? You tell me what you want me to do, and I'll do it for you."

"Oh, hell," said Molly. "Let him live. He's too pathetic to kill, now. And just maybe . . . he might know things that I still want to know."

"Stand back," I said to Coll. "Give me room to work."

I summoned up my armour, and it slipped around me in a moment. I felt faster, stronger, sharper; more than enough to deal with a living Horse god. I moved forward, to stand facing the closed front door. The sound of hooves was very clear, very close. The sound of a massive, gigantic Horse. Its every step shook the floor. The sounds approached the door, came right up to it, and then walked right through solid wood without even pausing. The hoof sounds were right there in the hallway with us, advancing steadily, and still I couldn't see the White Horse, even with the augmented Sight my armour gave me. Heavy steps filled the hall, shaking the floor and the walls. I looked back.

Coll hadn't moved. He just stood there and stared at the sounds, his face deathly pale, his eyes wide. I think perhaps he saw what I couldn't. I stood between him and the sounds of the advancing Horse. My hands clenched into golden fists, spikes protruding from the knuckles. Molly came forward to stand beside me, stray magics sparking and spitting on the air around her.

"You can't have him," she said, raising her voice. "He's a thug and a coward and a murderer, but vengeance is mine, not yours."

The horse sounds just kept coming; so loud now they hurt my ears, even inside my armour. The floor shook, and the portraits on the walls swung back and forth, slamming into each other. The White Horse had to be right in front of me now. I braced myself, ready to throw a punch the moment anything touched me. Molly raised her glowing hands. And the Horse went right through us, invisible, and intangible as a thought. The sounds were behind us. I spun round, just in time to see Hadrian Coll throw up his hands to ward off something only he could see. And then the light went out of his eyes, and he fell to the floor, and didn't move again.

The sounds stopped. No more sense of something else, so much more than human, in the hallway. Silence. I checked Coll's body. He was quite dead. Not a mark on him, anywhere, apart from the look of sheer horror on his face. The Horse had trampled his soul.

"It is a terrible thing, to look into the face of a living god," murmured Molly.

"Coll isn't the problem any more," I said, getting up. "The White Horse is the problem now. We can't let it run free. How do we stop something like that?"

Molly looked at the body of the man who had been her friend and her tutor, and there was nothing in her face. Nothing at all. She turned away.

"Do we really have to stop it?" she said, her voice entirely calm. "I mean, it's just a horse. Let it run free. Like a wild thing should."

"It didn't end up under that barrow by choice," I said. "Its own priests put it there. Like you said, we have to consider its state of mind. Imprisoned for centuries, then released by people who only wanted to control and use it. If it really has been building up its power, all these centuries, now it no longer has Coll to pursue. . . . It could trample the whole world under its hooves."

We left Monkton Manse and went outside. We could hear the White Horse running down on the beach below. I led the way to the edge of the cliff, and we looked up and down the beach; but there was no sign of the Horse anywhere.

"I thought you could See anything through your mask?" said Molly.

"So did I," I said. "I thought you could See anything with your witchy Sight?"

Molly frowned, thought for a moment, and then carefully pronounced a very old and powerful Word, not meant for human vocal cords. And just like that, the White Horse was there. Impossibly huge, bigger than Monkton Manse, running not on the beach itself, but several feet above it. Dazzlingly white, brighter than the moon, running wild in the night, its unnatural brilliance reflected across the dark waters of the heaving sea. Running for the sheer joy of running; beauty and grace blazing in its every movement. Just to look at such a thing seized my heart. A living idea, too pure and too perfect for this small and grubby world.

"All right," said Molly. "Now we can see it. What are we going to do?"

I armoured up, covering myself from head to toe in gleaming gold. "We go down to the beach," I said.

I led the way down the steps cut into the cliff face. Molly stuck close behind me, stray magics sputtering on the air around her. When we reached the bottom and moved off along the pebbled beach, the White Horse was still cantering along, ignoring us. It looked even bigger, up close. Wild and majestic, and utterly untamed.

"I have to wonder what it's still doing here," said Molly. "I mean, with Hadrian dead, all those who might have bound the Horse again are gone. If it's so keen to trample the world, like you said, what's it still doing here?"

"I don't know," I said. "Maybe it's just doing a lap of triumph round the Island. It doesn't matter. The White Horse is a threat to all Humanity, and I have to stop it here, while I still can."

"How the hell are you going to stop something as big as that?" said Molly. "Walk up and punch it in the ankle?"

"Drood armour isn't just about strength and protection," I said. "Watch, and learn. And keep your magics handy, just in case this all goes horribly wrong."

I concentrated on the strange matter of my armour, and a long golden line fell from my right hand, more and more of it falling in coils, until finally I had a long gold lariat in my hand. I formed a noose, and threw it high up into the air and right over the head of the massive White Horse. The golden lariat fell into place before the Horse even knew what was happening. The noose tightened around its great white neck, and the glowing golden line snapped taut.

Immediately, I was pulled forward by the sheer impetus of the Horse; but I dug my golden heels deep into the pebbled beach. The Horse dragged me on, so that I left two deep channels behind me in the beach; but the strength and power of my armour was more than a match for any living god. The White Horse slowed, shrinking all the time, until finally it was just a horse; and then it came to a sudden halt—shaking and shuddering, and tossing its head. I walked steadily forward, keeping a steady pressure on the golden line. Just a man and a horse now, and the bridle I'd made to break its spirit.

I called the golden line back into my glove, a few feet at a time, as I came to stand beside the horse. It stood very still. The long white face turned to look at me, with old, dark, very wise eyes. We looked at each other for a while. I heard Molly hurrying up to join me, but I couldn't look away. I reached slowly out, took hold of the golden noose around the horse's neck, loosened it, and pulled it over the horse's head. The golden lariat snapped back into my glove, and was gone. I armoured down, and nodded to the horse, as Molly came to stand beside me.

"You were never a threat to the world, were you?" I said to the horse. "Just to those few poor fools who were so scared of you, that they tried to break you to their will. The one thing a creature of the wild like you could never stand. That's why your old priests put you under the mound; because you didn't give a damn about being worshipped. You just wanted to run free. So, go. Run free, as you were meant to.

"My people are the Droods. If you ever get tired of running, and you'd like some company, come and find us. You'd be very welcome. We've already got a dragon. You would be safe there, I promise you; free from all harm. But for now . . . run free!"

The White Horse reared up, growing larger and larger, until he was as big as the night sky, and then he turned and ran off across the sea, his hooves pounding on the waves until he disappeared into the night.

"You old softy, you," said Molly.

"I've always had a fondness for wild things," I said. "How are you feeling now, Molly?"

"More like myself," she said. "I wanted answers, and I found them here; just like the Regent promised. But I can't say I'm any wiser, or happier. We have to go back, Eddie. I need to talk to your grandfather about all the things he did as the Regent of Shadows."

"Of course you do," I said. "I have a few questions I need to put to him myself."

"I know he's your long-lost grandfather," said Molly. "I know how much he means to you, and I know he's done a lot to redeem himself. But I still have questions."

"Take it from me," I said. "Answers aren't everything. Are you ready to go?"

"Hell, yes," said Molly. "I never want to see this place again."

"Then let's get out of the cold," I said.

I took out the Merlin Glass, and this time it worked perfectly. I shook the hand mirror out to full size, big as a door, and concentrated on the coordinates of the Regent's private office at the Department of the Uncanny. We both stepped through the dimensional door. And then we both stood very still, as the mirror snapped shut behind us.

We were standing in the Drood family Armoury, deep under Drood Hall, facing my uncle Jack, the Armourer. I glared at him.

"You interrupted the spatial transfer!" I said. "You diverted us here! I didn't know you could do that."

He smiled smugly. "I am the one who wrote out the operating manual for the Merlin Glass, remember? Which I am ready to bet you still haven't finished reading yet. It doesn't matter. Eddie, Molly—you need to come with me. You're needed. All hell has broken loose."

"Oh, not again," said Molly.

CHAPTER TWO

Half as Old as Time

Molly gave my uncle Jack her best cold hard glare, the kind that could punch a hole through a stone wall. The Armourer glared right back at her. And I quietly took several steps back to let them get on with it, because I knew better than to get involved. There was no way this was going to end well, for anyone involved, and the best I could hope for was to find something large and solid to hide behind, for when they started throwing things. There was nothing I could say that wouldn't just make things worse, so I removed myself from the firing range, and took a look around.

The Drood family Armoury looked much the same as it always did. Lots of sound and fury, signifying things going bang. Lots of white-coated lab assistants hurrying back and forth between workstations and testing grounds, trying out brand-new versions of weapons of messy destruction. You have to be brave and talented and a mechanical genius to work in the Armoury; but it does also help if you're completely lacking in self-preservation instincts. It's a wonder to me we haven't bred the lab assistant gene out of the Drood family, through extreme testing to destruction. But, there's always a long waiting list to get in, proving once again the triumph of optimism over experience. There's pride and honour and worth to the family to be found in the Armoury, if you last long enough.

One young woman was knocking chunks off a stone golem, using depleted-uranium knuckle-dusters. The golem was looking pretty peeved about it. Someone who'd turned himself invisible could be heard barging about and banging into things, while swearing loudly and bitterly at the world in general, because the field that stopped light getting out also stopped light getting in. So he couldn't see anything. Or even find the OFF switch . . . and two interns who'd developed a highly miniaturised and very powerful explosive device, and then dropped it, were scrabbling around on the floor on all fours, trying to find the bloody thing before the timer ran out. Just another day in the Drood Armoury. I always enjoyed my visits. As long as I was careful where I put my feet.

Reluctantly, I turned back to Molly and the Armourer, who were now standing face to face, eyeballing each other so closely they could hardly blink without entangling their eyelashes. It would have been funny if the emotions involved hadn't been so raw, and so dangerous. Molly had discovered what she'd always thought she wanted—the truth concerning the death of her parents. And it had stabbed her in the heart. Being Molly, she dealt with the pain by spreading it around.

"Give control of the Merlin Glass back to Eddie," Molly said flatly. "I have to get to the Department of the Uncanny. I have questions to put to the Regent."

"Ah," said the Armourer. And just like that the fire went out of his eyes, and he stepped back. He sighed, almost sadly. "You've found out, then."

Molly was so surprised, she almost forgot to be angry. "You knew?"

I was thrown, myself. "You knew the Regent of Shadows killed her parents? And you never said anything?"

"Of course I knew," said the Armourer. He sat down in a handy chair. I sometimes forget how old he is, and how sudden shocks can drive the strength right out of him. Like most of my family he's fine with violence, but has trouble with emotions. He looked suddenly tired, and frail. A tall and stooped man of more than middle age, wearing a grubby white lab coat with many chemical stains and burns, over a T-shirt bearing the legend BORN TO KILL PEO-PLE WHO NEED KILLING. Two shocks of tufty white hair jut-ted out over his ears, under a bulging bald pate. He always looked like he carried the cares of the world on his shoul-ders, and couldn't wait to do something really unpleasant to the people who put them there. He was an excellent field agent, in his day. Like his father before him, my grandfa-ther Arthur, the Regent of Shadows. The Armourer sighed heavily.

"I always meant to talk to you about this, Molly. But somehow it never seemed to be the right time. And you were so pleased to find your missing grandfather, Eddie; I didn't want to spoil it for you. But yes, I know. I've always known. I was still part of the family Council, back then, deciding policy, and enforcement . . ." He looked steadily at Molly. "You mustn't think too harshly of the Regent. He only ever did what the family asked of him. He still thought there was a chance he might be allowed to come home."

"That doesn't matter," said Molly. "Nothing matters, except getting to the truth. Right to the bottom of it."

"Hadrian Coll claimed my grandfather had a reputation for killing work," I said. "I don't like the sound of that."

"We're not responsible for the way the world is," said the Armourer. "But we are responsible for doing whatev-er's necessary to preserve it from those who would corrupt and destroy it."

"Stop," said Molly. "No excuses, no distractions. I don't care what the Droods' current emergency is . . ."

"Don't care was made to care," the Armourer said mildly. "Especially since the current emergency is mostly of your making."

"Oh, hell," I said. "What have I done now?"

"No!" Molly said fiercely. "I am not going to be reasonable, I am not going to listen to you, I am not going to be guilt-tripped by you! To hell with this. Keep your Merlin Glass; I'll teleport myself out of here." She looked at me. "Well?"

"You know I want to come with you," I said. "I don't want you facing the Regent alone. But, I think I ought to at least find out what this new emergency is."

"This is why you'll never be free of your family," said Molly. "Even after everything they've done to you, they still have a hold on you. The Droods just use people, Eddie; I thought I'd taught you that. Don't look at me that way . . . you stay if you want. I'm going."

She concentrated . . . and then looked shocked when nothing happened. The Armourer cleared his throat, in an almost apologetic way.

"The Armoury has very powerful shields, my dear. Nothing gets in, nothing gets out. It's safer for everyone, that way. . . ."

"Then lower your shields." Molly's voice had never sounded colder.

I slowly realised that it had grown unusually quiet in the Armoury. I looked carefully around me, and found that all the lab assistants had stopped what they were doing to watch the infamous and much feared Molly Metcalf go head-to-head with the Armourer. Some of them were quietly turning strange weapons and unusual devices in her direction. And, in mine. The assistants put their lives on the line every day, not just in service to the family, but in service to the Armourer. They admired and adored him, to a man and a woman. And they were more than ready to kill anyone who threatened him.

Sometimes, I forget that Molly had spent years at war with the Droods over the death of her parents. I had forgiven Molly her many sins, but my family hadn't. Still, if the family was determined to make me choose between them and my Molly . . . the family would regret it. I smiled easily around me, and was pleased to see several of the lab assistants flinch. I moved forward, to stand beside Molly. Her whole body was painfully tense, her face dangerously cold.

"Lower your shields," Molly said to the Armourer. "Or else."

It's always hard when you're forced to choose between people you love. Especially when there's a whole bunch of heavily armed people watching you with narrowed eyes, fully prepared to blow you into small meaty chunks if they don't like your decision. So I braced myself and stepped very firmly between Molly and the Armourer.

"Everybody calm the fuck down," I said. "Or there will be tears before bedtime."

"You just can't bring yourself to do it, can you, Eddie?" said Molly. "No matter how many times you leave the family, they always drag you back in, to do their dirty work."

"I'm trying really hard not to choose a side," I said. "I don't want to see anyone hurt."

"Well, tough," said Molly. "That's not an option. You're either with me, or against me. Don't try to argue! I'm not interested! I've waited too long for the truth about my parents' death to be stopped by anyone."

"It's been ten years," I said. "Can't it wait just a few minutes more . . . ?"

"You got your parents back!" said Molly loudly. There were tears in her eyes. "Mine are still dead! All I've got left is the truth."

I nodded, slowly, and turned to face the Armourer. "Let her go, Uncle Jack. Whatever this is, you don't need her. You need me. So let her go. I'll stay, if you let her leave."

"Honourable as ever, Eddie," said the Armourer. "You know I've always been so proud of you . . . but unfortunately being reasonable won't do it, this time. You both have to stay, because you're both needed. The family requires your assistance in this emergency."

"Okay," I said. "Stuff the family."

I armoured up, and the golden strange matter flowed

around me in a moment. Molly and I moved quickly to stand back to back, ready to stand off anything the lab assistants might throw at us. I showed them a golden fist, with heavy spikes rising from the knuckles. Molly raised one hand, and dark and vicious magics flared around it. Most of the lab assistants did the sensible thing, and ran for cover. The rest turned their guns and devices on us, with steady hands and wide scared eyes. And then the Armourer cleared his throat loudly, and everyone turned to look. He was holding up a small green plastic clicker, in the shape of a cartoon frog.

"I designed this for emergencies," he said calmly. "It shuts down armour and magic, temporarily. I can strip you both of what makes you strong; but I can't guarantee to give it back to you."

"You wouldn't," said Molly.

"Only in self-defence," said the Armourer.

Molly shot me a quick glance, and I shrugged quickly at her. "We haven't got this far by being sensible. I'm game, if you are."

"You're really ready to go to war with your family, over me?" said Molly.

"Looks like it."

"What about your old motto: anything, for the family?"

"I got a new one: anything, for you."

"My lovely hero. All right, let's do it. No magic, no armour; but . . . they still never met anyone like us. I've got a spare knife in my boot, if you need it."

"No!" said the Armourer. He lowered the clicker, though I noticed he didn't put it away. He looked quickly from me to Molly, and back again. "Please, just listen to what I have to say. Let me explain why your help is so necessary. If you don't agree, then you're both free to go."

It was my turn to look at Molly. "I would like to hear what all this is about. But if you really need to do this . . ."

Molly considered the matter for a worryingly long moment, and then shrugged, and relaxed, just a little. "You've fought your family over me before, Eddie. I know where you stand. I've no right to ask you to do it again. The Regent . . . can wait. Talk, Armourer."

I armoured down, and Molly let her magics dissipate into the air. The lab assistants lowered their various weapons, and wandered off for a quiet sit-down and a nice cup of tea, until the shakes wore off. The Armourer shook his head slowly, and put away his clicker.

"I swear to God, you two put years on me. Come with me now, and all will be made clear to you."

He led the way out of the Armoury, and I hurried after him, with Molly bringing up the rear. I moved in close beside the Armourer.

"You were bluffing with that clicker, weren't you, Uncle Jack?"

"I'll never tell," he said easily. "Good to have you back, nephew."

We passed quickly through the wide corridors and packed passageways of Drood Hall, past paintings and sculptures of incredible value and antiquity, by names you'd know; the loot of generations of Droods, presented to us by a presumably grateful Humanity. Luxuries and comforts everywhere, wood-panelled walls and thick carpeting, along with objets d'art and objets trouvés that went back centuries. It was good to see the old place again; my bad memories were mostly of the family, rather than the Hall itself. And it was all made much easier by the knowledge that whatever the family said or did, I wasn't staying.

People rushed back and forth, on missions of their own, and I spotted familiar faces here and there. Most of them seemed surprisingly pleased to see me. I hadn't been this popular when I was running the family. Perhaps especially then. I was beginning to feel distinctly uneasy. The only time my family is ever pleased to see me is when they need me to do something for them. Usually something really unpleasant and spectacularly dangerous.

"I had no idea I was this popular," I said dryly to the Armourer.

"You're not," he said, not even slowing his pace enough to glance around. "It's just that something really bad is coming, headed straight for us, and you're all we've got to put in its way."

"Situation entirely bloody normal, then," I said.

"Actually, no," said the Armourer. "This particular situation shows every sign of being so bad it's beyond the family's abilities to deal with it. We've had to call a Summit Meeting."

I just blinked at him for a while, utterly astonished. "But . . . that hasn't been necessary for . . . what? Decades?"

"Oh, at least," said the Armourer. "That's how important and scarily dangerous this situation is. Major threat, red alert, atomic batteries to power and turbines to speed. So bad, in fact, that we're already looking to you to pull one of your last-minute miracle saves out of the hat, one more time. Especially since this is all your fault anyway. You and Molly."

"I just knew this whole mess would turn out to be our fault," I said solemnly to Molly. "Didn't you just know it would all turn out to be our fault?"

"Might be your fault," Molly said briskly. "Not mine. Nothing is ever my fault. What's a Summit Meeting?"

"Panic stations," I said. "Whenever something comes along that's too big for any single organisation to deal with, they ring the alarm bell and circle the wagons, and send out a call to all the major secret organisations, to talk things over. And see if there's anything they can do together. And given how much these organisations distrust each other, and hate each other's guts, you can see how serious things would have to get before they'd agree to talk to each other."

"Should I be getting worried, about now?" said Molly.

"I passed worried long ago," I said. "I have already reached deeply disturbed, and am heading into pant-wetting territory."

"And you're the one who persuaded me to stay," said Molly. "I should have gone riding on the Horse."

*   *   *

We came at last to the Sanctity, the huge open chamber at the heart of Drood Hall. I relaxed a little, despite myself, as I strode through the open double doors and into the massive room. The whole chamber was suffused with a marvellous rose red light that sank into my bones and into my soul, like a blessing. Molly and the Armourer smiled too, because it's impossible to feel angry or scared or worried for long, in the presence of the Droods' other-dimensional entity, Ethel. She has no physical presence in our world, or at least none she'll admit to, but the rosy light is a sign of her presence. She manifests in the Sanctity as a feeling of contentment, love, and protection made real in the world. Ethel gives us our strange-matter armour, and is our very own guardian and protector. Probably. It's hard to be sure, with an entity that's downloaded itself into our world from a higher reality. She does seem honestly fond of us.

"Eddie! Molly!" her voice rose happily on the air. "Yes! It's so good to have you both back again! How was Scotland? Did you bring me back a present?"

"Not as such," I said. "You're so hard to buy for, Ethel. What do you give the other-dimensional entity who is everything?"

"It's the thought that counts," Ethel said sulkily. "I never get any presents."

"There might be a nice horsey in your future," said Molly. "If you're good."

"Ooh! Ooh! I love ponies!" said Ethel, immediately cheerful again.

"Let us talk about the Summit Meeting," I said determinedly. "To start with, where's the rest of the Drood Council?"

"They won't be joining us," the Armourer said immediately. "They don't need to be here. The debating is over. All future decisions will be made at the Summit."

"I'm still not clear on why this Summit is so necessary," said Molly. "I thought you Droods decided everything that mattered, and all the other groups just . . . specialised?"

"We do like to give that impression," said the Armourer. "And a lot of the time, it's true. But not always."

. "The Summit invites representatives from all the major secret organisations across the world," I said. "Including the ones we don't normally admit exist. Which goes a long way to explaining how rare these Summits are. Most of these groups would rather see the whole planet go up in flames than cooperate with a hated rival. We'll be lucky if a dozen groups answer the call."

"This Summit is necessary," said the Armourer. "The invitations have gone out, and some representatives are already on their way. The current situation is quite possibly the biggest and the worst problem we've faced in a long time. . . ."

"Oh, bloody hell," I said. "It's not the Loathly Ones again, is it? I thought we'd finished off the Hungry Gods?"

"Nothing so straight forward, I'm afraid," said the Armourer. He paused then, and his mouth twisted, as though bothered by a bitter taste. "This . . . is all about the Crow Lee Inheritance."

"What?" I said.

"What kind of inheritance?" said Molly. "Is there any money involved? Only I have been running a bit short lately . . ."

"How can you be running short?" I said. "What about all the gold bullion . . ."

"Hush," Molly said immediately. "He doesn't need to know about that."

"When you two killed The Most Evil Man In The World," the Armourer said patiently, "all his many followers, enemies, and rivals started fighting among themselves over who would gain control of what Crow Lee left behind. His hidden hoard of secrets, unimaginable wealth, objects of power, blackmail material . . . etc., etc. We've had to send field agents rushing back and forth all over the world, stopping warring forces and stamping out supernatural bush-fires before they can spread. In secret bases and subterranean galleries, in every major city you can think of, the word is spreading . . . that there is one hell of a prize to be won. We're being run ragged just trying to keep a lid on things, and the real war hasn't even started yet. The Major Players and Individuals of Note are holding back, for the moment, letting the lesser forces exhaust themselves on each other, but that won't last. Things are already bad, but they're going to get much worse."

"Hold everything," I said. "We have been through this before. The Independent Agent was supposed to have left a hoard behind. Treasure beyond belief, secrets that would shock the world, magical and super-science weapons powerful enough to make anyone master of the world. And none of that ever amounted to anything. All bluff and bullshit. Just part of the myth such people create. Are we sure this Crow Lee Inheritance really exists?"

"Were we mentioned in the will?" said Molly. "I have bills to pay."

"No, you don't," I said. "You're famous for not paying your bills. I have bills to pay—on your behalf."

"What's yours is mine," Molly said comfortably. "Though not necessarily vice versa, if you know what's good for you." She looked at the Armourer. "Was Eddie mentioned in the will?"

"There was no will!" said the Armourer. "Oh, God, I can feel one of my heads coming on. . . ."

"Me too!" said Ethel.

"You don't have a head!" said the Armourer.

"Might have," said Ethel. "You don't know."

"Anyway . . ." said the Armourer. "None of that matters. The point is, a great many important, significant, and horribly powerful people and organisations believe the Inheritance does exist, and they're prepared to go to open war over it. Either to gain it for themselves, or to make sure their enemies don't get it. We are looking down the barrel of a war so potentially far-reaching it's bound to spill over into the everyday world. And we can't allow that to happen. We're only able to operate so freely because the world doesn't know we exist. If Humanity ever finds out who and what they really share this world with, they will go batshit mental. Fighting in the streets, blood in the gutters, churches and governments burning in the night, for having kept so much secret for so long ... all the world's arsenals finally unleashed: nuclear, bacterial, chemical ... and God alone knows where it would go from there. No. We have to stop this dead, before it gets out of hand."

"And how exactly are we supposed to do that?" said Molly. "Eddie, he's smiling. Why is the Armourer smiling?"

"Because this is the part we really aren't going to like," I said.

"The Summit Meeting has been called to help us decide how best to defuse this situation," the Armourer said smoothly. "I am going, as Drood representative, and you two are going because you killed Crow Lee, and therefore have more immediate information about him than anyone else. And because it's all your fault, remember?"

"I thought we'd get back to that," I said.

"I gave up guilt for Lent," said Molly. "And never took it up again. You should try it, Eddie, it's very liberating."

"Molly and I were there when the family investigated Crow Lee's country house," I said. "They tore the place apart, and didn't find a single damned thing worth a second look."

"Or at least, nothing important," said Molly. "I mean, yes, there was a whole load of really weird shit, scattered all over the place, but nothing of any worth."

"Or you'd have taken it," I said.

"Exactly!" said Molly. "The point being, all Eddie and I know for sure about Crow Lee was that he was a complete bastard and an utter shit, and the world is better off without him. So what can we contribute to this Summit?"

"The house was empty because it had already been emptied of anything that mattered, before you got there," said the Armourer. "Which suggests ... that perhaps he saw his death coming, and made plans. Possibly involving a comeback. So as the last people to see Crow Lee alive, you become vitally important. You have to talk to the Summit."

"Will the Regent be there, at this meeting?" Molly said suddenly. "Representing the Department of the Uncanny?"

"No," said the Armourer. "Given his past, and his past reputation, and his closeness to the Establishment these days, it was felt his presence would be . . . divisive. You and Eddie can represent the Department."

I nodded. "Yes. I can do that. Since I've left the family."

"No one ever really leaves the family," said the Armourer. "You should know that, Eddie. *Anything, for the family.*"

I deliberately turned my back on him, to look at Molly.

"You don't have to do this, Molly. But, I don't want you facing the Regent on your own. So I think you should wait this one out, in the wild woods. I could join you there, once the Summit is over."

"No," said Molly. "I'm going with you. Someone has to watch your back."

We shared a smile. The Armourer smiled fondly on us. Ethel was singing *Love is in the air* . . .

"That's the trouble with you and your damned family," said Molly. "There's always some crisis going on. Never a chance to catch your breath around here."

"Never a dull moment," the Armourer said brightly. "Ethel, will you please knock that off!"

There was a pause. "I do requests," said Ethel.

"How long before everyone gets here?" I said quickly. "And we can get this Summit started?"

"Oh, the Summit isn't being held here, at Drood Hall," said Ethel, sounding faintly scandalised. "No, we're not considered neutral ground. Or even safe ground."

"You mean there are people out there who don't trust the Droods?" said Molly. "I am shocked, I tell you, shocked."

"That's all right," said the Armourer. "We don't trust most of them, either. Just because we're on the same side, mostly, it doesn't mean we aren't all ready to stab each other in the back first chance we get. We spend more time spying on our allies than we do on the enemy. You know where you are, with the enemy. It's the friends and partners you have to keep an eye on."

"It's all about survival. . . ." said Molly.

"Exactly!" said the Armourer, beaming.

"I like you better in the Armoury, Uncle Jack," I said. "Let you loose in the world, and you get downright devious."

"I was a field agent before you were born, boy," said the Armourer. "Mostly I prefer to forget all that, and hide away in my Armoury. Where all I have to worry about is the lab assistants . . . but sometimes, the world just won't leave you alone."

"What about the Nightside?" said Molly, suddenly. "That's been neutral ground, for all sides, for thousands of years!"

"No," the Armourer said immediately. "Droods aren't allowed in the Nightside. By long compact and binding agreements."

"I never did get the full story on that," I said. "If there are these ancient agreements, requiring us to leave the Nightside strictly alone, what do we get out of it?"

"I find it best not to ask questions like that," said the Armourer. "The answers would only upset you."

"So where is this neutral ground?" said Molly.

The Armourer beamed happily again. "We're going to Mars!"

"What?" said Molly.

"What?" I said.

"Hold everything, go previous, hit rewind," said Molly. "Mars, as in the planet Mars? You mean the Martian Tombs? My sister Louise was just there!"

"We know," said the Armourer, scowling. "And we're really not happy about that. If you ever find out how she got there, and how she got inside the Tombs, we'd really like to know. So we can stop her ever doing it again."

"There's no stopping Louise," said Molly. "That's what makes her so . . . disconcerting."

"Moving on . . ." I said, firmly.

"We use the ancient Martian Tombs for Summit Meetings," said the Armourer, "because there's nowhere left on Earth that's truly neutral ground. Every group and organisation lays claim to some territory. So we go to Mars, when we have to."

"Are you saying the family has its own rocket ship?" I said. "Blast off to Mars, and all that? Something worryingly old and unusual, like Ivor the steam Time Engine?"

"Well, I have been working on something like that," said the Armourer, not at all modestly. "Though it doesn't have rockets, and isn't really a ship, as such. . . . But no. We have a Door. A good old-fashioned dimensional doorway. Takes us straight to Mars, no stopping off along the way, no passport control, no chance to lose your luggage."

I looked at Molly. "He wants someone to make Ooh! and Aah! noises. You do it; I'm too tired."

"Wouldn't give him the satisfaction," said Molly.

"All right," I said. "Where is this Door? Back in the Armoury?"

"Actually, no," said the Armourer. "We felt we needed to keep it somewhere more secure than that."

Uncle Jack led Molly and me out of the Sanctity, and then out of the Hall, passing through the main entrance and on into the massive grounds that surround Drood Hall. Sweeping lawns, hedge mazes and ornamental lakes, peacocks and gryphons, and robot guns sleeping under the grass in case of unwanted visitors. A peaceful retreat for a family that's always at war with someone. The Armourer led us briskly along the gravel pathway, past the East Wing and round the corner . . . and for the first time I realised where he was taking us.

The old family chapel looked just as I remembered from all the times I'd sneaked out of the Hall at night, against all the rules and regulations, to visit with the disreputable old family ghost, Jacob Drood. The chapel was tucked away out of sight, though not always out of mind,

and didn't look particularly religious. An ugly stone structure with crucifix windows and a grey slate roof with holes
in it, the chapel didn't even try to look inviting. It gave every appearance of being Saxon, with maybe a touch of
Norman, but it was really just a nineteenth-century folly.
Back when it was all the rage to erect brand-new buildings
that already looked like they were falling apart. The Gothic
tradition has a lot to answer for.

These days, the family has its own peaceful and restful
and thoroughly multi-denominational chapel inside the
Hall. For those who feel the need. When you have to deal
with Heaven and Hell's cast-offs and spiritual droppings
on a daily basis, it makes you more thoughtful than anything else. We all believe, we have no choice, but we reserve the right to have serious doubts about just what it is
we're believing in. The old chapel is a left-over from more
traditional times, and strictly out of bounds. Not that such
limited thinking ever stopped me, of course.

"Isn't this where . . . ?" said Molly.

"Oh, yes," I said. "This is where I used to meet with the
only member of the family who was more of an outcast
than me. Mostly because he was dead, but damned if he'd
depart. With a family as old as ours, you have to take a
tough line on ghosts and the causes of ghosts, or we'd be
hip-deep in the bloody things. But Jacob was . . . different."

Uncle Jack paused by the door to let me look the old
place over. For a man who claimed never to look back, the
Armourer could be very understanding with those who
did. Most of the few happy memories I have from my childhood concern the times I escaped from my family, with
Uncle Jack in the Armoury, or Jacob the ghost in the
chapel. It seems like every time I come home, I get my past
pushed in my face. Like the family can't even leave my
memories alone. . . .

I took a deep breath, squared my shoulders, and looked
the chapel over. Ugly as ever—rough stone walls buried
under thick mats of ivy. The heavy greenery was already

stirring and murmuring restlessly, disturbed by our presence. I stepped forward and spoke to the ivy in a calm and friendly way, and it soon settled down again. Jacob's personal early warning system . . . still operating long after he was gone. The heavy door still stood half open, wedged in place. Swollen wood in a contorted frame. I put my shoulder to it, and the door creaked loudly as it slid reluctantly inwards. I led the way in.

The interior was the same old mess. All the pews had been pushed over to one side long ago, and stacked up against the wall. Dust and cobwebs and desiccated leaves scattered everywhere. The far end of the chapel was taken up with Jacob's old great black leather reclining chair, set before a massive old-fashioned television set on which Jacob liked to watch the memories of old television programmes. I could feel old memories welling up, like tears I was damned I would shed. Molly sensed my mood and moved in close beside me.

The Armourer looked around, and sniffed loudly. "Horrible old place. Horrible old man. But he was still family . . . and he did finally go to his end in an honourable fashion. Destroying the Hungry Gods. I come in here, from time to time, hoping he might have found some way to escape his doom. . . . Hoping against hope that he might find his way home again . . . But he never has."

"Why are we here?" said Molly, impatiently.

"Because this is where we keep the Door," said the Armourer, immediately all business again. "It's been here pretty much forever. That's why the family suffered Jacob to remain here all those years, instead of just exorcising him. He guarded the Door for us. Family ghost, family watchdog . . . Certainly no one was going to bother the Door while he was here."

"Are you going to get another guardian, now Jacob's gone?" I said.

"How do you know we haven't?" said the Armourer.

He spoke a Word of Power and gestured vaguely, and just like that the Door appeared before us. Standing still and alone, and completely unsupported, in the middle of the chapel. A heavy elm wood door with no handle or hinges, no knocker or ornamentation of any kind. No mystic symbols carved into the wood, nothing to suggest it was anything more than an ordinary, everyday door. Apart from the fact that just looking at it, you knew it was old. Really old. And that, just possibly, it was looking back at you. I studied the Door carefully from what I hoped was a safe distance. Molly strode right up to it, stuck her face close to the wood, and inspected it thoroughly. Did everything, in fact, but sniff and lick the damn thing. Molly never let caution get in the way of satisfying her curiosity.

"Old," she growled, not looking back. "And I mean really old. I can feel Deep Time in this, going back more centuries than I'm comfortable with. And . . . I think it knows we're here."

She backed away from the Door, not taking her eyes off it for a moment.

"How the hell did the family get its hands on this?" I said to the Armourer. "It doesn't have the feel of something one of our old Armourers might have cobbled together, while not in spitting distance of their right mind. This came from Outside. . . ."

"Forget Saxon or Norman," said Molly. "I'd say Celtic. Maybe even Druidic. It's got some of that old-time religion to it, that *Nail his guts to the old oak tree* vibe."

"Very good, Molly," said the Armourer, beaming. "Gold star on your report card, and extra honey for tea. We acquired this Door from the same place we got the Merlin Glass. From the same benefactor."

"What?" I said. "Merlin made this Door? Merlin knew about Mars?"

"Merlin knew about everything," said the Armourer. "That's what made him so dangerous."

"He gave us the Glass, and he gave us this Door?" I said. "Come on, Merlin Satanspawn was never known for his generosity. This doesn't feel like gifts, or even tribute; it smells a lot more like payment for services rendered. So what exactly did the family do for him, all those centuries ago? That he felt obliged to craft us such matchless gifts? What did we do, or what did we promise him, in return?"

"Excellent questions," said the Armourer. "If you ever find out, do let us know. I'd love to have one less thing to worry about. There's always the chance he might turn up in person one day, to present us with the bill."

"Merlin's dead," said Molly.

"That never stopped him before," said the Armourer, darkly. "So, everybody ready? Time to go to Mars, before the others get there."

"Why?" I asked bluntly.

"We can survive the Martian conditions in our armour, so we get to open up the Martian Tombs and turn on the machines," said the Armourer. "The old energy generators are still working, and can supply air and heat and gravity to Earth normal conditions, for the length of the Summit. And, we go first because it's traditional. Doesn't do any harm to remind the others that Droods always go first."

"Of course," I said. "The family runs on tradition. Don't smile, Uncle Jack. I didn't say that was a good thing."

"The Droods are always the hosts of the Summit," said the Armourer.

"Okay, my turn," said Molly. "Why?"

"Because we found the Tombs," said the Armourer. "And because we are best placed to keep the peace, if certain others start getting out of hand. Discussions have been known to get a bit . . . heated, in the past."

"So, everyone else goes along because they're afraid of us," I said.

"Isn't that what I just said?" said the Armourer. "I'd prefer to be admired and respected, but I'll settle for everyone else being shit-scared of us, if that means we can get the job done. Decisions have to be agreed on, one way or another. Now, ready yourselves, my children. Because once I open that Door, the red planet is waiting." He looked dubiously at Molly. "Eddie and I have our armour; are you sure you'll be all right . . . ?"

"I go to worse places than Mars for my tea-break," Molly said briskly. "I regularly visit clubs where you have to evolve into a more dangerous being just to use the toilets."

"It's true," I said solemnly. "She has. You wouldn't believe the things she brings home as party favours."

The Armourer surprised me then by laughing, and fixing Molly with a twinkling gaze. "Always knew Eddie would bring home someone . . . interesting."

Uncle Jack and I subvocalised our activating Words, and armoured up. Two gleaming golden figures stood facing each other in the chapel, and the confined space seemed suddenly that much smaller, and more shabby. Interestingly, the Door felt more real, more solid. There were differences between the Armourer's armour and mine. His was traditional, smooth, functional. Mine was more streamlined, detailed, personalised. There was a time all Drood armour looked the same, but since Ethel gifted us with her strange matter, we can shape our armour to fit our own needs and personalities. Uncle Jack was just a traditionalist.

We both looked to Molly, to see what she would do, and then we both stepped back quickly as a great leafy tree burst up through the flag-stones of the chapel floor. The tree surged upwards, and stopped only when its leafy head slammed against the stone ceiling. The tree toppled forward over Molly, and engulfed her in a brown-and-green embrace, until it was gone and only Molly stood before us. Wrapped from head to toe in skintight living tree bark, decorated here and there with strings of mistletoe. She looked like a wood nymph, or a dryad of old, with an elemental Druidic feel. The hole in the floor was gone, as though it had never been there, and possibly it hadn't. Molly turned to face Uncle Jack and me, and smiled. The gleaming bark stretched easily across her face, without cracking.

"I got the idea from you, Eddie," she said. "This way, I carry the strength and protection of the wild woods with me, wherever I go."

"You look amazing," I said.

"Treemendous," said the Armourer.

"Leaf it out," I said.

Molly shook her head sadly. "You don't deserve me; you really don't."

The Armourer turned to face the Door. "Mars!" he said loudly. The Door swung open, falling back before us, and a great red glare spilled through the Doorway and into the chapel. A whole new shade of red, unlike anything I'd ever seen before. Warm, almost organic . . .

"That's it?" Molly said to the Armourer. "You just shout where you want to go?"

"They liked to keep things simple, in Arthurian times," said the Armourer. "Now stay close, and don't go wandering off."

He led the way through the Door, and just like that . . .

We went to Mars.

Everything changed.

The light slammed down like a brick-red waterfall, and everywhere I looked, red planet Mars looked back. Even through my armour's protection I could tell I'd come to a whole new place, a whole other world. I stood very still, just looking around me. The bleak and dusty surface of the Martian plateau stretched away in every direction. A huge red plain, interrupted here and there with rocks and pebbles, but nothing else. No sign of life at all. The surface of Mars looked like the bottom of the ocean: a sea bed with all the water gone, long gone. A scene not just dead and lifeless, but lacking in any quality to suggest there might ever have been life here. Except for the city. Straight ahead of us rose a huge cliff face. Brick red, rising high as a mountain range, dominating the horizon. And there, cut deep into the cliff face itself, Someone or Something had carved a great city.

Not as we would understand such a thing, of course, but the shapes and structures, the entrances and windows, the long lines and the deep-etched details, all added up to something recognisable as a city. I couldn't even grasp the scale. I had to tilt my head right back, just to take in the jagged-towered top. There was nothing like it on Earth, in all of human history. The sense of . . . sheer scale, was utterly inhuman. I didn't know why I was so excited, why my heart was hammering so madly in my chest. I'd been to other worlds, other dimensions, other realities . . . but this was Mars. And Mars has always had a special place in the human heart. It had honestly never even occurred to me that I would ever get to walk on the Martian plains. Behind my golden mask, I was grinning so hard it hurt my face.

So, this was it. The Martian Tombs. All that remained to mark the presence of a race that was over, finished. A race gone to dust and less than dust before Humanity ever appeared on Earth. Our closest neighbour, our older brother. It felt like walking through a graveyard.

Molly moved in close beside me. "A rose red city, half as old as Time . . ."

"That's what most people say, the first time they see it," said the Armourer.

I glanced behind me and realised for the first time that the Door was gone. Not a mark left on the red ground, nothing to show the Door had ever been there. We were alone, on Mars.

"Don't worry, lad," said the Armourer. "It'll return, when it's called. It's a good Door."

Molly couldn't tear her eyes away from the deep red cliff face. "Look at it . . . it's magnificent! That's not even a human aesthetic, but it's obvious what it is. A Martian city . . ."

"No matter how many times I see it, it still takes my breath away," the Armourer admitted.

I turned to look at him. "You've been here before? You never said. How many Summit Meetings have you attended?"

"Three," said the Armourer. "Neutral ground like this is important. When important decisions have to be made."

"What sort of agreements are we talking about here?" I said. "I never heard anything about any of this, and I used to run the family! Or at least I thought I did . . ."

"We would have got around to telling you about things like this," the Armourer said vaguely, "if you'd stayed in charge a bit longer. . . . Do I ask you about all your secrets?"

"Yes!" I said. "All the time!"

"I'm allowed," said the Armourer. "I'm your uncle. I worry about you. When are you two going to get properly married, and make me a great-uncle? I'm not getting any younger, you know."

"No," I said. "But I bet you're working on it."

The Armourer shrugged easily. "Ask me something else."

"How are we hearing each other talk?" I said. "There's no atmosphere here."

"Armour speaks to armour," said the Armourer. "Though how Molly's joining in is frankly beyond me."

"Why did the Door drop us all the way out here, on the Martian plain?" said Molly. "It's a good half-hour's walk to that cliff. Why not deliver us safely inside the Martian Tombs?"

"Because the Tombs won't let it," said the Armourer. "This . . . is as close as the Tombs will allow."

"Who built the city?" I said. "And when?"

"We don't know," said the Armourer. "We just found it. The family, I mean."

"When?" said Molly.

"More centuries ago than I am comfortable considering," said the Armourer. "Our family does get around. . . . You must always remember that the Droods are very old and hold many secrets. All I can tell you is that our family's age is nothing compared to that city. The Tombs are really old. Millennia old. You're about to ask me how we came here and discovered the Tombs, aren't you, Eddie? Well, not even I know everything. Loath though I am to admit it. There's supposed to be a full report on the original discovery somewhere in the Old Library. But William hasn't found it yet. He says it's hiding."

I looked at Molly. "Are you all right, in your . . . bark? Breathing okay?"

"I'm fine, Eddie. Don't fuss. I've probably got more air

inside my woods than you have in your armour." She stopped to look at the Armourer. "Should we be hurrying? Didn't occur to me to wonder about your air supply."

"We have more than enough," the Armourer said comfortably. "But you're right; we should get a move on. The others will be here soon."

He started forward, across the great red plain, and Molly and I hurried after him.

My armour quickly adjusted to the different, lighter gravity, compensating for my every movement so I could walk almost normally, instead of just bouncing along. Molly quickly gave up trying, tucked her legs under her to sit cross-legged in mid-air, and floated along between me and the Armourer. There was no sound anywhere around us, just the faint thudding of our feet on the unyielding surface. No shadows, either. I looked up into the swirling dusty skies, where Martian sunlight fell through in fitful streams. It was hard to make out the sun at all, and the two moons were so small I couldn't see them anywhere.

Molly stopped suddenly and grabbed me by the arm, bringing me to an abrupt halt. "Eddie! Did you see that?"

The Armourer stopped too, and we all looked where Molly was pointing, at the base of the great red cliff. I zoomed in through my mask for all it was worth, but I couldn't see anything. Nothing moving at all . . .

"What?" said the Armourer, urgently. "What did you see, Molly?"

"I don't know." Molly's voice was small, doubtful. "I thought I saw . . . something moving. But there's nothing there now. Nothing at all."

We all stood and looked, for a while.

"Nothing there now," I said.

"It moved . . . strangely," said Molly. "Like nothing I've ever seen before. And I've been around."

"It's true," I said. "She has."

"Probably just a shadow," said the Armourer. "Nothing's lived on Mars for millions of years."

"You sure about that?" I said.

"Absolutely," said the Armourer. "Let's get inside. We'll be safer there."

"Safe from what?" said Molly.

"From jumping at shadows," said the Armourer, firmly.

"We will be safe, inside the Martian Tombs?" I said.

"Well . . . yes and no," said the Armourer. "We can't go far inside. The Tombs' hospitality is strictly limited. But we'll be safe enough in the entrance lobby. The only thing we really have to worry about are the other people coming to the Summit. Powerful organisations tend to send powerful representatives. Discussions can become heated, and it's not unheard-of for there to be a certain amount of . . . physical jockeying for position. A butting of heads, if you like, to determine seniority. And all that."

"Alpha males," said Molly, scathingly. "Evolution—I'm looking forward to it."

We moved on again, the Armourer leading the way. Slow plumes of crimson dust rose up with our footprints, settling gradually back again. I moved in close beside Molly.

"Did you really see something?" I said quietly. "Or were you just yanking the Armourer's chain?"

"I don't know," said Molly. "I saw something . . . but maybe it was just a shadow. In case you hadn't noticed, the shadows don't move here like they move on Earth. Even the light is weird. This whole place gives me the creeps. Don't you feel like there's something watching us?"

"All the time," I said. "Comes with being a Drood."

The closer we got to the cliff face, the more details I could make out in the crimson city. The whole cliff face was one enormous facade, all the pieces endlessly interlocking and connecting, and all of it made up of remorselessly straight lines. Not a curve, or a dome, or a circle anywhere. Every single detail was almost unbearably sharp and clear, after unknown millennia standing alone and forgotten. Standing firm, in the face of Time and the Martian elements. Any Earth city would have been ground to dust by now . . . I slowly realised that there were patterns in the face of the city, meaningful shapes within shapes . . . but none of them made any sense to me. The face of the city was an alien mask, inscrutable and unreadable to human eyes.

We came to a halt, finally, standing at the foot of the massive cliff face. Up close, I could make out lines of . . . markings, images. Might have been writing, or language. Though whether they were names, or instructions, or warnings . . . was beyond me. Each symbol was almost insanely intricate. Just running my eyes along them was enough to make my head ache, as though I was trying to assimilate concepts the human mind couldn't cope with. I pointed them out to the Armourer and he just shrugged.

"Don't ask me, lad. Haven't a clue. Don't know anyone who has. There's no one left to tell us what they might have meant. No Rosetta Stone, to help us translate them. The words of a lost race . . . their meaning lost, in Time."

I deliberately didn't look up the cliff face. The sheer size and scale of it seemed to hang over me, as though it may come crashing down at any moment. Usually, when I'm wearing my armour I feel like I'm ready to take on anything in the world, but I didn't feel like that here, on this world. My exuberance at making it to Mars was gone; I felt alone, in a strange place, beyond my understanding.

The Armourer leaned forward abruptly, studying a door-shaped design in the cliff face before him. It was huge, some thirty feet tall and maybe half as wide. Definitely not built to any human scale. The Armourer placed one golden palm flat against the brick-red surface. Dust fell in jerking rushes from the outlines of the door, and there was a sudden sense of movement and purpose to the door shape. As though we'd disturbed, or awoken, something. Molly lowered her feet to the ground and stood beside me, ready for action. The door seemed to stand out before us, more definite than ever, as though taking on a role. It slid suddenly, smoothly upwards, revealing a dark opening. Utterly dark, impenetrable even to my mask's augmented vision. I tried infrared and ultraviolet, and still couldn't make out anything beyond the door.

"Don't worry," said the Armourer. "I have powerful lights built into my armour."

"Of course you have," I said.

Two large lenses rose up out of my uncle Jack's shoulders, and blasted great beams of pure white light into the doorway. They blazed brightly, pushing back the dark, revealing a tunnel of dark red, almost organic material. Like staring into the body of some enormous beast. The white light was subtly comforting, after so much red everywhere. The Armourer strode into the tunnel, blasting his white light ahead of him, and Molly and I followed him in, sticking close behind. We didn't want to be left outside the light. The moment we were all inside, the door slid silently shut behind us. Locking us in.

The Armourer just kept walking, counting his steps under his breath. He moved his shoulders just enough to keep the lights ranging back and forth. The tunnel soon opened out into a huge, overpoweringly massive chamber. The sheer size of it was unpleasantly oppressive to merely human senses. The light from the Armourer's suit showed only brief glimpses of our surroundings. No human could ever be comfortable in such a place. The sense of scale was off the chart. They were bigger people, here. Back then.

The floor was made up of pale yellow squares that didn't look like stone or metal. Some kind of crystal, perhaps. Flat and smooth, they seemed to swallow up the sound our footsteps made as we trod on them. For all its antiquity the floor was completely unsullied and unmarked, with not a speck of dust anywhere.

"Is there nothing left here to tell us who and what the Martians were?" Molly said softly.

"No," said the Armourer. "Not a trace. They were long gone, millions of years gone, before the first Human set foot on Mars. Long and long before we found the Tombs. Of course, we haven't been able to explore much. The Tombs don't allow us to travel beyond this chamber. But as far as we can tell, nothing remains to even suggest what manner of creature the Martians were."

"Bigger than us," I said. "And, they built to last."

We were all talking quietly, respectfully. As though we didn't want to draw attention to ourselves. The darkness outside the Armourer's white light was still complete, and unfathomable.

"Why do you call this place the Tombs?" Molly said suddenly. "If you've never found any bodies?"

"Because that's what this place feels like," said the Armourer. "A place of the dead."

"And Louise was here on her own?" I said to Molly. "Your sister must have been scared out of her wits."

"Oh, nothing bothers Louise," said Molly. "Not if it knows what's good for it. If she really was here . . . I mean, she didn't leave any traces. Nothing missing, nothing broken. Which is not like Louise . . ."

The Armourer was still moving steadily forward, counting steps, or maybe panels, under his breath. And we went with him, to stay in his light. He finally stopped counting, knelt down and placed one golden palm on the floor, covering one particular crystal square. It lit up immediately, pouring out a pale yellow light, strangely unpleasant, like stale urine. The Armourer stood up, and shut down his shoulder lights. Crystal squares lit up all around us, pouring more light into the massive chamber. Great rumbling sounds started up deep beneath the floor. I could feel slow juddering vibrations through the golden soles of my feet. The whole floor suddenly blazed with yellow light, and then the walls, and the ceiling far above. The huge chamber made itself known all around us, appallingly large and entirely unsympathetic. The three of us stood close together, desperate for human contact and feeling, in the face of such . . . inhuman vastness. You could have stuck the whole of Drood Hall in this chamber, and it would have looked small and lost.

There was something wrong with the yellow light,

something subtly disturbing, as though it was meant for a different kind of eye, or sensibility. It was like being underwater, though I could make out every detail clearly enough. The light pulsed endlessly, moving in slow rolls or waves from one end of the huge chamber to the other, and then back again. It took me a moment to realise I wasn't casting a shadow. Neither was Molly, nor the Armourer. That spooked me, on some deep primal level. I wanted to ask the Armourer to put his lights back on, to have some sane white light to look at. But I didn't. First rule of a Drood in enemy territory: never do anything that might make you look weak. I craned my head back to look up at the ceiling; it had to be three, maybe four hundred feet above us. I felt a kind of reverse vertigo, as though I might fall upwards at any moment. I looked away.

There were no markings, no lines of alien symbols, on any of the walls. Just more flat crystal squares, like those on the floor and the ceiling: smooth and untroubled.

"Why did this place react to your touch?" I asked the Armourer. Just to be saying something. "Did you . . . ?"

"Hell no," said the Armourer. "None of this is anything to do with me. The Tombs created this room, for us. To serve our needs. Don't ask me why. It's a mystery. Ah, there! Can you feel that? Earth gravity has been established. That means this room now has Earth normal conditions. It's safe to armour down. In the sense that nothing in this room will actually try to kill us."

"You sure about that?" I said.

"Don't mess around, Eddie," said the Armourer, not unkindly. "I have done this before."

He armoured down, and the golden strange matter disappeared back into his torc in a moment. He was still wearing his messy lab coat, over his rude T-shirt, and looked extremely out of place. But then he always did, anywhere outside his beloved Armoury. He peered interestedly about him, apparently completely unconcerned, so I armoured down too. The air was flat and tasteless, and though I breathed deeply, I couldn't smell anything. The air was cool, and completely still. I turned to Molly just as the bark surrounding her disappeared. She shuddered briefly, despite herself, and then her head came up and she glared about her. Molly didn't believe in being impressed by anything. She shot me a quick grin.

"The wild woods I brought with me aren't gone, I just shifted them sideways. I can call them back at a moment's notice."

I looked at her, and then at the Armourer. "Her explanations are even worse than yours, Uncle Jack."

"What an appalling place this is," said Molly. "I have been in travel lodges with more character. Whole place looks like one big toilet."

"Don't you dare!" I said immediately.

She sniffed loudly. "It's all right for you. You can do it in your armour. Knew I should have gone before we left."

"What do you want me to do?" I said. "Extrude a golden chamber pot for you, from out of my armour?"

"You can do that?" said Molly.

"Well," I said, "I've never tried . . . but I suppose, in an emergency . . ."

"A little less chatter, children," said the Armourer, not looking back at us. "We're not alone, here. . . ."

Even as he spoke, machines or something that looked very like machines began to rise up out of the floor all around us. Utterly silent, with no discernable moving parts, formed from some strange kind of translucent metal, with an odd bluish tinge. Molly and I moved quickly to stand back-to-back. Just on general principles. The machines didn't seem to be doing anything, but the Armourer seemed pleased to see them.

"Will you two please behave?" he said testily. "I'll tell you when it's time to panic. Think of these things as the welcoming committee. I'd love to take one of them back with me to study, but the Tombs won't let anything go."

A single column of glowing crystal rose up out of the floor, right beside me. A small flat grey thing sat on the flat top of the column. It looked like a grey credit card, with no markings of any kind. I stood very still, and considered the object.

"Uncle Jack?" I said carefully. "What does this mean? What am I supposed to do?"

"Haven't a clue," he said, watching with great interest. Though I noticed he wasn't moving a single step closer. "This has never happened before. . . ."

The farther end of the crystal column tilted up, so that the grey card started to slide towards me, and in the end I had to grab it or let it fall to the floor. It felt flat and very smooth, and subtly cold to the touch. The moment I had it, the column sank back into the floor again.

"All right, take the bloody thing," said the Armourer. "Clearly the Tombs want you to have it. Never mind that I've hosted three Summits here, and it's never offered me anything. I'm not sulking at all."

Molly leaned in close for a better look. I offered her the grey card, but she declined. "Maybe it's a *Get out of jail free* card. I've always wanted one of those."

"Become a Drood," I said. "We have diplomatic immunity."

"This has never happened before," the Armourer said thoughtfully. "But then, you've never been here before, Eddie. Maybe you are special, after all."

"Don't," said Molly. "He's hard enough to live with as it is."

"Put the thing somewhere safe," said the Armourer. "And for God's sake don't lose it. I'll take a closer look at it when we get back."

I slipped the grey card carefully into my pocket, and on into the pocket dimension I keep there. For strange and valuable items, or things that might go off bang unexpectedly. Because you never know when you might have a use for such a thing. Although, a part of me was whispering *Beware of Martians bearing gifts . . .*

A table rose up out of the floor. A quite ordinary table: flat surface and four legs, some thirty feet long and ten wide. Made of the same crystal stuff as the floor. A set of human-sized, human-scaled chairs rose up next, around the table. They didn't look the least bit comfortable, but they were clearly intended to be used by beings of human proportions. I looked at the Armourer.

"Are you doing this?"

"No. This is what always happens at Summit Meetings. Whether one of our ancestors first arranged this, or whether the Tombs worked it out for themselves, I have no idea. Hmmm, that's interesting."

"What?" Molly said immediately. "What's interesting? Should I be worried yet? Guess what—too late . . ."

"I count nine chairs," said the Armourer. "And I was given to understand that only five others would be joining us, representing five organisations."

I gave him a hard look. "How does this room know how many places to set at table? Are we being watched? Are there computers here, or something?"

"Almost certainly something," said the Armourer. "Just go with the flow, that's my advice."

Another machine appeared, at the end of the table. Just a clear glass container, on top of another crystal column. No obvious controls or clues as to what it was supposed to do. The Armourer made a happy, satisfied sound; and I had to fight down the urge to dive for cover. Whenever my uncle Jack makes that kind of noise in his Armoury, it usually means something extraordinarily destructive is about to happen.

"About time!" said the Armourer, beaming happily on the new arrival. "I've been feeling a bit peckish."

"What is it?" said Molly, moving right up to the glass container and staring at it closely. Mention of food always draws her forward, like a moth to a flame.

"A machine to produce food and drink for Summit guests," the Armourer said happily. "Human food, mind, not Martian. Don't ask me how it does it, but this can supply anything you could ever want. Go on! Ask it!"

"You ask," I said. "We'll watch."

"I really have trained you awfully well, haven't I?" said the Armourer. He addressed the empty container with a clear carrying voice. "I'll have a Provençal truffle with grated Stilton; Siberian caviar on dry toast fingers; and a glass of pink champagne. Shaken, not stirred."

Two plates of food and a champagne glass appeared inside the glass container. The top disappeared, and the Armourer reached in and helped himself. He set them down on the table, and tucked in cheerfully.

"God, I miss being a field agent. And having unlimited expenses."

I moved forward and addressed the thing. "Beef madras curry, with pilau rice. And a bottle of Beck's."

And there it all was. Along with plain functional cutlery, made from the bluish metal. I took the steaming curry to the table, and sat down. The bottle was ice-cold. I tried a mouthful of food, followed by a mouthful of drink, and had to struggle to hold back delighted ecstatic sounds. Best I'd ever tasted. I studied the bottle carefully. The label gave every indication of being genuine. Maybe it was some kind of transporter, beaming things up from Earth . . . though the power involved would be almost inconceivable.

Molly confronted the glass container with the gleam of battle in her eye. "I want a beefburger, twelve ounces, medium rare, with cheese and onion and bacon, and a fried egg on top."

The burger appeared. It was a work of art; a thing of beauty and a joy forever. Molly grabbed it and bit into it, and grease ran down her chin as her eyes squeezed shut. She didn't even try to hold back the loud ecstatic noises. We all sat at the table, engrossed in our food. When we were finished, we all looked thoughtfully at the glass container. We were all thinking of second helpings, but no one wanted to go first and seem like a pig.

"How the hell does it do that?" said Molly.

"I have no idea," said the Armourer. "And I'm getting really tired of saying that. I've been trying to duplicate the thing in my lab for years, with only very limited success."

"How does it get everything so right, from such a basic description?" I said.

"I think something in the Tombs reads our minds," said the Armourer.

Molly glared about her suspiciously.

A viewscreen suddenly appeared, six foot by three, floating in mid-air above the table. It showed a view of the open red plain that we'd just crossed to get to the Tombs. The detail was so sharp I could see the trail our footprints had left.

"Ah!" said the Armourer, wiping his mouth on his sleeve. "This means our guests are about to arrive. Pay attention. You might learn something useful. The Summit Meeting, also known as the Consultation, has been going on, off and on, for centuries. It has outlasted many of the secret groups and organisations who originally founded it. So it's always interesting to see who actually turns up. No one ever wants to refuse the honour, but circumstances sometimes take their toll. When the call goes out, everyone who can attends. If only to make sure they don't get left out of having their say in whatever's decided."

Quite suddenly without benefit of dimensional Door, secret Gate, or any obvious means of transportation, a figure was walking across the red plain. Plodding steadily towards the city in a heavy suit of plate steel armour. Resolutely medieval in style, with boots and gauntlets, stylised greaves and main-gauches, and a great blocky steel helmet with a coloured feather sticking up: blue, with purple trimmings. The knight in armour wore a great sword on one hip, and a bloody big axe on the other. It was hard to judge scale at such a distance, but he gave every indication of being a really big fellow. He left a trail of deep footprints behind him, punched into the plain by the sheer weight of his armour.

"Sir Parsifal, representing the London Knights," said the Armourer. "I recognise the plume. An interesting choice, for a representative."

"You know him?" said Molly.

"Let's say, of him," said the Armourer. "Brave and true, honest as the day is long, arrogant and stuck-up and a real pain in the arse to work with."

"How can you be so sure, if you haven't actually met him?" I said.

"Because that sums up all the London Knights," the Armourer said flatly. "Think they're so big-time, just because they've been around almost as long as we have. They've been even more insufferable, just lately, ever since King Arthur returned to lead them again. Haven't got a dragon, though, have you, Parsifal? We've got a dragon!"

My gaze was jerked back to the floating viewscreen, as something dark and indistinct came hurtling down through the swirling atmosphere. Sir Parsifal didn't even pause to look. Even when the something slammed down into the red plain not fifty feet away, hard enough to raise great clouds of red dust. The clouds slowly settled, revealing a single human shape kneeling in the centre of a new crater. He was wearing what looked like some kind of steampunk spacesuit. Without waiting to be asked, the viewscreen obligingly closed in for a better look. The atmosphere suit had clearly been based on an old-fashioned diving suit, complete with a bulbous metal helmet, and weights attached here and there to compensate for the lesser gravity. Modern scuba oxygen cylinders had been strapped on to his back, while his chest boasted a large Union Jack flag. The figure slowly straightened up, got its bearings, and headed purposefully for the great cliff face.

"All right," said Molly. "I'll bite. What the hell is that tatty museum piece doing here?"

"That," said the Armourer, "is almost certainly the representative from the Carnacki Institute. They've been around for ages, and they never throw anything away."

"The Ghost Finders?" I said. "What business have they got at a Summit like this?"

"I have to wonder whether that might be their boss, inside that suit," said the Armourer. "Catherine Latimer . . . She and Crow Lee were something of an item, back in the day. Her insight on the nature of the Inheritance would be invaluable. But, she's a bit too old and too fragile to handle a landing like that. Must be one of her field agents. And don't be so snotty, Eddie! The Institute does valuable work."

"Okay," I said. "Now explain the spacesuit."

"From the original manned moon landing, back in Victorian times," said the Armourer. "We're not the only ones with a secret history."

"You just made that up!" said Molly.

"I wish," said the Armourer.

The view in the viewscreen shifted suddenly, whipping sideways across the great red plain at staggering speed, and then slammed to a halt to show a Door opening. It looked a lot more modern than ours, while still entirely basic and ordinary. A tall dark figure stepped through it, and the Door immediately slammed shut behind him, and disappeared. The figure looked around, taking his time. Molly and I looked at each other, sighed heavily, and shook our heads regretfully. We knew this one, by reputation. Everyone did.

Dead Boy was seventeen. He'd been seventeen some thirty years now, ever since he was mugged and murdered in the Nightside. And then came back from the dead to avenge his murder. He made a deal with Someone he still won't talk about, but he should have paid more attention to the small print. Because there was nothing in the compact he made about getting to lie down again afterwards. So now Dead Boy goes on and on, trapped in his body; a returned soul possessing his own corpse.

Tall and adolescent thin, he wore a deep purple greatcoat over black leather trousers, and scuffed calfskin boots. He wore a black rose on his lapel, and a large floppy hat crammed down on dark curly hair. He stood alone on the Mars surface, unprotected and unaffected by the local conditions because he was, after all, dead. He stared about him in an open, touristy way, and then jumped up and down a few times, to test the gravity. He looked like he was giggling. He strode off across the red plain, kicking red dust this way and that with happy abandon.

"Oh, hell," said the Armourer. "All the people the Nightside Authorities could have sent, and they chose Dead Boy? Why couldn't they have sent their new Walker, John Taylor?"

"Because he's on honeymoon," said Molly. "He married Shotgun Suzie, just recently. I read it in *Heat* magazine." I looked at her, and she shrugged self-consciously. "The Nightside edition. I'm a subscriber. Look, do I make comments when you watch *Testosterone Gear*?"

"I like *Top Gear*," I said. "It makes me feel manly."

"Pay attention, children," said the Armourer. "Someone else is arriving."

A bright light flared, out on the Martian plain, and suddenly . . . a four-foot-tall teddy bear was standing there, looking around him with great interest. He was wearing his famous blue tunic and trousers, and his big red scarf. He smiled at everything, and his bright intelligent eyes were full of wonder and delight. Every child's good friend, and companion in adventure, in the far off Golden Lands. Bruin Bear. From those wonderful stories we all read when we were young. I understand he's out of fashion and out of print, these days.

Kids today don't know what they're missing.

And there at Bruin Bear's side, his constant friend and companion, the Sea Goat. Tall and angular in his blue-grey trench-coat, human enough in shape, but topped with a large blocky goat's head, complete with long curving horns. He . . . didn't look particularly pleased to be on Mars.

Dead Boy went over to join them, and they were soon having a cheerful conversation. The lack of air didn't seem to bother any of them. Because he was dead, and they were fictional. Bruin Bear and the Sea Goat resided at Shadows Fall these days, a small town in the back of beyond where legends go to die when the world stops believing in them. An elephant's graveyard for the supernatural.

The Ghost Finder in his antiquated atmosphere suit came over to join them, and patted Bruin Bear fondly on the head. The Bear let him because he was, after all, everyone's friend. The Sea Goat gave the Ghost Finder a cold unwavering glare that clearly said *Don't even think about it* . . . and then they all walked on together, heading for the city in the cliff. None of them made any attempt to catch up with Sir Parsifal.

"Oh, bloody hell," said the Armourer. "Not Bruin Bear and the Sea Goat . . . I was sure Shadows Fall was going to send Old Father Time. Okay . . . hide everything valuable, including the cutlery; don't promise the Sea Goat *anything*; and if he starts any trouble, just hit him over the head with something solid. Don't worry, you can't hurt him; he's fictional."

And then, finally, the last arrival. A strange contraption appeared out of nowhere, some distance away from the others. A great cage of twisted silver bars, throwing off multicoloured sparks like a fireworks display. The cage shook and shuddered, like it might fly apart at any moment, and then abruptly settled down. The lights blinked off, and there, standing in the middle of the cage, was a tall Asian young lady, looking very formal and intimidating. She held herself like a Royal on a state visit, as though she was slumming just by being there. The silver cage disappeared, leaving her standing alone on the Martian surface, surrounded by a shimmering force shield. She was wearing a pink leather cat-suit, topped with a pink pillbox hat, over neatly trimmed black hair. She strode purposefully forward across the red plain, ignoring the others completely.

"Now, what is that little bitch doing here?" said Molly.

"You know her?" I said.

"Natasha Chang? Hell, yes. She still owes me money. She's a field agent for the Crowley Project. . . . Oh come on, Eddie, you must have heard of them! Nasty people, doing nasty things, always for a profit. Natasha is a Project field agent. A supernatural terrorist, serial nightclubber, rampant despoiler of fit young men who should know better, and eater of souls. And no, I am not even a little bit exaggerating. She eats ghosts, and digests their memories. I worked with her, a few times. On . . . matters of mutual interest."

"My girlfriend has a past," I said solemnly. "The horror, the horror . . . What's this Natasha Chang doing here?"

"The Crowley Project was originally founded by Crow Lee," said the Armourer. "The gaps in your background knowledge never cease to amaze me, Eddie. The Project kicked him out, eventually, so they could go their own unpleasant way . . . but they still know more about Crow Lee than anyone else. They kept him under constant surveillance, probably in self-defence. Which is why they have a seat at the table today. Because if anyone knows for sure what the Crow Lee Inheritance actually is, it's them."

"This is going to be a very noisy meeting, isn't it?" I said.

"Oh, you have no idea," said the Armourer. "We'll probably have to clean blood and hair off the walls before we can leave."

It took them all a while to arrive and assemble in the oversized entrance hall of the Martian Tombs. Sir Parsifal was the first, of course. The door in the cliff face didn't even wait for him to touch it, just slid rapidly upwards to get out of his way as he strode heavily forward. I sort of got the impression that if it hadn't, he would have walked right through it. There's no doubt the London Knights are the good guys, but they do like to think of themselves as the biggest dog on the block.

Sir Parsifal slammed to a halt at the foot of the long table, and studied us silently through the Y-shaped slit in the front of his helmet. His eyes were cold and grey and unyielding. He dismissed Molly and me immediately, and gave all his attention to the Armourer, who bowed politely. The Knight inclined his head slightly, and then removed his helmet to reveal a hard-faced man in his early thirties, with a blunt square head, a bald pate, and no eyebrows. His mouth was set in a thin straight line.

"I greet you, Jack Drood, in the name of King Arthur Returned," said Sir Parsifal. His voice was polite, but distant.

"I greet you, Sir Parsifal, in the name of Drood," said the Armourer. "Be welcome to this Summit Meeting. Allow me to present . . ."

"I know who they are," said the Knight. "The witch, and the renegade Drood."

He didn't seem at all pleased to meet me, so I made a point of giving him my most friendly smile, while holding Molly firmly by the elbow so she wouldn't throw herself at him. The Knight had already looked away.

"Please be seated," said the Armourer, "while we wait for the others. Refreshments are available."

"Not while I'm on duty," said Sir Parsifal. His mouth twitched slightly. Apparently that had been his idea of a joke. "I do not eat or drink, in enemy territory."

"I thought this was supposed to be neutral ground," I said. "That's why we came all this way."

Sir Parsifal kept his gaze fixed on the Armourer. "No such thing, boy. What are you teaching them at the Hall these days, Armourer?"

"You two know each other?" I said.

"Back in my field agent days," said the Armourer. "Everyone knows everyone, out in the field."

"That was back in the sixties," I said. "You don't look nearly old enough, Sir Parsifal."

"I don't believe in aging," said the Knight. "Do enough of it, and you die."

His mouth twitched again. Another joke. He was going to be a barrel of laughs, this one; I could tell.

I let go of Molly's elbow. She was still glaring daggers at the Knight, but even she had enough sense not to take on a Knight of the Round Table. Unless she had to. The London Knights exist to protect our world from Outside threats. They've fought off alien invasions, other-dimensional incursions, and gone head-to-head with gods and monsters and everything in between. And they've never lost a war. The Droods exist to protect Humanity from Earthly threats; the London Knights take care of everything else.

And on the few occasions when we overlap, we're all terribly careful to be very polite, and hide the fact that we can't stand each other.

"We had to take on the Hungry Gods ourselves," I said, just a bit pointedly. "Where were you guys when we needed you?"

"We can't be everywhere, boy," said Sir Parsifal. "It's a big universe. We're stretched thin, these days."

The steampunk spacesuit arrived next, stomping in through the entrance tunnel. Steam hissed loudly from the joints, and the lead boots made loud jarring sounds on the crystal floor. The suit waved cheerfully at us all, as the man inside peered out through the metal grille on the front of his diving helmet. And then the whole suit split open, right down the middle, from top to bottom, and the Ghost Finder stepped out. The suit crumpled to the floor, and lay there, as the man from inside strode forward to join us at the table.

Tall and dark and handsome, elegant and arrogant, in a blindingly white suit, the Ghost Finder had a rock star's mane of really long dark hair, and wore sunglasses so dark I was amazed he could see through them. He grinned cockily at all of us, as though he just knew he was the one we'd all been waiting for.

"J. C. Chance, Ghost Finder Extraordinaire, at your service," he said easily. "Don't all cheer at once, just throw money. I represent the Carnacki Institute, for my sins; officially licensed arse-kickers of the supernatural. Our motto: *We don't take any shit from the Hereafter.* Or anyone else, for that matter. We exist to investigate ghosts, and Do Something about them. I recognise everyone here, of course. We have extensive files, at the Institute. On everyone who matters and a great many who might. Hello, Molly. Been a while, hasn't it?"

I glowered at her. "Is this another of your dodgy exes?"

"Oh, please," said Molly. "Him? I wouldn't piss down his throat if his lungs were on fire. We just . . . worked together, a few times. That's all. Hello, J.C. Play nice, or I'll tell everyone what your initials really stand for."

"I stand for pretty much anything," said J.C.

And then he took off his sunglasses, and looked around.

His eyes blazed with a fierce golden light. He studied the massive chamber as though he was looking right through the crystal walls, at what lay behind, and when he turned suddenly back to look at me I actually shuddered, for a moment. There was something inhuman about that gaze. He slipped his sunglasses back into place, and we all relaxed, just a little.

"Those are seriously spooky eyes," I said. "What happened?"

"Laser surgery," said J.C. "I'm suing."

"He was touched inappropriately by Outside forces," said the Armourer.

"Good or bad?" said Sir Parsifal, immediately.

"Let me get back to you on that," said J.C.

"I was rather hoping to see Catherine Latimer," said the Armourer. "Given her . . . close relationship with Crow Lee."

"Sorry," said J.C. He didn't sound it. "She's busy."

"Busy?" said Sir Parsifal, loudly. "What could possibly be more important than stopping a war that threatens to tear the whole world apart?"

"You ask her," said J.C. "I wouldn't dare."

He flashed a wide meaningless smile at all of us, and took a seat at the table, adjusting his ice-cream white trousers carefully to favour the razor-sharp crease.

Next to appear was Dead Boy, swaggering in like he owned the place. Up close, he looked even more dead, even while he blazed with an unnatural vitality. His long greatcoat hung open at the front, revealing an old Y-shaped autopsy scar, a whole bunch of other injuries, and several bullet holes. Along with a great many stitches, staples, and the occasional length of black duct tape, to hold everything in. His long pale face had a restless, debauched, Pre-Raphaelite look, with fever-bright eyes and a sulky colourless mouth.

"God save all here, and call the Devil a bastard to his face," he said loudly. "No . . . can't say I know any of you. Don't much care, either. Sorry if I'm not much on manners, but it's hard to sweat the small stuff when you're dead. Let's get this over with, so I can get back to some serious smiting of the ungodly I've got lined up in the Nightside. Got to take your pleasures where you can find them, when your senses are a sometime thing. I was told there were refreshments. . . ."

The Armourer explained the glass container to Dead Boy, who studied it thoughtfully, with a most unpleasant smile. He produced a silver pillbox, and dry swallowed half a dozen pills, of various Technicolor hues.

"Got this marvellous Obeah woman, whips up these little treasures for me," he said. "Builds a fire in the cold, cold flesh so I can experience bodily pleasures. For a while."

He then ordered some of the most revolting food and drink I've ever heard of, piled it all up on the same plate, and pounded it down with great enthusiasm. He bent right over the table from his chair, pushing the stuff in with both hands, and everyone else edged their chairs a little bit farther away. Dead Boy studied us all with his burning eyes, and grinned.

"So, you two are Droods. I recognise the torcs. You're a London Knight; I recognise the armour. And you're a Ghost Finder; I recognise the complacency. And you're. . . . No. Sorry, girlie. Don't know you at all."

"I'm Molly Metcalf! The wicked witch of the wild woods!"

"Doesn't mean a thing. Don't really keep up with the tabloids any more."

"You'll have to excuse our friend," said a warm and fuzzy voice. "Because it's either that or hit him a lot, and he wouldn't feel it anyway."

Bruin Bear came forward to greet us, and we all had some kind of smile for him. He was that sort of Bear. Dead Boy laughed out loud and jumped to his feet. He ran over to hug the Bear fiercely. By then we were all on our feet, and Bruin Bear made a point of shaking hands with everyone. His paw was warm and furry and very firm in my hand. He smiled at me, and I had tears in my eyes. It's not every day you greet an old childhood friend of your early reading days, made real. I wanted to hug him too, but I had my dignity. Afterwards, I wished I had. I'm sure he wouldn't have minded. Molly patted his head and tugged at one of his ears, and he let her. Even Sir Parsifal had a real smile for the Bear, leaning right over to carefully enclose the fuzzy paw in one great steel gauntlet.

"Oh, no, don't mind me," said a figure in the doorway. "Ignore me, overlook me, I'm used to it. My lot in life, these days. It's just hard . . . when you're not a star any more. Unlike some people . . ."

The Sea Goat raised a bottle of vodka to his oversized mouth, and took a good long swig. He'd fallen far and fallen hard, and didn't care who knew it. Dead Boy laughed, threw an arm around the Sea Goat's shoulders, grabbed the vodka bottle away from him, and drank deeply.

"You think it's hard being dead," said the Sea Goat. "Try being fictional! I was a beloved hero of childhood fantasies, along with Bruin Bear. And now, no one gives a damn. Bloody kids don't read any more. . . . They should be made to read! I was big, I tell you! Big! It's just the books that got small. . . ."

"Why isn't Old Father Time here?" said the Armourer, just a bit plaintively.

"Apparently there's a major backup in the Chronoflow," said Bruin Bear. "And no, I don't understand that either. But he couldn't get away, so we volunteered. I've always wanted to see Mars!"

"I wanted to see Disneyland," said the Sea Goat, wrestling his vodka bottle back from Dead Boy. "But apparently they only let in their own characters." He grinned suddenly, showing large blocky teeth. "So I sneaked in! I had Snow White! Standing up on a roller coaster!"

"Is there anything more embarrassing than a legend that doesn't know when it's time to lie down and shut up?"

said the final arrival, in a polished, very private finishing school tone of voice. We all turned to look.

Natasha Chang stood facing the end of the table, sweet as cyanide and twice as deadly. The door to the entrance tunnel slid smoothly and very firmly down behind her. Natasha didn't even look back. A beautiful and exotic young lady in her pink leather cat-suit, with artfully bobbed black hair, heavy makeup to exaggerate her slanting eyes, and a teasing smile. Elegant and stylish, and aristocratically poised, but I couldn't help noticing that she was wearing enough heavy rings on the fingers of both hands to qualify as knuckle-dusters. Molly sniffed, quietly and dangerously, beside me.

"Try to force your eyeballs back into their sockets, Eddie. First rule when it comes to dealing with anyone from the Crowley Project is never relax for a moment. Because they'll steal your soul first chance they get, just to keep their hand in."

"Or eat it?" I murmured.

"Well, well!" said Natasha, deepening her smile to bring out the dimples in her cheeks. "The amazing Eddie Drood and the infamous Molly Metcalf . . . how nice! Are you here representing the Droods, or your new masters, the Department of the Uncanny?"

"Both," I said. "We get around."

"So I've heard," murmured Natasha, batting her heavy eyelids at both of us.

"Don't push your luck, darling," said Molly.

"How rude," pouted Natasha. She turned away, dismissing both of us, and swayed forward to stand before J. C. Chance. Who, to do him justice, stood his ground. He bowed to her sardonically, but something in his face, and perhaps his gaze, stopped her short. She pretended it was her own idea, and turned to Dead Boy.

"Love the look, darling," she said. "I could just eat you up."

"I'd only make you ill," said Dead Boy.

Natasha looked at Bruin Bear and the Sea Goat. "Oh, I see you've brought your pets you with. . . . Bless."

"Nasty woman," said Bruin Bear.

"Oh, yeah," said the Sea Goat, grinning unpleasantly. "Hey there, bad girl, want a suck on my Stoli?"

"Can't take you anywhere," sighed the Bear.

"As host of this Summit Meeting, I suggest we all take our seats at the table," the Armourer said loudly. "We have a lot to discuss, and not much time to do it in. For the moment no one knows we're here, but that won't last. The Martian Tombs are proof against eavesdropping, but there's nothing to stop other interested parties from dropping in to crash the party, once they realise something's going on here."

"I was going to mention that," I said. "I can't help noticing that all the groups gathered here are based in England. Where are the Americans, and the Russians? Not to mention the Chinese, the Indians, and so on and so on? This is a worldwide threat we're here to discuss."

"The word went out," said the Armourer. "It's not our problem if they don't take it seriously."

"They can play catch-up later," said Sir Parsifal. "I prefer smaller gatherings; decisions get made faster."

"I was hoping the Regent of Shadows would be here," said J.C. "A very useful person to have around when there's sudden death in the offing, by all accounts."

"His reputation does precede him," said the Armourer. "But it was thought his presence here might prove . . . divisive."

"Because so many of us would kill him on sight, for good reason," said Sir Parsifal. "Penance and good works in his old age are all very well, but some of us remember why he really had to leave his family."

I looked at the London Knight sharply, but he had nothing more to say. The Armourer looked uncomfortable, but remained silent. We all chose a chair and settled ourselves around the long table, allowing plenty of room between our various spheres of influence. The Armourer sat at the head of the table, as host, and looked hopefully about him ... but nobody seemed to want to get the ball rolling. And then J.C. took his sunglasses off again, and glared about with his terrible glowing eyes. We all started, and looked quickly around.

"Is anyone else Seeing what I'm Seeing?" said J.C.

I called my armour out of my torc and fashioned a pair of golden sunglasses to look through, and glared all around me ... but I couldn't See anything new. I glanced at Molly, and she shrugged quickly.

"This whole place looks weird to me," said Dead Boy. "I do feel sort of ... at home, here, but then I would. What are you Seeing, Ghost Boy?"

"We're not alone here," said J.C.

"You can See Martians?" said Bruin Bear.

"Not ... as such," said J.C. He put his shades back on. "I think the sooner we make our decisions and get the hell out of here, the better. And no, I'm not going to say anything else."

"Well, thanks a whole bunch for that," said the Sea Goat. "Unnerve us all, why don't you? Martians? Hah! Bug-eyed Monsters ... I eat stranger things than that for breakfast in Shadows Fall!"

"It's true," said Bruin Bear. "He does."

I looked around, one last time. The crystal walls blazed brightly ... and maybe it was just my imagination that made me think I glimpsed huge dark shadows moving beyond them. The Armourer said the Martians were dead and gone, long gone. But that didn't mean there was no one else here in the Tombs.

Louise wouldn't have come here for no reason.... I made the golden sunglasses disappear, and deliberately turned my back on the walls.

"Hold everything," said Molly. "Isn't there going to be anyone here from Bradford-on-Avon? It is supposed to be the most important town in the world."

"I thought that was Shadows Fall," said the Sea Goat.

"No, we're outside the world, strictly speaking," said Bruin Bear.

Sir Parsifal leaned forward, the joints of his armour creaking loudly. "The town you just mentioned . . . is best left to itself."

"We leave the town alone," said the Armourer, "and they leave the world alone. It's safer that way."

"Boring . . ." said Dead Boy.

Sir Parsifal glared at him. "Since when do we allow walking corpses to attend our Summits? We used to have standards. . . . The business of the living should be determined by the living. Not by dead bodies with delusions of grandeur."

Dead Boy punched Sir Parsifal in the head. The Knight's head whipped round under the force of the blow, and we could all hear the bones in Dead Boy's hand breaking. When Sir Parsifal turned back, his cold expression hadn't changed at all. Dead Boy snarled defiantly at him, and quietly pushed the bones in his hand back into place again.

The Armourer was on his feet. "Behave yourself, Dead Boy! Or I will throw you out of this meeting! You know I can do it. And then you can explain to the Nightside Authorities why you weren't present when the important decisions were made. And Sir Parsifal—apologise."

"He started it," said the Knight.

"You deserved it. You know the rules of the Summit. We all leave our personal feelings behind, the better to concentrate on the matter at hand. Now apologise to Dead Boy, or I'll put you out. And you know I can do it."

"Of course," said Sir Parsifal. "You would think that, wouldn't you?"

"We're Droods," I said. "We can do anything. Everyone knows that."

Sir Parsifal nodded. "Of course. You are quite right, Sir Armourer. I was forgetting. I apologise, Dead Boy."

"Fair enough," said Dead Boy. "Let's all be friends! Group hug?"

The Armourer sat down again. I was still watching Sir Parsifal. My uncle Jack had warned me about head-butting and jockeying for position, but I hadn't thought it would be so obvious. The Knight had pushed things, to see what he could get away with, and now he was sitting there quite calmly, looking around him, waiting for his next chance.

"The Meeting will come to order," said the Armourer, harshly. "First order of business: does anyone here know exactly what the Crow Lee Inheritance is?"

There was a lot of glancing back and forth, but no one said anything. Until finally Natasha Chang cleared her throat in a meaningful sort of way.

"No one in the Crowley Project has had anything to do with the nasty old scrote himself, since we booted him out all those years ago. Are you saying you don't know, Drood?"

"We know the Inheritance exists," said the Armourer. "We know that a great many powerful organisations and individuals are preparing to go to war over it. So whatever it might or might not turn out to be, we have to decide what to do about it, now. Before things get really out of hand."

"We've heard our fair share of rumours at the Institute," said J.C. "The Inheritance could consist of all the riches, secrets, unique items he acquired down the years. More than enough there to go to war over. The Boss allowed me to take a quick look through Crow Lee's file before I left. You wouldn't believe how many pages it runs to. . . . But there's nothing about an Inheritance. I don't think any of us expected him to die so suddenly. . . ."

He looked at Molly and me, almost accusingly. I looked right back at him. I wasn't going to let myself be ruffled. I was too busy keeping an eye on everyone else. I was starting to feel the undercurrents in the Meeting, all the dark and dangerous shapes moving just beneath the surface. I was beginning to get the feeling that not everyone present was singing from the same song sheet.

"Crow Lee made himself into a legend, in his own extended lifetime," Bruin Bear said slowly. "The Most Evil Man In The World. Now he's dead; I suppose it's always possible he might turn up at Shadows Fall. And then we could just ask him."

"No," said the Sea Goat. "Not going to happen. Shadows Fall is for legends that no one believes in any more. People still believe in Crow Lee."

"I don't understand Shadows Fall," said J.C.

"Not many do," said the Bear.

"Why are you here, Bear?" said Dead Boy.

"Because if the Inheritance is what some people think it is," said the Sea Goat, sounding suddenly sane and sober, "it's worth going to war over. A war that would threaten all of us. Shadows Fall is a refuge for the spiritually walking wounded, and we don't want its existence threatened."

"How very lucid of you," said Sir Parsifal.

"Up your poop chute, Knight," said the Goat.

"I may be able to contribute something useful here," said Natasha. Something in her voice made us all settle down and look at her. She smiled demurely. It wasn't very convincing. "Crow Lee left a . . . living will. The Project got its hands on a copy. Best not to ask how. I brought it with me. So, if you're all sitting comfortably . . . brace yourselves, darlings."

She produced something I immediately recognised as a memory crystal, and muttered over it; and just like that Crow Lee himself was standing at the far end of the table, smiling ghoulishly. A large and overbearing presence in a long white Egyptian gown, with a shaven head and bushy black eyebrows, and hypnotically fierce eyes. Broad-shouldered, barrel-chested, huge hands folded together before him. A nasty, despicable, fascinatingly ugly man, with a presence that wouldn't let you look away, even in death.

"If you are hearing this, then I have been murdered," said Crow Lee's image. "So, I leave the world my Inheritance. My greatest achievement, for those with the guts to go after it, and the will to master it. Whoever gains control of my Inheritance will have control over the world. Or, the means for its destruction. I have no way of knowing who will hear this—hopefully a great many people, and organisations. By all means, fight for the prize I give you. Tear civilisation apart to get your hands on my Inheritance. I promise you—it will be worth it."

He was still laughing when the image snapped off.

"Typical of the man," said the Armourer. "Do you have any further information, Natasha?"

"Not as such," she said, making the memory crystal disappear. "We have been assembling files on those most likely to go after the Inheritance."

"Including yourself, of course," said J.C.

"Well, of course, darling. But all we really have are theories, and educated guesses. We have interrogated a great many people, but to little useful effect. The possibilities do seem . . . seriously scary."

"But what is Crow Lee's greatest achievement?" I said. "Something he made, or had made for him, perhaps? We could be talking magic, or technology, or just his personal cache of secrets. I mean, he dabbled in everything at one time or another."

I looked to the Armourer, but he just shrugged. "Given some of the things Crow Lee's been known to use, the possibilities are worryingly endless. Information bombs, to rewrite reality. Words of Power, that could blow the whole world apart like a firecracker in a rotten apple. Blackmail information, to manipulate the movers and shakers in power. And let us not forget, he was responsible for the removal of Drood Hall from this world, for a time. No one's ever been able to do that before. Of course, we have since put new protections in place to ensure that can never happen again."

"Oh, of course," said Natasha. "Perish the thought."

"I can promise this much," said Sir Parsifal. "I can declare, on behalf of the London Knights, that anyone found in possession of the Crow Lee Inheritance will be punished severely."

"Typical Knight," said Dead Boy. "Still trying to bully the world into playing nicely."

"I'm sure the direct approach of the London Knights will be enough to put off all the right people," said the Armourer, diplomatically, "but, you're hardly ever here, are you? The Knights are always riding off to do battle, in worlds and dimensions beyond our own. You can make as many threats as you like, Sir Parsifal, but I fear it will fall to the Droods to back them up. And as you already said, we're all stretched a bit thin, these days. We can't be everywhere."

"Don't look at me," said J. C. Chance. "The Carnacki Institute exists to deal with threats from the Hereafter, not earthly villains with guns and armies."

"Right," said Dead Boy, nodding quickly. "Half the Nightside's already out looking for the Inheritance, with the other half standing by, to steal it from the first half when they find it. I'm sure the Authorities will do what they can. But that usually involves letting both sides fight it out, and then kicking the crap out of the winners. And I wouldn't be too ready to trust the Authorities, either. This is the Nightside we're talking about . . ."

"The Nightside will do what it always does," said Sir Parsifal. "Unleash the hounds of Hell, and the Devil take the hindmost. And no one in that unholy place will give a damn about all the innocents killed in the process."

"If they were really innocent they wouldn't be in the Nightside," said Dead Boy.

"You were innocent, once," said Bruin Bear, putting a paw on the cold dead hand beside him. "You weren't always Dead Boy."

"That was a long time ago," said Dead Boy. "I don't remember."

"If the Inheritance should turn up in Shadows Fall, we will sit on it until someone worthy comes along to claim it," said Bruin Bear.

"Right," said the Sea Goat. "No one messes with us. We've got things in Shadows Fall that make the Inheritance look like a wet paper towel."

"Strangely, that doesn't reassure me," said J.C.

"If the Crowley Project should acquire the Inheritance, you can all go to Hell," Natasha Chang said sweetly. "By the direct route."

"None of this deals with the main problem," the Armourer said severely. "How to prevent the war for the Inheritance from breaking into the everyday world. That would be bad news for all of us. The Droods have discussed this, at length, and we feel we have a plan that will work."

"Of course you do," said Sir Parsifal. "Droods always have a plan. And, their own agenda."

"It seems to us," said the Armourer, pressing on determinedly, "that the best way to stop all these people from fighting and intriguing over the Inheritance, is to destroy their economic base. You can't run a war without funds. Guns and armies cost serious money. So you can bet they'll all be looking to the Shadow Bank for loans and support. But, if the Bank should happen to be in such a delicate position that it can't afford to lend the money . . ."

"That would keep everyone quiet, until we could track down the Inheritance ourselves, and neutralise it," said Sir Parsifal.

"Now, that's what I call lateral thinking!" said J.C. "But how are we going to undermine a huge organisation like the Shadow Bank? I mean, they're big! Really big! And very well protected."

"Our plan is to infiltrate this year's Casino Infernale," said the Armourer. "Our agents will be Eddie and Molly. They will play the games, win big, and break the bank at the Casino, and thereby fatally weaken the Shadow Bank, who depend on these games for a large part of their income."

"Oh, terrific!" I said. "When were you planning to tell Molly and me about this amazing plan that will almost certainly get both of us killed?"

"I just did," said the Armourer.

Sir Parsifal rose suddenly to his feet, and glared coldly round the table. "If anyone is going to Casino Infernale and bring down the Shadow Bank, it must be a London Knight. Because only we are true and pure of heart enough not to be tempted. Money means nothing to us. We are Knights of the Round Table, of the Company of King Arthur Returned! We can be trusted."

"Yeah," I said. "But can you play cards?"

Sir Parsifal turned the full force of his glare on me. "Even the least of us is more trustworthy than a Drood who ran away from his family to serve that most despicable of creatures, the Regent of Shadows. Or a pagan witch who changes sides more often than her underwear."

I was immediately up on my feet and facing him. I knew what he was doing, but I had no choice.

"None of you would last ten minutes at Casino Infernale, Sir Knight, because you know nothing about gambling. About when to bluff, or take a risk. And you'd be spotted the minute you walked through the door, because you don't know how to pass. This is a job for a secret agent, not a knight in shining armour. And what's more, keep your mind off my girlfriend's underwear."

"Damn right," said Molly. "And the joke's on you anyway, Percy. I'm not wearing any!"

Sir Parsifal put his steel helmet back on, and stood back from the table. "The matter is not open to debate. The decision has been made. The London Knights will run this operation because none of you can be trusted to do the right thing."

I armoured up, and everyone else was quickly up out of their chairs, and backing away. Because it's one thing to have heard about Drood armour, and quite another to see it manifest right in front of you. To feel its power and potency beating on the air; its terrible significance. Everyone watched silently from the end of the table, while the Armourer did his best to calm things down. I gestured to Molly, and she reluctantly fell back to join them. Leaving Sir Parsifal and me staring at each other, from inside our armour. He turned slowly to face me, his joints making slow sinister noises, and his hand dropped to the heavy sword at his side. I stepped forward, and my armour didn't make a single sound.

"You can't be allowed to screw this up, Knight, through your own arrogance," I said. "This is too important. The whole world is at stake."

"Business as usual for the London Knights," said Sir Parsifal. "What's the matter, Drood; stakes too high for you?"

"This was supposed to be a chance for discussion, not ultimatums," I said.

"Typical Drood," said Sir Parsifal. "This is why none of the Big Names from around the world showed up for your little get-together. Because real Powers don't negotiate. I only came to see what you were up to. And now I know, I will take over. And do what needs to be done."

Uncle Jack armoured up, and came forward to stand beside me. Molly was quickly there too, on my other side.

"No," I said. "Thanks for the thought, but we can't have a London Knight thinking it takes more than one Drood to bring him down. We can't have these sanctimonious little pricks getting above themselves."

The Armourer leaned in close beside me, his voice murmuring inside my mask. "Nice words, Eddie. Excellent sentiments. Couldn't agree more. But, this is Sir Parsifal. A legendary warrior, undefeated fighter, and one of the most dangerous Knights in Arthur's Company. His strength is as the strength of ten, because he's too pure and single-minded to even entertain the concept of defeat. That sword he's carrying isn't Excalibur, but it is really old and horribly powerful, and soaked in martial magics. It might actually be able to cut through strange matter."

"Then I'll just have to make sure he doesn't have the chance to cut me with it," I said. "Thanks for the pep talk though, Uncle Jack."

"Anytime, nephew."

He moved back, taking Molly with him. She didn't want to go, but she didn't want me to look weak in front of the others.

I grew a long golden sword out of my armoured hand, and extended it out before me. Light as air, and sharper than a cutting word. Sir Parsifal drew his sword and the long blue-hued steel gleamed viciously. I could feel its presence, like a new arrival in the room. The two of us stepped forward, good men in armoured suits, fighting for what we each believed to be right. I was sure Sir Parsifal would honestly regret killing me, afterwards, but it wouldn't stop him. He thought he had to win, for the sake of the world. Trouble was, I thought that too.

We both lunged forward, and our blades slammed together and then jumped apart again. I could see surprise in Sir Parsifal's eyes; he'd expected his magic blade to shear right through mine. He knew nothing of strange matter. We cut at each other, again and again, stamping and thrusting, parrying and retreating. Circling each other, feinting and withdrawing, searching out weaknesses in the other's position and style. The two great swords hammered together, and neither of us would give an inch.

Sir Parsifal was fast and furious, incredibly strong and practised, coming at me from every direction; but he'd never met a Drood before. He didn't know how to fight dirty. So when I was sure I had his style down pat, I deliberately let my sword drop, just a little. He thought he saw an opening, and lunged forward, his sword leaping forward in full extension, to run me through the chest. I stood my ground, and the sword point hit my chest and bounced away, unable to penetrate. And while Sir Parsifal was shocked and caught off guard, I swung my sword with both hands, and hit him so hard on the wrist that his fingers leapt open, and his sword fell from his hand. I set the point of my golden sword at Sir Parsifal's throat, unprotected under his steel helm.

"Had enough?" I said.

"Well played, Drood," said Sir Parsifal, standing very still. "You took a hell of a chance, though. You couldn't have known your armour would withstand my sword."

"I gambled," I said. "And I won. And that's why I'm going to Casino Infernale."

"It isn't over yet," said Sir Parsifal. "Are you really ready to kill me, over this?"

"Yes," I said. "This matters."

"Then you are the right man for the job," said the Knight. "I yield. And I salute you, Sir Drood."

I stepped back, and he leant down and picked up his sword from the floor. He saluted me with his blade, and then put it away.

"You didn't really think it was going to be that easy, did you, darlings?" said Natasha Chang.

We all looked round, to see her standing away from the rest of us, covering us all with a nasty-looking piece of high tech in her hand. Energy weapon of some kind, presumably. She smiled happily.

"You should never have invited me here. I learned far more than I gave away; but just to be sure, I think I'll kill you all now. And then eat all your ghosts, and digest all your secrets. And then my people will come here, and make the Martian Tombs our own. And we'll find the Crow Lee Inheritance, and make that our own. It was always meant for us, anyway. Little people like you wouldn't appreciate it. I'm going to have it all, and there's nothing you can do to stop me!"

While she was still shouting and threatening us with her tech gun, the Sea Goat appeared suddenly behind her and hit her over the head with his vodka bottle. The glass shattered, and she slumped unconscious to the floor. J.C. moved quickly in to snatch up the weapon as it fell from her hand. The Sea Goat grinned broadly.

"No one ever notices me. Or takes me seriously."

"Did you have to break a bottle over her head?" said Bruin Bear. "You've got very coarse since you got real."

The Goat shrugged. "Stick with what works, that's what I always say."

"Can't take you anywhere," said Bruin Bear.

The Armourer and I armoured down, and then moved to one side to talk quietly together.

"This marvellous plan of yours," I said. "The one where we break the bank at Casino Infernale, to damage the Shadow Bank . . . correct me if I'm wrong, but hasn't this already been tried before? Many times, by many brave and experienced agents? And hasn't it always gone horribly wrong, never worked, and got everyone involved killed?"

"Well, yes," said the Armourer. "And, since they'll be looking for Drood field agents at Casino Infernale, you'll have to go in as Shaman Bond. But you and Molly do have this marvellous knack for winning against appalling odds. So, we're counting on that."

"But you're betting with our lives!" I said.

"Oh, no," said my uncle Jack. "Not just your lives, Eddie. They don't play for money at Casino Infernale. They play for souls."

CHAPTER THREE

Take a Chance on Me

We came home from Mars to find the old chapel waiting for us like a familiar pair of arms. It felt disturbing, but delightful, to go so quickly from an alien world to a place of such pleasant familiarity. The Armourer and I armoured down, and Molly sent her bark sideways again. She looked fine, but my uncle Jack looked . . . tired. Older. The three of us just stood together for a while, getting our mental breath back. Because even people like us need to take time out, now and again, to recover our bearings and recharge our batteries.

"Will everyone else get home okay?" I said, finally.

"Oh, sure," said the Armourer. "And the Tombs will shut themselves down."

"What if someone decides they want to hang around?" said Molly. "Dig out a few secrets?"

"The Tombs can look after themselves," said the Armourer. "You really don't want to outstay your welcome there."

"Louise did," said Molly. "She said she liked it there."

"Yes, but she's weird," the Armourer said kindly.

"What about Natasha Chang?" I said.

"I'm sure someone will give her a lift home, if she needs one," said the Armourer.

"I wouldn't worry about her," said Molly. "Take a lot more than a bottle over the head to slow that one down."

"Why would anyone want to help her, when she was ready to kill us all?" I said.

"Now, that was always on the cards," said the Armourer. "She is Crowley Project, after all. Bad Deeds R Us, where betrayal comes as standard. But . . . no one ever bears grudges over what happens at Summit Meetings. Not when you might need to work with them some day."

"What happens on Mars, stays on Mars," I said solemnly.

"Well, quite," said the Armourer.

And then he insisted we all beat our clothing, and stamp our feet hard, to shake off any Martian dust we might have picked up. He crouched down, his knees creaking loudly, and carefully brushed up what few grains he could find, before dropping it all into a small specimen jar, and sealing it very carefully. He straightened up, slowly. I went to offer a helping hand, and he stopped me with a hard look. I should have known better. He tucked the jar away, somewhere about his person.

"I'll study that later, then store it somewhere safe," he said happily. The Armourer does love his work.

"Excuse me," I said, "but what's so dangerous about Martian dust?"

"I don't know," the Armourer said darkly. "That's why I'm going to study it, and store it somewhere safe."

"You said . . . all the Martians are dead and gone," I said. "Long gone . . . so who else could there have been in the Tombs, watching us?"

"Beats me," said the Armourer.

"I could always ask Louise," said Molly, just a bit threateningly.

"Nothing lives in the Martian Tombs," said the Armourer, firmly.

"So what the hell did J. C. Chance See, with his horrible eyes?" I said. "Martian ghosts?"

"God, I hope not," said the Armourer. "Help me with this Door, Eddie. I'm not as young as I used to be."

Together, we pushed Merlin's Door into place against the chapel wall, and the moment we stepped back the Door just faded into the wall and disappeared, leaving nothing behind but an expanse of unbroken stonework. The Armourer sniffed loudly, turned away, and led us out of the old chapel. I was the last out, and I hesitated in the doorway, looking back. It would have been good to see the ghost of old Jacob, one last time. But there was no trace of him anywhere. There are miracles in my world, but rarely the ones you want.

I was just starting to turn away when the old television set suddenly turned itself on, and there on the screen was a ghostly image, grinning out at me.

"Jacob?" I said.

The television shut itself down. The screen was blank, the image gone—if it had ever really been there. It might have been him, or it might have been one last practical joke, arranged before he left. Jacob always did like to have the last laugh.

I left the old chapel, and heaved the door back into place. The ivy waved good-bye as I walked away.

The Armourer led us back through Drood Hall, heading for the Armoury. Like an old horse with the scent of the stables in his nostrils. He was clearly tired now, just plodding along with his shoulders bowed and his head down. People hurried back and forth through the corridors and hallways, and after a while I began to notice that they were looking at me. Not the usual *Oh God it's him back again . . .* but more . . . sad, concerned. As though they knew something I didn't and were commiserating in advance. I would have liked to stop and question some of them, but I didn't like the way the Armourer was looking. The trip to Mars had taken a lot out of him, and I wanted him back in the

Armoury where he belonged, as soon as possible. Hopefully, the familiar surroundings would invigorate him again.

Molly didn't give a damn how tired he was. She kept badgering him about the Regent, and demanding the Armourer return control of the Merlin Glass to me, so we could get back to the Department of the Uncanny, and she could pin the Regent to the wall till she got some answers out of him. The Armourer finally had enough, and turned his old head sharply to glare at her.

"The Regent isn't at the Department, just now. He's gone to France."

"What?" said Molly. "He didn't say anything to us . . . what the hell is he doing in France?"

"He went some time back, to prepare the way for our assault on Casino Infernale," said the Armourer.

"Why would the head of the Department of the Uncanny intrude on our mission?" I said. "And why has he gone personally, instead of sending his own people?" I was missing something here. I could tell.

"He had to go himself," said the Armourer, "because your parents have been at Casino Infernale for some time. Playing the games, putting pressure on the bank. Setting things up for you."

"But why is the Department of the Uncanny getting involved with Drood business?" I insisted, honestly confused.

"This is Summit business," said the Armourer. "My father, and your parents, are working with us on this case."

"Because . . . no one ever really leaves the family?" I said.

"You're learning, Eddie," said the Armourer.

Molly made a rude noise. "How is it you know so much about the Regent's business?"

"He's my dad," said the Armourer. "We keep in touch; always have. Even though we couldn't tell you, Eddie."

"Yes . . ." I said. "We are going to have words about that, Uncle Jack."

"It was for your own good, Eddie. Your protection."

"That whole *We know what's best for you* attitude is one of the main reasons I ran away from this family, first chance I got," I said.

"I feel the same way myself, sometimes," said the Armourer. "We will talk later, Eddie. About many things. I promise."

Back in the Armoury, everything looked much the same. Except for the bits that had exploded or caught fire in our absence. Sometimes I don't think of the Armoury as a scientific laboratory, more as evolution in action. It was raining very heavily in one corner of the Armoury, complete with thunder and lightning. A bit much just to test a new kind of umbrella. The Armourer seemed pleased to be back on his own territory again; stumbling along, not hurrying, smiling amiably about him at lab assistants who were usually much more preoccupied with whatever it was that was going horribly wrong right in front of them.

The Armourer finally sank down into his favourite old chair, complete with extra cushions and safety straps, in front of his personal workstation. He let out a long slow sigh of relief.

"Good to be back!" he said. "But then, the best part of a holiday is always coming home again."

"Didn't you enjoy being on Mars?" said Molly.

"I don't enjoy leaving the Hall much at all, these days, truth be told," said the Armourer. "It takes so much out of me. Don't even like leaving the Armoury, some days."

He started rummaging through his desk drawers, looking for food and drink and his private little bottle of pick-me-ups that he likes to think no one else knows about. I took a careful look around at the lab assistants, making sure none of them were getting too close. One young man was holding his melting arm over a sink, and swearing bitterly. A young woman was chasing frantically after a giant eyeball with its own heavily flapping bat wings, flailing about her with a really big butterfly net. The eyeball bobbed happily along ahead of her, always just out of reach. And two lab assistants stood quietly and thoughtfully at the edge of a combat circle, making notes on clipboards as their two shadows fought it out inside the circle.

Someone else was emptying the water from a fire bucket over a burning bush. I didn't ask. I didn't want to know.

I'd expected my uncle Jack to put the kettle on, and make us all a nice refreshing cup of tea. My family runs on hot sweet tea and Jaffa Cakes. Instead, he pulled out a bottle of Bombay gin and a glass, and poured himself a more than healthy measure. He didn't offer Molly or me one. He added a good measure of Red Bull to his gin, and then dunked a Jaffa Cake in it. Neither the drink nor the cake seemed to restore him much. It worried me to see him like this. Watching the Armourer host the Summit on Mars, standing tall and sharp and authoritative, had been like seeing the Uncle Jack I'd known as a child. The man who was, once upon a time, one of the best field agents the Droods ever had. Now, that much older man's fires seemed to have burned out. He looked up suddenly, and caught the expression on my face. He smiled, briefly.

"Don't get old, Eddie. It's hard work."

Embarrassed, I looked away. Molly stole two chairs from nearby workstations, and we pulled them up opposite the Armourer, and sat down. He finished his drink, and looked thoughtfully at the various bits of high tech and partially disassembled weapons scattered across his work surface. He reached out to pat his computer fondly, like a favourite pet. The machine was wrapped in mistletoe, and long strings of garlic. Which may or may not have added to its processing power.

"That's new," I said, pointing vaguely at something green and brown, in a pot. "What is that?"

"A bonsai wicker man," the Armourer said proudly. "Only one in captivity." His voice was firmer now, his eyes clearer.

Molly leaned in close, fascinated. "What do you burn in it?"

"Chestnuts, mostly," said the Armourer.

"Uncle Jack," I said, and he looked at me sharply. He knew I used his name only to put pressure on him. "I think it's time you told me what's going on, Uncle Jack."

"Yes, I suppose it is time, Eddie." He sat back in his chair, and considered me thoughtfully. "Very well. Down to business, eh? Good, good . . . Casino Infernale is being held in the city of Nantes, in France, this year."

"Hold it," I said. "With something this important, shouldn't I be getting the full briefing from the Council?"

"Thought you were in a hurry, boy? Still . . . caution; always a good thing. I'm telling you what you need to know, because I know more about this than anyone else. I was involved in one of the earliest attempts to break the bank at Casino Infernale, back in the mid-sixties. Don't ask me the exact date. I've never been good with dates. . . . Anyway, this particular mission was the first and only time I ever worked in the field with my brother James. We were both building a reputation, back then, and they'd already started calling James the Grey Fox. This was a carefully planned mission, with two very experienced field agents, and it still all went to shit in a hurry and we had to run for our lives. Hopefully, you two will do better." He stopped then, for a long moment, his gaze far away, lost in yesterday. He looked old again. Even frail. He roused himself, and continued. "It's been a long time since I was out in the field. Walking up and down in the world, changing history from behind the scenes. Now just hosting a Summit takes it out of me . . . which is why you get to go to Nantes, and not me."

"What went wrong?" I said. "On the mission, with you and James?"

"Casino Security was onto us from the start," said the Armourer. His mouth pulled back, as though bothered by a bad taste. "We thought we were being so clever, swaggering around hidden behind our brand-new identities and immaculately crafted disguises. But hotel security spotted our torcs the moment we walked in. They were just waiting for us to start something, so they could kill us both and prove they weren't afraid of no Droods. . . . We had no choice but to abandon the mission and take to our heels. Ended up being chased across the hotel roof by a whole army of heavily armed goons. Ah, the good old days . . . But you don't want to hear this."

"Of course I do!" I said. "You hardly ever talk about being a field agent, any more. When I was a kid, I used to love sneaking out of lessons to come down here and listen to all your stories."

"Glory days," said the Armourer. "You'll understand when you're older, Eddie. You can't afford to live too much in the past, if you want to get anything done. But the past can seem so much more tempting than the present, because that's the only place you can meet your old friends. . . . No. No; concentrate! I never told you this story before, Eddie, because we made such a mess of it. The Casino Security people threw everything they had at us: guns and magics, incendiaries and shaped curses. James and I would have liked to stand our ground and fight; show these cheap thugs what Drood armour and training could do. But we had to get away. We had to get the information home . . . that they could See our torcs. Not many could, then. So we headed for the roof, to make our escape.

"We were on the penthouse floor, you see. Casino Security couldn't touch us until we actually broke a rule. For fear of upsetting the other gamblers. If they thought Security thugs could just jump them any time, for no reason, they wouldn't come. Gambling, serious gambling, only works if it's protected by the rules. Anyway, word got to us that there was a hidden safe somewhere in the penthouse main office, with all kinds of useful information in it about Casino Infernale and the Shadow Bank that funded it. So James and I sneaked up there and broke in, trusting to our armour to hide and protect us. But the moment we opened the office door, every alarm in the world went off at once. And dozens of over-muscled, heavily armed, Security goons appeared out of nowhere. To drag us down, and haul us away for . . . questioning.

"James and I fought our way out, easily enough. Weapons and numbers were never going to be enough against Drood armour. We stove in chests and broke in heads with our golden fists, and threw huge men against the walls with such force that we broke the walls as well as the men. And laughed while we did it. Glorying in death and destruction. We were younger men then, and thought being the Good Guys justified anything. . . .

"We took the elevator to the roof. We couldn't go down, because it sounded like all the Security people in the hotel were coming up, with God alone knew how much heavy-duty weaponry. So we went up, to the maintenance level directly below the roof. The elevator slid smoothly to a halt, and James and I looked at each other. We knew there was bound to be massed nastiness waiting on the other side of the elevator doors. So, we smashed the door controls so the bad guys couldn't get in, and then bashed holes in the elevator roof. In films there are always inspection panels you can use to get out, but there aren't any in real life. Hollywood lies to you all the time. So, we burst up through into the elevator shaft, and then clambered up the cables to the roof exit.

"Once outside, we went to the edge and looked down. We were a very long way up. Tallest building in Nantes, by far. We could see right out across the city. The wind blew across the roof with savage force, enough to rock us back and forth on our feet even in our armour. I could hear feet hurrying up the stairs to the roof—lots of feet. James and I looked frantically about us, but there was no obvious way down . . . so we ran for the far edge of the roof, to buy us some time. Hoping we'd find something there we could use. A door burst open behind us, and armed men spilled out onto the roof, opening fire on us with every kind of weapon you could think of.

"James and I kept our heads down, and ran for all we were worth. When you're in the armour, Molly, you feel like you can run like the wind. We sprinted, faster than a racing car, golden arms pumping at our sides, and the roof just flew past. Bullets, and other things, ricocheted harmlessly off our armour. A few hit us hard enough to make us stagger, but we just kept going. We both knew surrender wasn't an option. They'd vivisect us alive, right down to the genetic level, to learn the secret of Drood armour. So we ran. I don't think either of us was laughing, any more.

"And, just like that, we ran out of roof. We skidded to a halt at the edge, our golden heels digging furrows in the concrete surface . . . and when we looked down it was the same dizzying drop, hundreds and hundreds of feet. No way down, and no way back. Bullets were still ricocheting from our armour, and blowing chunks out of the roof around us. We were trapped. Just standing there on the edge, looking down, made my head swim. Drood armour has many fine qualities, but flying has never been one of them. I looked at James.

"'We're going to have to jump,' I said.

"'Are you crazy? The fall will almost certainly kill us,' he said.

"'Let's cling to the word almost,' I said.

"'The armour will probably survive the drop,' said James. 'But I hate to think what the impact of the sudden halt will do to what's inside the armour. If they ever find a way to open it up, they'll be able to remove what's left of us with spoons.'

"'Not if we slow ourselves down,' I said.

"I jumped off the edge, not allowing myself time to think about it, and dug the fingers of both golden hands into the side of the building. They sank in deep, even as I plummeted down through all those hundreds of feet. James was right behind me. We fell, faster and faster, no matter how deep we dug our hands in, tearing two great jagged runnels down the side of the hotel. . . . But it did the trick. It slowed us just enough. We both hit the ground hard enough to blast out a great crater, but we walked away. Trembling like a stripper on opening night, but still alive. As soon as we got our strength and breath and wits back, we ran. And never once looked back.

"And that is what happened when James and I tried t
break the bank at Casino Infernale. Two great legends lik
us, and we never even got near."

I applauded loudly, and Molly joined in. The Armoure
shrugged, and made himself another large gin and Re
Bull.

"How did you get out of France?" I said.

"By train, under forged tickets and fake identities we'
tucked away on one side, just in case." The Armoure
smiled slowly. "I heard later that the Casino Security peo
ple came looking for us with cars and planes and boats
sniffer dogs and telepaths. Searching for teleport signs o
secret entrances to hidden underground ways . . . but i
never even occurred to them to stop and search the trains
Far too ordinary . . . James and I played portable Scrabbl
all the way to the coast, and then the invisible networ
smuggled us home. I have to tell you, Eddie—your uncl
James knew more rude words, and the correct way to spel
them, than any civilised person should. I was shocked,
tell you. Shocked.

"And that . . . was the only time I ever worked a missio
with my brother. The whole affair was considered such
cock-up that the then Matriarch split us up, and sent us of
to work in completely separate areas of the world. Suc
was the spying game, then.

"Now, Eddie, Molly . . . Casino Infernale is being hel
at Nantes again, this year. Right now. All the greates
games of chance, attracting all the most famous faces an
successful gamblers from all over the world. Fortunes t
be made and lost, every day and every night, while the Ca
sino takes its cut, and funds the Shadow Bank. Reputa
tions made and souls lost, on the turn of a card. And that
why we're sending you two.

"The Shadow Bank likes to move Casino Infernal
around, from city to city and from country to country. Fo
security reasons. They like some places better than others
because they're easier to defend, or control. That's wh
they're back in Nantes, for the third time in fifty years

You can expect the nastiest, most up-to-date, and fiendishly subtle security measures you've ever encountered. And then some. They will kill you if they find out who you really are. Just to be able to boast they've killed a Drood." He looked at Molly. "If Eddie dies, and you're taken, my dear, make them kill you. We wouldn't be able to get to them in time, and what they would do to you . . ."

"They wouldn't dare," said Molly. "My sisters would . . ."

"The Shadow Bank wouldn't care!" said the Armourer. "Even your sisters couldn't touch them. They do anything, because they can. Casino Infernale exists to help fund the Shadow Bank, but it's also about power and prestige. That's what pulls in the biggest and richest gamblers in the world every year, to play for the highest stakes. The Shadow Bank provides loans to all the secret people and hidden organisations. They provide utterly discreet banking services and launder money in every currency you can think of. Everyone owes them . . . favours. They regard themselves as untouchable . . . because they are."

"Why don't we just smuggle a really big bomb into the middle of Casino Infernale, and blow the hell out of everything and everyone?" said Molly, practical as always.

"Because we don't want to upset the Shadow Bank," the Armourer said patiently. "Not when we might need to go cap in hand to them, some day."

I looked at him steadily. "Are we by any chance already in bed with the Shadow Bank? Do we do business with them?"

"No," said the Armourer. "And we never have. But you can never tell what the future might bring. We just want to stop them supporting an inconvenient war, not destroy them."

"Such is the spying life," I said.

"Exactly," said the Armourer.

"I have done business with the Shadow Bank myself," said Molly. "Back before I met you, Eddie, of course . . . But they've always been something of a mystery. Who are they, really? Who owns the Shadow Bank? Who profits?"

"I don't know," said the Armourer. "Don't know anyone that does. They have the best security in the world."

"Better than ours?" I said.

He raised a bushy white eyebrow. "Neither side wants to press the point."

"How old is the Shadow Bank?" I asked. "Old as us?"

"Older," said the Armourer. "In fact, I have heard stories. . . ."

Molly and I waited, but he just stopped talking, staring at nothing in particular. After a while, he pulled himself together again and carried on, in a calm and considered tone of voice.

"Shaman Bond and Molly Metcalf are to go to Casino Infernale, and gamble at every game they can get into. Don't be afraid to lie and bluff, that's what everyone else will be doing. With the help of certain useful items, courtesy of these labs, you will play the games of chance, win, and win big. Big enough to break the bank. And hopefully drive a financial stake through the heart of whoever's running Casino Infernale this year. And, of course, stop the Inheritance war before it gets started. Yes. Any questions? Eddie, you're not in school any more, you don't need to raise your hand."

"How much money will we be given to work with?" I said. "On the grounds that I am sure as hell not funding this myself."

"I told you," the Armourer said firmly. "At Casino Infernale, it's never about the money. In the big games, you play for souls. There are lesser, introductory games, where you can play for money, or objects of power, or years of service. But those games are strictly for the small fry, and you won't be bothering much with them."

"I still see one major stumbling block to our getting in," I said. "Casino Security were able to See your torc, and Uncle James'. Our armour has changed since then, but certain people are always going to be able to See my torc. Hadrian Coll did, on Trammell Island."

"Never liked the man," said the Armourer. "You did

say he was dead, didn't you? Good, good . . . Don't worry about the torc. We think we have an answer."

"All right," I said. "What marvellous toys do you have for me to play with, this time?"

He actually winced. "I do wish you wouldn't call them that, Eddie."

"Do you have something to make sure I win, every time?" I said.

"Casino Security would spot anything that obvious in a moment," said the Armourer. "We have to be more subtle than that."

He rummaged around in one of his desk drawers, and brought out a very familiar-looking handgun, in a worn leather shoulder holster.

"We'll start with the Colt Repeater," the Armourer said briskly. "You've used this often enough before. Standard issue. No recoil, aims itself, and never runs out of ammunition. Fires steel bullets, silver, wood, and incendiaries. As required. The ammo teleports in from outside, so Casino Security shouldn't be able to detect the gun's extracurricular capabilities. . . ."

"They'll know it's there, though," I said. "Won't they just confiscate it?"

"Everyone at Casino Infernale goes armed," said the Armourer. "Or no one would dare turn up. Gamblers like to play rough, and they're always ready to defend themselves, and their winnings. As long as your gun is clearly for personal use, and apparently small and limited, Security won't bother you. All their staff will be much better armed, of course."

"Such as?" said Molly.

"Just assume the worst, and you'll be right more often than you're wrong," said the Armourer.

"Terrific . . ." said Molly. "I notice you're not offering me any weapons."

"Wouldn't dream of insulting you, my dear," the Armourer said gallantly, and Molly actually giggled.

"Why the shoulder holster?" I said, hefting the weight

of the gun and holster in my hand, dubiously. "Why can't I just keep it in my pocket dimension, until I need it?"

"Because we don't want the Security staff even suspecting you might have such a thing," the Armourer said sternly. "Keep the gun in plain sight, where they can see it."

I shrugged out of my jacket, and struggled into the shoulder-holster straps. I've never liked the bloody things. It's like trying to put on a bra, in the dark, backwards. In the end, Molly had to help me. She does have more experience in these matters, after all. Bras and shoulder holsters. By the time we were finished, and I had my jacket on again, feeling very self-conscious about the bulge over my left chest, the Armourer was waiting to present Molly and me with two thin glass phials, each containing a deep purple liquid that seethed and heaved as though trying to break through the glass. I couldn't help noticing that the phials were not just stoppered, but wired shut. This did not fill me with confidence.

"A simple memory enhancer," said the Armourer, beaming. "So you can count cards, calculate the odds, detect patterns in the run of play, and more . . . should give you just the edge you need, against even the most proficient and practised players."

I looked suspiciously at the bubbling liquid. "How long will the effect last?"

"Good question," said the Armourer. "No idea. Make a note of when the stuff stops working, and be sure to let me know."

"Has anyone actually tested this before?" said Molly.

"Oh, yes," said the Armourer. "Lots of people."

"Where are they!" demanded Molly. "Show them to me!"

"Don't be such a baby," said the Armourer. "Get it down you. Yes, right now! So it will have a chance to sink into your system, and Security won't be able to detect it."

Molly and I took one glass phial each. My phial felt unpleasantly warm to the touch. We looked at each other, for mutual comfort and support, and then carefully peeled away the heavy wire holding the stoppers in place. The purple liquid jumped wildly in the phial, as though sensing a chance to escape. I popped off the stopper, put the phial to my lips and knocked it back in one. My lips thinned back from the bitter over-taste, and then I swear to God my eyes squeezed shut so tightly, it forced tears down my cheeks. My throat tried to turn inside out. I have never tasted anything so foul in my life. Including that chalky white kaolin morphine muck they used to force on me when I was poorly as a kid. And too weak to fight them off.

God, it was bad! I wanted to rip my tongue right out of my mouth and throw it on the floor and stamp on it, in the hope that would stop the taste. I grabbed the Armourer's large gin and Red Bull and gulped it down, trying to cauterise my taste buds.

Molly waved her hands wildly, tears of pure horror jumping from her wide-stretched eyes. "Somebody bring me a dog's arse, right now! So I can chew on it, to get this taste out of my mouth!"

I handed her the Armourer's gin bottle, and she sucked it down hard.

"Big babies," said the Armourer.

The nuclear fallout in my mouth began to recede, and I was able to breathe properly again. Molly was still sucking at her gin bottle. I looked reproachfully at the Armourer.

"I am still working on the taste," he admitted. "But it could save your life, at Casino Infernale! I think . . . it works on the old principle of if it tastes bad, it must be doing you good. The effects should start kicking in after two, three hours. Don't worry about side effects."

"You mean there aren't any?" I said.

"No, I mean there's no point in worrying about them, because there's nothing you can do to ameliorate them. They don't last long. Just grit your teeth and hang on to something solid, until it's all over. Or, more likely, all over someone else."

"Let me kill him," said Molly, still hanging on to the gin bottle.

"Get in the queue," I said.

"You'll like this," said the Armourer, temptingly. He offered Molly and me two small objects: flat black plastic, like key fobs without the fobs.

"Look pretty damned ordinary and innocent, don't they?" the Armourer said proudly. "You each keep one, and make sure you keep them separate. Security won't even know you've got them. If anyone should challenge you, just say they're lucky charms. That always goes down well. They're completely innocuous, until you fit them together. Once joined and activated, this clever little device operates as a sort of top-rank can opener. Able to open any box or container."

"Such as a safe?" I said.

"You're learning!" said the Armourer. "Can I please have my gin bottle back, Molly? It may not be worth much, but it is of great sentimental value. Thank you. Oh, come on, the two of you; it wasn't that bad. . . ."

"Yes, it was," I said firmly.

"It was even worse than that," said Molly.

"Puts a nice shine on your fillings," said the Armourer. "Now, finally: a pack of playing cards. Look pretty damned normal, don't they?"

He thrust the pack into my hands, and I shuffled them a few times, and fanned out a few cards, to look them over.

"Marked?" I said. "Infrared, ultraviolet?"

The Armourer sniffed. "Nothing so obvious. This . . . is a chameleon deck. You can substitute it for any other pack of cards, and this pack will immediately take on all the characteristics of the pack it's replacing. Identical, down to the smallest detail. Except that this deck is preprogrammed to ensure you win, every time. Any game, any variation; the pack will provide you and you alone with the winning cards, every time. No matter who deals, or how many times the pack gets shuffled. But, you have to get really close to the deck you're replacing, for the chameleon aspect to kick in."

I put the cards in my jacket pocket. Molly glared at the Armourer. "I don't get any toys?"

"You don't need my help," said the Armourer. "You have your magic. But do be careful, Molly; Casino Security will go to great lengths to prevent you from using all your usual tricks and practices."

"Really like to see them stop me," said Molly.

"They will," said the Armourer. "Unless you're very subtle." And then he stopped, and looked at me, and something in his face changed. He looked . . . sad, and concerned, like all the people I'd passed in the corridors before. Who looked like they knew what was coming, and were sorry for me. The Armourer, my uncle Jack, was looking at me with something particular in mind, and he looked . . . guilty. "And now, Eddie," he said slowly, "we come to the unfortunate part. The necessary, unpleasant part."

"The memory drug doesn't count?" said Molly.

"I'm sorry, Eddie," said the Armourer, his gaze fixed on me, so sad, so sad. "I really am very sorry, but there's no other way to do this."

"What?" I said. "What are you talking about, Uncle Jack?"

I could feel the hairs on the back of my neck standing up. My stomach muscles tensed painfully. There was a sense of something really bad in the air, a foreboding of something awful just waiting to happen. I felt like I should be running. Molly glared quickly about her, looking for a threat. She could feel it too.

"Ethel!" said the Armourer. "Show yourself, please."

And just like that, the familiar comforting red glow appeared in the Armoury, confining itself to the Armourer's workstation. Warm rosy red light fell over me like a spotlight, picking me out; a spiritual pressure I could feel holding me in place, even as it embraced me. Ethel manifested in the Armoury, and immediately all the lab assistants stopped what they were doing and hurried forward from all sides. Many of them were carrying surveillance tech and recording gear, along with some other stuff I didn't even recognise. All of them eager for a chance to study our mysterious other-dimensional benefactor.

"Well done, boys and girls," said the Armourer. "Nice reaction times. Watch all you like, but don't get too close."

"And whoever's doing *that*, stop it immediately," said Ethel.

One particular piece of tech suddenly went up in smoke, and the assistant carrying it retired, coughing heavily.

"I like it here," Ethel said comfortably. "So many interesting things . . . and look at all the toys! I want to play with all of them!"

"What are you doing here, Ethel?" I said. "You never leave the Sanctity!"

"She's here because I need her to be here," said the Armourer.

And then he stopped. There was something more he wanted to say, but somehow he just couldn't bring himself to say it.

"Let me, Jack," said Ethel. "It's all right. He'll understand."

"Understand what?" I said. "What's going on here!"

"I have to remove your torc, Eddie," said Ethel. "It's the only way we can get a Drood into Casino Infernale."

"Oh, come on!" I said. "Can't you just disguise it, or alter it?"

"No," said Ethel.

"The kind of Security people you'll be dealing with would see through any disguise we might try," said the Armourer. He made himself look at me, and the naked sorrow and suffering in his gaze clutched at my heart with a cold, hard hand.

"Strange matter weighs heavily on the world," said Ethel. "All I can do is remove it completely."

Molly moved in close beside me. I don't know what was in my face, but she didn't like looking at it.

"Without your torc, you'll be completely unprotected," said the Armourer. "Nothing to stand between you and the dangers of the Casino. There's a good chance I'm sending you to your death, Eddie, and the only excuse I have is that it's necessary."

"You don't have to do this, Eddie," said Molly. She placed a comforting hand on my arm. "Tell them to go to Hell. Tell them to get someone else for their suicide mission. I'll stand by you. You know that. It doesn't always have to be you!"

"Yes, it does," I said. I hardly recognised my own voice. It sounded numb, shocked. "It does have to be me, because I have the best chance of succeeding and coming back alive. It wouldn't be fair . . . to hand this off to someone else. Someone less prepared, with a worse chance. This is too important to let someone else screw it up because they were second choice. So it does have to be me. Go ahead, Ethel. Do it."

"Eddie . . ." said Ethel.

"Do it!" I said. "Do it now, before I change my mind."

The torc disappeared from around my neck. Just vanished, drawn back into whatever unnatural place Ethel found it. I felt it go, and it felt like being skinned. Like having a layer of my soul ripped off. Afterwards, Molly told me I screamed. I don't remember. I think I made myself forget. I think I had to. The next thing I do remember, I was on the floor . . . on my knees, sobbing like a baby. Molly was on her knees beside me, holding me in her arms, rocking me back and forth and murmuring comforting words to me.

"You bitch!" I heard her scream at Ethel. *"What have you done to him?"*

"I'm sorry," said Ethel. "But I couldn't just take the torc away. Casino Security would still have been able to detect that it had been there. Strange matter leaves marks. I had to alter you right down to the genetic level, Eddie. So you're not just a Drood without a torc; you never were a Drood. Never have been a Drood. You're Shaman Bond, and you always have been."

"Just what I always wanted," I said, bitterly. "To have never been a Drood."

"When the mission is over, you come back here and Ethel will reinstate your torc," said the Armourer.

"Thanks," I said. "Thanks for everything, Uncle Jack."

I made myself stop shaking, with an effort of will. Molly let go and sat back. She brought out a handkerchief and wiped the cold sweat off my face. I don't think I've ever seen her look so angry. I started to get to my feet again, and Molly was quickly there to help me. She carried most of my weight, until I could carry it myself. I looked slowly about me. There were lab assistants everywhere, some of them recording my reactions, but none of them said anything. Molly glared about her, her hands clenched into white-knuckled fists. I wanted to say something, but I didn't have the words. I felt cold, and empty. Violated. I'd never felt so naked and vulnerable before.

"It's all right, Eddie," said Molly. "You've still got me."

"You've still got me," I said. "I'm still here. Most of me, anyway."

"I will make them pay for this," said Molly. "Make them all pay. . . ."

"No," I said. "Don't. Please. Anything for the family, remember?"

"I know what I've done to you," said Ethel. "Do you forgive me, Eddie?"

"Ask me later," I said.

She disappeared, her red glow gone in a moment. And what little comfort her light had given me went with her. Still without saying anything, the lab assistants turned and left, taking their tech with them. I would have liked to put their silent departure down to tact, and understanding, but I doubted it. There just wasn't any reason for them to stay any longer. So all that was left was Molly and me, and the Armourer. He sat down in his chair, looking older and more tired than ever. I sat down facing him, and Molly sat down beside me. She held my hand in both of hers, like she would never let me go. And for a while, we all just sat there and looked at each other.

"Was it really that bad, Eddie?" the Armourer said finally. "It looked bad."

"Yes," I said.

"I'm sorry, Eddie. There just wasn't any other way. You said it yourself. This mission matters."

"Oh, yes," I said. "I know. Anything, for the family."

He winced, and looked away from me.

"I hate your family, Eddie," said Molly. "Always have, and always will. Because they do things like this to people. To their own people."

"I would have taken your place if I could, Eddie," said the Armourer. "I would have given up my torc to take another run at Casino Infernale. I volunteered. Argued my case before the rest of the Council. I would have spared you this, if I could. But the family wouldn't let me go. Apparently, I'm too valuable to risk in the field. I had to fight them just to be allowed to take you to the Summit on Mars. I wanted you to have some fun first."

"It's . . . all right, Uncle Jack," I said.

"No, it isn't," he said. "It'll never be right between us again. I've poisoned what we had, for the family."

We sat a while longer, each of us lost in our separate thoughts. The Armoury seemed surprisingly quiet, subdued. Molly wouldn't let go of my hand. The pain was gone; the shock was gone. I just felt . . . cold. Finally, the Armourer forced himself up out of his chair, his face calm and composed again, as though nothing had happened. He was just a man with a job to do. He searched through the various drawers under his desk, brought out a hefty buff envelope, and handed it to me. I made myself take it, and look inside. Molly looked too, and wrinkled her nose at the wad of documents and papers.

"What's this?" she said. "You want him to sign a disclaimer, so he won't sue you?"

"This is what those in the field call a legend," he said, ignoring the anger still dripping from every word she spoke. "Spy talk for a complete set of documents, all the paperwork an agent needs to support his identity in the world. Driving license, photo IDs, credit cards, old letters and photos, everything to prove Shaman Bond has a real history in the world. Normally, Eddie wouldn't need it. He's a familiar face in the scene. But this is Casino Infernale, so we don't take chances."

I leafed quickly through the various papers, and then distributed them here and there about my person.

"Don't I get a legend?" said Molly. Her voice made it clear that while she hadn't forgiven him, she was ready to play the game again if I was.

"Use your own," said the Armourer. "Just be yourself. They'll have heard of you. In fact, you're exactly the kind of person they'd expect to turn up for the games. And, hopefully, your infamous reputation will help to hold everyone's attention, and distract the Security people from seeing your companion as anyone but the shifty and shady Shaman Bond. You shine brightly, so he can hide in your shadow. . . ."

"Is that it?" I said. "Are we done now?"

"Not just yet," said the Armourer. "I was wondering if you might like to leave the Martian artefact with me. The one the Tombs forced on you? I would like to study it."

"No," I said. "The Tombs wanted me to have it."

"You see?" said the Armourer. "I'd find that worrying."

There was one more stop before Molly and I could leave the Hall. The Armourer took it upon himself to personally lead us back through the Hall, and accompany us all the way to Vanity Faire, the Droods' very own costume department. (Named after the novel, not the magazine.) A great store full of clothes and costumes and outfits suitable for every occasion, in every culture and country. Field agents have to fit in, if they want to go unnoticed.

The Armourer threw the door open with a flourish, revealing row upon row of clothing racks, groaning under the weight of more good tatt and schmutter than you could shake a fashionable stick at. It looked like the world's biggest jumble sale, or a going-out-of-business sale. The Armourer looked at me hopefully. It was obvious he'd brought me here to try to cheer me up. So I did my best to play along.

"I don't normally get to use this place," I said.

"Because you hardly ever come home," said the Armourer. "You can't go to Casino Infernale looking like that, now can you?"

"What's wrong with this?" I said, looking down at myself. "This is my best casual outfit."

"That's so casual it's downright careless," said the Armourer. "You look like you're wearing your favourite old suit so your wife can't throw it out. You need something more fitting, more glamorous, to make the scene at Casino Infernale. You have to dress up if you're going to mix with gambling celebrities and Major Players. A Drood wouldn't, but Shaman Bond would."

"What about me?" Molly said immediately. "Do I get a new outfit too?"

"Of course!" said the Armourer. "Help yourself to anything you fancy!"

"Oh, you will regret saying that," I said.

Molly gave the Armourer a hard look, to show she wasn't finished with him yet, and then gave me a searching look. Asking without asking whether I'd be okay on my own. I nodded briefly. Molly gave my hand one last squeeze, and then went charging into the costumes department with the light of battle in her eyes.

"Caradoc!" the Armourer said loudly. "Where are you, man?"

"Is he still in charge?" I said. "He's a bit . . ."

"He's a lot," said the Armourer. "But everyone in the family has the job that fits them best, and this is his. He reads all the fashion magazines, you know. . . ."

Caradoc Drood came striding forward to greet us. He knew everything there was to know about outfitting a field agent with just the right look, to blend in. Though looking at Caradoc, it was hard to think where he might ever blend in. Tall and spindly, with his overlong arms and legs, Caradoc was wearing a bright pink frock coat over white leggings and court shoes, and all in all he looked very much like a mad flamingo. He had long, slicked-back white hair, a sharp angular face, and piercing blood-red eyes. He stopped before us, struck a pose, ruffled his cravat of gold cloth with the long fingers of one hand, and looked down his nose at me.

"So!" he said, in a dark dramatic voice. "You are the incredible Edwin Drood! I was hoping they'd let me run up something special for you, to mark you as the family's new head, but you didn't last long enough. Hey ho . . . alackaday. And now you're off to France, home of la belle couture. I am so jealous I could just spit. Well, well . . . what are we to make of you, so that you can walk through Casino Infernale with your head held high, Mr. *Shaman Bond*?"

If Caradoc were any more artificial, he'd be an android.

"I'm sure my measurements are on file here somewhere," I said.

"Oh, we have everyone's measurements," said Caradoc. "If only so the shroud will fit . . . what am I going to do with you? Is there time for plastic surgery? My little joke . . ." He considered me for a long moment, tapping at his chin with one slender finger. And then he turned and darted back into the clothes rack, disappearing into the rows. I looked at the Armourer.

"He's got worse, hasn't he?" I said.

"Hard to tell," said the Armourer. "Admit it, though, you are having fun."

"For all the wrong reasons," I said. "Now hush— Caradoc returns from the clothing jungle."

Caradoc deigned to offer me several outfits in a row, all of which I dismissed out of hand, just to watch his nostrils flare. I might have to play dress-up doll, but I wasn't going to make it easy for anybody.

"Far too everyday and acceptable," I said loftily. "Shaman Bond wouldn't be seen dead in anything so . . . mundane."

"This is the kind of thing they will be expecting at Casino Infernale," said Caradoc.

"Then they're going to be disappointed," I said. "Which

is as it should be. Shaman Bond has a long history of disappointing people."

I strode forward into the racks and started taking things off, rejecting them, dropping them in crumpled heaps on the floor, and moving on. Caradoc hurried after me, grabbing up the clothes and hugging them to his chest, while making loud bleating sounds of distress. I was actually starting to feel a bit better. My mood always improves when I get to torment authority figures. As authority figures went, Caradoc didn't go far, but he was present, and annoying me, so he would do. He really shouldn't have looked down his nose at me. That's always dangerous.

Molly kept reappearing with something big and bold and horribly expensive-looking, hanging around just long enough to say *I'm having this!* before dropping whatever it was onto a growing pile, and then darting back in for more. Every now and again I could locate her exact position in the fashion jungle through loud squeals of delight and the odd cry of *New shoes!*

I finally settled on a black goatskin leather jacket, over a blindingly white shirt, and black slacks. A bit stark, but it suited how I was feeling. Molly came back out of the clothes racks wearing a Little Black Dress, took one look at me, muttered something about not being a member of the Addams Family, and went back in again. I admired my new look in a full-length mirror, and then looked at the Armourer.

"Well?" I said. "What do you think?"

"Words fail me," said Caradoc, bitterly.

"You'll certainly make an impression," said the Armourer.

Caradoc insisted on offering me a display of Old School Ties, everything from Eton to John of Gaunt, Cambridge to Oxford. On the grounds that they might impress somebody. I dismissed all of them. Shaman Bond wouldn't wear such a thing, unless he was running a con. His past is a mystery, and quite deliberately so, so that he could claim to be from anywhere, as needed.

"Have you got any bow-ties?" I asked Caradoc. "Bow-ties are cool. The Travelling Doctor said so."

Caradoc raised his eyes, to address the heavens. "I'm being punished for something, aren't I? I'll go and look. . . ."

He stomped off just as Molly returned, wearing a marvellous burgundy red evening gown, complete with all sorts of expensive accoutrements. She did a twirl for me, and the Armourer and I applauded politely. Molly grabbed up all the dresses she'd dumped in a pile, and hugged them to her.

"Designer labels, all of them! And they're mine, all mine! Don't they look amazing?"

The Armourer and I exchanged a look. We didn't speak fashion.

"Wonderful," said the Armourer.

"Charming," I said.

"You'd better pick out some spare socks and underwear, and things," the Armourer said vaguely. "No telling how long you'll have to spend at the Casino. I'll go round up some decent luggage for you. Leather, with straps. You can never have too many straps. . . ."

He disappeared into the frocky depths of the department, in search of the still missing Caradoc. Molly looked me over.

"Not bad . . ."

"Scrub up nice, don't I?" I said.

"We can still drop everything and run," said Molly, perfectly seriously. "They'd never find us."

"I want my torc back," I said. "And, I want to be the one who breaks the bank at Casino Infernale."

All too soon we were back in the old chapel and standing before the retrieved Door, dressed to the nines, with a whole bunch of heavy designer luggage. Most of it Molly's, though I had a pretty good idea who'd end up carrying it. I'd settled on a burgundy red bow-tie, to match Molly's dress, and then broke Caradoc's heart by insisting on a clip-on.

"I still don't see why we can't use the Merlin Glass," I said. "At least then we'd have a way out if we need it."

"You can't use the Glass," the Armourer said patiently, "because Casino Security is set up to recognise the presence of anything that powerful. Its ownership would be a dead giveaway as to who you really are."

"I could always say I'd stolen it," I said. "They'd accept that, from Shaman Bond."

"Shaman might possess the Merlin Glass, but he wouldn't know how to keep himself safe from the Glass' defences," said the Armourer. "No, Eddie. Best not to risk it. The Glass stays here."

He stepped back from the Door, shouted *Nantes! France!* at it, and the Door swung open at once, revealing a bright, sunshiny city view. The Armourer gestured frantically for us to go through, so Molly and I quickly gathered up our luggage and made a run for it. The Door slammed shut behind us the moment we were safely on the other side, and then disappeared itself.

We were standing on an old bridge, looking out over a river. Don't ask me which one. Very blue waters, with barges tied up at regular intervals. Bright sunshine, midday from the look of it, and the air smelled wonderfully fresh and clean. Well-preserved historical-looking houses on all sides. On the whole, I approved. People passed us by, paying us no attention at all. Which was just a bit odd, considering that as far as they were concerned, we must have appeared suddenly out of nowhere. I mentioned this to Molly, and she just shrugged.

"Part of the Door's magic, I suppose. I'm sure they'll start noticing us in a moment. They'd better. I didn't squeeze into this dress with the help of a crowbar and a warm spoon just to be ignored."

"No one would dare," I assured her.

She looked at me steadily. "How do you feel, Eddie? Really?"

"I don't know," I said. "I never felt like this before. Naked to the world, with all its threats and dangers. Maybe this is what being Shaman Bond really feels like. If so, he's a braver man than me."

"I wish you wouldn't talk about Shaman as though he was someone else," said Molly. "He's just your cover! You're both the same man!"

"It doesn't always feel like that," I said. "Do you love Shaman the same way you love Eddie?"

"Of course!" she said. "They're the same person!"

"No," I said. "They're not. You're always much easier around Shaman, because you still hate Droods. . . ."

"You are a psychologist's dream," said Molly. "Or his worst nightmare . . . Someone's looking at us."

I looked round quickly, and sure enough one particular young man was heading straight in our direction. A happy, smiling sort in a striped jacket, over a Johnny Hallyday T-shirt, with battered blue jeans and cowboy boots. Smart and handsome, and just full of joie de vivre. He wore a black beret, with a cigarette protruding from a corner of his mouth. He couldn't have looked more like someone trying to look French. As he drew nearer, still smiling determinedly, it seemed to me that he had far too much character for his own good. I was pretty sure I knew him from somewhere. . . .

He came to a halt before Molly and me, bouncing up and down on his springy soles, nodded to me and winked to Molly. He leaned forward to kiss me on both cheeks, and I stopped him with a hard look. He turned to Molly, and quickly thought better of it.

"Welcome to Nantes, *mes braves*," he said, in a fake French accent that wouldn't have fooled a deaf person. "François Greyson, at *votre* service."

"Oh, bloody hell," I said, as the penny finally dropped. I finally recognised the face, and the bad acting. "François, my arse. You're Fun Time Frankie."

"Well, yes, if you insist," said Frankie, in a posh English accent that was just as fake in its own way. "Just trying to blend in, old bean. . . ."

Molly looked at him, and then at me. "Is this a good or a bad thing?"

"Hard to tell," I said.

"Why . . . Fun Time Frankie?" said Molly.

"Because this disreputable little toad never met a party he didn't like," I said. "Been everywhere, had everyone."

"That is an awful rumour, only spread by people who know me," said Frankie.

"A useful enough tour guide, I suppose," I said. "Just don't turn your back on him."

"You're too kind," said Frankie.

"No, I'm bloody not," I said. "You're really the best local contact the family could provide?"

Frankie then provided an excellent version of the Gallic *Couldn't give a damn screw you move along* shrug. "I'm the only one in the area, just now. The Droods really are being run ragged, trying to keep the lid on things. Even friendly associates such as I are in short supply. Frankly, you're lucky to have me. I know the area, I know the local underground scene, and I have direct knowledge of Casino Infernale. Which I'm happy to provide. For the just about generous fee your family is currently providing."

"Frankie is another of my uncle James' half-breed offspring," I explained to Molly. "Dear God, that man did put himself about. Half the up-and-comers in secret organisations and hidden underground bunkers have his eyes."

"I am a Grey Bastard and proud of it!" Frankie said cheerfully. He spat the cigarette out the side of his mouth, over the side of the bridge and into the river. "Never did care for Gauloises. . . . Welcome, welcome; what can I do to help?"

"To start with, you can carry the bags," I said.

Molly looked at Frankie in a thoughtful way that made him visibly uncomfortable. "So," she said, "another Bastard . . . like Hadrian Coll."

"Trickster Man?" said Frankie. "Splendid fellow! You know him?"

"He tried to kill us," I said.

"And now he's dead," said Molly.

"Never liked the man," Frankie said briskly. "Welcome to Nantes! France's sixth biggest city! Lots of nightlife here, if you know where to look, and some fantastic restaurants. . . . We get a lot of tourists here, particularly when Paris gets a bit crowded. No Crazy Horse, as such, but I'm sure we can find you something a bit tasty, if your tastes run that way." He winked roguishly at us, took in our expressions, and hurried on. "Nantes was built along the River Loire, at the confluence of the Rivers Evdre and Sèvre. . . . Why are you looking at me like that and I really wish you wouldn't."

"Do we look like tourists to you?" I said.

"Not really, no," said Frankie. He scuffed his cowboy boots in an awkward sort of way. "I learned all that specially, too. . . . Still! Never mind, eh? Always happy to do work for the exalted Drood family. If the price is right. Come along with me, everything is prepared."

"Hold it," said Molly. "Information first. I want to talk with the Regent of Shadows. I was told he was here, at Casino Infernale."

"Well, yes," said Frankie. "He was here, but he's already left. Gone back to the Department of the Uncanny, I suppose."

"He's avoiding us," said Molly.

"Can't think why," I said.

Molly rounded on me. "This is serious, Eddie! This matters to me!"

"Of course it does," I said. "I'm sorry, Molly. But . . . do try to remember I'm Shaman Bond here."

Molly sighed, and stepped forward to place both her hands on my chest, her face close to mine. "We've both been through a lot, haven't we? Let's just get this mission over with, so we can get our lives back. Shaman."

I looked at Frankie, who was shifting uneasily from foot to foot. Clearly he could tell that something was wrong, and equally clearly, he didn't want any part of it. I glared at him, and he stood still.

I put Molly carefully to one side, so I could give him my best cold dangerous stare. "There's something you're not telling us, Frankie." I had no evidence, but with Fun Time Frankie it was always going to be a pretty safe bet. "I think you should tell us everything. Right now."

"I was going to get you settled at the hotel first," said Frankie, clinging desperately to his winning smile. "Let you have a nice cold drink, take it easy. . . . All right! All right! I'll tell you everything you want to know—just please let go of my lapels and put me down! Really, you don't know where this jacket's been. . . ."

I put him down. My temper was running on a really short fuse.

Frankie swallowed hard. "I'm afraid . . . things have already gone horribly wrong. The Regent's shadow agents, Patrick and Diana, arrived here with the Regent some days ago. Before I was even involved. The Department of the Uncanny was starting its own run on breaking the bank at Casino Infernale. That's what persuaded the Droods to have another go."

"You'd think I would get used to my family keeping things from me, by now," I said. "Go on, Frankie. And don't try to clean it up. I want to know everything."

"Patrick and Diana bet big at the games, and lost big," said Frankie. "They didn't just bet and lose their own souls. They lost yours, too."

"What?" I said. "Players are allowed to bet other players' souls, as well as their own?"

"Well, yes," said Frankie. "If they can demonstrate that they and you are directly linked by blood, which apparently you are. . . . Would you care to explain to me how that's possible?"

"No," I said.

"You haven't actually lost your soul, as such. It's just that the Casino, and therefore the Shadow Bank, now have primary claim on it. It's up to them to find a way to enforce that claim, though to be fair, that doesn't seem to have been much of a problem for them, in the past. So basically, you're still the captain of your soul . . . just not the owner of it. Sorry."

"I don't feel well," I said.

"Purely psychosomatic," said Frankie. "It'll pass."

"How do they collect on a gambled soul, if the owner's still alive?" said Molly.

"They have their ways," said Frankie. "Really horribly unpleasant ways . . ."

"Where are the shadow agents Patrick and Diana, right now?" I said, and something in my voice made him hurry to answer me.

"Incredibly missing," said Frankie. "They went on the run the moment their losses became clear, so they couldn't be obliged to make good on their souls."

"Are they still here in Nantes?" said Molly.

"Unknown," said Frankie. "I rather doubt it. In fact, if I were them, I wouldn't even still be in France. I would be in another world, in another dimension, hiding out under an assumed species. The Shadow Bank has very far-reaching friends and influence. They never give up on a debt, and have been known to enforce them on succeeding generations, when the original loser escapes them. With interest."

"Wonderful," I said. "Screwed and blued before I even start. What else can go wrong?"

"I have made out a list, if you're interested," said Frankie, reaching for an inside pocket. He stopped when he saw my look.

"You're so good to me," I said. "Does anyone at Casino Infernale have any idea who I really am?"

"Not as far as I know. Your cover alias is still solid." Frankie looked at Molly. "Your reputation precedes you."

"I get that a lot," said Molly. She didn't sound particularly disappointed.

"As long as I'm still safely Shaman Bond, we still have some time to work with," I said, thinking hard.

"Yes," said Frankie. "But not a lot."

"So, I have to win at the games, and win big, and win

fast," I said. "No pressure there. But what am I supposed to bet with, if I can't use my own soul?"

"There is still Molly's soul," said Frankie, very carefully.

"What?" said Molly, extremely dangerously.

"Yes, I admit it is a somewhat compromised soul, with many claimants already attached," said Frankie, even more carefully, "but it's all you've got to work with, Shaman. You're not blood relatives, but you are . . . attached. They'll accept that, at the Casino. As long as Molly goes along . . ."

"I am going to turn you into a small squishy thing with your testicles floating on the surface!" said Molly. "And then stamp on you!"

"Please don't let her turn me into a small squishy thing," said Frankie, hiding behind me.

"Not in public!" I said to Molly.

"Never get to have any fun any more," grumbled Molly.

"Are you sure about this?" I said to Frankie, as he reluctantly appeared again from behind me.

"Unfortunately, yes," said Frankie. "Souls are currency at Casino Infernale. And before you ask, no you can't bet with my soul. It's already . . . under contract."

"Doesn't surprise me at all," I said. I looked at Molly. "I can't do this to you. I can't risk you losing your soul."

"You have to," said Molly. "It's the only way to get your soul back. I give you my permission, Shaman."

"You're going to hold this over my head for the rest of our lives, aren't you?" I said.

"Bloody right I am," said Molly.

We shared a moment.

"Warms the cockles of my heart, to witness such true love," said Frankie. "I may cry."

"I will stamp on your cockles if you piss me off any further," said Molly. "Take us to the nearest first-class hotel. I want a shower and a whole bunch of drinks, not necessarily in that order. And I think Shaman could use a little lie-down. . . . Why are you looking at me like that?"

"Weren't you told?" said Frankie. "Didn't you get any

kind of briefing before they sent you here? Maybe they were afraid to tell you, in case you wouldn't go. . . . All players at Casino Infernale are required to stay at the Casino hotel. It's a condition, if you want to play the games. So no one can sneak out on their debts."

"Like Patrick and Diana just did?" I said.

"Yes!" said Frankie. "It's supposed to be impossible to get past Casino Security! They're still tearing their hair out trying to figure out how that happened. Anyway, you two already have a room booked at the Casino hotel. As Shaman Bond and Molly Metcalf."

"Just how long ago did my family commit themselves to this mission?" I said.

"I didn't ask, and they wouldn't tell me if I did," said Frankie. "I find it best not to ask the family questions because the answers are always going to upset you. I got you a really nice room! At a really good rate."

"For a really nice kickback," I said.

"Well, naturally," said Frankie. "I have a reputation to live down to."

"Have you at least arranged for a car to take us there?" I said.

Frankie winced. "I want it clearly understood that none of what is to follow is in any way my idea. The Regent left a car for you. He had it imported, specially, just for you. Did you by any chance do something to make him really mad at you?"

"It's always possible," I said. "What's wrong with the car?"

"Oh, see for yourself," said Frankie.

He gathered up as many of our bags as he could, and I took the rest, because Molly doesn't do things like that. Says it's bad for her image. Frankie led us off the bridge. He shot a look back at Molly.

"Did you really . . . ?"

"Almost certainly," said Molly.

"I was afraid of that," said Frankie.

Off the bridge and around the corner, parked in a space

all by itself because nothing else wanted to be anywhere near it . . . was a 1958 scarlet and white Plymouth Fury.

"Oh, no . . ." I said.

"Told you," said Frankie.

"Yes!" said the car. "It's me! Back again, by popular demand! The Scarlet Lady, her own sweet self. I knew you wouldn't be able to cope without me, so I volunteered to come over and help you out! Aren't you glad to see me?"

"Words fail me," I said.

"I heard that!" said the car.

"Oh, I am so glad you can hear that thing talking," said Frankie. "I thought it was just me. . . . Is it an Artificial Intelligence?"

"I don't know if I'd go that far," said Molly.

"I am wise and wonderful and know many things!" said the car happily. "What am I? I'll never tell!"

"So," said Frankie, "you three have a history?"

"We've worked together," said Molly. "And my nerves may never recover."

"You're just saying that," said the car.

"She's very impressive," I said. "In her own loud and vulgar and utterly appalling way. She helped us bring down Crow Lee."

"The Most Evil Man In The World?" said Frankie. "Well, colour me officially impressed."

"Knew you would be!" said the car.

Frankie and I loaded the baggage into the trunk, and then he hurried forward to pull open the driver's door. But when he tried to get behind the wheel, the Scarlet Lady flexed the front seat and threw him right back out again.

"You get in the back, underling, where you belong," said the car. "I know all about you Grey Bastards."

Frankie picked himself up off the curb, recovered as much dignity as he could, and got in the back seat. I settled in behind the wheel, and the car started her engine while Molly was still taking her place beside me as shotgun. We both fastened our seat belts immediately. We'd never been able to forget what it was like, riding with the Scarlet Lady.

Much as we'd tried. The car lurched forward and out into the traffic, driving herself, slamming through the gears in swift succession, her engine roaring like a predator let loose among unsuspecting livestock.

"Just sit back and leave the driving to me," the Scarlet Lady said cheerfully. "It's all right, I know the way. I have SPS. Supernatural Positioning Systems. Satellites? We laugh at Satellites!"

We roared through the narrow city streets, the Scarlet Lady's engine revving for all it was worth, while the rest of the traffic hurried to get out of our way. But we hadn't been driving for long before we realised we were driving down an empty street. All the other vehicles had disappeared down side streets, thrown themselves into back alleys, or hid themselves in cul-de-sacs. Leaving the road entirely to us.

"Slow down," I said, and the car reluctantly did so. I looked around me.

"Where has everyone gone?" said Molly. "Do they know something we don't?"

"Almost certainly," said Frankie. "Word gets around fast when the Casino's in town."

"Incoming!" shouted the car.

I leaned forward, peering up through the top part of the windscreen, and discovered that the sky overhead was full of prehistoric flying reptiles. Massive creatures with twenty-foot wingspans, grey-green scales, and long, toothless beaks ending in sharp points. Their narrow, vicious heads were balanced by long backwards-pointing bony crests. Their huge wings cupped the air as they glided back and forth above us.

"What the hell are those ugly-looking things?" said Molly.

"Hush," said Frankie, from the back seat. "They might hear you."

"They're Pteranodons!" I said, grinning despite myself. "I used to love dinosaurs when I was a kid. Though strictly speaking, Pteranodons are reptiles, not dinosaurs. . . ."

I broke off, as I realised there were people riding on the backs of the winged reptiles. Sitting bolt upright in silver saddles, controlling their Pteranodons with glowing silver bridles and reins, were large blonde warrior women in SS Nazi uniforms. All of them perfect Aryan types, with harsh, laughing faces. Even as I watched, they dug silver spurs into the scaly sides of their mounts, and drove them down out of the sky, heading straight for us.

The warrior women all had heavy-duty machine guns mounted securely at the front of their saddles, and every single one of them opened fire on the Scarlet Lady as they swept past us, hitting us from every side at once. The car threw herself back and forth, while all around us sustained gunfire chewed up the road, blew up lengths of pavement, and blasted great holes in storefronts on either side of the street. Fires blazed up, and black smoke billowed out of gutted buildings. Some of the bullets must have been incendiaries. The flying reptiles punched right through the black smoke, and went banking up and around in a great turn, to come round at us again. Their riders reloaded from bulging panniers, while the Pteranodons screeched back and forth in the air above us, riding the thermals, sweeping round and round in great arcs. The flying reptiles screamed rage and fury as their riders forced them into long machine-gunning power dives again.

There were more of them than I could count, coming at us from every direction at once, guns blazing.

"Who are these crazy women?" shouted Molly.

"Pan's Panzerpeople!" Frankie shouted back, from where he was lying prone on the back seat. "Fourth Reich Femmes, the Bitches From Hell!"

"You know them?" said Molly.

"Everyone knows them!" said Frankie. "Mayhem for hire, all proceeds going to fund the return of the glorious Fourth Reich!"

"Mercenaries . . ." I said. "Who sent them?"

"How should I know?" said Frankie. "I only just met you and I wish I hadn't. It could be anybody. . . . And no, I am not going to sit up and talk to you. I am staying down here where it is relatively safe. If there was a glove box back here, I'd be hiding inside it."

"Control yourself!" said the Scarlet Lady. "I don't care how frightened you are, you make a mess on my upholstery and I will make you clean it up yourself!"

"Could be worse," said Molly, peering out the windows. "Could be dragons."

"How could dragons be worse?" said Frankie.

"Dragons breathe fire," said Molly.

"Everything they say about you is true," said Frankie.

"If someone's paying mercenaries to kill us, even before we get to the Casino," I said, "does that mean someone knows who I really am?"

"Why do you keep asking me questions, when you must have figured out by now that the best you're going to get is an educated guess?" said Frankie, just a bit shrilly. "Somebody might know, or they might not. It's a Casino! Place your bets! Choose whichever answer will make you feel better. I'm going to keep my head well down and sob for my life."

"When I find out who wished you on us as our local contact," said Molly, "I will riverdance on their head."

"Fine by me," said Frankie.

"Death from above!" howled the car, throwing all of us over to one side as she charged down a side street, and then plunged back out onto a main street again. The Pteranodons stuck with us, chewing up our surroundings with long strafing runs. The odd bullet ricocheted from the Scarlet Lady's reinforced exterior, but didn't even slow her down. The car radio started playing "Ride of the Valkyries," while the car hummed happily along. Molly and I braced ourselves and hung on to our seat belts with both hands, as the car rocked this way and that. From somewhere deep in the back seat came plaintive noises of distress.

The Scarlet Lady roared up and down half a dozen back streets, taking lefts and rights at random, trying to shake off the Pan's Panzerpeople. But the Pteranodons wheeled majestically overhead, tracking us easily from above, raking the streets with vicious gunfire. Buildings blew up as we shot past them, flying debris bouncing off the car. A lamp-post was cut in half by savage fire, and the top end crashed down onto the car's roof. The metal didn't even buckle under the weight, and the steel post fell away in a series of sparks as the car pressed on, laughing savagely.

I couldn't help noticing that while all the cars and trucks and other vehicles had disappeared, there were still any number of pedestrians still walking up and down the pavements, who didn't seem to be paying any attention to the end of the world going on all around them. Fire and bullets and collapsing buildings to all sides, sometimes right in front of them, but never any reaction from the poor souls caught up in it.

Even when some were shot dead, or brought down under falling rubble.

"Frankie?" I said.

"I'm not coming out!"

"Why are all the pedestrians blind to what's happening?"

"Casino Infernale has half a dozen major league telepaths just sitting around their basement, doing nothing but broadcasting *Don't Notice Anything Out Of The Ordinary*, very loudly, in eight-hour shifts. All of the day and all of the night, until Casino Infernale is over. Huge payoffs take care of everything else. The price of doing business in a tourist town."

"But people are dying out there!" said Molly.

"No one will give a damn," said Frankie. "No one will even notice anything, until much later. By which time Casino Security will have cleaned up the mess and hauled away the bodies, and silenced the relatives. One way or another. At best, there'll be some vague story about terrorists, for the outside media. No one wants to scare off the tourists."

"Could the Casino be behind the Pan's Panzerpeople?" I said.

"Stop asking me about this! I don't know!"

"Don't make me come back there," I said.

"All right! All right, let me think. . . . It's unlikely. If Casino Security knew who you really are, they'd have blown you away the moment you arrived. Taken you out with a nuclear grenade, or a hit demon. Made a real mess of you as a warning to others. But, I mean, come on! No one with any sense would try to take down a Drood with bullets! Shaman Bond, on the other hand . . . This kind of overkill has all the hallmarks of a pre-emptive strike, by some other gambler who sees you as a threat."

The Pteranodons slammed down out of the sky in waves, again and again. Ugly flying reptile things with gun girls on their backs, sweeping in from left and right to try to catch us in a crossfire. The Nazi warrior women called out to each other in harsh guttural voices, laughing raucously, their bony Aryan faces full of the joy of battle and slaughter. They didn't care how many innocent people they killed, how many pitiful corpses and broken bodies they left lying in the streets. Heavy bullets slammed into the Scarlet Lady's chassis, over and over, rocking the car back and forth but never breaking through.

"I've had enough of this," I said. "No more innocents dying, not on my watch. Car, do you have any built-in weapons systems?"

"Of course!" said the car. "Your uncle Jack gave me a good going over on his last visit. Lovely man. Lovely hands . . ."

"Hold everything," said Molly. "What was the Drood Armourer doing, installing Drood weapons in a Department of the Uncanny car?"

"Can we please concentrate on the matter at hand?" I said. "Car, can you fire back at these Nazi bitches?"

"I have front-mounted cannon," said the car. "But they're all aimed at ground level. Everything else has to be controlled by the passengers. Rules."

"Fine by me!" said Molly. "Show me something!"

"Love to," said the car.

The dashboard suddenly rolled over, to be replaced by

a complete computerised weapons system.. Controls for automatic weaponry, car-to-air missiles, front- and rear-mounted flamethrowers. Molly and I both reached for the missile control systems, but she got there first. She activated the tracking systems, grabbed the joy-stick provided, and locked on to the nearest rider in the sky. Molly fired the missile, and it blasted off from the rear of the car to blow both the Pteranodon and its Nazi gun girl out of the sky in one great explosion. Blood and flesh fell through the air like hellish confetti. Molly kept working the controls, targeting one Pan's Panzerperson after another, but she could take out only one at a time, and I just knew there weren't going to be enough missiles in the car's armoury to take out all the targets.

"Missiles won't do it," I said to the car. "What can I do?"

"I don't know," said the car. "What can you bring to the party?"

"I have a Colt Repeater!"

"That'll do nicely," said the car.

A sliding panel opened in the roof above me, while the front seat sank down into the floor. I stood up, and the upper half of my body passed easily through the space provided. I drew my Colt Repeater from its shoulder holster, called for standard steel ammo, and let the gun do the rest.

I braced myself as the car plunged back and forth, and screwed up my eyes at the wind that battered my face. I felt cold and alone and very vulnerable. No torc, no armour, no protection. If a bullet hit me, I would die. Simple as that. I wanted to sit down again. Let Molly and the car do all the hard work. But I couldn't just sit there in safety while innocent people were being killed. Because of me. So I turned the Colt Repeater on the nearest flying reptile, and opened fire.

The first bullet hit the rider of the Pteranodon coming straight at me. Slammed right through her left eye. Her head snapped back and blood and brains spilled out through the exit wound, flying off into the slipstream. The pink and grey streamers seemed to just fly away forever.

Until the dead warrior woman fell off the Pteranodon, and tumbled bonelessly through the air. The Pteranodon screamed angrily, and just kept coming; so I shot that through the left eye too. The skull was probably bony enough to deflect a bullet. (I did the general aiming; the gun took care of the rest.) The Pteranodon plunged from the sky like a dead plane, and smashed through the roof of a *boulangerie*.

Sometimes the bullets hit hard enough to punch a Pan's Panzerperson backwards out of her saddle. Sometimes I couldn't get a clear shot at a Pteranodon's eye, and then I'd blow holes in their leathery wings until they couldn't stay aloft, and they fell scrabbling from the sky to slam into the ground, and spread their guts across the road. Sometimes, if I killed the rider the Pteranodon would just flap away, and I'd let them go. It wasn't their idea to be here.

The cold rushing air beat me in the face, as I steadied my right wrist with my left hand. The Colt's aiming system could do only so much. I kept firing, and women and reptiles kept dying. Molly was still working the missile controls, so that the sky above was full of flames and dark clouds, and bloody bits and pieces falling through the air. Bullets still came pounding in from every direction, ricocheting from the sides of the car and sparking from the roof, some increasingly close to me.

I'd never felt so scared. There had been times before when I'd been separated from my torc for a time, but I'd never had to go into battle without my armour's protection. I flinched every time a bullet flew away from the roof. Sometimes I cried out, involuntarily. My stomach ached from where the muscles had been clenched for so long. It was hard to get my breath. I could have sat down. Said I'd done enough. But I couldn't, as long as there were still Nazi killers in the air and people dying in the streets. And because if I did sit down, I knew I'd never get my nerve back.

I needed to prove to myself that torc or no torc, armour or no armour, I was still me. With a Drood's training and a

Drood's duty. I may not always have believed in my family, but I have always believed in what they were supposed to stand for.

That's usually been the trouble between us.

I switched from steel ammo to incendiaries, summoning them into the Colt from wherever the hell it stores the damn stuff, and the gun made sure I never missed. I killed the Nazi killers, one by one, and dead Pteranodons fell as blazing carcasses from an increasingly empty sky. Falling bodies slammed into burning roofs, and smashed through storefronts, while others hit the ground hard and did not move again. Until finally there was only one Pan's Panzer-person left, standing up in her silver stirrups as she raked the Scarlet Lady with machine gun fire, screaming obscenities that were mostly lost in the rushing air.

She sent her Pteranodon circling round the car in a tight curve, so that I had to keep turning in my enclosed space to track her. And then she brought the flying reptile all the way round, and urged it hurtling down. The Pteranodon flew straight at the car, just a few yards above the ground. Collision course.

"I've run out of rockets!" Molly shrieked at me. "There's nothing more I can do!"

"And the reptile's still too far off the ground for my front-mounted cannon to do any good!" said the car.

"Hold yourself steady," I said.

I leaned forward, across the car roof. The Pan's Panzer-person was speeding towards me, hunched over her Pteranodon. She saw me aim my gun at her and laughed raucously. She and her mount flew right at me, as she fired her machine gun in short steady bursts. Bullets sprayed all around me, ricocheting harmlessly from the car's roof. Reptile and rider drew closer and closer, while I waited for a clear shot, and then I aimed the Colt Repeater as carefully as I could, and shot the Nazi warrior woman right between the eyes. Her head snapped back, her hands flying away from the mounted machine gun. She fell sideways, out of her silver saddle, but one foot remained caught in the silver stirrup. The Pteranodon flew on, its dead rider dangling beneath it. I couldn't get a clear shot at either of the Pteranodon's eyes as it headed straight for us, screaming with rage.

"Nothing more I can do," I said. "Coming back in, car."

The front seat reappeared below me. I sank back into it, and the roof panel closed over my head as I sat down. I slipped the Colt Repeater back into its shoulder holster. I was shaking, shuddering, from reaction. Looking through the windscreen, I could see the Pteranodon flying straight at us, growing bigger and bigger. Its great wings flapped viciously as it built up more and more speed. I fastened my seat belt again, and put my hands on the steering wheel.

"Give me control, Scarlet Lady," I said.

"Are you sure about this?" said the car. "If you're thinking of dodging that thing, my reflexes are a lot better than yours."

"No," I said. "I don't think dodging would work."

"And I really don't think you should assume that you or I would survive a head-on collision with several flying tons of enraged flying dinosaur!" said the car.

"Just give me control! I've got an idea!"

"Oh, well, that's different," said the car.

The steering wheel came alive under my hands. I kept us on course, straight towards the Pteranodon.

"This better be a really good idea," said Molly.

In the back seat, Frankie was singing "Abide With Me." The car joined in.

I waited till the very last moment, until the Pteranodon was committed and plunging down out of the sky, straight at us. And then, I slammed on the brakes. The car screamed to a very sudden halt, black smoke belching out from the wheel arches. Molly and I were thrown forward against our seat belts. (No airbags. Not that kind of car.) But we slammed to a halt much faster than any modern car could have managed. And the Pteranodon slammed head first into the road, exactly where we would have been if I hadn't hit the brakes. The impact broke the reptile's neck, and it tumbled over and over across the ground before sliding to a halt right in front of us.

Dead as a dodo.

I put the car in gear and rode over the reptile, taking my time, just to be sure. I drove on, and then gave control back to the Scarlet Lady. And only then did my hands start shaking again. Molly leaned over and put an arm across my shoulders, hugged me, and kissed me on the cheek.

"My hero," she said.

The missile control disappeared, as the dashboard revolved back into place again. The car radio started playing "Give Peace a Chance," while the car hummed along. Frankie slowly reappeared in the back seat, looking very pale as he checked himself for bullet holes. The car moved steadily along at a sane and reasonable pace, and bit by bit the general traffic reappeared to accompany us. Driving calmly and easily, as though it had never been away. The whole city seemed entirely calm and peaceful again, as though there was no fire and black smoke rising up in the car's rearview mirror.

"Is there a bar anywhere in this vehicle?" said Molly.

A bar immediately appeared in the dashboard before her, and Molly opened it up and poured herself a very generous brandy. She offered one to me, but I shook my head, tight-lipped. I felt like I needed to stay sharp, in control. I held both my hands together in my lap, and they gradually stopped shaking. I'd risked my life before, in the field. Just never so . . . nakedly. Frankie looked pleadingly at Molly, and she passed him back a brandy. He downed it greedily, and made loud grateful noises.

"They did warn me about you two," he said, after a while. "But I didn't believe them. . . ."

"How are they going to remove all those dead reptiles?" said Molly.

"Fork-lift trucks, I expect," said Frankie.

"I still want to know who sent those Pan's Panzerpeople after us," I said. "I want a name. You must suspect someone, Frankie."

"This is Casino Infernale," Frankie said patiently. "It could be any number of people. Experienced players weeding out the weaker opponents is not only expected, it's actively encouraged. This was a bit over the top, admittedly."

"Can we expect more of this?" said Molly.

"Of course," said Frankie. "Nothing so obvious, or straight forward, once we're safely inside the Casino itself, but . . ."

"Then in future," said Molly, "I think we should get our retaliation in first."

"You're going to fit right in," said Frankie. "You stand up to them, girl. I'll be right behind you. Hiding."

"This all happened a bit too soon for my liking," I said. "This was all arranged; waiting for us. But who knew exactly where and when we'd be arriving, and what car we'd be using?"

"Good questions," said Frankie. "I'd try to find out, if I was you."

"Have you got an ejector seat?" I asked the car.

CHAPTER FOUR

Dinner Theatre

For a supposedly secret location, Casino Infernale didn't believe in hiding its light behind any kind of bushel. We could see the Casino long before we got anywhere near it. The massive building rose up into a cloudless blue sky like a mad cathedral monstrosity on the very edge of the city. Like a mountain manufactured in steel and glass, shining brighter than the sun. The Scarlet Lady tinted her windscreen till the car's interior was gloomy as a tomb and the light still blasted through. Less and less traffic accompanied us as we approached our destination, until finally we were the only vehicle left heading down the single narrow road to Casino Infernale. The shops were all closed, and even boarded up, and finally disappeared completely, until there was nothing left to look at but the massive structure filling the horizon before us. I was concerned the lack of traffic might indicate another attack, but Frankie quickly put me right.

"This whole end of town is strictly off-limits to everyone but expected guests. The telepaths in the cellar see to that. No one comes here by accident; you only get this close if your name is on the list. No tourists, no gate-crashers, no one who isn't . . . the right sort."

"I have never been the right sort in my entire life," Molly said immediately. "And proud of it!"

"We have so much in common," I said. "I have to say, I don't see any obvious security measures in place. . . ."

"You wouldn't," said Frankie. "Until it was far too late."

I looked across at Molly. "Without my torc, I don't have the Sight any more. Elves could be fighting a war with alien Greys up and down this street, and I wouldn't know anything about it. Are you Seeing anything?"

"No," said Molly, frowning. "And since I very definitely should be Seeing *something*, I can only assume somebody is interfering with my Sight. And there's not many who can do that."

"The Shadow Bank doesn't just depend on telepaths to keep Casino Infernale's secrets under wrap," said Frankie. "They also spend big money on major sorcerers, future science tech, and things fresh out of laboratories or straight from the testing bench. If you can name it, they've almost certainly got it on the payroll here somewhere. Hopefully on a strong leash. Major league gamblers only come to Casino Infernale because they know they'll be safe and protected from outside threats. Of course, no one protects the gamblers from each other. You're all fair game, to each other. That's part of the fun."

"Have you ever been inside Casino Infernale yourself?" said Molly.

"Well, no," said Frankie. "Not as such."

"Then just how dependable is all this information you've been feeding us?" said Molly.

"Want me to electrocute the back seat?" said the car, cheerfully. "That should get some straight answers out of him."

"You can do that?" I said.

"Wouldn't take me long to rig something up," said the car.

"I talked to the staff!" Frankie said quickly. "The waiters and the maids and the cleaning staff! All the little people, that the Big Names don't even notice. You'd be amazed what Major Players will say to each other, right in front of the hotel staff. Who are all so badly paid they're always ready to spill the beans in return for cold cash and a warm smile. Revenge and retribution have always been a big part of the class war. If the Casino paid their staff a decent wage, they wouldn't talk, but that would mean Casino management admitting their hotel employees were people of real value. Casino Infernale only cares about the games and the gamblers. Idiots. Penny wise, pound foolish, and a boon to spies like us."

I nodded. "That's why there aren't any staff at Drood Hall. We do everything ourselves, pretend it's character-building, and make a virtue out of necessity. They made me clean the brass when I was small, over and over again. You wouldn't believe just how many brass objects accumulate in a Hall as old as ours. I can get horrible flashbacks, just from the smell of Duraglit. Do I really need to tell you that I don't own a single brass object?"

"Go on, dear, let it all out," said Molly. "Vent. . . ."

As we finally approached the front entrance of Casino Infernale, the massive structure revealed more and more of itself. A huge futuristic building made of steel and glass, gold and diamond, rising hundreds of stories up into the sky. Big enough to hold a dozen standard hotels, and a whole army of security people to protect it. The building's aesthetics were . . . odd. The exterior was made up of long curves and circling lines, endlessly interacting, with great waves of glass rising and falling across the front. I couldn't help but be reminded of the Martian Tombs—all straight lines and no curves. It did make me wonder whether the Casino building was . . . from around here.

"It looks like some alien starship that's crash-landed on the outskirts of Nantes," said Molly.

"Funny you should say that," said Frankie, leaning forward across the back seat. "The whole thing is supposed to be built around stolen alien tech, though no one's willing to talk about just where the Casino might have acquired such materials. The whole structure teleports from one location to another, with a blast of such power that space at the other end just sort of shuffles around to make room for the new arrival. Well, wouldn't you? That Casino is big enough to intimidate Moby Dick's big brother."

I pushed Frankie back into the rear seat, and leaned across to talk quietly with Molly. "I can't help being reminded of Alpha Red Alpha.... The Armourer was pretty damned sure we had the only teleport machine of its kind anywhere in the world. I think we owe it to ourselves to take a really close look at whatever it is the Casino uses to jump itself around. And, if need be, shut it down with extreme prejudice and really bad language. I am not happy with the idea that there might be anything in this world capable of sending Drood Hall on its travels again."

"I thought the Armourer said that he'd taken measures to ensure that couldn't happen," said Molly.

"Yes, well," I said. "The Armourer says lots of things. . . ."

"What are you two talking about?" said Frankie, cautiously, from the very back of the rear seat. "Aren't we all for one, one for all, and all that?"

"You wish," I said.

"That is a very big building," said Molly.

"Size isn't everything," I said.

"You wish," said Molly. And then she elbowed me in the ribs, laughing at the look on my face. "I meant the building, sweetie! Look at it! You could swing Drood Hall around like a cat inside that thing!"

It was big, and seeming bigger all the time, as the Scarlet Lady headed straight for it like a bullet from a gun. The hotel rose up and up before us, an overpowering, overbearing presence that seemed to look right through me and know everything I didn't want it to know. Which was probably the effect the designers had in mind. The car finally slammed on the brakes, spun the wheel, and parallel parked with a vengeance, bringing us to a juddering halt square in front of the main entrance door. All the other vehicles parked in the vicinity just coincidentally discovered a need to move a little farther away, to give the Scarlet Lady plenty of room. For safety's sake. Pride, status, and authority just vanished in the face of the Scarlet Lady's brutal intransigence.

I undid my safety belt with surprisingly steady hands, and clambered out of the front seat. I would have liked to say a great many things, but I didn't. Never show weakness in front of an ally. I looked up the front of the building, and immediately wished I hadn't. I had to crane my head right back, and still couldn't make out the top floors. I felt a kind of reverse vertigo, as though I couldn't be sure of my grip on the ground, and might go sailing up into the sky at any moment. I looked down at my feet, and then squeezed my eyes shut for a moment. The vulnerabilities of being without a torc struck me at the strangest moments. Molly moved in close beside me. She didn't say anything, but her hand slipped into mine as she pressed up against me.

"That really is very impressive," she said. "And we've been to Mars. . . ."

Frankie slammed his door shut as hard as he could, just to make a point, and then hurried forward to join us when the car growled at him.

"Try not to look like tourists," he said kindly. "That's not going to impress anyone. It's only a good, or more properly bad, reputation that's going to keep the rats away in a place like this. You look even the least bit vulnerable, and you can just bet someone will try to take advantage. You practise looking world-weary and dangerous, while I haul the bags out of the trunk."

Uniformed staff were already hurrying out of the main entrance doors to welcome us. In much the same way that strip club bouncers welcome you by grabbing your arm and hustling you inside, while assuring you that the first drink is on the house. The porters all had perfect smiles, showing off perfect teeth, and they all wore the same uniform of smart black with red trimmings. They headed for our bags like a bunch of piranha in a feeding frenzy. Frankie stopped unloading our luggage, and snapped his fingers imperiously at the uniformed flunkies.

"Help yourself, boys," he said grandly. "Don't drop anything; all breakages will come out of your wages. And if anything goes missing so will favoured parts of your anatomy."

A tall and muscular fellow in the same snazzy outfit snapped to attention before Molly and me, and flashed us a perfectly meaningless smile. "Park your car, sir and madam? Just toss me the keys, and I'll put her away for the night."

"In your dreams, sonny!" snapped the car. "I can look after myself!"

The uniformed flunky jumped just a little, despite himself. The car sniggered.

"But still—stick around, sonny. I do like a man in uniform. . . ."

I looked at the flunky. "Run!" I said. "Flee, you fool. Get away, while you still can."

"That's all right, sir," said the flunky. "I have been specially trained to deal with all the most . . . eccentric forms of transportation. Including Artificial Intelligence systems. I can handle anything."

"Oh, I like him," said the Scarlet Lady. "He's got possibilities. . . ."

She opened her front door invitingly, and the poor fool actually dropped me a wink as he slipped in behind the steering wheel. He'd barely got his legs inside before the door slammed shut and locked itself, the engine roared and the steering wheel spun madly, and the car took off at great speed. In what might or might not have been the direction of the underground parking. I could hear the flunky screaming, the sound quickly diminishing as the car disappeared.

"She will eat him alive," said Molly.

"I'm sure she'll let him go," I said. "Eventually."

The other flunkies blinked at us respectfully, and handled our baggage with even more care. Just in case our bags also had more personality than was good for them. It took a good dozen uniforms to handle everything that had emerged from the car's trunk, and transfer it through the main doors and into the lobby. Either they were making very heavy going of it, in hope of a bigger tip, or the bags really were very heavy. I wasn't actually sure what was in most of them, but I was pretty sure most of it wasn't mine. For all I knew they could be full of bricks, courtesy of the Armourer, just to ensure a good first impression. Appearances are everything, in the field.

Inside the lobby, it was all very rich and luxurious and ostentatiously expensive. The kind of look that says, if you aren't independently wealthy . . . boy, are you in the wrong place. The dimensions alone were big enough to intimidate most people. The lobby stretched away far and wide, with a ceiling so high you'd have a hard job hitting it with a cricket ball. Fortunately, Molly and I had just returned from the Martian Tombs, which were big enough to make the lobby look like a poor relation. Glass and steel everywhere, decorated with gold and gems and pockets of impressive tech, held together with gleaming expanses of brightly coloured plastic. Not a spot of wood or marble anywhere. The only organic touches were the dozen or so tall potted plants set out across the lobby at strictly regular intervals. Though, of course, they weren't any kind of plant I recognised, and I've been around. Everything I could see, from the furniture to the fittings, to the boutiques selling overpriced tatt, were all determinedly futuristic, designed to impress rather than make you feel comfortable.

You didn't come to Casino Infernale to feel comfortable; you came to play the games.

"Someone clearly watched too much *Star Trek* at an impressionable age," said Molly. "And, oh dear Lord, listen . . ."

I did, and winced. The lobby Muzak was playing tasteful orchestrated versions of old Rolling Stones songs. Someone's idea of the classics.

There were quite a few people standing around the lobby: men and women of every age and nationality and culture, and even more varying ideas of what constituted formal attire. They all looked Molly, and then me, up and down before quickly deciding that no, we weren't anybody. Or at least, no one important enough to worry about. They didn't relax, as such, but they did go back to just staring around or talking quietly in small groups. Some of them leaned against walls, or pretended to browse the boutique displays, but everyone ignored the very uncomfortable-looking chairs. But wherever they were or whatever they pretended to be doing, they all kept a careful watch on the main doors, waiting for someone who mattered to arrive so they could rush forward and offer their services. Like the dedicated little parasites they were, or aspired to be.

"Don't stare," Molly said briskly. "They're no danger to anyone, or they wouldn't be allowed to hang around the lobby. They won't be playing the games, so we won't be mixing with them. There's no one more snobbish, more elitist, more fixated on caste and status than a big-time gambler."

"They can still be useful sources of information," said Frankie, eager as always to be of assistance. "These people have come a long way to offer themselves to their perceived betters, to perform various services and functions. Think of them as the remora fish, allowed to swim safely through the shark's jaws, to pick crumbs of food from its teeth. Of course, you don't need them; you have me. They can't do half the things for you that I can! I can get you anything! There's a reason they call me Fun Time Frankie. . . ."

"And not a good one," I said. "Talk to them when you get a chance. See what you can learn."

The porters finished placing our bags very carefully before the high-tech reception desk, and Molly and I strode

unhurriedly forward to meet the concierge. He drew himself up to his full height, which was impressive, the better
to show off how fashionably thin he was in his tightly fitting formal suit of black with red trimmings. He had an
unhealthily pale face, cold dark eyes, and a lipless smile.
He looked like he should be starring in commercials for a
cut-price undertaker. Old atavistic instincts made me want
to throw something at him and run.

"Your names, sir and madam?" he said, in a deep sepul-
chral tone.

"Shaman Bond and Molly Metcalf," I said grandly.
"You're expecting us."

The concierge looked down his nose at me, as though
very much not expecting any such thing, and turned to the
computer screen before him. His oversized and very hairy
hands scuttled over the keyboard like a pair of spiders, and
then his thin smile widened as he studied the information
on the screen. He withdrew his hands, turned back to
Molly and me, and did his best to seem even taller, so he
had even further to look down on us.

"Your names are not on the list. We have no record of
any rooms reserved for you. As far as our computers are
concerned, you don't exist."

I just stared at him blankly. I didn't know what to say.
No one had ever looked me in the face before and told me
I didn't exist.

"We have reservations!" Molly said loudly, and just a
bit dangerously. "Look again!"

"The computers are never wrong."

"I could make you not exist," I said.

"Threats will get you nowhere," said the concierge.

"You sure about that?" said Molly. "They always have,
before."

"Threats, backed up by extreme violence," I said.

"Well, obviously," said Molly.

Frankie leaned in helpfully. "He wants a bribe. . . ."

"He wants a good kicking," I said. "And he is going to
get one if he doesn't change his tune, sharpish."

"Can I change him into something?" said Molly. "I'm in a mood to be innovative. And extremely distressing when it comes to deciding on the details."

"Security!" said the concierge, in a loud and carrying voice.

Molly and I turned quickly around to stand with our backs to the desk, as a dozen over-muscled thugs in ill-fitting tuxedos came hurrying forward from every direction at once, all of them smiling unpleasantly in anticipation of blood and mayhem. Very big and impressive, and probably quite scary, to anyone else. Molly and I looked at each other, and shared a quick smile.

"I'll take the starch out of them with a few simple transformations," said Molly. "How do you feel about sea anemones?"

"Sounds sufficiently unpleasant to me," I said. "Anyone gets past you, I'll kick them half-way into next week."

"You pace yourself," Molly said tactfully. "Remember, you're not as . . . strong or as protected as you used to be."

"Thank you, I hadn't forgotten," I said. "I can still look after myself."

"Of course you can," said Molly.

She gestured sharply at the nearest Security goon, and nothing happened. Molly blinked, tried again, swore dispassionately, and turned back to me.

"Okay, we're in trouble. There's a null zone operating here, covering the entire lobby. Presumably generated by Casino Security. Magic won't work here. Any magic."

I glared at Frankie, who'd already backed away a fair distance. "You might have warned us!"

"I thought you knew! You said you'd been briefed! And don't look to me for help . . . I do not do the violence thing. And anyway, if the two of you can't cope with a few muscle-bound bouncers you won't last five minutes inside Casino Infernale. So, I'll be over there, by the newsstand, hiding behind something, wishing you well. Unless you lose, in which case I never saw you before."

And he departed, at speed. Leaving Molly and me to

face the rapidly approaching Security goons. They were almost upon us, grinning nastily and flexing their large hands, eager to do something really nasty to some guests. Instead of just bowing to them and taking their shit.

"Okay," I said to Molly. "You take the six on the left, and I'll take the six to the right. First to pile up all six in a bloody heap shall be entitled to Special Treats in the bedroom department."

"No offence, Shaman," said Molly, "but are you sure you're up to this?"

"I was trained to fight by my family," I said. "Armour's all very well, but you need real fighting skills to get the most out of it. How about you, without your magics?"

"Are you kidding?" said Molly. "I grew up with Isabella and Louise! And I am just in the mood to hit someone. . . ."

"Never knew you when you weren't," I said.

Molly beamed at me. "Nicest thing you've ever said to me."

And together we went forward to face the Security goons, and something in the way we held ourselves, and something in our smiles, slowed them down for just a moment. Which was all we needed.

I put aside my usual practised fighting skills; they needed my armour's strength and speed to back them up. Instead, I fell back upon the basic scrapping skills drilled into me from a very early age by the family Sarjeant-at-Arms. As children, we weren't allowed to use our armour against him in the practise ring; he shut down our torcs and made us fight barehanded. We all learned to defend ourselves quickly, because it was either that or get the crap knocked out of us on a regular basis. No use complaining to the family—they just said it built character. They said that about a lot of things I hated, but there was no denying the Sarjeant-at-Arms taught us how to fight. It was all that kept us out of the family hospital.

Remember: nuts and noses, hit their soft parts with your hard parts, and whenever possible trick an enemy into using his own strength against him. And never hit a man when he's down; put the boot in. It's safer, and more efficient. I could hear the Sarjeant-at-Arm's voice in my head as I went to meet my enemy. That horrid, implacable voice.

I ducked the first goon's punch, and used the second goon's overextended blow to throw him over my shoulder. I tripped a third, and took the fourth's blow on my shoulder. It hurt like hell. I wasn't used to taking punches any more. I let the pain drive me on. I grabbed the fourth goon by the lapels of his tuxedo, pulled him forward, and head-butted him in the face. He cried out as his nose broke, and blood splashed across my face. I threw him away from me, ducked a punch from the fifth goon, kept moving, grabbed up a tall potted plant, and threw it at the sixth goon. He caught it automatically, and I lunged forward and sucker-punched him in the throat through the foliage. He fell backwards with the plant on top of him, making horrible choking noises.

Fists hit me from every direction, hitting hard, and it was all I could do to keep moving, and try to take the blows in places that wouldn't put me down. The pain took my breath away, but I kept bobbing and weaving, ducking some punches and doing my best to block the rest. I caught one overextended hand in mine, twisted the man around, and threw him face-first into the wall. He hit hard, and slumped to the floor, twitching. A really big goon lunged at me with both arms outstretched, his hands going for my throat. I let him come forward, let his hands fasten around my throat, and then kneed him in the groin with great thoroughness. His breath shot out of his mouth, his grip loosened, and his head lowered. I rabbit-punched him on the back of the neck, just to be sure, and he was unconscious before he hit the floor. Another goon grabbed me from behind; two huge arms closing around me, forcing the breath from my lungs. I stamped hard on his left foot, and felt the bones break in his toes. He cried out in pain and outrage, but his grip didn't loosen. So I stamped down hard again, grinding the broken toes under my heel, and this time his grip loosened enough for me to surge forward and then back, slamming the back of my head into his face. I felt warm blood splash across the back of my neck. I broke his hold, and spun round to see blood gushing from his smashed mouth. It made me feel good. I hit him hard, just under the sternum, and all the colour went out of his face as my fist compressed his heart. He fell to the floor, and curled into a ball.

The one remaining goon on his feet decided he wanted to box, his huge fists held out before him. He looked like he'd done it before, so I decided I wasn't going to play. I took off one of my shoes, and threw it in his face. And while he was distracted, I kicked him good and hard in the nuts with the foot that still had a shoe on it. He bent right over, as though bowing to me, and I viciously back-elbowed him in the kidneys till he went down.

The trouble with being big and strong is that you often don't feel the need to learn how to fight. You just assume that being the biggest man in the room automatically makes you the winner. Well, no, not if you're up against someone who's been trained by a family who've spent centuries refining the art of fighting dirty. And, if you are someone who has learned how to take on the Drood Sarjeant-at-Arms and walk away reasonably intact, nothing is ever going to frighten you again.

I stood for a moment, bent half over, struggling to get my breathing back under control. It felt surprisingly good, to know for a fact that I wasn't dependent on my armour to get things done. Nothing like proving to yourself that you can still hold up your end of a ruck to raise the old self-esteem. It's the man, not the armour. The family always tells us that, but we never really believe it until we find out the hard way.

I put my shoe back on, and then looked around for Molly. Five unconscious and somewhat bloody Security goons were piled up in one corner of the lobby, and Molly was stabbing two stiff fingers into the eyes of the sixth. He screamed briefly, and put both hands up to protect his face. Molly kicked the goon hard enough in the left knee to dislodge the knee-cap, and he fell to the floor, still screaming. Molly kicked him really hard in the head, and he stopped screaming. Molly smiled sweetly, and looked round to see how I was doing.

We moved slowly and just a bit painfully towards each other. She saw the blood on my face, and I quickly raised a hand to assure her it wasn't mine. We stood together, face to face, not leaning on each other because we didn't want to appear weak in the face of so many potential enemies. We smiled at each other, as we learned to breathe more deliberately, and our heartbeats fell back to something closer to normal. And then we both turned to look at the concierge behind his desk.

We smiled at him, just daring him to try to run. And then we walked back to the desk, taking our time, while he stared at us with wide, frightened eyes. I stood before the concierge, took out my Colt Repeater, and placed the long barrel right between his eyes. The concierge went even paler, and made a high whimpering noise.

"Check the reservations again," I said. "Perhaps there's been an error."

"An error! Yes, of course, sir and madam! Ha-ha!" said the concierge, smiling desperately. "Here are your names: Shaman Bond and Molly Metcalf! They were here all along—please don't shoot me."

"You didn't even look," said Molly.

"You are very definitely booked into this hotel!" said the concierge. "Here is your electronic door key. Do please enjoy your stay."

"We'd better," I said.

I stepped back, and made the Colt disappear back into its holster, while the concierge gestured urgently for the baggage boys. A dozen or so quickly gathered up our suitcases between them and headed smartly for the escalators. Molly sniffed loudly.

"They'd better not all be expecting a tip."

"I've got a tip for them," I said. "But they probably wouldn't want to hear it."

Molly looked at me thoughtfully. "How much money have you got on you, sweetie? I mean, actual cash? We're in France . . . they have Euros. I haven't got any Euros. Have you?"

"Now that you mention it, no. A field agent usually receives a wodge of local cash along with his legend, but this all happened in a bit of a hurry. Can't you just conjure some up?"

"Not the kind of bank-notes that will fool Casino Security, no!"

I looked around for Frankie, who was still lurking by the newsstand, and he hurried over to join us, smiling shamefacedly.

"Get us some cash," I said, before he could say anything. "All denominations. And no, you can't put it on my credit card. Use your intuition. Go wild. And don't get caught."

He nodded quickly, and hurried away. I headed for the elevators, Molly at my side.

"You do know your Colt Repeater wouldn't have worked under a null zone?" Molly murmured in my ear.

"I did rather suspect that, yes," I said, just as quietly. "But the concierge didn't know that. And I could always have clubbed him over the head with the specially weighted butt. That's a design feature."

"You're a class act, Shaman," said Molly.

"Bet your arse," I said.

We were both pleased to discover we'd been assigned a whole suite to ourselves on one of the higher floors. Molly and I investigated happily, while the baggage boys dumped all our suitcases in one place, and then gathered together by the door to stare at us meaningfully. I was just considering whether Mr. Colt needed to reappear, when Frankie returned and stuffed folding money into every outstretched hand. The baggage boys disappeared quickly, smiling broadly, and Frankie slammed the door shut in their faces. He then produced large bundles of bank-notes from every pocket, and pressed them into my waiting hands. I riffled quickly through them, but they all looked much the same to me. Foreign currency usually does. I handed half to Molly, stuffed the rest into various pockets, and nodded briskly to Frankie, who all but wriggled like a dog who's just had his head patted.

"That should last you!" he said grandly. "Try to be generous with the staff; it makes a good impression if you don't seem to care about money. I do get to put this all on expenses, don't I?"

"Write it all down," I said. "And keep receipts."

Frankie sighed, heavily. "I don't know why I bother."

I looked at him thoughtfully. "Why do you bother? The family can't be paying you enough for all the danger involved."

"Why does any Bastard like me work for the Droods?" said Frankie. "We all want to earn the right to join the family. We all want to come home."

"It rarely works out well," I said, not unkindly.

He just shrugged, so I turned away and joined Molly in looking over the many wonders of our new suite. Wide open with lots of room everywhere, the suite had even more rooms, leading off, and Molly and I spent a happy time running in and out of the side rooms, and sharing reports with each other. There was a double bed big enough to invite several friends in, and what looked like genuine antique furnishings. Bright golden sunshine streamed in through huge bay windows, with a fantastic view out over the city. Every luxury you could think of, including a mini-bar bigger than the fridge freezer in my old flat. Molly ended up running round and round the main room like an over-excited puppy, touching things in passing with trailing fingertips, while whooping at the top of her voice. She finally threw herself onto the double bed, rolled back and forth, and then clambered to her feet and jumped up and down, laughing happily.

"Quick, Shaman! Find things to steal! I'm not leaving this hotel empty-handed!"

She must have realised I wasn't paying attention, because she broke off abruptly, and came over to stand beside me. I was staring out the massive bay window, not looking at anything in particular. Her hand stole into mine, and squeezed it comfortingly.

"What is it, sweetie?" she said. "What's wrong?"

"My own father and mother sold my soul, to gamble with," I said. "How could they do that to me?"

"I'm sure they had a good reason," said Molly.

"Strangely, that doesn't make me feel any better," I said. "I'd only just got my parents back . . . and they do this to me."

"Don't be too quick to judge them," said Molly. "Not until we've got all the facts. We don't know what happened here. Everyone knows things can happen in a Casino that would never happen anywhere else. The stakes are so high here—and it's not like they were gambling for themselves. . . ."

I turned away from the window to look at her. "Will you forgive the Regent, my grandfather, if he turns out to have a good reason for murdering your parents?"

Molly sighed, and cuddled up against me. I put an arm across her shoulders. And we just stood together for a while. As we often did. Us, against the world.

"We don't have easy lives, do we?" Molly said eventually.

"Wouldn't know what to do with them, if we did," I said.

"Come lie with me on the bed, sweetie," said Molly.

"Don't mind me!" Frankie said quickly. "I can always nip out for a bit, make contact with the wrong sort of people, make myself useful. . . ."

"I meant lie down and rest, you horrible little man," said Molly.

"Damn," I said, solemnly.

Molly laughed, pushed me away from her, and went to lie down on the bed. She crossed her long legs, and looked thoughtfully up at the ceiling. I opened the mini-bar and took out a bottle of champagne and two glasses. Domestic, but it would do. I opened the bottle and poured two glasses. I gave the bottle to Frankie, laid myself out on the bed beside Molly, and handed her a glass. We braced our heads against the padded headboard, and sipped our champagne. I'd been on worse missions. I looked at Frankie, and he snapped to attention.

"All right," I said. "Make yourself useful. Brief us on all the things we need to know that we should have been briefed on before this."

"Well, to start with," Frankie said carefully, "you should both be very careful about which names you use. There are listening bugs and recording devices everywhere, magical and tech. Not *everywhere*, obviously, but it's safer to assume the worst and speak wisely. Everyone knows Security is listening—all part of being "protected"—but you should choose your words carefully, Shaman and Molly. Just in case."

"Got it," I said. "What else do we need to know?"

"And keep it short and to the point," said Molly. "Or I will heckle. And throw things."

Frankie took a long drink from his bottle, wiped his mouth with the back of his hand, and smiled brightly. "Lecture mode! This year, Casino Infernale is being run by an up-and-coming, and very ambitious, representative of the Shadow Bank: one Franklyn Parris. Word is, he got where he is today by being even more vicious and ruthless than all the other ruthless and vicious bastards he met on the way up. Coldhearted, too intelligent for his own good, with all the natural charm of a rabid rat with bleeding haemorrhoids. Look, he's a big-time banker! What else do you need to know?"

"He's in charge of everything here?" I said.

"He makes all the decisions," said Frankie, "but he's still answerable to the managers of the Shadow Bank."

"Tell us more about the Shadow Bank," said Molly. "All I have is gossip."

"They have branches everywhere, underground," said Frankie. "In the Maldives, the Cayman Islands, Switzerland; all the banking whores of the world. They provide financial practices and services for all their many and varied clientele. Including places to hide or go to ground, where absolutely no one will find you. The Shadow Bank keeps this all very private, very secret and secure, so that all the hidden organisations and secret individuals can keep their finances under the world's radar. The Shadow Bank makes organised supernatural crime possible."

Molly looked at me. "Then why don't the Droods . . ."

"If it wasn't them," I said, "it would only be someone else. Better the devil you know . . . and can lay hands on, if necessary."

Molly gave Frankie a hard look. "Do you know who's behind the Shadow Bank? Who owns it; who's really in charge? Who profits?"

"Well," said Frankie, "to be honest, for a long time a lot of people just assumed it was the Droods . . . but of course no one believes that any more. The truth: these days, no one knows. A lot of very powerful people have made some very determined efforts to find out, but the Bank's internal Security really is first class. May I continue with the briefing? Thank you.

"Casino Infernale is always run by the Shadow Bank's finest young sharks, determined to make a name for themselves. The Casino is where those most desperate to prove themselves get their chance to show what they can do, and jump several rungs up the promotions ladder. They run all the games here, make sure all the right people get invited, and make sure the Casino runs at a very generous profit.

"Franklyn Parris is here to make sure that everything goes as it should, and to stamp down hard on anyone who looks like they might be trouble. He is personally responsible for all Casino Security. Casino Infernale is a major money earner for the Shadow Bank, as well as a major source of prestige. So a blow to the eye of the Casino is a kick in the balls to the Bank. And God help the Casino manager who screws up. If anyone were to break the bank here, Franklyn Parris would be lucky to keep his life. Or his soul."

"Let us think of that as a happy bonus," I said.

"Yes, let's," said Molly.

"You are not taking this nearly serious enough!" said Frankie. "The Big Names, the Major Players, the really big-time gamblers, all come to Casino Infernale to show off . . . to wipe out the opposition and make or lose fortunes overnight. Often just on the turn of a card. If you can beat these people at their own games, you could wipe out any number of Major Players and Big Names, most of whom have very definitely got it coming to them. And if you can, by some absolutely amazing chance, break the bank here, it would be a severe blow to the Shadow Bank.

"At least, temporarily. It would cost them a lot of money, undermine their prestige and dependability, as well as putting them in a position where they wouldn't be in any position to loan money to anyone . . . but you must realise, it wouldn't last. Just slow them down a bit . . ."

"A win," I said.

Molly and I toasted each other with our glasses of champagne. Frankie took a quick drink from his bottle, and then cleared his throat, meaningfully.

"I do feel I should point out that this is all purely theoretical. It's never actually been done. Never! No one has ever broken the bank at Casino Infernale. Not even come close. Not since it began, hundreds of years ago."

"How many hundreds?" said Molly.

"No one seems too sure," said Frankie. "The origins of the Shadow Bank, and all its works, are cloaked in mystery. And you can be sure the Shadow Bank likes it that way."

He and Molly both looked at me, and all I could do was shrug.

"I'm sure someone in the Drood family knows," I said carefully. "But don't look at me. I only know what I need to know to get the job done. And I'm only interested in the present, not the past."

"Try to damp down the enthusiasm, sweetie," said Molly.

"Need I remind you that I was chosen for this mission because I have a reputation for winning against the odds?"

"You never met odds like the ones at Casino Infernale," said Molly. "Get cocky around here, without your usual protections, and you could get both of us killed."

"And me!" said Frankie. "So let us all be *very careful*. Word is, Franklyn Parris is determined that nothing will be allowed to go wrong on his watch, this year. His first in charge. Casino Infernale is going to run smoothly and perfectly or someone is going to pay for it. To make sure of this, he has hired some very special Security muscle: the Jackson Fifty-five."

"Oh, wow," said Molly. "I've heard of them! Fifty-five clones of the same highly experienced and very deadly mercenary, Albert Jackson. Biggest, blackest fighting man ever. So they say . . ."

"Are we talking about a group mind, operating in fifty-five bodies simultaneously?" I said. "Or fifty-five separate versions of the same fighting man?"

"The latter, I think," said Frankie. "No one's ever got close enough to ask, and survive."

"Well, that's all right, then," I said, returning my attention to my glass of champagne. "For a moment there, I thought we might be in trouble."

"Fifty-five!" said Frankie, loudly. "Which part of *fifty-five* are you having trouble with?"

"Maybe we can trick them into fighting each other," said Molly.

"Of course, the sudden disappearance of Patrick and Diana has put Franklyn Parris on his guard," said Frankie. "Which will only make things even more difficult for you two."

"Nonsense," I said. "What are the chances of two sets of people coming here determined to break the bank? They'll never see that coming. Especially since, as you already pointed out, no one has ever done it before."

"The point is," Frankie said doggedly, "Parris will have already ordered his entire Security staff to be on the lookout for anyone and anything out of the ordinary!"

"In this place?" said Molly. "Good luck with that . . ."

There was a knock on the door. We all froze, and looked at each other. Frankie became extremely tense. I got up from the bed and faced the door, and Molly was quickly there beside me. We drank off the last of our champagne, tossed the glasses carelessly onto the bed, and glared at the door. None of us made any move to answer the knock.

"Are we expecting anyone?" I said.

"No," said Frankie, very definitely.

"Assassins?" said Molly.

"They'd hardly knock, would they?" I said. "Hello, we're the polite assassins! Would you mind awfully if we killed you now, or should we pop back later?"

"Could be complimentary room service," said Molly. "But it doesn't seem likely, does it?"

"I am feeling a bit peckish," I said.

"Then you open the door," said Molly.

"Not that peckish," I said.

"Well, someone's got to answer the door!" said Frankie. "Unless we're all going to hide under the bed. And I don't think there's room."

"You looked!" Molly said accusingly.

I drew my Colt Repeater, stepped towards the door, and said, "Come in!"

The electronic lock worked from the other side, the door swung open, and a very civilised gentleman strolled confidently in. Medium height and weight, middle-aged and distinguished, very well-tailored, calm, smiling, courteous. I distrusted him immediately. He raised an eyebrow at my Colt, but didn't appear particularly impressed. He smiled at Molly, and when he spoke to her his English held only the faintest and most charming of French accents.

"Hello. I am Jonathon Scott, the hotel manager. I understand there was, regretfully, some degree of unpleasantness earlier, at reception. I am here to apologise on behalf of the hotel, and make it very clear that we will not tolerate any rudeness to our guests. The concierge is gone. You will not see him again."

I couldn't help noticing that he was paying nearly all of

his attention to the infamous Molly Metcalf, and only glancing occasionally at the merely notorious Shaman Bond. Which was, of course, as it should be. Frankie didn't even get a glance.

"You know who I am," said Molly.

"Of course, Miss Metcalf. Your reputation precedes you. Welcome to the Casino hotel! Please don't break it. It's the only one we've got, and it is of great sentimental value."

"Casino Infernale's reputation precedes it," I said. "You'll pardon me if I don't put the gun down. I wouldn't want to be suddenly gone, like the concierge."

"Of course, Mr. Bond," said the manager. "I have heard of you. And we will be counting all the cutlery before you leave."

"We're here to play the games," I said. "And we're here to win."

"Of course, sir," said the manager. He turned back to Molly. "May I ask, very politely, whether your sisters will be joining you here at any point?"

"Unlikely," said Molly.

"Oh, good," said the manager.

"I get that a lot," said Molly.

"As a mark of our regret for the earlier unpleasantness, I have been instructed to inform you that all your food and drink is on the house, for the entirety of your stay," said the manager.

"Instructed?" I said. "By Franklyn Parris, perhaps? Has the big man himself taken an interest in Molly and me?"

"We've all heard of Molly Metcalf," said the manager. It wasn't an answer, but he made it seem like one. Scott smiled graciously. "The games will begin in one hour, madam and sir. Five p.m. sharp. Please note that full Security will be in place throughout the games, for the protection of the hotel. Not the guests. We expect the guests to be able to fend for themselves."

"Oh, we can fend," I said. "We can fend like crazy if we have to."

"Suddenly and violently and all over the place," said Molly.

The manager smiled briefly at Molly, nodded to me, and left, closing and locking the door behind him. I put my gun away.

"Did you see how he completely ignored me?" said Frankie. "That's class, that is!"

"He didn't pay that much attention to me," I said.

"I did notice," said Molly.

"He couldn't do enough for you," I said.

"I noticed," said Molly. "Still—free food and drink . . ."

"Best kind!" said Frankie.

"All a bit easy, though, I thought," I said.

"He doesn't know the real you," said Molly. "I'm sure you'll have an opportunity to make him wet himself before we leave."

"He was a bit smug and overbearing," I said. "How would you like to help me burn this place down, later?"

"Love to," said Molly. "He was rude about my sisters."

"Okay," said Frankie. "You two are making me very nervous. So I think I'll leave you to your own devices, or whatever it is you've got in all those suitcases, while I go take a quick look around before the games start. Get a feel for the place, and the players."

"Go," I said.

He left. Molly and I busied ourselves opening the suitcases. Clothes, clothes, and more clothes. Molly had clearly been very busy in the Drood wardrobe department. She threw dress after dress onto the bed, smiling happily, and after a while I just let her get on with it. Until finally she produced a magnificent tuxedo outfit, with all the trimmings, and threw it at me.

"We are changing for dinner, and the games," she said.

"I could eat," I said.

We both took our chosen outfits into the bathroom, and started stripping off. It took a while, as we both kept stopping to wince at pains acquired during the fight. When we were finally both naked, we stopped to look at each other.

I had bruises all over me, already shading towards purple. Molly had bruises too. We'd both taken our lumps in the lobby. And being who we are, tried to hide it from each other. Molly stood before me, and ran her fingertips lightly over my bruises. I let my fingertips drift gently over hers. Molly took a cloth from the sink, wet it under the tap, and gently mopped the dried blood off my face, and from the back of my neck. I stood still, and let her do it. And then we just stood there and held each other for a while.

Then we got dressed for dinner.

We stood before the full-length mirrors, admiring ourselves. I thought I looked rather fine in my tux, but Molly looked magnificent in her full-length evening gown of gleaming gold. Molly brushed invisible dust motes from my shoulders, patted me down, and then moved to stand behind me, her arms around my waist, looking over my shoulder to take in my reflection in the mirror.

"I can still see your Colt Repeater, bulging under your jacket," she said.

"I think that's the point," I said. "To warn the others off. And I can see all sorts of bulges under the front of your dress."

She slapped my shoulder playfully, and came forward to stand beside me. I thought we looked pretty damn good together. Exactly the kind of high-rolling gamblers who would turn up at Casino Infernale. It took me a moment to realise Molly wasn't smiling any longer.

"You do realise," she said, "that all of this . . . is just a distraction. Something to keep me busy. The Regent is not forgotten, nor forgiven."

"Of course not," I said. "Neither are my parents. But for now, let's just do the job. And try to enjoy ourselves, as much as we can."

"You still have your soul, sweetie. I can See it. All the Casino has . . . is a claim on it, if they can enforce it. You should see the list of those who've got a claim on mine. Or think they have."

"You can See my soul?" I said. "Your magics are working again?"

"Oh, sure," said Molly. "The null zone only covered the lobby, as a Security measure. I felt my magic come back the moment I stepped into the elevator. There's bound to be more null zones, scattered across the Casino . . . to secure the games and keep the peace. But I'm pretty sure I could break a null zone. If I really had to . . ."

"Of course," I said.

You don't have to be in a relationship long to discover that being economical with the truth is nearly always going to be the better part of valour.

We went back down to the lobby, where everyone present went out of their way to give us plenty of room. A few even ran away and hid. There was a new concierge in place behind the desk, smiling desperately at us. Molly and I stuck our noses in the air and strode straight past him, following the hand-written signs to the hotel restaurant. Which turned out to be very large and very civilised, and probably quite impressive if you weren't used to places like the Casino.

Molly and I . . . have been around.

The great open space was packed with tables, under brightly gleaming white tablecloths, with only the narrowest of trails left between them. Most of the tables were occupied, but there was barely a murmur of conversation anywhere. The guests just sat quietly at their tables, very obviously on their best behaviour. None of them wanted to risk being thrown out of Casino Infernale for something small.

Molly and I stood just inside the doors, waiting for someone in a waiter's outfit to acknowledge us. There was a head waiter, standing tall and proud behind a podium, but he clearly wasn't even going to admit we existed until we were on our way to a designated table.

I couldn't help noticing that most of the guests were sitting alone. Some with food, some with drinks, just staring off into the distance. A few groups here and there, but even only two or three to a table. And everyone studying everyone else, surreptitiously. I pointed this out to Molly.

"People don't come here to make friends," said Molly. "It's entirely possible you might end up having to kill anyone you meet here, given that everyone else is a potential threat. Or rival. You wouldn't want to hesitate at the killing point, just because you liked someone."

A waiter finally slouched over to stand before us, a surly young man in a dazzlingly clean white uniform and apron. He jerked his head in our direction and then plunged into the maze of tables, leaving us to hurry after him. Molly and I exchanged an amused glance and went after him, quietly plotting future revenges. As we passed the head waiter, he raised his head just long enough to announce Molly's name, and mine, in ringing tones. What conversation there was in the room stopped immediately as everyone looked up, heads turning to consider us thoughtfully. Most of them looked at Molly, rather than me, and none of them looked for long.

The waiter finally stopped before an empty table by the far wall, and gestured impatiently for us to sit down. He pulled a chair out for Molly, but didn't bother with me. *This boy gets no tip,* I thought. I considered the possibility of a reverse tip, where I picked his pocket and stole his wallet. But I didn't want to push my luck with the Casino establishment. Not this early, anyway. The waiter dropped two oversized menus onto the table, and then shot off before we could actually order anything.

"Wait a minute!" said Molly. "The little bastard . . . he's sat us right next to the toilets!"

"Good," I said. "I hate a long walk to the loo. I always feel like everyone's watching me."

I gave my full attention to the menu. Which was ugly and laminated, with all the entries handwritten in half a dozen languages. With thoughtful descriptions and tactful warnings for the inexperienced. No prices anywhere, of course, but in a restaurant like this you wouldn't expect any. As the old saying goes: if you have to ask, you can't afford it. But the hotel manager had said all our food and drink was on the house, so . . . I decided to order big portions of everything, just on general principles. And the very best wines. And ask for a doggie bag.

"Oh, look!" said Molly. "They've got Moebius mice; they stuff themselves. I love those! Dragonburgers, flame-grilled, with a twist of lemming . . . Mock Gryphon soup. Baked baby chupacabra . . ."

"Oh, that's not nice," I said. "It's things like that make me feel like becoming a vegetarian."

"Try that here and they'd probably serve you a triffid," said Molly.

In the end we both settled for an old favourite: thunder-bird paella. Lots of meat and lots of rice, and a whole bunch of other things absolutely guaranteed to be bad for you. (The thunderbird is a huge winged creature from the deep South of America. Supposedly extinct, but there's always someone who can get you a carcass, for an extortionate price. I think they clone them. . . .) I looked around for our waiter and eventually spotted him leaning against a wall, in desultory conversation with another, equally bored, waiter. They looked like they were trying to out-sulk each other. I raised a hand to catch our waiter's attention and he deliberately turned his head away, so he could pretend he hadn't seen us.

"He is going to regret that," I said.

"It's another test, like in the lobby," said Molly. "If you can't master a lowly waiter . . ."

I picked up the knife set out for me, hefted it a couple of times to get the balance, and then threw it with practised skill and uncommon force, so that it sank half its length into the wall right beside our waiter's head. He jumped back with a startled shriek, and looked wildly around. I waved and smiled at him.

"Just think what I could do with the fork," I said, loudly.

The waiter hurried over to take our order, almost dropping his little notebook trying to get it out. He crashed to a halt before our table, and smiled at Molly and me in a wobbly sort of way.

"Ready to order, sir, madam?"

"What do you think?" I said.

"I think they'll let anyone in these days," said the waiter, defiantly. "I'm only doing this job to raise enough money to put myself through college. What do you want?"

"Molly," I said. "I don't think this young man is sufficiently impressed. Take out his appendix, the hard way."

"I could do with a starter," said Molly. "I'm told it goes very well with some garlic butter and black pepper."

"All right, all right!" said the waiter. "Look, this is me, being impressed! Just give me your order. No respect for the working man . . ."

We told him what we'd settled on, and he wrote it down in nice neat handwriting.

"Five minutes, tops," he said. "They don't sweat the simple stuff here. And by the way, my appendix is in a jar at a Paris hospital."

He grinned at me, and I couldn't help grinning back.

"What wine would you recommend?" I said.

"Avoid the clarets, they're an abomination in the sight of God. And the Médocs are all malignant. Everything else is overpriced and an abuse of your taste buds. I'd stick to the house red, if I were you. That's what we drink, in the kitchen. It'll get you there."

"Bring us half a dozen bottles," I said. "And, I need a new knife."

"Right away, sir," said the waiter.

And just like that he was gone, off and running before his fellow staff could accuse him of fraternising with the enemy.

While we waited for our food to arrive, Molly and I stared openly around us. Everywhere I looked there were familiar faces with bad reputations. Big Names and Major Players from every scene, in every city. It soon became clear to me that I knew pretty much everyone in the restaurant by face or reputation. And not in a good way.

"I didn't realise how much I knew about this place," said Molly. "I mean . . . I never wanted to come to Casino Infernale before. Not my thing. But the stories and legends that surround the Casino are just so big, so pervasive, they sort of force their way into everyone's conversations. Casino Infernale, where you can test whatever nerve and skills you think you have, against the biggest and most dangerous gamblers in the world. I do see the attraction. . . ."

"Oh, dear God," I said. "Look over there! Is that who I think it is? Is that Jacqueline Hyde?"

"Yes . . . poor thing," said Molly. "What the hell is she doing here?"

I knew Jacqueline Hyde's story. Everyone in our line of work does. It's one of the great cautionary tales from the Nightside. Jacqueline started out as a Society girl, happy spending Daddy's money, leading the most comfortable of lives, partying till she dropped . . . until she couldn't resist trying this marvellous drug: Hyde. It had been around for ages, in one variation or another. Harvested from the body of Edward Hyde (because that was the body Dr. Jekyll died in), the drug had been doing the rounds in various strengths and mixes ever since. Bouncers and thugs for hire used a much diluted strain as a kind of super-steroid. Others mixed and matched the drug with other chimerical compounds, so they could turn into other people. For commercial or recreational purposes. Hyde was a vicious and unforgiving drug, and hardly anyone was stupid enough to take the original formula. Jacqueline knew better, but she never could resist a dare. And so she became Jacqueline Hyde, a Society girl and a monstrous man, bound together, forever.

Her family disowned her. Daddy cut her off without a penny. She went from party girl to homeless in a matter of weeks. She had no idea how to look after herself. Spent some time living on the street, in Rats Alley, along with all the other unwanted monsters of the Nightside. But that isn't the real tragedy.

Jacqueline and Hyde are in love with each other, but

they can only meet and experience each other in that extended moment when one turns into the other. The long love letters they write and leave for each other have turned up in most of the major auction houses of the Nightside. They're collectible.

Jacqueline Hyde—a lot of people have found a use for her, and him, and their fortunes have fallen and risen many times. But neither of them were ever rich enough to attend Casino Infernale.

"Someone's funding her," said Molly. "But why?"

"Another distraction?" I said. "A wild card thrown into the mix . . . or, just possibly, she knows something we don't."

Jacqueline herself was small, painfully thin, neurotic; sitting uncomfortably at her table, scrunched up and eyes down as though trying not to be noticed. Her dress would probably have looked attractive on anyone else. She had a sharp-boned face with piercing eyes, a tight-lipped mouth, and ragged mousy hair. She didn't bother with her appearance, because she never knew how long she'd stay that way. Hyde came and went. She glanced about the restaurant, but never looked at anyone for long. She had a bottle of whisky on the table in front of her, and was drinking steadily through it, one glass at a time. Didn't seem to be affecting her much, but then, once you've had Dr. Jekyll's Formula, everything else is always going to seem like a poor relation.

And then I saw who was sitting at the table beyond, and I forgot all about Jacqueline Hyde.

I knew the face, and the reputation, from Drood files. Earnest Schmidt, current leader of the reformed Brotherhood of the Vril. Back in the day, the original organisation was a mystical supergroup, and a major supporter of the Nazis. The Vril supported Hitler on the way up, and once he was in power, he showed his appreciation by supplying them with all the warm bodies they wanted for their special experiments. Sometimes, they let him watch.

The Vril loved being Nazis, and playing with innocent lives and deaths. But once the war was over they quickly discovered they had no friends and a hell of a lot of enemies, so they just grabbed as much loot as they could and disappeared into the jungles of South America. Along with so many other war criminals.

The Brotherhood of the Vril split and schismed so many times, they effectively neutered themselves. But just recently they'd shown signs of pulling themselves together again. They'd run out of war loot long ago, but they were finding new funds from somewhere . . . which might explain what a Nazi scumbag like Earnest Schmidt was doing here, at Casino Infernale.

A portly, dark-haired man in his early forties, he sat stiffly at his table in a tuxedo almost the match of mine. Though he didn't wear it nearly as well. He held his head high, as though to make clear to everyone present that he was not a man to be trifled with. His eyes were a pale blue, his mouth a flat line, and he had a single glass of brandy in front of him that he didn't touch. Nazis always were big on self-denial, except for when they weren't. Schmidt didn't wear a single swastika or Gestapo death's head. Or even the SS double lightning bolts. He might have passed for just another successful businessman, here for the games and the thrills . . . except for the look in his eyes. The way he looked down on everyone else in the room for not meeting his exacting standards.

"Vril," said Molly. "I hate those little shits. You think he set those Pan's Panzerpeople on us, on the way here?"

"He does seem to be looking at everyone else in the restaurant apart from you and me," I said.

I picked up the croissant by my plate, and threw it at Schmidt with devastating accuracy. It bounced off his head with enough force to make him cry out. He put a hand to his head and looked round sharply and saw me smiling at him. He sat very still, and then turned away again. Saying nothing, doing nothing. Perhaps because he wasn't prepared to acknowledge the existence of such an obvious inferior as myself.

I reached for the water jug. Molly put a hand on my arm to stop me, smiling even as she shook her head.

"Why not?" I said. "I can hit him from here."

"Because we don't have any proof he was behind the attack," said Molly. "And because you never know who you might need as an ally in a place like this."

"Him?" I said. "The only use I'd have for that evil little turd is as a human shield. Or possibly a battering ram."

"Anywhen else, yes," said Molly. "But this is Casino Infernale. The rules are different, here. You never know when you might need to make a deal against someone else. Someone worse, or just more immediately dangerous. You must remember, *Shaman*, we can't depend on our usual protections. Either of us. We really don't want to start a fight we can't be sure of winning."

"You're no fun when you're right," I said.

I looked around for someone else to interest me, and immediately recognised a person of interest I knew from Drood files. A large and fleshy man in a scarlet cardinal's robes, smiling easily about him. Smiling constantly at some private joke on the rest of us. His face was kind and calm, even serene, until you got a good look at his eyes. Fanatic's eyes, fierce and unyielding. I knew his story, too.

Leopold, the famous gambling priest. The man of God who went from one gambling house to the next, playing every game of chance there was to raise money for his Church. The priest who never lost because he had God on his side, murmuring in his ear. Or so he claimed. He certainly had a hell of a reputation for winning against all the odds. Backed by the Vatican banks, Leopold had spent the last twenty years cutting a swath through all the great gambling houses of the world, and taking them to the cleaners. Not for him, never for him. All the money he won went straight to his Church. But this was the first time I'd ever heard of him attending Casino Infernale.

"Maybe the Vatican wants him to break the bank here, to bring down the Shadow Bank," said Molly.

"Unlikely," I said. "The Vatican banks and the Shadow Bank have a relationship that goes back centuries."

And as I watched Leopold watching everyone else, it

occurred to me that everyone in the restaurant was looking at everyone else, in their own quiet, surreptitious ways. A lot of people were looking at Molly, and some were even looking at me. The only completely detached person in the room was Jacqueline Hyde. And, maybe Leopold, who seemed to find the whole situation deeply amusing.

The food arrived. Two huge plates of richly steaming paella. It looked and smelled amazing, and I had my knife and fork in my hand before the plates even hit the table. But Molly stopped me with a harsh look, and I made myself sit back and watch as Molly produced a long thin bone needle from somewhere about her person. Unicorn horn—a simple and effective test for poison. Molly thrust the bone needle deep into the paella before her, and we both watched grimly as a purple stain rose up the white bone. She tried my plate, and the poison was there, too.

The waiter backed away from the table, shaking his head rapidly, to make it clear that none of this was anything to do with him. Molly rose to her feet, but before she could even accuse anyone, the whole restaurant went insane.

The spaghetti in front of the man next to us shot straight up into the air, and tried to strangle him. White ropy stuff whipped around his throat and tightened, stretched taut and immovable in a moment. More and more of the stuff sprang up into the air, wrapping itself around his head, burying his face under layers of ropy pasta. He grabbed at the white ropes with his hands, but couldn't break them. His eyes bulged, and his mouth stretched wide as he gasped for air.

Earnest Schmidt's salad exploded upwards, growing and shaping itself into a single massive green arm, studded with razor-sharp thorns. The green hand grabbed the front of Schmidt's suit and lifted him right out of his seat and into the air, shaking him viciously. He grabbed at the green arm with both hands, only to cry out as he cut himself on the vicious thorns.

Jacqueline Hyde was quickly on her feet and backing away from her table, as the steaming curry in front of her took on new life. A horribly monstrous form, all hot steaming flesh, with reaching hands and snapping jaws. It towered over the small woman, a monstrous thing of bestial angers and appetites; and then it stopped, abruptly, as Jacqueline became something much worse.

Leopold's baked baby chupacabra rose up off its plate, levitating on the air. The tiny stitches holding its mouth and eyes shut all snapped at once, and it fixed the gambling priest with terrible glowing eyes as he rose abruptly to his feet. It said something awful to him, in Spanish. Leopold stood his ground, his face twisted with loathing, and began an exorcism in old-school Latin.

The thunderbird exploded right out of the paella before Molly and me; all the meat slamming back together to reform the great flying bird it had once been, with a long bony beak and flapping skinless wings. It was dead and it was alive and it stabbed viciously at me with its beak. Screaming horribly, as though seeking revenge for its death, for our meal. I dodged the beak and punched it in the head, and hurt my hand. Molly yelled for me to get out of the way, and hit the thunderbird with a fireball. It scrabbled across the tabletop, burning fiercely, flapping its fiery wings, not dying because it was already dead.

"Why isn't the hotel dropping a null zone on all this?" I said.

"I don't know!" said Molly, hitting the flapping bird with another fireball. "Maybe they approve of competitors thinning out the herd, before the games start."

I looked quickly about me. The whole restaurant was in an uproar, with everyone fighting off what had been their meals just a moment before. No one was trying to work together, and no one was interested in helping anyone else.

I grinned at Molly. "I've got an idea!"

"About time! These fireballs are barely slowing it down. What's your idea?"

"Grab a wing!" I said.

And we both grabbed a flapping wing, gritting our

teeth against the flames, and ripped the wings right off the firebird. The fight went out of it. Slowly, it stopped struggling, and then it just lay there on the tabletop, a very overdone piece of blackened meat. The wings turned into mists in our hands, and disappeared. And the burns on our hands disappeared, too. Which made me wonder just how real the whole experience had been, anyway.

I looked to Jacqueline, but she was gone. Hyde was there. A squat, ugly, barrel-chested figure, with a dark face and a beast's eyes; an angry vicious brute that hated everything in the world, except the one person he could never have. He tore the curry monster to pieces with savage exuberance, laughing aloud as he did it. It was a horrid sound that raised all the hairs on the back of my neck. Hyde looked around, knowing he was feared and hated by everyone else in the restaurant, and loving it.

He turned back into Jacqueline, and for a moment I seemed to see both of them at once, two people superimposed on the same spot. It looked like they were holding hands. And then Jacqueline was back; her head down and her shoulders slumped. As though she carried the weight of the world on her shoulders.

And then everything stopped. The food attacks crashed to a halt, as all the food went back to being food again. And that was when I realised Leopold had finished his exorcism. We all looked at him, and he looked coldly back at all of us. He didn't look calm or serene any more.

"Yes," he said. "I saved you. Not because any of you are worth saving, but because there's no fun in winning against second-raters."

He turned his back on all of us, and strode out of the restaurant, his scarlet robes swirling around him. Molly turned to our waiter, who was still standing by our table, shuddering and quaking. She smiled sweetly at him.

"Could we order something else? I don't think this paella agrees with us."

CHAPTER FIVE

Gambling with Your Life

Uniformed staff arrived with stretchers to take away a dozen or so dead bodies. Presumably the official report would read food poisoning, although food attack would be more accurate. The staff had to hold the stretchers up to head height to manoeuvre them past the people still sitting at their tables. Some guests had left the restaurant, if only to change their clothes, but the vast majority had stayed. Some were actually eating the meals that had just tried to kill them. I suppose you have to have a strong stomach to be a gambler. No one looked at the stretchers, or the bodies on them. Presumably, in case such bad luck might rub off. Molly and I ordered lasagne. It seemed the safest thing on the menu. And the excitement had left us with an appetite.

"Just as well no one ordered the dragonburger," Molly said finally. "That could have got really out of hand."

"But, what was the point of all that?" I had to ask.

"I think someone just wanted to see whether we could defend ourselves," said Molly. "And get a look at what kind of protections people had going for them. You saw

Jacqueline turn into Hyde. Which was . . . pretty nasty, actually."

"Do you want to look at the dessert menu?" I said.

"Of course! It's free!"

"I think I just want to get started on the games," I said. "You might remember you found poison in our food even before it rose up and attacked us. Which suggests to me two different attackers. I really don't feel safe here."

"Of course we're not safe here," said Molly. "This is Casino Infernale!"

And that was when the manager finally turned up. Jonathon Scott just came strolling in, as smart and casual and urbane as ever. Apparently entirely unconcerned with what had just happened. He clapped his hands smartly, to draw everyone's attention.

"The Introductory Games are about to begin," he said, bestowing an avuncular smile on one and all. "Might I respectfully remind all of you that attendance is mandatory this year for all of our guests who have not attended Casino Infernale previously."

Everyone rose up from the their tables, sometimes abandoning half-finished meals or desserts, and headed for the exit. Scott stepped quickly back to get out of their way, still smiling his managerial smile. I was ready to go too, but Molly put a hand on my arm to stop me.

"Not yet," she said. "Frankie isn't back. I want to hear what he has to say, before we venture into enemy territory."

I scowled. "I hate going on missions where I haven't been properly briefed."

"Only so you can lecture everyone else," said Molly.

"True," I said.

"I do know a few things about the Introductory Games," Molly said carefully. "I mean, a girl does hear things. . . ."

"Go on," I said, resignedly. "Tell me what you know. And we will discuss how you came to know it later."

"The opening games are the only ones where money still matters," said Molly. "I had hoped we'd be able to skip them, but it seems Parris is playing strictly by the book this year. The Introductory Games are for newcomers, to sort out the wheat from the chaff; make sure you're wealthy and worthy enough to be here. And, to test your nerves. Because if you can't cope with these, you sure as hell aren't ready for the big games."

"What are we going to gamble with?" I said. "The cash Frankie got for us won't go far, not in a place like this. We need to be able to bet big, to win big."

"I do have an account with the Shadow Bank," said Molly. "With quite a bit on deposit . . . Don't look at me like that! How do you think I funded myself before I hooked up with you?"

"Stealing things," I said.

"Well, yes, but . . ."

Perhaps fortunately, Frankie turned up at that point. He slipped past the head waiter at his post with a nod and a wink, and the head waiter didn't even look at him, never mind announce his name. Frankie pulled up a chair and sat down at our table without waiting to be asked, and Molly and I quickly filled him in on what we'd been discussing. He nodded quickly.

"You can't use the money in your account," he said immediately to Molly. "It's strictly cash in the Introductory Games. Though you make the most money in side bets, gambling with the crowds on how well you'll do in the games. But listen, you need to know this. I've been wandering around, talking with the staff, renewing old friendships and spreading a little bribery and corruption in all the right places, and the word is, the fix is in. The house will be taking even more liberties than usual this year, and squeezing the odds till they squeal. Apparently Parris is determined that this will be the most successful and profitable Casino Infernale ever, so he can take all the credit. Once you're in there, watch your backs, and be prepared for treachery from all quarters. You can't trust the games or the players or the staff this year."

"Just our luck," I said.

*   *   *

Frankie led us into the Arena of Introductory Games. With such a grand title, I was disappointed to discover it looked much like every casino and gambling house I'd visited in my time as London field agent for the Droods. No real difference from any of the after-hours drinking and gambling parlours that infest parts of the West End. Where you can get in only if you're a member, but fortunately they sell memberships at the door.

There were roulette wheels, card tables, dice; all the usual means to part a sucker from his money. Deep pile carpeting, neutral-coloured walls, a general sense of opulence and comfort, but nothing distinctive enough to distract you from what you were there for.

The huge room was packed with people, expectation heavy on the air. Though soon enough that would be replaced with the heavier scents of perspiration and desperation. You don't come to places like this to enjoy yourself; it's all about the winning and the losing. After you've put a few hours in, and nothing's gone to plan, and the people around you are betting more and more wildly to win back the money they've lost, that's when eyes go cold and hearts grow desperate, and the wise man just chalks it up to experience and gets the hell out while the going is good. And your soul is still your own.

Casinos exist to take everything you've got.

Most people were just milling around, seeing what there was to see, not yet ready to commit themselves to a game until they'd seen what everyone else was doing. Waiting for someone else to take the plunge. There were no Big Names or Major Players here. They wouldn't lower themselves to play this kind of game, in this kind of company. There was a continual low murmur of conversation, as people worked up the nerve to bet everything they had, and then beg for credit to lose even more. No one bets heavier than the man who can't afford it and is desperate to hide that fact from everyone else. Pride, and face, are everything in the gambling world.

There's no sportsmanship in games like these, and certainly no sense of fair play. It's all dog eat dog, and devil take the hindmost. As far as the Casino management was concerned, these people weren't even players. Just lambs to the slaughter, and sheep to be sheared. Games at this level were designed to bring out the worst in people, to tempt them and watch them fall. And then laugh in their faces when they begged for another chance.

I had been in places like this before, but I'd always had the good sense to stay away from the games.

"It feels . . . like walking into a room full of enemies," Molly said quietly.

"We are," I said. "No one here is on our side but us." I looked at Frankie, who was smiling and nodding easily about him, perfectly at home. "You know this bear pit better than us, Frankie; where do you recommend we start?"

"Depends on your strategy," said Frankie. "You do have a strategy, don't you?"

"Win big, win fast, then get the hell out of here and on to the games that matter," I said.

"Well," said Frankie, "it's risky, but . . . that's your best chance, right there. Russian roulette."

We looked across at the single table, standing empty and alone, with the gun lying on it. Two chairs, but no one sitting on them, yet. A group of people were slowly gathering around the table, looking at the gun with hot, expectant eyes and talking animatedly. While being very careful to stay well away from either of the chairs.

"It's the old game," said Frankie. "Two players, one gun, one bullet. Spin the chamber, take your turn, and hope you get lucky. It's risky, but the odds are really no worse than most of the games here, and the side bets can make you a lot of money in a hurry. As long as your nerve holds out."

"I can't believe you're even considering this!" Molly said angrily to me. "You are, aren't you? We didn't come here to die! It's just another mission!"

"They have my soul," I said. "I want it back."

"No, Shaman," said Molly. "I can't let you do this.

You're still thinking like you have your armour to protect you. If anyone's going to do this, it should be me."

"No," I said. "You can't risk it, Molly. Not with your soul already owed to so many. I will do it, because I have just had a really sneaky idea. My Colt Repeater has no bullets in it because the gun teleports appropriate ammo into place, as necessary. You can tap into that magic, quietly and discreetly, and apply it to the Russian roulette gun. Any time a bullet threatens me, you just make it disappear."

"I can do that," said Molly. "But I can't keep the gun empty all the time. Someone would notice. You might have to shoot someone, Shaman. Kill your opponent, to win. Could you do that?"

"He'd shoot me, if he could," I said. "Are you in?"

"It's sneaky," said Molly. "I love it. Let's do it!"

"You haven't wasted any time getting into the swing of things," Frankie said admiringly. "You'll do well here."

But I still hesitated. Molly was right. The whole point of Russian roulette is that you only really win when the other player dies. What was one man's life, against the success of my mission? And any other game, you could get up and walk away when you'd had enough. I was pretty sure that wouldn't be allowed in this game.

"I know what you're thinking," said Molly. "You always were too ethical for your own good. That's why I should do this. Pulling the trigger won't bother my conscience. I don't have one."

"They'd detect your magic if you worked it at the table," I said. "So it has to be me."

"I really wouldn't worry about it," said Frankie. "The kind of person you'll be facing, you'll be happy to see them die."

I moved quickly forward before I could change my mind, pulled out one of the chairs, and sat down at the table. I looked at the gun before me, but didn't touch it. All around me, people began talking excitedly in loud breathy voices. They looked at me with admiring, condescending eyes, as though I'd just volunteered to go over Niagara Falls in a barrel. And some of them were looking at me in an eager, anticipatory way, because they had come to this table to see someone die. A few of them knew Shaman Bond, by reputation at least, and sent my name racing round the circle. And then my opponent pulled back the chair opposite me, and sat down hard on it, and the buzz of his name was much louder than mine had been. Because everyone here knew Gentleman Junkie Jules.

He didn't smile or even nod to me, didn't even acknowledge my presence. Just stared at the gun, like there was nothing he wanted more in the world. I'd met Jules before in some of London's more up-market early hours clubs, but I was pretty sure he wouldn't remember me. Gentleman Junkie Jules was wearing an expensively tailored suit that had seen much better days, like its owner. It hung shapelessly about him, as though it was a few sizes too large, draped unflatteringly about his spindly frame. No doubt the suit fit perfectly when he first bought it, but Jules had been through a lot since then. His face was thin and pinched, and unhealthily pale. His eyes were fierce and fever bright, and his colourless lips pulled back in a mirthless smile.

Word was, Gentleman Junkie Jules was a remittance man these days. Paid regular sums by his very well-off family, but only on the understanding that he would never come home to embarrass them. Jules was never that good a card player, but he always had enough money to get into the big games, and lose it all. Until the buzz of high stakes cards just wasn't enough any more and some kind friend introduced him to chemical heaven. And Jules found out the hard way that heroin is a harsh mistress. Given how much he'd abused his luck all his life, I was amazed he was still around. But it did make perfect sense that he would be sitting here, opposite me, ready to play Russian roulette. He'd been playing it all his life.

I had to at least make a gesture, for my conscience's sake. I raised a hand, to draw the attention of the manager

Jonathon Scott as he drifted by. He immediately changed direction to approach the table, and the crowd opened up just enough to let him pass. While still staying close enough that they wouldn't miss a word.

"Is there a problem, sir?" said Scott.

"I object to Jules as my opponent," I said. "This man isn't fit to play. I mean, look at the state of him."

"As long as he can pick up the gun and point it in the right direction, he can play," said Scott. "That's all the rules there are in this game."

"And it's the only way I can raise enough money to get out of this shit hole, and back into the real games where I belong," said Jules, in a dry, uninterested voice. He looked at me for the first time and he didn't see me at all. I was just something to be overcome. Something in his way. "Stop wasting my time. Let's get this done so I can get on with my life."

"Do you even know who I am?" I said.

"Shaman Bond," said Jules, just a bit unexpectedly. "I remember you. Always hanging round the edge of the scene in London looking for some small-time trouble to get into. Scrambling for crumbs from the rich man's table. How did someone like you even get in here?"

"This is wrong!" said a loud carrying voice, and we all looked round sharply. Leopold the gambling priest was standing nearby, glaring at us all impartially. "Suicide is a mortal sin," the priest said flatly.

"And gambling isn't?" said Scott, quietly amused.

"Not the way I do it," said Leopold.

"Butt out, priest," said Jules. He'd gone back to staring at the gun again. "No one wants you here; no one wants to hear what you have to say. This is what I want."

"Of course it is," said Leopold, his voice suddenly kind. "When you've abused your body with as many drugs as you have, only the biggest thrills can even touch you any more. But it's not too late to step away. You can lean on me, if you wish."

"Of course it's too late," said Jules. "It was too late the day I was born."

Leopold nodded slowly, and walked away. Heading for the big games, where he belonged. The manager went with him, perhaps just to see that the priest kept going. Cheating and assassination attempts were all very well, but nothing and no one could be allowed to interfere with the games at Casino Infernale.

A uniformed flunky turned up, to oversee the Russian roulette. A small characterless man with a brisk, efficient manner. He picked up the gun from the table, and showed it to the crowd. A Smith & Wesson .45, much used, brightly polished, well maintained. The flunky opened the gun's chamber, to show it was empty, and then produced a single bullet, and pressed it into place. He closed the chamber, spun it, and placed the gun back on the table, exactly halfway between me and Jules. People pressed in close around the table, determined not to miss a thing. Some looked at the gun, some looked at Jules, and a few even looked at me. They wanted to be in close, for the kill.

They looked . . . hungry.

They disgusted me. Jules didn't even notice them. He had eyes only for the gun. He rested his hands on the green baize tabletop. They weren't shaking at all, but beads of sweat were already appearing on his face. I felt sick to my stomach. I was the only one there who knew the fix was in; that I had already condemned this poor broken man to death. For the mission. But there was no other way . . . I couldn't even get up and walk away now. The Casino wouldn't permit it, not now that I'd committed myself. If I tried, at best they'd throw me out of Casino Infernale. And then the plan would be a bust, and there would be a war in the streets over Crow Lee's Inheritance. Blood and slaughter, inevitably spilling over into the everyday world, all because of me.

I looked Gentleman Junkie Jules in the eyes, and it was like there was no one there, looking back. Or was that just what I wanted to believe?

The flunky put his hand on the gun, and sent it spinning round and round with a practised movement. It wasn't the first time he'd done it. Wasn't the first time two men had sat down at this table, and only one of them had walked away. How many men had died, sitting in my chair? All the surrounding sound stopped, as everyone watched the gun spin round and round, gradually slowing, finally coming to a halt with the long barrel pointing in my direction. I sat up straight. Jules picked up the gun, with a steady hand. The crowd made a small, almost intimate sound. Jules aimed the gun at my head, right between my eyes. I sat very still. I knew the gun was empty, knew it had to be empty, but still my heart was hammering in my chest, and my breathing was fast enough to be painful. Jules' hand was entirely steady. His overly bright eyes were fixed on me now, and he was still smiling his lipless smile, showing dirty yellow teeth. He didn't seem to be breathing at all. He pulled the trigger, and there was a hard firm click as the hammer fell on an empty chamber.

The crowd let out the breath they'd been holding, with a sound that was almost orgasmic. Jules looked at the gun as though he couldn't understand what had just happened. And then he slowly lowered the gun and placed it on the table before me. There was a loud buzz of conversation round the table, as money changed hands in the first run of bets, and everyone hurried to bet again. I waited for the flunky to give me the nod, and then I picked up the gun, spun the chamber, pointed the gun at Jules, and pulled the trigger. Again, an empty chamber. I put the gun down. Jules hadn't moved, hadn't flinched, barely seemed aware that anything at all had happened. The sound from the crowd seemed angry, this time. I'd cheated them out of the drama they craved. I didn't care.

More money changed hands; more bets were made.

Jules picked up the gun again. He held it a while, considering it, and then he spun the chamber with a hard, angry motion. He aimed the gun at my left eye. I didn't move. Didn't react. The crowd had gone silent again. Jules' face was slick with sweat, but his hand was still steady. I looked down the barrel of the gun. I'd never seen anything so fascinating. I knew the gun was empty, believed with all my heart that it was empty, but I didn't trust the gun or my heart. The flunky gave the nod, and Jules slowly pulled the trigger. On another empty chamber.

There was a fierce babble of sound all around us. The crowd was really getting into it now. Jules slowly lowered the gun onto the table, and took his hand away. I looked around. Money was changing hands freely, as many bets were paid off. Voices were raised, and hands waved excitedly as new odds were set for the next round. I could see Molly and Frankie moving quickly through the crowd, making the rounds, taking bets wherever they could, backing me to win. I hoped they were getting good odds.

I picked up the gun. The butt was wet with sweat from Jules' hand. I put the gun down again, took out a handkerchief, and carefully wiped the butt clean. Jules said nothing. I put the handkerchief away, and took up the gun again. It felt heavier now, as though just the significance of what we were involved in added to its weight, its reality. I spun the chamber, aimed the gun at Jules' flat unwavering gaze, waited for the flunky, and then pulled the trigger. Nothing.

I put the gun down hard, almost snatching my hand away. I didn't like the feel of it—how it made me feel. I hated the gun. Hated myself for what I was doing. I carefully didn't look at Molly, but I couldn't help thinking, *Don't stretch this out. Put the bullet in the chamber, get this over with. Let the poor bastard die. Don't torture him like this. Don't torture me.*

Jules picked up the gun. He hefted it, almost thoughtfully. We looked into each other's eyes. He could see me now. The gun had made me real to him. The man who might kill him. The contact between us was direct, without barriers, almost intimate. I knew what he was feeling; he knew what I was feeling. Two men, bound together by a death that hadn't happened yet. I had killed men before, when it was part of the job. I prided myself they were all people who needed killing. That the world was a better, safer place without them in it. But I'd never had to sit opposite them, stare them in the eyes, while I did it. I could feel sweat on my face now. Jules and I were both breathing hard, almost in time with each other. As though we were both complicit in whatever happened next.

The crowd had fallen silent again, caught up in the moment. Their breathing was oddly synchronised, as though they had become one great organism. All of them stretched taut, by the painful anticipation of killing to come. I couldn't see Molly. I couldn't look away from Jules, and the gun. There was a bullet in it. I could feel it. And to my surprise, that made the moment easier to bear. Made it better. The danger felt very real and I was getting into it. All my life, the armour had been there to protect me. But now, sitting here, staring death in the face, I had never felt so alive. But . . . I only had to look into Jules' horribly fascinated eyes to see where that kind of feeling led you. Jules wanted to be here, but not to win. He wanted to play. He pointed the gun carefully at my right eye, and his hand was shaking now, just a little. With the thrill of the moment.

And then Jonathon Scott shouted, "Stop!"

Jules looked round sharply as the manager's hand came down out of nowhere, and forced Jules' hand down onto the table. Scott forced Jules to let go of the gun, wrestling it out of his hand. Jules suddenly stopped fighting him. The moment was broken. The manager picked up the Smith & Wesson, and stepped back from the table. There were raised angry voices to every side—men and women cheated of their sport. The manager glared coldly about him and the voices fell silent.

"This game is suspended," said Jonathon Scott. "Jules is disqualified, for cheating."

I sat back in my chair. Breathing hard, shaking in every limb. Adrenalin was still rushing through me, and my heart was pounding painfully. And all I could think was *I made it. I'm alive. I'm alive. . . .*

The game's uniformed flunky put his arms around Jules, and held him still, while Scott searched roughly through Jules' pockets. He soon found what he was looking for. He held up a small bone amulet so that everyone could see it. The crowd murmured angrily.

"A hidden charm, to affect the bullet in the gun," said Scott, in a loud and carrying voice. "It didn't work, of course; this whole room is covered by a null zone, cancelling out any magics that might affect the games. But it was such a small charm it took us a while to work out who had it, and what it was doing." He looked at Jules contemptuously. "He was trying to force a bullet into the chamber of the gun when it was facing him. Because he wanted to die. Not just because he owed more money than he could ever hope to pay back. But because he saw this pathetic death as the ultimate thrill.

"As the injured party, Shaman Bond is hereby declared the winner. All bets placed shall be paid off in his favour."

He gestured to the uniformed flunky, who dragged Jules out of his chair with surprising strength, and hauled him away. Jules tried to fight him, tried to pull away, and couldn't. There was a more than natural strength in the flunky's hands. Gentleman Junkie Jules was dragged from the room, kicking and screaming all the way. The doors slammed shut behind him, cutting off his hysterical voice. A low heavy murmur moved through the crowds, as all bets were settled. They weren't sure whether they felt cheated or not. They hadn't seen a man die, but the unexpected drama had been almost as satisfying.

I looked at Scott. "What will happen to him? Will you have him killed, for cheating?"

"Of course not," said Scott. "I have a much better punishment in mind. Jules will be thrown out of Casino Infernale, and then we will pass on the word, to ensure that he is banned from every other major gambling house. As a proven cheat. Let him live with that. We won't kill him, Mr. Bond. That's what he wants. We're not here to do people favours."

He smiled briefly, meaninglessly, and drifted away. The crowd went with him. I sat in my chair, looking at the gun on the table. Molly and Frankie hurried forward to join me. Molly was stuffing handfuls of assorted bank-notes into a red leather reticule that Frankie was holding for her. There looked to be a hell of a lot of money there, but I couldn't bring myself to care. I looked dully at Molly.

"The manager said there was a null zone. No magics would work here."

"I know!" said Molly. "Found that out the moment I tried to work one. But there was nothing I could do to warn you, not once you'd sat down at the table. I'm sorry, Shaman, but you played two rounds of Russian roulette for real."

"I know," I said. "I think . . . I need a drink. A lot of drinks."

"Me too," said Molly. "Let's get a bottle. Each."

"I'm afraid there's no time," said Frankie, forcing the last of the money into the reticule and snapping it shut. "You need to keep playing while you're still hot and people are still interested in you. We have to keep the side bets going! Remember, it's the privilege of winning, as well as the money, that will prove you worthy to leave here and rise to the next level!"

"You chose Russian roulette," I said to Frankie. "I'll choose the next game."

I stood up and looked around the room. I was back in control again, awake and focused. I studied my surroundings with an experienced eye, and the first thing I noticed was that there weren't nearly as many people gathered around the roulette wheel as I would have expected. People like to play roulette. They think it's glamorous and exciting, and fun to play, because they don't really understand the rules, or the odds. But those who were standing around the wheel and the table were studying it with far more than usual fascination. They studied every move of the ball and the wheel, as though their lives depended on it. In fact, I would have said they looked scared shitless.

"Explain to me," I said to Frankie, "what is going on with that roulette wheel?"

"Ah," he said. "You've noticed. That's not your usual, everyday game of roulette. You use chips to gamble there, but they don't represent the cash you paid for them. You bet years of your life."

"What?" said Molly. "How the hell does that work?"

"Oh, it's very ingenious," Frankie said earnestly. "A game unique to Casino Infernale. You bet red and black, you see, and the number you choose is how many years of your life that you're betting. Not the years you've lived, but your future years, the years you still have left to live. You're betting your future. If the wheel turns, and your number doesn't come up, you lose the number of years you've bet. To the house. That's the Casino's cut. So if you bet, say, twenty-one on red or black, and you lose, you become twenty-one years older. But if you bet on twenty-one and you win, then you gain twenty-one years of extra life!

"See? Not at all complicated, once you get your head round it, is it? All right, yes, the odds are stacked against you right from the start . . . but this is roulette we're talking about."

"So you can die right there at the table of old age, if you keep losing?" I said.

"Happens all the time," said Frankie. "That's part of the thrill of playing—to watch someone else check out, right next to you."

"Is everyone here crazy?" I said, loud enough to turn several heads in my direction. "Why on earth would any sane person want to play a game like that?"

"This is Casino Infernale," said Frankie. "The risk is part of the attraction. Sane people don't normally come here."

"How does the wheel work?" said Molly, tactfully changing the subject while I calmed myself down again.

Frankie shrugged. "Some kind of future tech. Fell off the back of the Nightside. Supposedly, it started out as some kind of medical technology, where a future doctor could give you extra years of life, topping you up as and when needed. Trust Casino Infernale to make a game of chance out of something intended to save lives. This roulette wheel is a game of life and death; but then, aren't they all?"

"Don't get smug," I said, "or I will slap you a good one and it will hurt. Right here, in front of everyone."

"Don't blame the messenger for the message, boss," said Frankie.

"I get to play, this time," said Molly, very firmly. "You took all the risks before, even the ones you didn't know about. Look at you, you're still shaking. I won't let you put yourself through that again."

"I'm not arguing," I said. "You're right. I'm not in any shape to play sensibly."

"Do you want to go back to our room and lie down?" said Molly.

"And leave you to play alone?" I said. "Not going to happen. Too many sharks in these waters. Besides, someone's got to keep an eye on Frankie while he's handling the money from the bets."

"Well, really," said Frankie. "Anyone would think you know me. . . ."

We wandered over to join the crowd round the roulette wheel. Just in time to see someone bet on Red twenty-one, and the ball jump into the slot at Black twenty. The whole crowd made a sound as though they'd been hit, and we all turned to look at the poor loser—a woman of a certain age in a dress and makeup far too young for her. Even the man she'd clearly come in with backed away from her, as though she'd suddenly become contagious. The woman shot him an angry look of betrayal, and then turned reluctantly back to face the croupier. He was smiling, and it was not a good smile. He held up a small hour-glass, and everyone around the table held their breath. The croupier turned the hourglass over, and as the sands started falling, the woman grew older. Twenty-one years weighed down on her, cruelly and implacably. Her face wrinkled, and her body shrank in on itself, until an old woman stood beside the roulette wheel, weeping helplessly for her lost years. No one did anything, said anything, to help her. Most of those watching were smiling a smile very like that of the croupier. This was what they were there for. The old woman stumbled away from the table, and left the room. Alone.

I looked at the roulette wheel. "If it was up to me I'd smash that bloody thing into splinters . . . I don't like this, Molly. Far too many random factors involved."

"But if you win big here, you win really big," said Frankie. "Extra years of life, handfuls of cash from the side bets, and major prestige. And it's not like any of the other games are going to be that much easier, or fairer. Winning against the odds is the whole idea."

"And we do have an edge, this time," said Molly. "An edge that can't be affected by any null zone. Remember the potion the Armourer gave us?"

"Remember it?" I said. "How could I forget? I'll still be able to taste that muck when I'm dead and six months in my grave!"

"A potion to let us see the patterns in any game," Molly said patiently. "Just looking at this game, I can sense the weight of the ball and the stresses in the wheel. All the patterns that decide where the ball turns up. I am pretty sure I can predict which number the ball will choose, every time. And since the potion is a part of our system, the Casino won't be able to spot it, and the null can't affect it."

I looked at the roulette wheel, and she was right. I could see the patterns in the play, clear as day. Given the mechanical workings of the wheel, predicting the outcome was child's play. It was like reading a pack of marked cards. I could feel the weight of responsibility sliding off my shoulders.

"Okay," I said. "Go play, Molly. Have fun. Bet big, and take that smiling little croupier for everything he's got. And Frankie, get the best odds you can from the crowd."

"No problem," said Frankie.

He moved off into the crowd, grinning and glad-handing everyone who didn't run away fast enough, while Molly elbowed her way forward into a prize position at the side of the table. I hung back. I wasn't sure why. It wasn't as though anything could go wrong, this time. But I didn't trust that feeling any more. People at the table realised they were standing next to the infamous wild witch Molly Metcalf, and quickly fell back to give her room. She smiled sweetly at the croupier, and exchanged a whole wad of money for a single chip to play with. The croupier smiled and nodded and went out of his way to flatter her, and Molly slapped him down with a single look.

People came hurrying forward from all over the room as the word spread that Molly Metcalf was playing roulette. Some clearly wanted her to win, some just as clearly wanted to see her lose hard, and most just wanted to see the wild witch in action. Frankie moved among them like a shark with his mouth open, taking them for everything they had. The people might admire Molly and her reputation, but no one believed she could beat the wheel.

Molly took her single chip and placed it firmly on Red twenty-one. Biggest bet you could make: twenty-one years of your life. One way or the other.

The croupier looked round the table. "Place your bets, ladies and gentlemen!"

Everyone played, but no one else wanted to place a chip beside Molly's. The croupier spun the wheel, the ball went whirling round and round, clattering from place to place, and finally ended up in Black seventeen.

"No!" I said. "That's not possible!"

No one paid me any attention. They were all looking at the small steel ball, and then at the young woman who'd just lost twenty-one years of her life. I was the only one there who knew just how wrong it was. Given that ball, in that wheel, there was no way it could have ended up in Black seventeen. Until I looked really hard—and saw the hidden mechanism behind the wheel. The croupier cheated.

Molly looked slowly around her. Everyone was backing away from her. Partly so none of her bad luck would rub off on them, partly so they could get a better look at what was about to happen. The croupier smiled at Molly, and held up his hour-glass. Molly looked coldly back at him.

"Do your damnedest. My sisters will avenge me."

A shudder ran through the crowd at that, and even the croupier balked for a moment. The croupier had cheated, diverted the ball, and looking into Molly's eyes, he knew that she knew. But who would believe her? I knew, but how could I prove it without revealing how I knew? Without revealing I was a Drood, and throwing away my mission?

I was here to prevent a war. To save who knew how many lives. I couldn't risk my mission, just to save Molly from something she could probably undo herself, given time. She would understand. The croupier held up his hour-glass and waggled it in front of Molly, taunting her. And I reached for my Colt Repeater. Because no one messed with my Molly.

And that was when a harsh, buzzing artificial voice shouted out, *"Cheat!"*

The croupier glared around him immediately. "Who dares call me cheat?"

"That would be me," said the Thirtieth Century Man. He stomped forward, with loud crashing footsteps. An incredibly tall, broad, and heavy man, in an outfit that seemed to consist mainly of black leather straps. His marble white flesh was whorled with long streaks of steel, the meat and the metal fused seamlessly together. He was a cyborg, from some unknown future; a mixture of living and nonliving materials. His face was a collection of flat surfaces, with glowing golden eyes. I'd encountered him before, wandering through the sleazier flesh pits of old London town, trying to find something to interest him. He didn't know how he ended up in our time, and was desperate to find a way back. People said he had an affinity for all things mechanical, and could see how anything worked at a glance.

(Other, less kind people said he was queer for machines.)

He gestured roughly at the roulette wheel, with one oversized hand, and the ball jumped from one slot to another as the cyborg worked the hidden mechanism, calling out each number in advance. The croupier's face went white, and he started edging away from the table, looking for the nearest exit . . . but Jonathon Scott was already walking towards him, with two large Security men.

"This . . . is intolerable," said Scott. "Two proven cases of cheating in the first hour of Casino Infernale! This could damage our reputation beyond repair! And that it should be one of our own staff who is caught this time . . . ladies and gentlemen, allow us to make proper recompense."

He gestured to his two Security men, who moved quickly forward to grab the croupier by the arms and hold him still. He didn't even try to struggle. He was already in enough trouble. Scott took the hour-glass from the croupier's hand, and held it up so everyone could see it.

"This man is the guilty party, so it is only proper that he should pay for his crime. Molly Metcalf, please allow the Casino to pay you the twenty-one years you rightfully won, courtesy of the man who cheated you."

He turned the hour-glass over with a dramatic flourish, and as the sands began to fall, so the extra years fell upon the croupier. He was a young man, and he cried out miserably as the best years of his life were taken from him; until a middle-aged man stood slumped between the two Security men. Weeping silently, for what he'd lost. I might have felt sorry for him if I hadn't seen him enjoying it so much when it happened to other people. I looked at Molly. She threw back her head and laughed out loud. She didn't look any younger, but she practically glowed with new energy. I turned to thank the Thirtieth Century Man, but he was already gone.

"This roulette wheel is closed," said Scott. "Until we can have it replaced. Please continue with the other games! Enjoy yourselves!"

He strode away, and the Security men dragged the still sobbing croupier after him. A number of people who'd played the wheel before hurried after him, raising their voices. Scott just kept going. I cautiously approached Molly.

"How do you feel?" I said.

"I feel great! Marvellous! Full of energy . . . I feel like I could take on the whole damned world!"

"Never knew you when you didn't," I said, and she laughed and calmed down a little.

"There was no way the croupier was running that scam on his own," she said briskly. "The Casino made him the scapegoat to avoid awkward questions. Frankie was right. We can't trust anyone here."

"So," I said, "does all this new energy mean you'll be able to break the null zone from now on?"

"Unlikely," said Molly. "Doubt it. I don't think the Casino would give me anything I could use against it."

"Good point," I said. "Does it mean you'll live twenty-one years longer now than you would have?"

"I don't know . . . in theory. But in practice, given the kinds of lives we lead . . ."

"I know what you mean," I said. "I really don't like this place, Molly. I think it's bad for us. Whether we win or lose."

"What did you expect?" said Frankie, sauntering over with another red leather reticule, bulging with cash. "This is a place of temptations. Win or lose, it's bound to affect you."

I looked round sharply as the Thirtieth Century Man came over to join us. I hadn't heard him leave, and I hadn't seen him come back. Which, given the sheer size and weight of the man, should have been impossible. I was thinking vaguely about cloaking shields when he nodded brusquely to me, and addressed me abruptly with his buzzing artificial voice.

"I thought you should know, you have friends here. From the Department of the Uncanny. But this is the only time I can assist you openly. Can't help you again without risking my cover, and I have my own mission."

"What are you doing here?" I said. "Did the Regent . . ."

"Hush," said the Thirtieth Century Man. "Not a name to use in a place like this. Point is, he got word there might be a working time-travel device tucked away here, somewhere. Just a rumour, nothing solid. But one, we don't want people like this to have it. And two, it could be a way home for me. So, you continue with your mission, and leave mine to me."

He strode away, and we watched him go. It wasn't like we could have stopped him to ask more questions, even if we'd wanted to. I looked at Molly and Frankie.

"That's twice we've been saved at the last moment, by someone else. I think we're pushing our luck."

"Come on!" said Frankie. "It's a casino! Pushing your luck is what it's all about. So, what next?"

"A chance to catch my breath would be nice," I said. "But I think the sooner we're out of here, the better."

We looked around the room. None of the other games appealed to me, for all kinds of reasons. Too small, too slow, too risky . . .

"You only need one more big win," said Frankie. "I suppose . . . there is always the Arena."

"You have gladiators here?" said Molly.

"Not as such," said Frankie. "They call it the Pit. Just a big hole in the ground, really. The usual: two men enter, one man crawls out barely alive. Everyone else bets on the outcome, and makes lots of money. It's win or die, hand-to-hand fighting, no weapons allowed."

I remembered looking down the gun at Jules, wanting him to die so I could win.

"I'm an agent," I said. "Not an assassin. I came here to gamble, not kill people."

"I don't think anyone here cares what you want, sweetie," Molly said carefully. "But you're right. This isn't for you. You don't have the killer instinct. So I'll do it. I can take care of myself in a fight, and the way I feel right now I could kick anyone's arse!"

"And that's why you can't do it," I said. "All those extra

years have gone to your head. I'll do it. But whoever they put against me, I won't kill them unless I have to."

"You'll have to," said Frankie.

Through the far doors and out beyond the Arena of Introductory Games . . . there was a really big hole in the ground. Just like the man said. A pit, some ten feet deep, with a packed earth floor and walls. Surrounded by a huge baying crowd, several ranks deep, all of them pushing and shoving each other in their excitement, struggling for a better view of what was going on down in the pit. Molly and I forced our way to the front, with a lot of elbowing, while Frankie stuck close behind. I looked down into the pit, and there was Jacqueline's Hyde, fighting a French savate kick-fighter. The Frenchman was fast and skilled and vicious, just a blur in his movements as he danced back and forth. Sweat gleamed on his bare chest, over jodhpurs made from the French flag. His blows came out of nowhere, savage kicks striking home again and again. And none of it meant anything, because he was fighting Hyde.

Everyone in the watching crowd hated Hyde. They booed and hissed him, screaming obscenities, men and women alike. Just the sight of Hyde seemed to infuriate and unhinge them. I could understand why. It wasn't just that Hyde was ugly, though he was. Brutish, short, and powerfully muscled, hunched over by the sheer mass of musculature in his back. His square bony head thrust forward, dark feral eyes glaring from under a protruding brow. Long black hair fell down around a face marked with every sin that man is heir to. Just to look at him was to hate him, because he was everything inside us that we hate about ourselves. Only he gloried in it. He loved being what he was. Free of all inhibitions and restraint. I wanted to draw my gun and shoot him dead, just for the sin of being what he was. Just for existing.

Robert Louis Stevenson put it best. He said Edward Hyde had the mark of Cain on him.

Fresh blood dripped from Hyde's hands and arms. He'd fought other men before this in the Pit. I could see bits and pieces of them scattered across the packed earth floor. And great dark splashes of blood all over the earth walls.

The bloodlust in the watching crowd filled the air; hot and vicious and overwhelming. They wanted to see a death. Preferably Hyde's, but deep down they weren't fussy. They'd reached the point where anyone would do. The Frenchman hit Hyde again and again, terrible blows that slammed into him with devastating force and speed and accuracy. Just the sound of the impacts was enough to make me wince. But no matter how hard the Frenchman hit Hyde, or how often . . . he couldn't hurt him. Hyde took every blow without flinching, not trying to evade any of them. He didn't react at all, taking no pain or damage that anyone could see. He just smiled at his opponent—a cold, crafty, infuriating smile. Waiting for his moment.

And eventually, inevitably, the Frenchman tired and slowed, and one great gnarled hand shot out and fastened on to the Frenchman's ankle, stopping a blow in mid-kick. The Frenchman looked at Hyde with wide, startled eyes; caught in mid-move with one leg fully extended. And then Hyde just ripped the leg right off. Casually, as though it was the easiest thing in the world. The leg came away with a terrible tearing sound, and blood spurted thickly on the air from the awful open wound at the Frenchman's hip. He crashed to the ground, and lay there, shaking and shuddering, too shocked even to scream as his life's blood ran away to sink into the earth floor. The crowd were utterly still, and silent, watching with avid eyes as the Frenchman died. No one was interested in helping him. By the time I realised that, and started forward, the man was dead.

Hyde leaned against the earth wall, and ate big chunks of meat from the leg he was holding. This was too much, even for a Casino Infernale crowd, and they screamed and shouted abuse at him. Those at the front surged forward, as though they would jump down into the Pit and attack Hyde, overwhelm him by sheer force of numbers. But the

Casino Security people got there first, and forced the crowd back. Because no one could be allowed to interfere with the games.

Hyde threw what was left of the leg away, wiping his bloody mouth clean with the back of his huge hand. He smiled arrogantly up at the crowd. Soaking up their rage and hate like approbation. And then, quite casually, he turned back into Jacqueline. There was no great transformation of the flesh; she just seemed to rise out of him, as though her presence had been implicit in him all the while. And, perhaps because I was watching so closely, in the moment when they changed . . . I saw Jacqueline and Hyde touch fingertips tenderly, just for a moment.

Jacqueline Hyde looked round the blood-soaked Pit, holding the tatters of her dress to her. If what she saw bothered her, it didn't show in her face. The crowd watched silently. Looking on in awe at this small slender woman, who held a monster inside her. Jaqueline moved slowly over to the single iron-runged ladder that was the only way in and out of the Pit, and climbed out. When she reached the top, no one offered her a helping hand, or tried to push her back in. They just fell silently away, to give her space. Out of something like respect. A uniformed flunky came forward to offer her a robe. At arm's length. Jacqueline accepted the robe, without saying anything, and wrapped it around her. She walked away, and everyone let her.

In case Hyde might come back.

More uniformed flunkies filed down into the Pit to recover the dead body and gather up the body parts scattered across the earth floor. It took them a while to manhandle everything back up the ladder.

The barker in charge of the Pit came forward—a large cheerful fellow in a chequered suit. He grinned around him, as though he knew us all, and knew what we were there for.

"Hello, hello, boys and girls! Come on in, you know you want it! Welcome to the Pit, where the killing's easy and the dying is hard, and you get to enjoy every last bit of it!

So step right up; who's going to be our next volunteer? For the winner: prestige, and the sheer joy of being alive! Let me tell you, you never feel more alive than when you stare death in the face and head-butt him!"

I looked at Frankie. "That's it? Just the prestige, and happy to be alive? No prize money?"

"Not here," said Frankie. "People play this kind of game for the fun of it, to show courage and gain instant respect. If you win. There is a lot of money to be made in the side bets, but this is really all about courage and skill and being completely fucking insane."

"And this is your idea of what we should do next?" said Molly.

"It's risky, yes, but a good win here would be more than enough to guarantee you access to the next level. Whilst also ensuring that everyone you meet there would be seriously scared of you."

I nodded, and strode forward. Before I could get a rush of good sense to the head and change my mind. I made myself known to the barker, and he flashed me a wide and knowing smile, clapped me on the shoulder, and roared out my name to the waiting crowd. They managed a few good-natured cheers as I climbed down the iron-runged ladder into the Pit. There were a few taunts and insults, but I ignored them. I wasn't here for the crowd. I walked slowly round the Pit, getting the feel of the place. It was surprisingly cold, and the air stank of blood and spilled guts, of sweat and testosterone. It felt like a bad place to die.

And then my opponent came swarming down the ladder, jumping the last few rungs in his eagerness. He spun round to face me, smiling coldly, and my heart sank. I knew him. And not in a good way.

The Dancing Fool strutted round the Pit, bouncing on his feet to test the resilience of the packed earth floor. The fastest fighting man in the world. He could hit you so fast you wouldn't even know you'd been hit till you woke up in hospital. He liked to claim his particular brand of martial arts was based on old Scottish sword dances, which was bullshit, but it didn't stop him from always wearing a kilt. In a tartan I knew for a fact he wasn't entitled to. His edge came from his very own special gift: to know what you were going to do, before you did it.

Déjà fu.

He was big and broad, and moved like the professional he was. He had dark hair, dark eyes, and a darker heart. And he knew Shaman Bond was really a Drood, because we'd worked together before.

It hadn't ended well.

Lots of people in the crowd recognised the Dancing Fool, and roared his name approvingly. Just by being here, he guaranteed a show—blood and death in the grand manner. He smiled and waved at all the hot watching eyes, and I just knew the odds against me were going through the roof. Hopefully Molly and Frankie were keeping on top of it. The Dancing Fool finally strode forward to face me, and I sighed, and nodded to him.

"Hello, Nigel."

His smiled disappeared in a moment, and he scowled fiercely at me. "Don't call me that, *Shaman*. Only my friends get to use my given name, and you never did qualify. Even when I thought we were both working on the same side. Never thought you'd see me again, did you, *Shaman*?"

"You're looking well," I said. "Considering Walker shot both your knee-caps off at Place Gloria."

He sniffed loudly. "You can get anything repaired, if you have enough money. And if you're motivated enough. I swore I'd have my revenge on you, *Shaman*! And so when a little bird told me that you'd be coming here . . . and that you wouldn't have your precious armour to hide behind . . . well! How could I resist? A fair fight at last. I'm going to tear you to pieces, *Shaman*."

"Walker was right," I said. "I should have let him kill you."

And I went straight for him, even before I'd finished talking. There was no point in hanging about, and there was always the chance I'd catch him off guard and get one good punch in. But of course he was expecting it, and he was so very fast. . . . My fist whooshed through the empty air where he had been just a moment before, and he hit me in the side, hard. I staggered away, clutching at myself, half-blind with pain and gasping for air. I was fast and skilled, well trained and experienced, versed in all the really dirty tricks . . . but he was just so damned *fast*. I spun round, head down, hands up to defend myself.

I never stood a chance.

The blows came out of nowhere. The first fist slammed into the side of my head, and the earth floor jumped up and hit me in the face. I didn't even realise I'd fallen until he kicked me again and again in the ribs, to get me moving again. I heard ribs break, felt splinters grind in my side. I coughed hard, and blood filled my mouth. Not a good sign. I forced myself up onto my hands and knees, and a fist came flying down, hitting me so hard in the back I was slammed right back to the earth floor again. I couldn't move, couldn't think. The pain blotted out everything else. I squirmed around on the floor like a fish hauled up out of the water, hardly able to breathe. The only thing that saved me was that the Dancing Fool took time out to go strolling round the Pit in a lap of honour, smiling and waving to the screaming crowd.

I spat out a thick mouthful of blood, and forced myself up onto my feet. I was swaying, and I could barely raise my fists without crying out, but I was up. The Dancing Fool looked around, saw me, and laughed delightedly. He got to play some more. He came at me again, impossibly fast, dancing round and round me, hitting me wherever and whenever he wanted. Every blow hurt like hell, and every blow did damage, but I stood my ground and took it and wouldn't go down again. Because I had a plan.

I was outclassed, and we both knew it. I was a good scrapper, but he was a professional. I'd only ever beaten him before because my armour protected me, and made me as fast as he was. Now all I had was stubbornness, and one desperate plan.

At first, the crowd cried out and applauded every time he hit me, yelling out suggestions on the best ways to break and kill me. But as I rocked back and forth, taking the punishment but stubbornly refusing to be beaten, parts of the crowd came round to my side, yelling out encouragement. They did love an underdog, even if they wouldn't bet on one.

I staggered back and forth across the increasingly bloody earth floor, protecting my head as best I could, because one good shot to the head would leave me dazed and vulnerable. And that would be the end of it. More bones broke, more blood flew on the air, as the Dancing Fool spun and stamped around me, enjoying himself. My left arm hung broken and useless at my side, and I couldn't see out of one eye. I hoped it was just puffed shut. And still I wouldn't fall, wouldn't give in. Because bit by bit the Armourer's potion was kicking in. Showing me the patterns in how the Dancing Fool moved and held himself and planned his attacks.

Until I could read the cocky little bastard like a book.

I put my back against the wall, as though I hadn't known it was there, as though I had nowhere else to run. The Dancing Fool came in close to throw a punch, and I saw it coming. His fist slammed towards my head with incredible speed, and I turned my head aside at just the last moment, so that his fist flashed by my head and buried itself deep in the earth wall behind me. Just as I'd planned.

I heard bones crunch as they broke in his hand. I saw the look of shock, and then pain, in his face. And then more shock, as he discovered his hand was trapped, buried deep, locked fast in the earth wall. And in that brief moment, as he put all his attention into trying to pull his hand free, I summoned up the last bit of strength I'd been saving and punched him savagely in the throat. I felt his trachea break, felt his windpipe collapse. Blood shot from his mouth, and all the sense went out of his eyes. He was still trying to pull his hand out of the wall, even as he made horrid choking sounds. I hit him again, with my one good hand; a vicious blow that slammed in right under his sternum. Hit a man there hard enough, and you can disrupt the rhythm of his heart. The Dancing Fool fell to his knees, his face blank, his eyes rolling up. One arm still stretched above his head, from where his hand was still trapped in the wall. He couldn't breathe, and his heart was struggling. I looked down at the exposed back of his neck, and I rabbit-punched him.

The first blow probably killed him. I hit him six more times, as hard as I could, just to be sure.

I killed him. Not because he might have revealed who I really was and put an end to my mission. Not because he was a professional killer who needed killing; not because the world would be a better place without him. No. I killed him because he hurt me so badly, and because he would have killed me.

The crowd was going wild at the unexpected victory. Jumping up and down, clutching at each other, screaming and shouting like they'd never stop. I could barely see them, and the sound seemed to be coming from a long way away. I didn't care. I was looking at Nigel, lying dead before me on the cold earth floor. A small, broken, pathetic thing. I leaned over, and spat blood on his face. And then I turned away and limped slowly back to the iron ladder. It took me a long while to climb back up, with only one working arm.

Molly and Frankie were waiting for me at the top. Molly looked at the mess the Dancing Fool had made of my face, and swallowed hard. She and Frankie helped me over the edge of the Pit, and then held me up between them as they half-led, half-carried me away. I tried not to cry out, but every movement hurt so much. Molly put my good arm over her shoulders, so she could carry more of my weight. Her face was white with shock, and her eyes were full of rage. Wherever she looked, people fell back to give her more room.

"Hell of a fight, Shaman!" said Frankie. "Hard core!"

"Shut up," said Molly.

People came forward to congratulate me from every side, and Molly drove them back with hard looks and harsh language. Frankie left us for a while to collect the winnings from his side bets. He came back laughing.

"You wouldn't believe how much money we've made, betting on you!" he said happily. "No one thought you stood a chance!"

"Shut up," said Molly.

"Is that it?" I said. "Have I done enough to get through to the next level?"

"Hell, yes!" said Frankie. "Major prestige! Dangerous prestige! But I have to say . . . you look like crap. Just saying, but . . . maybe you should quit now? While you're still ahead?"

"No," I said.

"Let's get you back to our room," said Molly. "Once we're out of the null zone, I can work my healing magics on you."

"Sounds good to me," I said, or thought I said. After a while, I managed a small smile. Blood leaked from the corners of my mouth.

"What?" said Molly.

"Those were just the Introductory Games," I said. "Can't wait to see what the next level's like. . . ."

CHAPTER SIX

Robbery with Attitude

don't remember how they got me to the elevators. I remember drifting in and out, sudden flashes of pain, of people and places, and Molly yelling at Frankie to support more of my weight. I remember the taste of blood in my mouth, and light that hurt my one working eye, and voices that seemed to come from far, far away. I was broken. I knew that, but I couldn't seem to care.

I remember being in the elevator, and Molly crying out with relief as the null lifted and her magics returned. She quickly cast a levitation spell on me so I could hang in midair, unsupported. It felt like being carried on the backs of angels. Molly leaned tiredly against the wall of the elevator, getting her strength back. The front of her dress was covered in blood. My blood. Frankie stood at the back of the lift, sulking because Molly had yelled at him. I looked down, and saw blood dripping steadily off me, to form a widening pool beneath my floating feet.

The elevator doors finally opened onto our floor, and Molly quickly floated me out of the elevator and down the corridor to our suite. I settled into the embrace of the levitation spell, like snuggling into bed. It felt good, peaceful, distant . . . far less painful than being hauled around. Any sudden movement meant fresh pain, sudden spikes that jolted me out of my protective daze, waking me up. I didn't want to wake up. Molly opened the door to our suite and sent me floating in with a wave of her hand. I caught a glimpse of Frankie looking quickly up and down the corridor, to see if anyone was watching, and then he hurried in and locked the door behind him.

Molly lowered me onto the bed as carefully as she could, but I still cried out despite myself. Even the soft and supportive mattress was enough to put pressure on my broken body, and set all my wounds crying out again. Molly sank down onto a chair by the bed. She looked exhausted, and bad as I felt there was still enough of me left to worry about her. A simple levitation spell shouldn't have taken that much out of her. Frankie dithered at the foot of the bed, hardly able to look at me, as though what he saw disturbed him.

"Should I ring for the hotel doctor?" he said. "I really think I should ring for a doctor. I mean, look at the state he's in!"

"No doctor," said Molly. "I can see how bad he is. I'm not blind! But I wouldn't trust any doctor this hotel might provide. We can't have anyone knowing how bad he is, and there's always the chance the doctor might be able to tell who and what he really is. . . . You'd better be right about the surveillance bugs in this place, Frankie, because I am getting really tired of having to talk in circles. Anyway, we don't need a doctor. I can heal him. As soon as I get my second wind. There's something wrong here. . . . I think there's a low-level null working everywhere in this hotel, hidden under the surface. Just enough to make every kind of magic an effort, and slow the players down. Give the Casino an advantage. . . ."

"You can sense that?" Frankie said dubiously.

"I can feel the extra effort involved," said Molly.

"Can you still heal him?"

"I once brought him back from the shores of death," said Molly. "This is just damage . . . I can fix damage. Go outside, Frankie, you're a distraction. Guard the door, warn me if anyone's coming, and don't let anyone in unless I tell you otherwise."

Frankie nodded quickly, and left.

"I thought he'd never go," I said.

Molly levered herself up out of her chair and leaned over me, her face close to mine. "Hush, sweetie. I didn't realise you were awake or I'd have put you under with a sleep spell."

"No," I said. "Don't. I'm afraid to sleep. Afraid to let go, in case I don't wake up again. This is bad, Molly. Really bad. I can feel . . . broken things, grinding together inside me."

"That little bastard really did a job on you," said Molly. "Who was he? It looked like he knew you, and you knew him."

"An old friend," I said. "And an old enemy. That's the spy game for you, mostly."

"I know, sweetie. Now shut the hell up so I can work on you."

"Yes, doctor," I said.

"We can play doctors and nurses later," said Molly, trying to smile. "When you're all better."

"Can I be the doctor, for a change?"

"If you're good."

She kissed me briefly on the forehead, and then stood back, facing the bed. She frowned intently, her whole face a mask of concentration. She didn't wave her hands around or chant incantations; most of that stuff is strictly for the rubes. She just gathered her strength, and drew energy from the hidden worlds so she could do what she needed to do. And just like that my body became transparent wherever she looked, so she could See inside me, and See how bad the damage was. The spell must have leaked at the edges, because I could See what she was Seeing.

My left arm was badly broken, in three places, splinters of shattered bone piercing the torn skin. Ribs were broken and shattered, all down one side. Some of them had pierced the lung. I could See great areas of internal bleeding, moving inside me like slow dark tides. Molly looked at my head.

I couldn't See what she Saw, but it must have been really bad, judging by the look on her face. It was actually something of a relief, to know I had good reason to feel this bad.

I was breathing as shallowly as I could, because even the smallest movement hurt so badly I had to fight to keep from crying out, when Molly finished her scan and shut off the spell. She sat down in her chair again. She was crying, silently. Great fat tears, rolling down her cheeks. I wanted to reach out a hand to her, but I couldn't.

"Don't," I said. "Don't, love, please."

"Dear God, you're a mess," said Molly, sniffing back her tears so she could try to sound professional again. "I can't believe how much damage you took in that fight. I can't believe you hung on that long, to take him down."

"Growing up with my family," I said, "you learn to take punishment and keep going. I had to kill him, Molly."

"Hush. . . ."

"I had no choice! He had to die, because he knew who I was, knew me from before. He would have told everyone if I'd let him live."

"You had no choice," said Molly. "He would have killed you. And if you hadn't killed him, I would have. For what he did to you."

"Can you fix me?" I said. "If there is a null operating here . . ."

"Low level," said Molly. "I spit on their null. It'll just make the job that little bit more difficult, that's all. Means I'll have to do it the hard way. And I'll have to put a screen over us, to block out the bugs. Can't have anyone watching this. Now shut the hell up and let me concentrate."

"Yes, dear," I said.

She spoke Words of Power over me, and I could feel her presence growing in the room, eclipsing everything else. I could feel her, as closely as I felt myself. Her mind, her soul, reaching out to me. Linking herself to me. And then she healed me, by taking my injuries into herself. She lay down on the bed beside me, taking my hand in hers, and one by one she took every broken thing inside me . . . and made them hers. I heard the bones in her left arm break, three times, but she never made a sound. My arm was immediately whole again, and I felt the magic course through her, as her bones healed in a moment. She stirred and stiffened on the bed beside me, sweat running off her face as she concentrated, taking my hurts and making them her own, so she could mend them inside herself. Because an injury shared is an injury halved, or at least weakened, and easier to deal with. My pain disappeared as she embraced it, and then rejected it. And she never cried out once. I knew what she was feeling because I'd felt it first, and I could only marvel at her strength.

And her love, that she would put herself through such hell, for me.

It took the best part of an hour to take on all my hurts and damage and put it right. I held her hand as tightly as I could. It was all I could do, all the support I could give her. In the end we lay on the bed together, side by side, still holding hands, staring up at the ceiling, breathing hard with the effort of everything we'd been through. Just . . . luxuriating in the peace and comfort that comes with not hurting any more. I was whole again. I could feel it.

"Well," Molly said finally, "there went all the extra years of life I won at the roulette wheel. Just burned right through them to power the healing."

"You're going to hold that over me for the rest of our lives, aren't you?" I said.

"Oh, yes," said Molly. "You'd better believe it. You even miss one birthday and you are a dead man. God, I feel tired."

"You feel tired?" I said. "I feel like I've been to hell and back."

Molly laughed briefly. "I've done that, and it wasn't as bad."

We turned and cuddled up against each other. I held her to me, and we lay together on the bed for a long time. Trying to give each other strength, and support.

Eventually, we both sat up and stretched slowly. My joints creaked loudly, but everything seemed to have settled back into place. We rolled off the bed and got to our feet. My side of the bedclothes was soaked in blood. I looked down at my clothes, and there was more there, too. I looked at Molly. Her clothes were stained with blood from where she'd touched me. Molly stripped the sheets off the bed, while I headed for the bathroom. I pulled off my stained clothes as I went, dropping them to the floor. I didn't want anything to do with them again. I turned on the lights in the bathroom and looked at myself in the mirror. In the harsh unforgiving light, I looked hard and grim and maybe ten years older. I got in the shower, and hunched under the steaming hot water for as long as I could bear it, before I started soaping the dried blood off my unbroken skin. After a while, Molly got in and joined me.

I'll say this—Molly's breasts have never been cleaner than when she showers with me. They positively glisten.

Afterwards, we got dressed in the clothes we'd arrived in. I think we'd both had enough of dressing to the Casino's standards. Now that we'd seen what the Casino was really like, we just wanted to look like ourselves. We stood together before the full-length mirror and looked ourselves over. We looked . . . pale, but determined. I put an arm across Molly's bare shoulders, and she slipped an arm round my waist. We both looked like we'd been through the mill, but it would still have been a brave or foolish man who would have gone up against the people I was seeing in the reflection.

"Do you still want to go on with this?" said Molly. "Are the games, and the mission, really worth all this? No one in your family can expect you to put yourself through such punishment. . . ."

"They don't," I said. "I do. We're stopping a war, and saving untold lives. Doing the right thing. It's always been important to me that now and again I take on a mission with no . . . ambiguities."

"Doesn't have to be us," said Molly. "Doesn't have to be you. Let somebody else do it, for once. Sir Parsifal would be only too happy to step in and take over."

"He'd only screw it up," I said. "He's honourable. He

wouldn't stand a chance against the kind of tricks they pull here. They'd take him to the cleaners."

"Then call in someone else from your family!"

"They're not here, and I am," I said. "By the time I could bring them up to speed, it would be too late. We can do this, Molly."

She smiled, and leaned her head on my shoulder. "You always were too ready to take the weight of the world on your shoulders."

"Someone has to," I said.

"But what he did to you . . ."

"Just makes me that much more determined to give some of it back," I said. I wasn't sure whether I was trying to convince her, or myself. I was strong and sound in body again, but I did wonder . . . whether some important part of me might still be broken. Whether my nerve . . . was everything it should be. Whether I might hesitate in the crunch. I couldn't have that. So, if the horse throws you, punch it in the head and get right back in the saddle again. And if the world hurts you, take the fight to the world.

"Come on," I said cheerfully. "Let's get this show back on the road. Lots to do, and lots of bad people to do it to. Call Frankie back in here."

Molly laughed, kissed me quickly, and went to the door, while I peered into the mirror and gave myself a stern look. Drood is as Drood does.

Frankie hurried in the moment Molly opened the door, and looked quickly around for me. He seemed openly shocked and taken aback to find me standing easily before him. He looked me up and down, then looked at Molly, and finally settled for a baffled shrug.

"You look better!" he said brightly to me. "Quite amazingly better . . . Just as well, you'll need to be strong, and I mean in tip-top shape, to go far in the Middle Games. You are ready to dive back into the Games?"

"Hell, yeah," said Molly. "Are the Games ready for us?"

Frankie winced. "Confidence is good, attitude is better, but overconfidence will get us all killed. In slow and lingering ways. They don't deal in money in the Middle Games; they deal in souls. You've proved yourselves worthy opponents in the Introductory Games, and that buys you entrance. You've earned major prestige and enough money that they'll take you seriously . . . and when they see how you've bounced back from the beating you took in the Pit, that will definitely help to impress all the right people, but . . . these are the Middle Games. Only Major Players, now. From this point on, it's all about how many souls you can bring to the table. And unfortunately, all you have to wager with is Molly's much-mortgaged soul. You lose that, on the wrong bet, and it's Games over."

"I've been thinking about that," I said. "I think it's time for a change in tactics. I've had enough of playing the Casino's games, by the Casino's rules. Where they have all the advantages."

"What do you have in mind?" said Molly. "Does it involve cheating, bad sportsmanship, and gratuitous violence?"

"Remember the little gift my uncle Jack gave us before we left home?" I said. "The thing in two parts? I say we use it to burgle Franklyn Parris' office, break open his safe, and steal every secret he has."

"Yes!" said Molly, punching the air. "Oh, Shaman, you always have the best ideas!"

"No! No! No!" said Frankie, waving his hands around frantically, and miming people listening.

"Relax," said Molly. "I already laid down a spell to garble our words to anyone who might be listening in. As far as any eavesdroppers are concerned, we're just sitting around singing show tunes."

"You can't be sure of that!" said Frankie. "And anyway, it is still a really, really bad idea! The Casino Security people have installed major security devices and weapons throughout the building, but especially on the penthouse floor, and in Parris' office. We are talking top-of-the-line, best-you-can-buy, magical and scientific defence systems, and any number of really nasty weapons!"

"Such as?" I said, interested.

"I don't know!" said Frankie. "They're secret! So secret none of the people I talked to know anything about them! That's how secret they are! And, they're backed up by Parris' personal security men, the Jackson Fifty-five. Remember them? Allowed and indeed actually encouraged to kill, maim, and dismember anyone they encounter who isn't where they're supposed to be!"

"Please," I said. "Remember who you're talking to. I have broken into places that don't actually exist, to steal things you can't even detect with human senses."

"It's true," said Molly. "I haven't seen them."

"That was when you had your armour," said Frankie, still looking around surreptitiously.

"I'm still a Drood," I said. "A trained field agent."

"And I'm still me," said Molly.

"I'm not sure which is scarier," I said.

Molly beamed at me. "Nicest thing you've ever said to me."

"Parris' safe is bound to contain all kinds of useful information," I said. "On the players, and the games. More than enough to move the odds in our favour."

"Cheat codes!" Molly said happily. "Hidden back doors, blackmail information on the other Players, maybe even passwords to circumvent these bloody annoying null zones!"

"The safe," said Frankie. "If there really is one in Parris' office, which has never been confirmed, is on the penthouse floor. That's dozens of stories above us! You'd have to defeat the defensive systems on each floor, one after another, all the way up. Which would take forever! And someone would be bound to notice!"

I looked at Molly. "Burgling the office is what my uncles Jack and James tried, back in the day. They thought it was a good idea."

"Didn't work out too well for them, though," said Molly, judiciously.

"So, I think we'd be better off trying a different approach," I said. "I say, start at the top. Break in through the roof of the hotel, and access the penthouse floor that way."

"Brilliant!" said Molly. "How do we get up to the roof?"

"Still working on that," I said.

"It does have the advantage of never having been tried before, to my knowledge," said Frankie.

"There you go, then," I said.

"That doesn't mean it can be done!" said Frankie.

"Watch us," said Molly.

"We are, after all, professionals," I said.

"How are you going to get up to the roof?" Frankie said loudly. "You don't have your armour to work miracles for you. The elevators are very heavily guarded, so Molly's magic won't work. Or were you perhaps planning to revitalise one of the dead Pteranodons, and fly up there?"

"Now you're just being silly," I said.

"He may not have his armour," said Molly, "but he still has me. And the elevators are far too obvious anyway. I could teleport us up there, once I've got my strength back. There can't be a null zone on the roof, or the hotel's magical protections wouldn't work there."

"No," said Frankie, very patiently, "but there are all kinds of nulls in the hotel, that could confuse your teleport, and send you somewhere else. And even if you could punch through the nulls, there are all sorts of protections in place on the roof, just to detect things like unauthorised teleports! You'd set off more alarms than World War III!"

"Keep the noise down, Frankie," I said. "I've got a headache. And, I have an idea. We need to talk with the Scarlet Lady."

"Oh, no," said Frankie, miserably.

We sent Frankie off to do loud and annoying things in public to hold the Casino Security's attention. Which he actually preferred to having to meet the Scarlet Lady again. Molly and I took the elevator down to the lobby. It played us orchestral versions of old Blue Öyster Cult standards, until Molly blew the speakers out. The moment we stepped out into the lobby, everyone there stopped talking and stopped what they were doing, to stare at me. Many of them openly took a double take, and there were wide eyes and dropped jaws everywhere I looked. Apparently no one had expected to see me reappear this soon, let alone so manifestly uninjured and undamaged. A few people actually applauded. Others surreptitiously made signs to ward off evil spirits. I smiled easily about me, and headed quickly for the side exit, Molly walking haughtily along beside me. We weren't in the mood to answer questions. Everyone hastily fell back, to give us plenty of room.

A private elevator on the far side of the lobby gave access to the underground car park. Exactly where Frankie had said it would be. The door said STAFF ONLY, but it opened easily to the access codes Frankie had provided. He really did know everyone on the hotel staff. An excellent example of the advantages to be found in good fellowship and generous bribes. The elevator descended rather longer than I was comfortable with, but eventually opened onto the private car park underneath the hotel. Just a large concrete cavern, with row upon row of parked cars, illuminated by harsh fluorescent overhead lighting. Molly and I had a good look round, before we ventured into the massive cavern.

"Where's the Security?" said Molly. "I don't see any Security people down here."

"Most of these cars can probably look after themselves," I said. "Frankie assured me there were only a few basic staff here, to raise the alarm if the automatic systems failed."

"This is a hell of a lot bigger than I expected," said Molly. "In fact, I would say this cavern is actually bigger than the hotel it's situated under. Look at all these cars! How are we going to find the Scarlet Lady in the midst of all this?"

She had a point. Parked cars stretched away in every direction. I didn't even know where to start looking.

"This is probably the result of bigger on the inside than it is on the outside tech," Molly said wisely. "Pretty much comes as standard in the Nightside these days. It's the only way they can pack everything in."

"I do wish you'd keep out of that place," I said. "You know I don't approve."

"That's why I do it," said Molly. "And anyway, you know you hate hen nights. Hey! I just noticed—there's no null zone down here! Not even a low-level one, like in our suite!"

"Presumably because it might disagree with some of the vehicles here," I said.

"I've spotted some basic security cameras," said Molly. "And spelled them not to notice us. As long as we don't hang around here too long."

"Then we'd better get a move on," I said.

I led the way through the maze of parked cars, being very careful not to touch anything, or even get too close to some of the more arcane vehicles. Depressingly, most of them were just the obvious muscle cars and restored classics. Typical cars of the super-rich and up-themselves celebrities. Overpriced, fancy, bought by people with more money than sense. Or style. A few really old makes that looked like they were held together by only faith and baling wire. And just a few seriously futuristic jobs, floating serenely in their parking spaces as though wheels were beneath them. But given the number of Major Players, there was nothing that really stood out. No pink Rolls-Royces, or Black Beauties. And no sign anywhere of the Scarlet Lady.

"Shouldn't there be chauffeurs lounging around?" I said vaguely. "Waiting to be called to bring the cars to their owners?"

"Hotel Security doesn't allow other people's staff to just hang around," said Molly. "I asked Frankie. All personal staff are holed up in their own rooms till the Games are over. The guests have to believe that everywhere in the hotel is secure, or they wouldn't come. Look at these cars . . . ugly, Technicolor monstrosities. Nothing here with a touch of character. Nothing worth stealing. Just, *Look at me! I'm expensive!* I feel like exploding the lot of them. Just on general principles."

"Let's finish the mission first," I said. "You can blow the whole hotel up once we're finished. I'll help."

"It's good when couples have interests in common," said Molly.

I dug out my cell phone, and dialled the Scarlet Lady's private number. Molly looked at me.

"The car has its own number?"

"Of course," I said. "Comes as standard, when my uncle Jack has worked on a car. Hello? Scarlet Lady! This is your lord and master!"

"You wish," said the car. "What do you want, big boy?"

"Sound your horn and flash your lights so we can find you," I said.

"I'm right behind you," said the car. "I've been watching you for ages."

She blasted her horn, and half a dozen rows down, there she was, the Plymouth Fury herself. Parked in her own little area of open space, with all the other cars packed up tightly together as though they were scared of her. Which was only common sense, really. I hurried over to join her, with Molly bringing up the rear and glancing suspiciously in every direction.

"I'm glad you've come down here," said the car. "It's so dull! Nothing to do, no one to talk to. Have you tried talking to a car? It's boring! These cars have no character, and no conversation. And the few hotel staff on duty down here won't come anywhere near me, after what I did to that uniformed twit who tried to park me."

"What did you do to him?" I said, resignedly.

The car giggled, a deep, dark, disturbing sound. "He was a real disappointment, in every department. So I chased him round the parking bays a few times and then out the back entrance. Last I saw, he was still running. Teach him to disappoint a lady."

"What are you, really?" I said.

"I'll never tell!" said the Scarlet Lady. "An old broad like me needs to keep a few secrets. But you wouldn't believe some of the things I can do. . . ."

"Can you fly?" I said, bluntly.

"Fly?" said the Scarlet Lady. "What makes you think I can fly? I'm a car!"

"I talked to my uncle Jack," I said.

"Oh, him." The car sniffed loudly. "Armourers should be like doctors—sworn to keep confidences. All right, yes, I can fly."

"Really?" said Molly. "As in, up into the wild blue yonder?"

"Yes! Really!" said the car. "I am marvellous and amazing and can do many things. Though not for long, my power coils aren't what they used to be."

"I'm not going to ask," I said.

"I wouldn't," said the car. "It would only upset you."

"Can you fly us all the way up to the top of the Casino building?" I said.

"Without being noticed," Molly added quickly.

"Oooh . . ." said the car. "I do love a challenge. . . . I would have to say: yes and no. Yes, I can quite definitely get you up there, but my stealth fields are no match for the Casino's security systems. I'd be bound to show up on their sensors."

"You get us up there," said Molly, "and I'll keep us from being noticed."

"Deal!" said the car. "When did you have in mind?"

"Right now," I said.

"Ah," said Molly. "In broad daylight?"

I looked at her. "Is that going to be a problem?"

Molly scowled, considering. "The cover of darkness would have made it easier. . . . Let me think. There are all kinds of null zones scattered throughout the building, of various strengths. So any spell I might cast could fail, at any time, without warning. So, time to get creative. And just a bit sneaky. Frankie told us the Casino has a whole bunch of telepaths down in the cellar, broadcasting *Don't Notice Anything Unusual* . . . I can tap into that, and wrap the field around the car. The null zones must be programmed not to override the denial broadcast."

"You're right," I said. "That is seriously sneaky. Go for it."

Molly gestured briefly, and the Scarlet Lady rocked back and forth. "Hey! That tickles! Kinda like it, though . . ."

"You are a deeply disturbing vehicle," I said.

"You don't know the half of it, big boy," said the car.

"Get in the car, Shaman," said Molly. "There's no telling how long my override patch will last and somebody notices something."

I got in behind the wheel, Molly took shotgun, and the Scarlet Lady drove quietly through the underground car park, careful not to draw any attention from the few hotel staff, who weren't supposed to notice us any more. Once outside, the car roared back up the entrance road, putting some distance between us and the hotel. *So I can get a good run at it,* said the car, when I was unwise enough to ask. An answer which to my mind did not actually inspire confidence. She finally slowed, spun round to face the hotel building again, and then accelerated for all she was worth. We slammed down the road, faster and faster, our surroundings a blur, while Molly whooped happily. The hotel grew larger and larger before us, and I couldn't help but notice that for all our impressive speed, we weren't actually leaving the ground.

"Going up, soon, would be good," I said. "On the grounds that the hotel is getting really very near. Going up, really soon now, would be a really good idea! Go up! Up!"

"Front-seat driver," said the car, dismissively. "Atomic batteries to power, turbines to speed, Thunderbirds Are Go!"

The car's crimson and white bonnet rose up abruptly, and the car leapt into the air, leaving the road behind. Sheer acceleration forced Molly and me back into our seats. The great curving front of the Casino building loomed before us, but the car's bonnet kept rising until suddenly we were flying vertically parallel to the hotel front, whipping past the windows so fast they were just one long gleaming blur. The Scarlet Lady laughed loudly, blatting her horn triumphantly.

Molly laughed along with her, beating both hands on the dashboard in a sharp paradiddle.

Sometimes I think I'm the only sane one on these missions.

"Pardon me," I said to the car, "but I can't help noticing . . . we seem to be slowing. As in, not going nearly as fast as we were. Are you running out of power? Are we actually going to reach the top of this building? Do I really want to know the answers to these questions?"

"Let's all try to be optimistic," said the car. "Think happy thoughts."

"Are there any parachutes in this car?" said Molly.

"Safety features are for wimps," said the Scarlet Lady.

She shot over the top of the hotel, and the bonnet came down sharply. All four wheels hit the roof at once, and there was a loud squeal of brakes as we hurtled towards the far side of the roof. I gripped on to the steering wheel with both hands, for comfort's sake, while the deceleration pressed me back into my seat again. Black smoke spilled out from under the rear arches as we slowed and slowed, along with a hellish stink of burning rubber, until finally we slammed to a halt just a few feet short of the far edge. Molly and I bounced back and forth in our seats, and then slumped with relief. The Scarlet Lady engaged reverse, and moved us back a few yards from the edge of the roof.

"There you are!" she said. "Told you I could do it! Never doubted I could! Not for a moment. Now for the bad news. I don't have enough energy left to fly us back down again."

"Now you tell us?" said Molly.

"Be fair," said the car. "You didn't ask. Nice view, isn't it?"

"I am going to have my uncle Jack reprogramme your personality with a sledgehammer," I said. "Now, Molly and I have work to do. You, stay."

"I love it when you're all masterful," said the car.

I got out of the car, slamming the door with more than necessary violence, and looked around. The hotel roof was flat and wide and open, with no one about. A cold wind whipped across the roof, ruffling my hair and tugging at my clothes. Molly came forward to join me.

"Are we still protected by your distraction field?" I said to Molly.

She shrugged, quickly. "It's not an exact science. As long as we stay reasonably close to the car, probably."

I walked over to the edge of the roof and looked down. It was a really long steep drop to the ground far below. I started to feel a bit dizzy, so I made myself keep looking until the feeling went away. Molly came and stood beside me. The drop didn't seem to bother her at all.

"So, here we are," she said brightly. "Part One of our Really Desperate Plan has been achieved. Really looking forward to seeing what Part Two might consist of."

"Look at that drop," I said. "I can't believe Uncle Jack and Uncle James just jumped off here, and trusted to their handholds on the building to slow them down. I wouldn't like to try it even now, with Ethel's improved armour."

"Which you haven't got," said Molly. "And, I think we should at least consider the possibility that your uncle Jack might have been exaggerating, just a bit."

"Hard to tell, given all the things he really did do back in the day," I said.

"If they really did do it, you can bet good money that there are security options in place now, to make sure no one ever does it again," said Molly.

"Can you See any hidden security systems up here?" I said.

She looked around. "No. Nothing. Which is . . . odd. You'd expect *something* . . . if only to dissuade people like us."

"There are no people like us," I said firmly.

Molly stamped her foot on the roof a few times. "Seems solid enough. How are you planning to get down into the penthouse floor without the use of major explosives, which I don't happen to have about me?"

"There's a trapdoor," I said, pointing. "But that's far too easy, and far too obvious. Bound to be alarmed."

"Agreed," said Molly.

I looked back over the edge of the roof. "I was always very good at climbing," I said. "I used to climb around the exterior of Drood Hall all the time, when I was a kid. So I could get to all the places I wasn't supposed to go."

Molly grinned. "Like the girls' dormitory, after lights out?"

"No," I said. "I've always been the shy and retiring type."

"I have noticed," said Molly.

I lowered myself onto one knee and studied the exterior face of the hotel, with all its sweeping curves. There was a cold hard knot in my stomach.

"You want to climb down *that*?" said Molly. "Are you sure about this?"

"Absolutely," I said. "But feel free to try to talk me out of it."

I swung down over the edge before she could say anything. I needed to do it to prove to myself that I was physically fit and fine again . . . and that my nerve was everything it should be. I couldn't go through life hesitating and worrying, armour or no armour. I was a field agent, and that was all that mattered. I grabbed tightly on to every extruding curve, and forced my feet into every place where one rounded design met another. And step by step, foot by foot, I lowered myself down the side of the building. It was a lot harder than I remembered from my youth, but then, I'd been a lot smaller and lighter in those days. And, I'd had my armour. And, the drop had only been a few stories. I didn't look down, just concentrated on finding new foot- and handholds. The cold wind whipped around me, blowing my hair in my eyes and tugging peevishly at my clothes. Trying to pull me away from the hotel face, and throw me down. I pressed myself as flat against the building as I could, and kept going.

No armour to protect me, nothing to depend on but my own strength and skill. I grinned to myself. I was going to have to do this, anyway, so I might as well enjoy it.

A line of closed and apparently secure windows

stretched across the building, marking my arrival at the penthouse floor. The glass was opaque everywhere, so that Parris and his kind could look out on the world, but the world couldn't see them. Which meant I had no way of knowing whether there was anyone home, and maybe watching me. I would have shrugged, but it didn't seem like a good idea. I lodged my feet carefully, and tested the frame of the window with my fingertips. No obvious locks or hinges, or anything I could get a grip on. I could have smashed my way in with an armoured fist, or broken the seal with armoured filaments, but now . . . I was still considering the problem when I realised Molly was standing beside me, hovering in mid-air. I looked at her for a long moment.

"What?" she said. "You didn't ask. I could have carried you down, if you'd asked."

"I have my dignity," I said.

"Don't touch the glass itself," Molly said briskly. "It's alarmed. I can See the protections. Major-league stuff, too. Expensive."

"Give me your half of the Armourer's lock-breaker," I said.

I fished out my half, being very careful with every move I made. Molly handed over her half. The two pieces fitted easily together, clicking into place to form one smooth black square. No obvious controls, or protrusions, so I just pressed the thing carefully against the frame of the window. And the window opened, swinging smoothly outwards.

The solid glass pushed me away from the building with a firm, remorseless pressure, forcing me backwards. My feet scuffed and slipped on the curved surfaces, and I scrabbled helplessly for a hold on the smooth window frame. I'd just started to fall backwards when Molly grabbed me from behind.

"I can carry you in," she said. "Or you can embrace your dignity, all the way to the ground."

"Carry me," I said.

Molly flew me in through the open window. I snatched the lock-breaker at the last moment, and the window swung smoothly shut behind us.

Inside, it was at least a fair bit warmer, away from the cold wind. Molly placed me carefully on my feet, and I nodded my thanks. A quick look around suggested we'd hit pay dirt first time out. We were inside a massive, sprawling office, packed with every luxury and comfort.

"I love it when a plan comes together," I said.

"I love it when pure blind luck hands us a free pass," said Molly. "You really should have left the window open in case we need to make a sudden exit."

"You've done this before," I said.

"I did have a life, before I met you," said Molly.

"I know," I said. "I try not to think about it."

We both moved cautiously around what I very much hoped was Franklyn Parris' office, careful to touch nothing. Very plush, very comfortable, thick carpeting, paintings on the walls. But somehow, still impersonal. No character, no individual touches. Just a place to work. Molly studied the paintings carefully, and then sniffed loudly.

"Bought by the yard," she said. "Ordered out of a catalogue, to look good. No taste, or design. Just there to impress the visitors. And I can tell you for a fact, that Dalí there is a fake. I stole the original years ago."

"That was you?" I said. "I'm impressed. But the paintings are just that little bit too obvious, to hide a safe behind. Keep looking."

I moved over to the large and impressive office desk, just bursting with all kinds of futuristic tech. I hadn't even got within arm's reach when Molly spun round and yelled at me.

"Stop! Don't move! Don't even breathe heavily! I'm sensing alarms everywhere!"

I froze where I was. "Have I activated anything? Am I in any danger? Should I start running?"

"You activated a whole bunch of silent alarms and

weapons systems just by getting too close to the desk," said Molly.

"Weapons *systems*?"

"Relax! I shut them all down the moment I sensed them coming online. They keep trying to turn themselves back on . . . but I think I've got control now."

"Can I move yet?"

"As long as you're careful," said Molly. "I don't trust this office. It's hiding things from me. . . ."

"This would be so much easier if I still had my armour," I said.

"You don't need your armour," said Molly. "You've got me."

She strode over to the desk while I was still unclenching my muscles, and kicked it a few times, thoughtfully. She sank into the very comfortable swivel chair, bounced up and down a few times, and then spun round and round in it, laughing happily. Two steel clamps sprang out of the chair's arms, and snapped around her wrists, holding her in place. I tried not to laugh. Molly spat out a Word, and the metal clamps exploded off her. Molly surged to her feet, turned on the chair, and tore it apart, throwing the pieces every which way. She finally stopped, breathing heavily, and glared at me.

"I have nothing to say," I said quickly. "Not a word."

We moved around the office, inspecting everything thoroughly, while being extremely careful not to touch anything. No trace of a hidden safe, or a hidden anything, anywhere. We went back to the desk, and considered it again. Molly gestured at the desk drawers, and they all popped open, one at a time. Molly leaned over, and peered into them. I knelt down, and looked under the desk. And that was when I spotted that one particular square of the fitted carpet that looked just a little bit more worn and used than the others. I gestured to Molly, and she came and knelt down beside me. She frowned at the carpet square, while I wished impatiently for the Sight my armour used to give me. She shook her head quickly.

"No alarms, no sensors, but there's something off here . . . as though I'm not being allowed to See something."

I took a cautious hold of the edge of the carpet square, and peeled it back a few inches at a time. We were both tense, ready to jump back at a moment's notice. And then, finally, with the carpet out of the way, I could see the steel safe set square into the floor. I smiled triumphantly at Molly.

"Beginner's luck," she said, loftily.

I examined the safe carefully. Gleaming steel, a high-tech combination lock, very impressive. Molly whistled, impressed.

"That . . . is a Hockler-Strauss safe. Most expensive on the market, most complicated locking system, absolutely no way of opening it without a whole lot of really expensive equipment, which I don't happen to have with me at the moment."

I grinned, and held up the Armourer's lock-breaker. "Never leave home without one. Thank you, Uncle Jack."

"That's cheating," said Molly.

"We're spies," I said.

I set the lock-breaker on the steel surface, right next to the combination lock, and the locking system made a number of really upset noises as the numbers spun madly round. There was the sound of inner bolts drawing back, and then the door to the safe clunked open. I grabbed the handle and pulled the door all the way open, leaning it back on the thickly carpeted floor. Molly and I both leaned forward eagerly to peer inside. The safe was empty, apart from a single piece of paper. I reached in and took it out.

The note said: *Nice try. By opening this safe you have set off a silent alarm that cannot be countermanded or shut down. Better luck in your next reincarnation.*

"Oh, shit," said Molly. "I hate it when they think they have a sense of humour."

I tossed the paper back into the safe, and slammed the door shut. "Is there really a silent alarm? Can you tell?"

"I can now," said Molly.

"Run," I said.

Heavy reinforced steel shutters slammed down, covering all the windows and the only door.

"Run where?" said Molly. "We're sealed in! Listen . . . can you hear that? Can you hear running feet in the outer corridor, heading our way?"

"No," I said. "But I'm ready to take your word for it. Can you teleport us out of here? Just as far as the roof?"

"We're in a major null zone," said Molly. "It slammed down the moment the alarm went off. I could probably push some minor magics through it, if I really had to, but that's all. Eddie, we can't afford to be caught here."

"I know," I said.

"I mean, we really can't afford to be caught and identified, Eddie! They won't just kill us, they'll make an example of us!"

"I know!" I said.

"Well, don't just stand there—think of something!"

"It would be easier to think if you weren't yelling at me! You know, for an ex-professional burglar, you don't half panic easily."

I drew my Colt Repeater, called for heavy-duty incendiary bullets, and opened fire on the shutter covering the window we came in through. And then Molly and I both had to drop to our knees and duck and cover behind the desk, as the blazing bullets ricocheted back at us, unable to penetrate the reinforced shutter. Several small fires started up, as the bullets set fire to some of the furniture and parts of the carpet. And then the sprinklers kicked in, covering the whole office. The fires were put out, and Molly and I got drenched. She glared at me.

"Wonderful. You have actually managed to make the situation worse. I'm soaked!"

"Have you got a better idea?" I said, putting the gun away. "Because I'm perfectly willing to listen to one. Can't you at least turn the sprinklers off?"

"Which part of *major null* are you having trouble understanding? Do something! The security systems are all putting themselves back online!"

I took out my cell phone and called the Scarlet Lady.

"What do you want?" said the car. "I'm busy having a perfectly lovely time shooting down pigeons."

"The brown smelly stuff has hit the fan!" I said. "It's all gone horribly wrong, and we're trapped inside the penthouse floor. Can you do anything to help?"

"Oh, sure!" said the car. "I still can't fly you down . . . but, if you can get out a window, there is something I could try. . . ."

"Do it!" I said. "Whatever it is, do it. I'm sure it's a perfectly reasonable plan, and I love it to death. Now get moving!"

"People are always in such a hurry," said the car.

I put the phone away, just as Molly's head came up sharply.

"Weapons systems are back online!"

"Shut them down again!" I said.

"I'm trying!"

Energy guns appeared in the ceiling above us, and beams of sharp dazzling light stabbed down, shooting holes through the furniture. Molly and I threw ourselves underneath the desk, figuring Parris wouldn't let his defence systems shoot up his special desk. The energy beams got as close as they could, blasting holes through the floor and setting fire to the expensive carpeting. The sprinklers went into overdrive, and then shut down one by one as they ran out of water. That was something.

I reached up around the desk, and attached the lockbreaker to the side of the desk computer. It immediately turned itself on, and the monitor obligingly opened up all its files to me. I cautiously raised my head enough to see what I was doing, found the file responsible for the weapons systems, and shut them down. All the energy beams snapped off. Molly and I emerged cautiously from behind the desk. The air was very still, and smelt strongly of ozone.

"I was almost there," said Molly.

And then we both looked round, as we heard heavy footsteps outside the office door. They stopped abruptly, there was a pause, and then I could just make out agitated voices arguing about how were they supposed to get in when the lowered shutter had closed off the only door. There then followed a certain amount of arguing and raised voices, over who was going to have to go back and get the cancellation codes to raise the shutters.

I grinned at Molly. "Okay, that buys us some time."

"To do what?" said Molly. "All right, stop grinning; you've had an idea. Show me."

I hurried over to the shutter covering the window we'd come in through, and slapped the lock-breaker against the window frame. The lock-breaker overrode the locking system, and the shutter rolled up. Fresh sunlight spilled into the room. I opened the window, and looked out. And there was the Scarlet Lady, parked in place next to the window.

"Just enough power left to cling to the wall!" she said cheerfully. "Sort of anti-antigravity. Don't ask me to explain, I'm just a car. Get in while it's still working, whatever it is."

Molly and I scrambled out through the window. The car opened her doors, I threw myself into the front, and Molly scrambled into the back seat. The doors slammed shut, and I hauled myself sideways into the driving seat.

"Go! Go! Go!" I said.

The Scarlet Lady shot off down the side of the building, as easily as if she was driving down a somewhat bumpy road, accelerating all the way. Floor after floor shot past us, and the ground came flying up towards us.

"Keep going!" Molly yelled from the back. "I'm out of the null, and pumping out *Don't Look At Us!* at full volume!"

We roared down the side of the building, the passing windows just a gleaming blur.

"Tell me you've got a plan!" I said loudly to the car. "Tell me you've got a very specific plan about what to do when we hit the ground! Preferably something that doesn't involve actually hitting the ground!"

"Of course!" said the Scarlet Lady. "I am known for my plans! Hang on, you're going to love this!"

And at the very last moment, with the ground leaping up to smash the car right in the radiator grille, the Scarlet Lady's bonnet rose up and leapt away from the building. She revved her engine for all it was worth, and we flew away from the wall and out onto the road. All four wheels hit hard, and we rocked back and forth before straightening out and heading off down the road.

"Let us all praise self-regenerating power coils!" said the Scarlet Lady, cackling loudly. "And just enough power for a last-minute save!"

I sat slumped in my seat, trying to get my breath back. "I am going to rip off your bumpers and piss in your petrol tank," I said, eventually.

"Get in line," Molly said feebly, from the back seat.

"Humans don't know how to have fun," said the car.

CHAPTER SEVEN

Mind Games, and Others

The Scarlet Lady drove us back to the hotel. Molly and I sat slumped in our seats, getting our second wind back. A successful mission fills you with pride and adrenalin, and it's champagne all round and party till dawn. A complete balls-up, on the other hand, takes all the energy out of you, until all you really want to do is go to sleep and forget all about it. Molly and I didn't have that luxury. The overall mission wasn't even half over, and we still had the Medium Games ahead of us. Still, even though breaking into Parris' safe hadn't provided us with anything useful, I was glad I'd done it. Because it proved I didn't need Drood armour to act like a field agent. And, that I could still take calculated risks without my armour to protect me. I mentioned this to Molly but she wasn't in the mood to see the funny side, just yet. She was still glaring at me. I was still pretending not to notice. Of such helpful compromises are successful marriages made. The Scarlet Lady dropped us off outside the main hotel entrance, and we left her to find her own way back to the underground car park.

"There's enough of my denial field still clinging to you,

that no one will notice your return," said Molly. "In fact, they shouldn't even have noticed you've been gone."

"Like I care," said the car. "Anyone down there even looks at me wrong, I'll run them over and park on them."

"I wish you were even a little bit joking," I said. "The whole point of a secret agent, and their car, is not to be noticed."

"I do not do the modesty thing," said the car. "I prefer to intimidate people with my magnificence."

"Well, that's one way of putting it," said Molly.

"I heard that!" said the car. "See you later. If you should happen to get into trouble again . . . feel free not to call me. I shall be terribly busy, indulging in some serious me time."

And she sped off, revving her engine unnecessarily. Molly and I looked at each other, considered saying many things, and then just gave up and headed for the main entrance. Before we could even venture inside the lobby, Frankie came running out the doors to intercept us. He looked flustered and alarmed and not at all happy. He slammed to a halt before us, paused a moment to get his breath back, and then glared accusingly from me to Molly and then back again.

"Where have you been?" he said, just a bit hysterically. "What have you been doing?"

"You don't even want to know what we've just been through," I said. "I was there, and I don't want to know."

"What are you so upset about, Frankie?" said Molly. "Did one of your bribes run out at an awkward moment?"

"All hell's breaking loose in the Casino," said Frankie. "Alarms going off everywhere, more sirens and flashing lights than the civilised mind can cope with, and a general security clampdown. You need to get back in the lobby before they seal off the hotel completely!"

"Then what are you doing keeping us hanging around here?" I said. "Holding us up with unnecessary explanations? Really, Frankie, you are letting the side down. . . ."

"Very unprofessional," said Molly.

We strode past him, through the doors and into the lobby. Frankie followed close behind, growling under his breath. Inside, the lobby was packed full of all kinds of people, from legitimate players to obvious hangers-on, all of them milling around and chattering loudly, forming into small groups and then breaking up again, as they tried to find someone who knew what the hell was going on. Though with everyone clamouring at the top of their voices, it was a wonder any of them could hear what anyone was saying. There was a definite feeling of unease on the air, and more than a hint of hysteria.

Someone had misbehaved, that was clear, and punishments were in the offing. There was so much commotion no one even noticed Molly and me returning, along with a seething Frankie. But we'd barely got inside the door when the hotel manager, Jonathon Scott, came striding into the lobby, accompanied by half a dozen large and muscular gentlemen, carrying machine pistols at the ready. Scott looked coldly furious, and his muscle men looked coldly professional. And just like that, everyone in the lobby shut the hell up to watch Scott's every move with wide, watchful eyes, like frightened children.

The men with Scott all looked exactly the same. Big black men in quasi-military uniforms. With exactly the same face. I didn't have to be told who they were; that I was finally getting a clear look at living examples of the legendary Jackson Fifty-five. Their dark scowling faces all showed exactly the same expression of practised intimidation, and they all moved in the same way, with an eerie synchronicity. They spread out across the lobby, covering the crowd with their guns. Some people took one look at the infamous mercenary soldiers and ran, heading for the nearest exits, but still more Jacksons appeared, spilling out of every door and exit with guns at the ready, to herd everyone back again. They didn't say anything; they didn't have to. A sense of imminent danger hung heavily on the air—a feeling of blood and death ready to happen at any moment.

I looked carefully around me. All the ways out of the lobby were very thoroughly blocked off. If Scott should order the Jacksons to open fire, it would be a massacre.

"They don't look that tough," said Molly.

"But they are," said Frankie. "Please don't start anything."

"Is there a null operating?" I said quietly to Molly.

"Oh, like you wouldn't believe," she said. "Major null. I couldn't produce a bunny out of a top hat."

"Then let's not start anything, just yet," I said.

"What do we do if they open fire?" said Molly.

"Hit the floor first, and hide under the bodies," I said.

"What if they fire through the bodies, to make sure?" said Frankie.

"Well, hopefully by then I will have thought of something else," I said.

One of the Jacksons noticed we were still talking, and came forward to glare at us. Molly and I moved to stand close together, and regarded the Jackson thoughtfully. He stopped, and looked at us. He'd been a soldier for many years, you could see it in his movements and in the way he held himself, and he knew a real threat when he saw one. I could tell just from looking at him that he'd seen pretty much everything bad the world had to offer, and that he hadn't got where he was today by taking unnecessary risks. He gave us his best scowl, checked we weren't obviously armed, and decided he was as close to us as he needed to be.

"Pay attention!" said Scott, into the silence of the lobby. He didn't sound like a manager, all calm and patient and dedicated to the comfort of his guests; he sounded like a man who served Casino Infernale. "I regret to say . . . that there has been a major breach in hotel security. Someone has betrayed the trust placed on you, as guests. Someone has broken into Franklyn Parris' private office."

A short anticipatory murmur ran through the crowd at the name of the man in charge of the Games, but it was quickly shut down by threatening looks and movements from the Jacksons. Everyone looked quickly at everyone else, in search of a culprit. But since everyone there looked equally suspicious, and equally guilty, that didn't really help much. There was also a certain look of admiration on many faces—that anyone had dared take on the man in charge. Of such things are reputations made. Frankie looked at Molly with something very like horror.

"How close did you come to getting caught?" he said, very quietly.

"Shut up," said Molly. And she stamped on his foot, hard.

"Mr. Parris is extremely annoyed at having his privacy invaded," said Scott. "He has therefore authorised me to punish someone. Since we cannot know who the guilty party is, and it seems unlikely that they will do the decent thing and own up, I have decided that someone will be punished . . . right here. Right now. Someone chosen entirely at random. To make the point that no one defies the rules at Casino Infernale."

Scott produced a gun from inside his jacket. A simple, brutal handgun. Another quick murmur rose and fell, as the crowd realised they were going to see someone die. That Scott was just going to pick one of them, and shoot them dead. Just to make a point. Some of those present looked quite excited at the prospect. Scott moved forward, and everyone fell back before him. The manager swept his gun back and forth, quite unhurriedly, his cold gaze moving almost impartially over the people packed together before him. Here and there, men and women tried to back away, but either the people behind them wouldn't let them, or there were armed Jacksons in place to prevent them. Scott paused before one man, who made a high-pitched hysterical sound, and then dissolved immediately into a tower of water that splashed to the lobby floor and ran away.

"Now that's what I call nerves," said Molly. "He wet himself."

There was a sudden burst of nervous laughter, but it

didn't last long, in the face of so much tension and a very real threat. Scott was still pressing forward, moving his gun back and forth, taking his time, savouring the moment. The Jacksons were still standing solidly in place, making sure no one got away. Men and women flinched and clutched at each other as the gun targeted them. Some cried out, involuntarily. A few begged and pleaded shamelessly until the gun moved on, and then they cried bitter tears of relief and self-disgust. Some tried to hide behind other people, who fought them savagely off. Scott looked at me. I stepped forward, to put myself between him and Molly. I didn't think about it; just did it automatically. Molly quickly shouldered past me, to stand between me and the gun, shooting me an angry glance to remind me that I didn't have my armour's protection any more. That honestly hadn't occurred to me. I glared at Scott. I didn't know what I'd do if he settled on Molly, but I knew I'd do something. Frankie hid behind both of us. And Scott and the gun moved on, leaving us behind.

Someone was about to die, because of something Molly and I had done, but I didn't even consider confessing. Partly because I still had a war to stop, and partly because just by being here, at Casino Infernale, all of these people were guilty of something. I'm not normally that cold, or at least I like to think not, but these people deserved everything that happened to them.

And then Scott suddenly raised his gun and shot a man in the head. Quite neatly and proficiently, straight between the eyes. The man's head jerked back, as blood and brains spattered the faces of the people behind him. They cried out in shock, but they didn't say anything. The man crumpled bonelessly to the floor, his face blank and empty. He hadn't even had enough time to look surprised before he was dead. Silence lay heavily across the lobby. Some people looked angrily at Scott, some looked relieved, but nobody looked shocked. This was Casino Infernale, after all. You had to expect things like this. Sudden death. Unfair death. It was part of why people came. Scott nodded briefly, satisfied, and put his gun away. He gathered up the Jacksons with his eyes, and led them out of the lobby.

Everyone else relaxed, and started talking again. Chattering loudly and excitedly, laughing nervously, speculating wildly on what might have been behind what just happened. If anyone there knew the dead man, no one was admitting to it. They all stayed well back, giving the body plenty of room. Quiet uniformed staff came forward, bearing a stretcher, and removed the body with casual ease. They had clearly had to do it before.

"Who was that?" said Molly, to Frankie. "Who was it who just died?"

"No one important," he said, coming out from behind us now the danger was over.

"How can you be sure?" I said.

"Because if it had been someone important," Frankie said patiently, "I would have known them. Mr. Scott chose his target very carefully, and not at all at random. He couldn't afford to kill a Major Player, or even a potential Major Player, because of all the money and prestige such people bring to the Games. And, because you can't kill a Major Player that easily with just a gun, even inside a major null. They always have some hidden protections. No, Scott had to kill someone, for the pride of the hotel, and Franklyn Parris, so he chose a nobody. Someone whose death wouldn't matter. He was just making a point, after all."

"I really don't like this place," said Molly. "Such small evils, such petty malice. I'd expected something more . . . romantic, from a big operation like Casino Infernale. Tragic betrayals, major reverses, souls lost and won on the flip of a coin . . ."

"Please," said Frankie, "it's just a business." He paused to look at us both accusingly. "Did you really . . . ?"

"Yes!" said Molly. "Of course we did! We told you we were going to!"

"I didn't think you'd really do it!" said Frankie. "And I

certainly didn't believe you'd actually be able to get into his office!"

"Bit of a failure, there," I said. "We cracked his safe, but there wasn't anything useful in it. Parris knew we were coming. Just like before . . ."

"What?" said Frankie.

"Never you mind," said Molly. "The point is, Parris knew someone was coming. I don't think he suspects us, personally, especially since I dried us out from the sprinklers; because if he did he'd have had all fifty-five of the Jacksons open fire on us the moment we reappeared. Take us out while we weren't expecting it."

"That might even have worked," I said.

"Please," Frankie said pleadingly. "No more burglaries. They're bad for my nerves."

"Didn't do mine any good," I said.

"The Medium Games are already under way," said Frankie. "You need to make yourselves known there, while there's still time."

"Why are they called the Medium Games?" Molly said innocently. "Is it because if you lose, you can only complain through a medium?"

"You worry me," said Frankie.

He led us over to the elevators, nursing a grim silence like a reprimand. We rose slowly through the hotel, and stopped at the fiftieth floor. The doors opened onto a really long corridor, stretching away before us into the far distance. There were no doors leading off, no side turnings, just the corridor, heading far and far away. Frankie raised his head and squared his shoulders, and set off. Molly and I went after him. And it was only then that I realised both walls of the corridor were lined with faces.

Hundreds, maybe even thousands, of living faces staring out of simple wooden frames. Held in place behind polished glass, staring out at the world with knowing, horrified eyes. Their mouths moved with words I couldn't hear. Young and old, all races; just faces now, trapped behind glass. No children. I don't think I could have stood it, if there had been children. The faces watched us pass, with helpless eyes. Like so many insects pinned on a collector's board, still endlessly suffering. So many trophies of Casino Infernale. I looked hard, but I didn't recognise anyone. I think a few might have recognised me.

"Are these . . . ?" I said, finally.

"Yes," said Frankie, striding along, staring carefully straight ahead. "These are the gamblers who lost their lives and their souls to Casino Infernale."

"Are they in Hell?" said Molly.

"Might as well be," said Frankie. "This is what happens when the Casino makes good its claim on your soul."

"What does the Casino want all these souls for?" I said.

"There are a great many theories about that," said Frankie. "Though of course the Casino, and the Shadow Bank, and whoever's behind them, aren't talking. The most common belief is that souls are currency, in the Great Game between Heaven and Hell. And that the Shadow Bank can trade in the souls it owns, to make deals with Above and Below. Don't ask me what kind of deals; the general feeling is it doesn't bear thinking about."

"I have seen similar faces, trapped under glass, in Crow Lee's country house," I said. "After he was dead, I set them free."

"But they were still alive," said Molly.

Frankie paused to look back at both of us. "You really did kill Crow Lee. The Most Evil Man In The World. Damn . . ."

"I am not leaving these people like this," I said. There was a cold anger in my voice, and Frankie flinched away from it. "I will free all these people before I leave Casino Infernale. I don't care who they were, or what they might have done, this is just wrong."

"You didn't mind standing by while Scott shot a man for something you did," said Frankie.

"I couldn't save him," I said. "I couldn't do anything, then. I can do something here. And I will."

"Don't make promises you can't keep," said Frankie. "You never know who might be listening. These souls . . . are spoken for."

"Like yours?" said Molly.

"I'm not going to talk about that," said Frankie. "Let's just say I don't think you need to worry about ever seeing my face here."

"I will free these people," I said. "Even if I have to bring my whole family here to help me do it."

"Of course you will," said Molly. "That's what you do."

"You worry me," said Frankie.

We walked on down the corridor for some time, for a lot farther than should have been possible inside the hotel. More and more faces watched us pass, silently pleading. I didn't make eye contact. It was the only way to cope. And finally a door loomed up before us, blocking off the end of the corridor. Molly leaned in close beside me.

"We're being scanned," she said quietly. "Act natural."

"I wouldn't know how," I said.

The door was so big we could see it long before we got anywhere near. Just a huge steel slab, with no obvious handle or hinges, or details. As we finally drew near, two over-sized thugs in formal clothes appeared out of nowhere to block our way. They stood before the steel door, looking us over, arms folded tightly across their massive chests, daring and defying us to get past them.

"Keep walking," Frankie murmured, while falling casually back to allow Molly and me to take the lead. "Show no weakness; they can smell fear."

I headed straight for them, smiling widely. I'd faced down club bouncers before, in parts of London that would have scared the crap out of all fifty-five Jacksons. I let my hands close slowly into fists. I was just in the mood to hit someone who needed hitting. And they looked like they qualified. Molly leaned forward, grinning nastily. The two Security thugs held their post till the very last moment and then stepped aside. The door slid sideways, disappearing into the left-hand wall, and Molly and Frankie and I strode straight through.

"It's all about confidence," said Frankie. "And brass nerve. If you haven't got those, you don't belong in the Medium Games anyway."

"We've never been short of either," I said, and Molly nodded solemnly.

As we actually passed through the open doorway, Molly's head came up sharply.

"This is a dimensional door," she said. "Like the one we used earlier today. It could be taking us anywhere. Anywhere at all."

"Of course," said Frankie. "The Medium Games are far too dangerous, and too private, to take place inside the hotel building."

And then we all stopped walking as we realised we'd arrived somewhere new. I looked back, and there was no sign of the steel door, or the corridor, or the hotel. We were standing on the top of a small grassy hill, with wide grassy plains all around. Down below us lay an Arena—an open circle of stony ground, surrounded by row upon row of circular stone seating, in raked ranks. Like . . . a miniature Colosseum. The stone looked old and beaten and worndown. As though it had been here, and much used, for some time. No seats, just low stone walls, so people could sit on them and watch what was happening in the Arena, right in front of them. There were already some people in place, in strikingly modern clothes, sitting and waiting patiently, while others wandered back and forth between the raked rows, talking animatedly. No one went anywhere near the open circle at the centre.

The dying ground.

"Okay," said Molly, after a while. "I am thinking gladiators, and not in a good way. And, I'm picking up another major null operating here. Covering everywhere, except for the circle in the middle of the Arena."

"Exactly," said Frankie. "No magics or psychic influence possible anywhere, except on the fighting ground. So the audience can be sure no one can cheat or interfere in the Games."

Molly gave me a hard look. "You are not Pit fighting again. I had a hard enough job putting you back together again last time."

"I would rather avoid that, if possible," I said. "I don't like what that kind of Game brings out in me." And then I stopped, as something caught my eye. "Hold everything, people, and look up."

We all looked up. At a night sky full of unfamiliar constellations. Stars burned fiercely, in all the colours of the rainbow, and three huge moons glowed bitter yellow against the dark. It was actually disturbing, to suddenly see a night sky so different from the one I was used to. It felt as though someone had ripped the world out from under my feet, while I wasn't looking. I glared about me. It all seemed bright as day. I looked down, at the ground. The grass beneath my feet had a definite purple tinge to it, among the dark green.

"Those aren't our stars," said Molly. "We're not in Nantes any more, Toto."

"Just how much power does the Casino have?" I said. "To power a dimensional door like that? To transport us to a whole new world just to play Games?"

"Why do you keep asking me questions, when you must know by now that I'm not going to be able to answer?" said Frankie. "No! I don't know where we are! No, I don't know how we got here, or how they do it. For all I know it's all done with mirrors. The important thing for both of you to concentrate on is that the only way for us to get back is for you to win at the Games."

"And win big," said Molly.

"Well, obviously," said Frankie. "That is why we're here."

He led us down the hill to the Arena, and the purple-green grass crunched dryly under our feet. Rows of stalls had been set up around the outer perimeter, offering complimentary champagne and mulled wine, along with the usual assortment of civilised nibbles. All taste and no substance, but absolutely guaranteed to be packed full of everything that was bad for you. I walked straight past the stalls, dragging Molly along with me when she showed signs of being tempted. My gaze was fixed on the Arena. There was something about the bare, brutal sensibilities of that open stone circle, surrounded by open stone seating, that made it seem just as brutal as the Pit. A very old game, and a very old spectacle, designed to appeal to our most basic emotions. To bring out the beast in us.

Frankie strayed towards one of the stalls, and I grabbed him by the arm and hauled him back again.

"Hey!" said Frankie, not actually fighting me. "I could use a little something for the inner man! I have been on the go all day. . . ."

"Never trust goblin food," I said.

Frankie looked at Molly. "What?"

"You can never tell where goblin fruit has its roots," Molly said briskly. "He's being paranoid and so should you. I don't like this place. It doesn't feel like a place where people come to play games. This is where people come to fight and kill and die, while other people watch and bet on the outcome, and have a good time."

Frankie shrugged. "That's what Casino Infernale is all about. That's what all casinos and all gambling is about. They're just a little bit more honest about it here."

"Talk to me, Frankie," I said. "Tell me things I need to know. What kind of Games do they play in this place?"

"Just a handful of actual Games, really," Frankie said quickly. "It's more about the side bets. And remember, from now on, it's all about the souls. The Casino makes all such transfers possible, and enforces the outcome, and of course the house always takes its more than generous cut along the way. Cheaters really don't prosper here."

"But what Games are there?" I said. "What should we choose?"

"I don't know," said Frankie, looking interestedly about him. "I never made it this far before."

He broke off abruptly, as both Molly and I grabbed him by the arms and swung him round to face us.

"Then what use are you to us?" Molly said bluntly.

"I know the general rules!" Frankie said quickly. "And I have talked to a lot of the staff about the Medium Games. They hear all kinds of things. . . . Look, I know how the Games work, and I know how they do things here. Basically, you have to challenge someone, before someone challenges you."

I looked back at the Arena. Stone seats, surrounding a stone circle of death. More and more people arriving, presumably from other dimensional doors. They filled the rows, usually in small chattering groups, eating and drinking and laughing, ready for the spectacle to come. Like so many predators with their nasty smiles and hungry eyes. And part of me wanted to kill every single one of them just on general principle.

I was right, this kind of Game really did bring out the worst in me.

A uniformed flunky approached us, and we all turned to face him. He stopped a respectful distance away, and bowed courteously. The uniform was basic; the person inside it even more so. Average height, average weight, all within acceptable parameters. It was the face that gave everything away. He had no hair on his head, no eyebrows, no trace there had ever been any hair on his face. And his features were strangely blank, utterly lacking in character. Almost a generic face. A generic uniformed flunky. Except, the clothes looked somehow wrong, on something that wasn't actually human. Like dressing up a dog. He started speaking, in a calm uninflected voice, and I paid careful attention.

"Mr. Shaman Bond, I regret to inform you, sir, that if you are contemplating wagering your soul in any of the Medium Games, that cannot be allowed. Our records show that the Casino already has a claim on your soul. It was used as collateral, some time earlier, by another player in another Game. It was lost to the Casino."

"I know," I said. "I have already been told that and I would like the Casino to know that I am not at all happy about it. I would, in fact, very much like to see the Casino try to collect. But, that's a matter for another time. I'm not betting my soul. I'm betting hers."

And I nodded at Molly, who smiled brightly at the flunky.

"Hi there!" she said sweetly. "I'm Molly Metcalf!"

The flunky bowed again, briefly. "We know who you are, miss. Your arrival here set off all kinds of alarms. Including a few we didn't even know we had, until you woke them up. Our records indicate that there are already a number of claims in place on your soul."

"Yes," said Molly. "But not by the Casino!"

"True," said the flunky. "Very well. There are . . . precedents. You may continue in the Games, sir and miss."

"You didn't mention Frankie's soul," I said.

"We wouldn't accept anything that soiled, sir," said the flunky.

"Excuse me," I said. "But, I have to ask . . . are you human?"

"I am a generic human template, sir," said the flunky. "Grown here at the factory farms, on behalf of Casino Infernale. I live to serve."

"This isn't planet Earth, is it?" said Molly.

"I do not know the name, no, sir and miss," said the generic flunky.

"Then where are we?" I said. "Exactly?"

"Sector Seventeen, sir. Home to the Medium Games. I have not been programmed with any further information on these matters."

"Doesn't the Casino have a . . . representative here, to run things?" I said.

"No, sir. This is our place, given over to us. We run things here in return for being left alone."

"And, when there are no Games?" said Molly.

"There are always Games, miss. We are made to serve."

"Can't you say no?" I said.

"We are not allowed that privilege, sir," said the flunky. "It is not a part of our programming. The best we can hope for is that while some of us run the Games, some of us are left alone."

"I will not stand for this," I said. "I will do something about this."

"Many people have said that, sir," said the generic flunky. "But we are still here."

"You never met anyone like me," I said.

"That's enough, Shaman," Molly said quickly. "You do like to promise things, don't you?"

"People manufactured to be slaves?" I said. "I'm not having it!"

"The Games," Frankie said urgently. "You have to make a start, get your challenge in, before you're noticed by some of the sharks operating here."

"If you'll excuse me, sir and miss," said the flunky, "I have my business to be about."

He bowed, and left. There wasn't even any character in the way he walked, or held himself. More like a toy that had been wound up and left to run.

"The more I learn about this place, the less I like," I said. "I don't think my family knows nearly enough, about the Casino, or the Shadow Bank, or the people behind them . . . if they are even people. Dimensional doors, people factories . . . Once this mission is over, I will get some answers. . . ."

"First things first," said Molly, soothingly. "We have to win here, and win big enough to get us into the Big Game, if we're to break the bank. And get your soul back. That is why we came here, remember?"

"If you survive the Medium Games," said Frankie.

Molly tapped me urgently on the arm, and pointed out a familiar figure moving casually through the stone seating, meeting and greeting with professional ease. Earnest Schmidt, current leader of the reformed Brotherhood of the Vril. He seemed in no hurry; happy to talk his poison to anyone.

"Maybe I should challenge him," I said. "Nothing like kicking the crap out of a Nazi to brighten up your day."

"Don't aim so high," Frankie said immediately. "He has many souls, and he knows his way around the Medium Games. You want someone who's as unfamiliar with everything as you are. Someone like the individual currently heading our way."

A somewhat less than medium height, very slender, and very striking figure was striding confidently towards us. Dressed in full formal attire, complete with top hat, gloves, and spats, and a monocle screwed tightly into the left eye. He stopped before us, nodded jerkily, and then had to pause to stuff his monocle back into its eye socket again. He struck a haughty pose, and did his best to look down on me. Which is not easy, when you're at least a head shorter.

"I say!" he said, in a high breathy voice. "You're that Shaman Bond chappie, aren't you? I'm told you did frightfully well in the Introductory Games, even if you were mostly saved from your own folly by the assistance of others. You do understand that won't happen here."

"And you are?" I said.

"I am the Little Lord!" snapped the aristocratic figure. Somewhat taken aback and even affronted at not being immediately recognised. "Aristocrat of the Nightside and Gambler Supreme! Winner of many Games, and my soul is still my own! Not a mark on it . . ."

"Do you know which planet we're on?" I said.

He sniffed, dismissively. "As though that matters. I'm a gambler, not a tourist!"

Molly leaned forward suddenly, to get a really close look at the Little Lord, and then crowed triumphantly. "I knew it! You're a woman!"

"What?" I said.

"Shut up!" said the Little Lord.

"You're a woman!" said Molly. She put both her hands on the Little Lord's chest, and had a good feel. "You've got breasts! You're female!"

"Not officially!" said the Little Lord, backing away sev-

eral steps. She glared at me. "And I challenge you, Shaman Bond, to a game of Change War!"

Molly gave every indication of going after the Little Lord again, possibly to pull her clothes open for a fuller investigation. I grabbed Molly by the arm and pulled her back.

"Behave, Molly!" I said sternly. "You're not at home now."

Frankie murmured urgently in my ear.

"Accept the challenge. It's a simple, basic Game, one on one, win a soul or lose one. A good introduction to the Medium Games, and a chance to make a good impression in front of the crowds."

"Very well," I said to the Little Lord. "I accept your challenge."

"Wait a minute," said Molly. "We don't even know what the Game involves yet!"

"Too late, old dear," said the Little Lord, smiling frostily. "Mr. Bond, I shall make you pay for these indignities, sir!"

And she hurried away, heading for the Arena.

"Little Bitch," said Molly.

The Little Lord's back stiffened, but she pretended not to hear and kept going. Striding down through the stone seats, heading for the circle at the heart of the Arena. Top-hatted head held high. I considered blowing a raspberry after her, but decided against it. I had my dignity to consider. I looked at Frankie.

"All right," I said. "What have I just agreed to, on your advice?"

"Change War," said Frankie. "You both take a potion, provided by the Casino, a mixture of classic Hyde formula and Chimera Venom. Gives you both the short-term ability to transform your body into absolutely anything your mind can conceive of. You both change shape repeatedly, trying to outmanoeuvre and overwhelm each other, until one of you turns into something the other can't match. Basically, you just keep fighting in one form after another until there's a clear winner. And a loser, of course."

"Didn't I see this in a Disney film once?" said Molly.

"The thought of you watching a Disney film feels frankly unnatural," said Frankie.

I thought about it. "Is there any way I can get out of this Game?"

"No!" said Frankie. "No, really, you don't want to do that! This is a good deal! You're a trained fighter, and a Drood, so you're bound to have encountered far weirder and more dangerous things than the Little Lord! You can outclass and outfight her and . . . and walk all over her!"

"If it's such a good deal, why are you getting so loud?" said Molly.

"I don't want to kill the Little Lord," I said to Frankie.

"You won't have to," he said quickly. "Just . . . overpower her. We can get really good odds on you, in the side betting!"

I looked at Molly, and she nodded reluctantly. "Do what you have to do, Shaman."

"Good thing Jacqueline's not here," I said. "To see what they've done with Hyde formula."

"Don't be naive," said Frankie. "Who do you think sold the details of the formula to the Casino in the first place? In return for an invitation, and enough money to play with?"

I took my time walking down through the stone seating, towards the circle. I really didn't want to fight anyone, after what I'd been through in the Pit, but there was no denying the idea of Change War intrigued me. I had some experience in changing the shape of my armour, but to actually change my body . . . into someone or even something else . . . I made myself smile and nod easily to everyone I passed. The crowds were really gathering now, filling the stone seating, pressed shoulder to shoulder. Many were already discussing Shaman Bond and the Little Lord with cold familiarity, like two racehorses. Bets were being placed. It all seemed very sporting and civilised, until you remembered they were wagering other people's souls. I stopped, right at the edge of the circle. The Arena. Nothing could happen, nothing could begin, until I stepped into the Arena. The Little Lord was already there, strutting up and down, waving to the crowd in a haughty, affected manner. As though they were privileged to be watching her. I suppose, if you're going to play a part, play it all the way.

Another uniformed flunky appeared, seemingly out of nowhere. He stepped into the circle, bearing a silver salver with two champagne flutes on it. No point in putting it off any further. I strode out into the circle, and the crowd cheered me in a mostly good-natured way. The Little Lord came forward, and we both stood together before the Casino's generic flunky.

"Have we met?" I said, peering into the familiar characterless face.

"No, sir," said the flunky. "An easy mistake to make. I am told we all look alike to you. Please, drink. So that Change War can begin."

The Little Lord snatched one of the champagne flutes from the tray, and tossed the clear liquid back. She slammed the glass back onto the tray and walked quickly away. I picked up the remaining glass and studied the contents carefully.

"How long will this stuff last?" I said, to the flunky.

"As long as it needs to, sir. The act of winning, or losing, acts as a psychic trigger to shut down the potion's effects. It's all been very carefully worked out, sir. We have done this before. Win, and the Little Lord's soul is yours. Lose, and your opponent takes control of Miss Molly's soul. I am not permitted to take anyone's side, but I believe I am allowed to say 'Good luck, sir.'"

He bowed, and stepped back. Not a trace of emotion anywhere, in his face or voice. Just waiting for me to drink so the Game could get under way. I looked out into the crowd and there was Frankie, moving quickly back and forth, nailing down those important side bets. I hoped he was getting good odds. I looked round and there was Molly, standing right at the front of the crowd, in the first row. I moved over to stand before her, still holding my champagne glass. We stood and looked at each other for a long moment.

"What are you doing here?" I said.

"You don't have to do this," said Molly. "I could do this for you. I've as much experience as you, and I can hold my own in a fight. You know that."

"I have to do this," I said steadily. "If the horse throws you . . ."

"Then you shoot the bloody thing in the head and move on!" said Molly. "You don't have to prove anything to me, Shaman."

"Perhaps I have something to prove to myself," I said. "You don't know how close I came to losing against the Dancing Fool. I had to descend to his level to win. I don't like how that made me feel. I need to win this, Molly, and I need to win it . . . in a good way. To be myself again."

"Oh, hell," said Molly. "Just . . . don't get chivalrous. Kick the crap out of the Little Tranny, and come home safely."

"Now there's a sentence you don't hear every day," I said.

I smiled at Molly, and she smiled at me. And then I turned away from her and strode out into the stone circle, to where the generic flunky was waiting patiently for me. The Little Lord was standing stiffly in place now, impatient to get started. I toasted her with my champagne flute, and gulped the clear liquid down. After my horrid experience with the Armourer's potion, I didn't want the stuff lingering in my mouth any longer than necessary. I braced myself, ready for some really horrible taste, some open assault on my taste buds . . . and was surprised to discover that the potion had no taste at all. I might as well have been drinking tap water.

I looked suspiciously at my empty glass, wondering whether someone might have cheated, and slipped me water instead of the potion, but no, I could already feel the stuff working within me. Feel the potential opening up of all the things I could be. The generic flunky took the empty glass away from me and left the circle, but I barely noticed.

I felt like I could be anything, anything at all. That I could rise up into the sky like a giant and drag down one of the moons, or dissipate into a deadly mist that would poison everyone who breathed it in. Turn myself into anyone or anything I've ever met. And I've been around. All the possibilities jostling within me, just bursting to get out . . .

I looked across at the Little Lord as she carefully removed the monocle from her left eye and tucked the glass safely away in an inside pocket. And then she looked at me and smiled, coldly and dismissively. As though she'd already worked out every possibility in her mind, and won every time. And all that was left now was the formality of playing it out. I had to smile at that. I had been places, and seen things, and done things, far beyond her imagination. The Little Lord wasn't going to know what hit her. Except, I didn't want to play the Game that way. The Casino's bloody, brutal way.

So I just sauntered around the perimeter of the circle, bouncing along full of life and energy, ignoring my opponent to wave and smile at the crowd, who didn't quite know how to take that. It sure as hell wasn't *We who are about to die, salute you.* Fighting in the Arena was supposed to be a grim, deadly affair. That's why they came. You weren't supposed to have a good time in the Arena. . . . My actions seemed to actually incense the Little Lord, who had to keep turning just to face me.

"You're not taking this seriously!" she said, accusingly.

"I've had enough of serious," I said brightly. "Not really my thing. It's supposed to be a Game, isn't it? Then let's play! Let's enjoy ourselves; have some fun!"

"This isn't a game," said the Little Lord. "It was never meant to be a game! Just a contest of skill, with souls on the line!"

"Doesn't mean we can't still have a good time," I said, reasonably. I slammed to a halt and looked steadily at her, my hands thrust casually in my pockets. "Why did you challenge me, rather than anyone else? Did you see me fight in the Pit?"

"You fought in the Pit?" said the Little Lord. "And won?"

"Well, obviously," I said. "If I hadn't won, I wouldn't be here, would I?"

"I chose you at random," said the Little Lord. "Because I didn't know anything about you. Therefore, you weren't a Major Player. I couldn't risk that. Not after I sacrificed so much to get this far. I will beat you!"

"Why?" I said. "Why is winning so important to you?"

"Because it's my only way to get home again!" said the Little Lord, harshly. "I want to go home!"

"You'd take my soul to do that?" I said.

"I'd take a thousand souls!" said the Little Lord. "And that's the other reason why I chose to challenge someone I didn't know. So that whatever happens to you, it won't bother me so much."

The Little Lord stamped her foot hard, and her formal clothes burst apart as her body exploded into tightly stretched flesh and muscle. She rose up before me, a huge and powerful figure, a living engine of destruction. The Little Lord had gone for the most obvious choice: a Hyde. But not a female Hyde, not just an evil version of herself. Like Jacqueline before her, the Little Lord had taken the formula at face value. She had become the legendary bogeyman; the biggest, strongest, most deadly man she could think of. A real man, at last. I could see the proof hanging down, between the dark tatters of what had been her exquisitely tailored trousers. And I couldn't help but grin. The Little Lord might be living her dream, right now, being all a man could be ... but I was ready to bet that she hadn't thought it through. That there was one part of being a man that she hadn't considered, because she'd never had to.

So I didn't even bother to change into anything else. I just walked right up to the Hyde, smiling sweetly. The Hyde reared up before me, his huge hands opening and closing, smiling his own harsh smile as he got ready to tear me into little pieces. He reached out to me and I lunged quickly forward, inside his reach, and kicked him good and hard in the nuts.

The Hyde tried to cry out in pain, but he couldn't force a sound through his closed-off throat. He'd never felt anything like it before, as the Little Lord. Never knew there could be a pain like it. His eyes bulged, tears coursing down his stricken face, hurting so bad he couldn't move a muscle. He didn't even have the sense to fall down. So I lined up and kicked him in the groin again, putting all my strength behind it. A large part of the crowd cried out in sympathy. The Hyde finally fell down, as all the strength went out of his legs, hitting the hard stone of the circle floor with a crash, and then curling up into a foetal ball. And in the end all he could do, to get away from the pain, was turn back into the Little Lord again.

Round One to me. If I had to fight, I'd fight my way.

I did a lap of honour around the Arena, smiling and waving, acknowledging the cheers and laughter from the crowd. And then that broke off, as loud voices cried out a warning. I turned around, to find the Little Lord had changed shape again. And once again, she'd gone for size and strength.

If anything, she was even bigger than before. A good ten feet tall, her lithe body covered with dark grey fur. Her great head rose up, her face lengthening into a muzzle full of blocky teeth and savage canines. Great pointed ears, eyes yellow as urine. Her back hunched, bending her half over with great ridges of muscle under the grey fur. Her feet were paws, her hands viciously clawed. She'd made herself into a werewolf. Or at least, her idea of one. A huge shaggy figure towering over me, her mouth stretched in a wide hungry smile. The thick doggy scent of her, rich with blood and musk, was almost overpowering. The Hyde had been threatening; the werewolf was actually dangerous.

So I just stood my ground, nodded casually to her, and thought about it. I could have turned into something equally monstrous; God knows I've seen worse things in my travels. But I was still determined not to play the Casino's Game in the Casino's way, rending and tearing and spilling blood, for the amusement of the crowd. No head-to-head brutality . . . I would win this one with a little lateral thinking.

The werewolf padded forward, yellow eyes gleaming fiercely, clawed hands reaching out to tear my flesh. And I just stood there and smiled, with my hands behind my back. The Little Lord should have had enough sense to be suspicious, but she was all wolf now, driven by the beast's needs and instincts.

I remembered when Ethel first gifted the Droods with her own strange matter armour, and how we learned to change its shape to suit our needs. I had, on occasion, extended the armour of my golden hands into long golden sword-blades. So, as the werewolf lunged forward, I concentrated on my hands. I could change any part of my body now, into anything I could think of, and right then . . . I was thinking of silver. I waited till the werewolf was almost upon me, lunging for my throat, and once again I stepped forward inside her reach, brought my hands out from behind my back, and showed her the silver blades where my hands had been.

She knew them immediately for what they were, but there was no time for her to stop. She just kept coming, and I thrust both silver blades deep into her heart.

The impact as we closed drove me backwards, but I was expecting that, and kept my balance. The werewolf cried out horribly. I ground both blades deeper into her chest, into her heart, and we skidded to a halt. I pulled both blades out, and jammed them both into her gut. The werewolf cried out again, and collapsed onto the unforgiving ground. Her dark blood pumped thickly on the stone floor. She was dying, and she knew it, so she did the only thing she could. She turned back into the Little Lord, shrinking away from my silver blades, away from the things that were killing her.

I let her do it. She scrambled away from me on all fours, holding the tatters of her clothing to her. It was obvious to anyone who cared to look, now, that the Little Lord was a woman . . . but no one in the audience cared. They were all leaning forward, smiling eagerly, to see what would happen next. They'd never seen a Game like this.

The Little Lord changed again, quickly, desperate to regain the advantage. The stone floor of the circle blew apart as she made contact with the ground beneath, and turned herself into a huge archetypal female figure. A Gaia woman, an earth goddess, rising up and up, growing huge and powerful as she drew on more earth for her body from under the Arena. She towered over me, vast and potent, an overwhelmingly female figure. Big enough to stamp me into a bloody mess on the stone floor, or grab me up and hug me to her earthy bosom, and smother me in dirt. But I . . . was thinking about the man I'd seen earlier, in the hotel lobby. Who'd been so scared of what the manager Jonathon Scott might do that he dissolved into water and ran away. I thought I could do better than that.

So I turned myself into a great spring of water, pumping up out of the ground, rising up into a massive boiling fountain with all the pressure of a fire hose behind it. I hit the earth goddess in the face, with enough force to blow her features off. And then I hit her with so much water, I just washed her away. She fell apart, running like thick mud, collapsing in on herself, until there was nothing left of her but mud, spattered across the Arena.

It took us both a while to come back from that. Remembering what a human shape was, and why it was important. Re-forming our human bodies from the elemental forms we'd taken. But I still remembered duty and honour, because I was never free of them, and so I was the first to pull myself together. I stumbled forward to stand over the Little Lord as she took her original shape again. I still had my clothes, intact, because I didn't think as literally as she did. This time, I didn't wait for her to change first; I just bent down and slipped one arm round her neck as her head came up, and tightened my hold. Cutting off the air to the throat, and the blood flow to the brain.

Chokehold.

She turned into a horse, and I clung grimly to her neck

as she reared up, kicking out her front legs and shaking her great head, trying to throw me off. When she found she couldn't, she changed again, becoming a massive grizzly bear. I pushed my face deep into her dark fur, tightening my hold. She clawed at my back with her great paws, and I cried out as they raked my flesh to the bone; but I just healed myself and hung on. She became a huge snake, bucking and coiling and writhing, slamming me against the stone floor, over and over. But I wouldn't let go. I grabbed my arm with my other hand, tightening the hold still further, holding on with all my strength. Until she couldn't breathe any more, or the blood couldn't reach her brain, and she passed out.

I lay on the cold stone floor, breathing hard and shaking, my arm locked so tight around the returned Little Lord's neck that I could barely feel it. I could have maintained the hold until she died, but I couldn't see the point. I let go of her and stood up, and a generic flunky was quickly there, to raise one arm above my head, as the winner.

The crowd cheered and applauded, happily enough. There hadn't been much blood, and no death, but they'd been entertained. I jerked my arm away from the flunky, and looked down at the unconscious Little Lord. Such a small, pathetic figure, in the tatters of her suit. The top hat long gone. She could have won if she'd just thought to turn into something that didn't need to breathe, or require blood flowing to the brain. But she'd never encountered anything like that.

I walked steadily out of the Arena. The crowd had already stopped applauding. They'd hoped for more, from me and the Little Lord, but I was glad to have disappointed them. As I reached the front row of the stone seats, I could feel the change potion vanish within me, all the possibilities dropping away, until I was just me again. I was glad to feel them go. It's hard enough just being me.

Molly was there, in the front row, waiting for me. She threw her arms around me as I left the circle and hugged me tight, as though she'd never let me go. I held on to her. The only thing in my life that always made sense in my ever-changing world. We finally let go, and stood back, and I grinned at her.

"The old legends are always the best. Did you get good odds on me?"

"Hell, yes!" said Frankie, joining us. "Mostly from people who'd never heard of Shaman Bond."

"We won over three hundred souls betting on you!" said Molly.

"Three hundred and twenty-two," said Frankie.

Molly glared at him. "Isn't that what I said?"

"What are you planning on doing with all these souls?" I said.

"Use them as collateral for future bets," said Molly. "We're here to break the bank, remember? Can't do that, if we haven't got the souls."

"I'm still concerned about what happens to these souls afterwards," I said.

"Well, of course you are, because that's you," said Molly.

"Don't think about it," said Frankie, quite seriously. "You can worry about all that later, if there is a later. For now, please concentrate on the Games before you. Because from now on any lack of concentration will almost certainly get you killed. Change War was an easy Game against a relatively unskilled opponent. It gets harder, and more complicated, from now on."

Another generic flunky approached me. I didn't bother asking if we'd met before. He bowed briefly, and presented me with a single small coin. I hefted it in the palm of my hand, and could barely feel the weight of the dull metal.

"All right," I said. "I'll bite. What is this?"

"An obol, sir. A chit from Casino Infernale representing one soul. The soul of the Little Lord, won in the Change War."

I looked at the coin again. Small, roughly milled edge, the markings almost worn away. "This is a human soul?"

"Yes, sir."

"It's not very big, is it?" said Molly, leaning over for a closer look. "Rather humbling, I suppose, when you think about it."

"The obol represents the soul," said the flunky. "Your receipt, sir, if you like. Don't lose it. Casino Infernale is not obliged to offer a replacement."

"We didn't get any coins from our side bets," said Molly.

"The Casino keeps a record of all such exchanges and transactions at the Games, miss," said the generic flunky. "Even if it's not immediately obvious. The Casino sees all, knows all. The record is all you need, to make further wagers. The obol is . . . ceremonial. A prize, to the winner of the Game. Apparently, humans value such things. I am told I wouldn't understand."

"I'm not sure I do," I said. I put the obol away, carefully, in an inner pocket.

The flunky bowed, turned, and departed. I looked out into the stone circle, where two other uniformed generic flunkies were dumping the still unconscious Little Lord on a stretcher. They carried her out. Some of the crowd laughed at her, and booed, for letting the side down. I hoped the flunkies found her top hat.

"She would have taken your soul, if she'd won," said Frankie, trying to be kind.

"An obol," Molly said thoughtfully. "Isn't that the coin the ancient Greeks used to put on the eyes of their dead to pay Charon the Boatman to ferry their souls across the river to the land of the dead? Maybe you're not the only one here who's thinking about the old legends."

"You've been watching the History Channel again," I said. "Because you have to say something at moments like that."

I looked back into the stone circle. The Little Lord was gone.

"What will happen to her?" I said to Frankie.

"She has nothing left to bet with," he said. "She lost her soul to you, so she can't play in any more Games, or wager on them. The Casino will hold on to her until the Games are over and her final fate can be decided."

"Don't get sentimental," said Molly, sternly. "She would have been quite happy to see that happen to you."

"She just wanted to go home," I said. "Where will they put her, Frankie?"

"There's a place in the hotel," Frankie said carefully. "Somewhere safe and secure, for all the losers."

"As a face, in the corridor?" said Molly.

"No," said Frankie, immediately. "Those are the souls the Casino owns. They don't own the Little Lord's soul. You do, Shaman."

"Liking the Medium Games less and less all the time," I said.

"You have to play, to win," said Frankie. "If you really are going to break the bank."

"My turn now!" Molly said briskly. "Come on, Frankie, we need to escalate things. What's a good Game for winning big?"

Frankie pointed across the rows of seating at a short cheerful-looking black man, wearing a Hawaiian shirt and khaki shorts. He had close-cropped white hair, a hardworn face, and an easy smile. And yet the people all around him still seemed to be going out of their way to give him plenty of room.

"That," said Frankie, in a surprisingly respectful tone of voice, "is the Bones Man. Got his name from old triumphs with the dominoes, which were always known as bones in the Caribbean community of old London. Do I really need to tell you he's a voodoo practitioner?"

"I don't know the name," I said, frowning. "Not really my territory. . . . Is he dangerous?"

"Of course he's dangerous!" said Frankie. "Or he wouldn't be here. He's not a good man to play Games with; he has a reputation for needless cruelty. Likes to play with his victims before finishing them off. A bit too nasty, even for this crowd. I think they'd like to see him take a fall, but they'd still bet on him. Which is something we could take advantage of . . . You have a pretty bad reputation yourself, Molly, enough to perk the interest of the crowd. Challenge the Bones Man and win, and we could be talking serious souls."

"What game?" said Molly. "Change War?"

"He wouldn't lower himself," said Frankie. "Far too entry-level, for someone like him. No, I recommend you challenge him to a Game of World War."

"Hold everything, go previous," I said. "That sounds . . . excessive."

"Not that kind of World War," said Frankie. "This is all about creating worlds, right there in the Arena. Whoever creates the realest world, with the most dangerous and most threatening inhabitants, wins. By overwhelming your opponent's world."

"I can do that," said Molly. "I've been around."

"That's true," I said. "You have. But are we talking about real worlds here, or imaginary creations?"

"Little bit of both," Frankie said cheerfully. "It's all about what you bring to the circle. That's what makes the Game so exciting."

"One world overwhelming another," I said. "To the death?"

"Can be," said Frankie. "Usually . . . but you can always submit. Yield to a greater player."

I looked at Molly. "Don't be proud. If you're losing, quit. We can always play another Game."

"You never did have the knack for pep talks," said Molly.

And before I could say anything to stop her, or even slow her down, Molly strode off through the stone seats to confront the Bones Man. He knew she was coming, even though he had his back to her, and stood up to turn and face her at the very last moment. Still smiling his calm, implacable smile. I was already hurrying after her, determined not to be left out, with Frankie in my wake, but I stopped far enough short that she wouldn't think I was fussing over her. Molly could get very upset if she thought that.

"Molly Metcalf," said the Bones Man, smiling almost fondly on her. His voice was rich and dark, almost avuncular. "Your reputation precedes you, me girl. What is it you want with me, now? You think to challenge me, little witch?"

"Yes," said Molly. "To a game of World War. You up for it?"

"Well, well," said the Bones Man. "I think that might be fun. And an honour, to take on one of your many accomplishments. I shall enjoy beating you. I shall enjoy making you bleed, and scream, and beg for mercy. Before you die. And your soul shall make such a fine addition to my collection." He looked past her, at me. "You understand, of course, that your companion cannot aid you in the circle. No matter what happens to you."

"Now, then, you had to go and spoil it," said Molly. "You were doing so well, all old-time villain with a sadistic streak . . . and then you let yourself down by showing how scared you are of Shaman and me. I don't need any help to walk all over you, conjure man. I have had dealings with the loa; they know me and I know them. I don't think you've got any surprises for me, old man."

The Bones Man was still smiling, even though it must have been a long time since anyone spoke to him that sharply. "Perhaps, me child. But you'd be surprised how many Games are won here in the audience before the Games even start. It's all in the mind, me girl. After you . . ."

"I don't think so," said Molly. "After you."

He laughed, and made his way unhurriedly down through the stone seats and into the Arena. Molly took the time to kiss me quickly, and then hurried out into the circle after him. She smiled and waved cheerfully to the crowd, as a generic uniformed flunky came forward to announce the Game, and the names of the competitors, to the crowd. There was general good-natured applause, and even a few cheers for Molly. The crowd might respect the Bones Man, but it was clear he wasn't . . . popular. I sat down in the front row, while Frankie went off to work the crowd, for the best odds. I let him do it. I had eyes only for

Molly and the Bones Man. More and more people were arriving, filling up the seats and talking excitedly, looking forward to a really good match. A good game, and a good death. That's what they were there for. You could almost smell the anticipation in the air.

And all I could do was sit there and watch.

It wasn't that I didn't trust Molly to win. I had absolute faith in her abilities, and I would back her against anyone and anything, up to and including Elder Gods and Ancient Ones. But I didn't trust the Games, or the Casino, or the Bones Man, to play fair and by the rules. I had already decided that if I saw anything that looked like cheating, or even if she just looked like she was losing, I would set this whole world afire to protect her. She'd be mad as hell at me for interfering, but I'd rather have her alive and shouting at me than dead and silent.

Frankie sat down on the seat beside me, just for a moment, out of breath from running back and forth in the crowd, pushing the odds as far as they would go.

"Just checking in," he said. "How many of the souls we've won do you want me to wager?"

"All of them," I said.

"Are you sure? You don't want me to hold some back, just in case . . . ?"

"All of them," I said.

"You're the boss!" And he was gone, flitting through the crowd, making instant new friends and jollying them into betting more than was sensible.

A large thug in tailored combat fatigues suddenly loomed over me. I looked up, and he scowled at me. A very thorough scowl. Probably practised it in front of a mirror.

"You're in my seat," he said.

"No, I'm not," I said.

"That's the best seat, so it's my seat," said the thug. "So move. Or I'll move you."

I sighed, quietly. There's always one. I stood up, kneed him in the groin, waited for him to bend over, and then rabbit-punched him on the back of his exposed neck. He fell to the ground. I sat down again and put my feet up on his unconscious body. Everyone else left me alone, after that. They could tell I didn't want to be bothered.

The generic flunky, or one very like him, gestured for Molly and the Bones Man to retreat to the far ends of the circle. They did so; Molly still waving to the crowd, the Bones Man walking slowly and calmly, as though in a deep concentration. The flunky then left the Arena with more than usual speed, and the crowd went suddenly quiet, watching intently, not wanting to miss anything. I leaned forward in my seat. I'd seen Molly do many amazing things with her magic, but I'd never seen her create a world.

The Bones Man started first, while the flunky was still leaving the Arena. He gestured, quite calmly, and a huge dark jungle immediately filled his half of the circle. Tall trees bowed down with heavy luxuriant foliage, interlocking branches high above forming a giant canopy, blocking out the light. A menacing place, full of moist sweaty heat that spilled out across the first few rows of the audience. An oppressive jungle, with closely packed vegetation, and fat pulpy flowers, burning with phosphorescent fire like unhealthy ghosts. Things moved in the jungle the Bones Man had made. Horrible things.

Dead birds crawled across the jungle floor, broken wings drooping as they hauled themselves along. Crippled animals, warped and twisted by unnatural forces, lurched out of the shadows, burning pus dripping from their empty eye sockets. Great swarms of insects buzzed loudly on the hot still air, sounding mindlessly vicious and hungry. Even the great trees moved slowly under the Bones Man's will, creaking loudly in sudden jerks. Everything seemed rotten and diseased, and even the light seemed poisoned. And then, the final touch, as dead men came walking through the jungle, heading straight for Molly, in her half of the circle.

She didn't budge an inch. "Zombies?" she said loudly. "How very . . . traditional!"

She stamped her foot once, and winter fell upon her

half of the circle. A terrible winter, of snow and ice and blazing sunlight. It hit the jungle dead on, and stopped it in its tracks. The freezing cold laid its powerful touch on everything at the jungle's edge, painting it white with frost and ice. Freezing it in place. Vegetation shattered, and fell apart. The cold surged on, freezing everything it touched. Even the trees cracked, and fell apart, invaded by the awful cold. The vegetation died, the animals froze to death, and the insects fell lifeless from the bitter air. And the walking dead men slowed and stopped, frozen in place, and fell on their faces on the frozen ground. All of the jungle was winter now, white shapes in snow drifts. Except for the Bones Man himself, standing in his own small circle of unaffected ground.

He dismissed the frozen jungle with a wave of his hand, and the circle was empty again. He frowned, and surrounded himself with a new world, or perhaps more properly an old one. The familiar dimly lit back streets and alleyways, the Caribbean territory of his childhood, when new immigrants were packed into substandard tenements and left to make their own world. He stood in the darkest streets of old London, heavy with shadows because half the street lights had been smashed. The shadows were everywhere—deep and dark and full of menace. Not real things, these streets, probably, but how the Bones Man remembered them.

Shadows seemed to move with a life of their own. The few remaining street lights hummed loudly and then exploded in showers of sparks, one at a time. Making more shadows. Dead rats with broken backs heaved themselves forward into the light, dragging lengths of pink intestines behind them, followed by cats that had been turned inside out. Just because someone in those streets had a taste for suffering. Windows in the surrounding buildings glowed unnaturally bright, and foul, and dark shadows moved like demons glimpsed in Hell's light. The Bones Man looked just as at home in this new hell as in his jungle.

And once again, dead men came shambling forward,

heading straight for Molly, with old appetites stamped deep in their rotting faces.

Molly snapped her fingers, and a great sandstorm rose up out of nowhere and swept forward, slamming into the dark streets. Brick red dust, from a red planet. More appeared around her, filling her half of the circle. The ancient overwhelming sands of the Martian plains, older by far than this world, and far less forgiving. The red sandstorm blasted through the dark streets the Bones Man made, scouring through the open spaces and blowing the zombies apart. The sands smashed the windows and the foul lights went out, and nothing moved there any more. And for the first time, the Bones Man took a step backwards. Because he'd never encountered anything like old Mars.

He braced himself, surrounded by one small area of his own darkness, untouched by the sandstorm. And Molly smiled at him. She snapped her fingers, and Mars was gone. Replaced in a moment by the one place she knew best. The wild woods.

Tall trees surrounded her, old trees and ancient, even primordial. From when we all lived in the forest, because there was nowhere else. Green grass and green leaves, and living things everywhere. All the triumphant vegetation of old England, untouched by human hand. Bright sunlight, full of life, shining down through the trees in great golden shafts. Birds singing, filling the air with joyous noise. And all the old creatures of England's past: the wolf and the boar, the bear and the stag, the lion and the unicorn.

England's Dreaming.

The sunlight blazed forward, into what was left of the Bones Man's darkness. Throwing back the dark and dispersing the shadows. And where the clean light touched the broken creatures, it healed them. The rats and cats ran away, into the woods; turning their backs on the dark in favour of a new wild freedom. The last buildings disappeared, replaced by trees, and the Bones Man backed away, bewildered, as his world was destroyed.

In Molly's woods, birds came flying down to dart and

circle around her. The beasts bowed down to her, and she patted their faithful heads. My heart ached to see the world she'd given up, for me. A single squirrel hopped forward forward to stare at the Bones Man. He glared down at it, and raised a foot to stamp on it. The squirrel fixed him with a cold eye.

"Don't even think about it, rube."

It hopped back into the woods. The sunlight blasted forward, and the dark was gone. Leaving the Bones Man standing alone, blinking dazedly, in his half of the circle.

He tried to call up one world after another, but they all failed and fell apart, in the face of the wild woods. He had nothing half so strong or half so vital. He had nothing to offer, in the face of the woods we all came from. So he just gave up. He bowed to Molly, and sank down on one knee. Molly looked at him for a long moment, and then nodded briefly. The birds and the beasts left her, and the wild woods faded slowly away. Nothing left but an empty stone circle, with a beaten man and a triumphant woman. The audience made a soft sound, as though they hadn't wanted Molly's woods to go.

She strode forward to face the Bones Man, who rose smoothly to his feet again to face her.

"So," said Molly. "I own your soul now."

"Hardly, me child," said the Bones Man. "I would not be so foolish as to risk my own spirit on a game of chance. You have merely won the souls I won in earlier games. And much good may they do you, being the small and pitiful things they are. Be careful, little witch; some of them are . . . restless. And watch your back, for I will revenge myself upon you for this humiliation."

"Go for it," said Molly. "I mean it; right now. You'll never have a better chance."

"In a time of my choosing," said the Bones Man. "The lords of the loa will tear your soul apart."

"Oh, piss off!" Molly said loudly. "Sore loser!"

The Bones Man gathered up what little of his dignity remained, turned, and strode away. The crowd booed him and cheered Molly. A uniformed flunky came forward and presented Molly with her obol, her symbol as winner of the Game. And while she was distracted with that, the Bones Man attacked. The crowd cried out a warning, and Molly spun round to see the Bones Man transform himself as he took on the aspect of the voodoo loa he served: Damballah, the snake god. He rose up, growing larger, becoming huge and swaying, a massive serpent . . . and Molly braced herself, stray magics discharging around her raised hands. I was already up and running forward, my Colt Repeater in hand. But before either of us could do anything, a dozen flunkies appeared out of nowhere, surrounding the massive serpent in a great circle. They didn't speak, or move, but the snake collapsed, falling in upon itself, becoming just a man again.

The Bones Man stood alone, surrounded by things not wholly men.

"We have been given power in this place," said one of the flunkies, "to enforce the rules of the Games. Such behaviour as this cannot go unpunished."

"You think you can hurt me?" said the Bones Man. "You small, stupid, artificial things?"

"We can do more than that," said the generic flunky.

And just like that, the Bones Man lost his shape. His face melted away, replaced by simple, characterless features. His hair fell out, his name disappeared, his existence reworked. Made over, into just another generic flunky. He stood there helplessly, not knowing what he should do yet. The flunky who'd spoken turned to Molly and me.

"We will take care of him until he is ready to take on his duties here. The rules of the Games must be followed."

He looked at the gun in my hand, and I put it away. The flunkies left the circle. I hugged Molly tightly, and she hugged me back, and we left the circle arm in arm.

"You weren't worried, were you?" Molly said cheerfully. "He never stood a chance."

I looked at her thoughtfully. "What was all that about *I*

know the loa, and they know me? Is there anyone you didn't make a pact with to gain power when you were starting out?"

"I don't think I missed anyone," said Molly. "I was very thorough, and very motivated."

"Some day your past is going to catch up with you," I said. "And all those pacts will have to be honoured. And on that day, I don't know if even I will be able to protect you."

"Worry about that when it happens," Molly said briskly. "Ah, Frankie's here. How did we do in the betting?"

"One thousand, four hundred and thirteen souls!" Frankie said proudly. "Can't speak for the quality, of course, but . . ."

"Do we have enough to get us into the Big Game?" said Molly.

"Not yet," said Frankie. "But one more really big win should do it."

"So, what next?" I said. "Who do I have to challenge, and what do I have to play?"

"I think everyone here knows enough now to be wary of both of you," Frankie said carefully. "So you'll have a hard time getting anyone to go up against you, one on one, in any game. And that affects the odds I can get. . . . But, there is a Game, a group Game, where we could still get really good odds. It's a bit risky, but . . ."

"The Games we just took part in weren't risky?" said Molly.

"Not compared to this," said Frankie. "Because the Game I'm thinking of is a free-for-all. Anyone can enter, and it all comes down to Last Man Standing. Or at least, last person still alive."

"Okay," said Molly. "That doesn't sound too bad; what makes it so specially risky?"

"Most people who participate in this Game are lucky to get out alive," said Frankie. "You can't take any weapons in with you, but anything else goes. It's all about survival. But outside, you can bet on any number of things! How long you'll last, what kind of damage you'll take, as well as whether you last long enough to win. This isn't a Game I'd

recommend to most people, because with so many partici-
pating, anything can happen. But you do seem to have that
certain lucky something going for you. . . ."

"How do I get into this Game?" I said.

"Just apply to one of the flunkies," said Frankie. "And
then make out your will."

"If this is a free-for-all, then why don't we both enter?"
said Molly. "Should help the odds on us winning, if we're
in there together to watch each other's back."

"You could both enter," said Frankie, "but the rules say
there can only be one winner. You'd have to kill, or at least
seriously maim, the other to be declared winner."

"Then we won't do that," said Molly.

"It's down to me," I said firmly. "You're an excellent
fighter, Molly, but I'm the one trained on how to survive
against all the odds."

"This is the Pit, all over again," said Molly. "I had a
hard enough time bringing you back from the brink after
you fought the Dancing Fool! And now you want to take
on a whole bunch of people just like him? Are you crazy?"

"There is no one like the Dancing Fool," I said. "And I
promise you, I have absolutely no intention of fighting
fairly this time. I plan to use lateral thinking and a hell of
a lot of ducking and weaving."

"Well," said Molly. "That's more like it."

We went in search of a generic flunky, and I told him I
wanted to take part in Last Man Standing. He just nodded, and led us out of the Arena, and out across the grassy
plain, to a tall round stone Tower standing on its own. Not
very tall, and not very large, three or four stories at most,
but with a great many windows in the curving exterior
wall. Lots of other flunkies were leading even more people
towards the Tower. As we drew nearer, I could see there
were open doorways at the base of the Tower, and a great
many viewscreens floating in mid-air, giving views of the
interior. A large audience was assembling around the circular base of the Tower, from every direction. Just sitting

there in the grass, staring eagerly at the viewscreens. Our flunky stopped us just short of the doorways, and looked at me pointedly.

"The rules of the Game are quite clear, sir. You can only take in whatever is yours, and you must enter the Tower naked."

I glared at Frankie. "You didn't mention that part."

"Didn't I?" Frankie said innocently. "Must have slipped my mind."

"Don't worry," said Molly. "I'll mind your clothes."

"Strangely enough, that isn't what's worrying me," I said. "There's all these people . . . I don't like to."

"Oh, get on with it!" said Molly.

I looked around and saw that everyone else was stripping off. And since they didn't seem too bothered, and no one was making a fuss about it, I did so too. The wind felt very cold, and I felt very vulnerable, as I finally stood naked and shivering before an open doorway. No one else seemed to be paying me any attention; they all had their gaze fixed on the Tower, their minds set on the Game.

"See?" Molly said brightly, hugging my clothes to her chest. "Not a scar to be seen, anywhere. I do good work!"

"Not bad," said Frankie. "Though I have seen better . . ."

"Hey!" said Molly. "You keep your eyes off my property!"

The generic flunkies began ushering everyone through the open doorways, and into the Tower. By now there was a whole crowd of players, dozens of us. All types and sizes, most of them in pretty good shape. And watching us, all around the base of the Tower, an audience of hundreds gathered to watch us fight and hopefully die, entertainingly, on the floating viewscreens. Frankie waved a quick good-bye, and moved off into the crowd to do what he did best. Molly waved, and then the generic flunky pushed me politely but firmly through the open doorway.

The inside of the Tower was just a great empty hollow, surrounded by a curving stone interior wall. People were filling up the empty space from all sides, hurrying in through the doorways. Some smiling, some serious, no one saying anything. And every one of us naked as the day we were born. Some it bothered, some it didn't; a few stared openly. I looked up, to the top of the Tower. A single stone step protruded, at the very top. According to Frankie, just before the Game began a flunky would appear there, holding the sacred staff. He would drop it, and one of us would catch it. And then, we would all fight it out to see who could hold on to the staff. While everyone else tried to take it away, by any and all means necessary. Last Man Standing. And that, Frankie had assured me, was all there was to the Game. Be the last man, with the staff. No other rules.

The hollow interior filled up pretty quickly, but the flunkies kept pushing in more and more competitors. Even after we were all packed uncomfortably close together, still the competitors kept arriving. Forced through the doorways by firm, implacable flunkies. Until finally we were all packed so closely together, we could hardly move. No room left for modesty when we were all back to back, belly to belly, face to face. The heat inside the Tower, generated by so many bodies in such a confined space, quickly became intolerable. And then got worse. We were all of us sweating like fury, but the perspiration running down our bodies was the only lubrication we had, to allow us to move. And it didn't take me long to realise that not everyone else in the Tower was entirely human.

Fur brushed up against bare skin, as werewolves and werebears and other furred halflings insisted on their presence. Unnaturally pale people with sharp teeth and crimson eyes—vampires, hiding their true walking corpse status behind flickering glamours. And from the smell of it, several ghouls, too. And on top of that, several only vaguely human shapes that might have been aliens or demons, or anything in between. Some had scales, some had bony carapaces, or vicious bone spurs protruding from their elbows, and some had too many arms. It would appear that invitations to Casino Infernale went really far and wide. I couldn't help feeling at something of a disadvantage, in being only human. Except, that I had one very special ace, not at all up my sleeve.

We finally reached a point where the generic flunkies couldn't force another body through the doorways and that was when the flunky appeared on the top step high above us, holding out the sacred staff. He called out once, to get our attention, and then just dropped the staff.

It seemed to float almost tantalisingly on the air above us, turning end over end as it fell. A hundred hands thrust up, eager to grab it, mine among them. The staff fell and fell, and finally one hand grabbed it out of the air. I turned towards it and someone kicked my feet right out from under me. I fell, slipping through the greased bodies around me, and hit the floor hard. And straight away everyone else trampled all over me, as the crowd surged back and forth in pursuit of the sacred staff. All kinds of feet slammed into me from every direction, knocking the breath right out of me. It didn't take me long to realise that if I stayed down, I would be trampled to death.

So, I delivered short vicious punches, and back-elbows, in every direction; cracking bones and breaking ankles, until enough people crashed to the floor to allow me enough space to fight my way back onto my feet again. Bruised, and bloodied, but intact. Some more applied viciousness opened up a little more space around me, but there were any number of punches and back-elbows coming my way too, as we all surged this way and that, a hundred and more naked bodies fighting it out for one wooden staff.

Please don't let me get a hard-on, I thought. *People are watching. It would be so hard to explain, afterwards.*

I could hear the crowd outside, enjoying the fighting. Watching it all on the floating viewscreens, laughing and cheering and applauding. They cheered especially loudly when they saw someone die. I couldn't see the bodies on the floor, but I could feel them when my feet slammed into something hard and unyielding.

I could see the staff, held above our heads, being snatched from hand to hand. It didn't look like much, just a length of wood covered with engraved runic symbols. Most people used it as a club to beat other people about the head with. It quickly became covered in gore and hair, dripping blood. Someone waved it back and forth triumphantly, and drips of blood flew into everyone's faces. Until the holder was beaten down by everyone around him.

Fists were flying everywhere. Knees came up, and feet kicked. We were all shouting and screaming at the top of our lungs, till the sound was actually painful. All of us caught up in the fighting frenzy, everyone against everyone else. Someone head-butted me in the face, but by the time I lashed out in return, my attacker was already gone, carried away by the movements of the crowd, and I punched out someone else instead. It didn't matter. I had no friends here, only enemies. Blood dripped from my nose, but it didn't feel like it was broken. I spat a mouthful of blood into someone's face, and their returning fist shot past my head and punched out someone behind me. That was the Game.

More and more space was opening up, as more and more bodies crashed unconscious or dying to the floor. Just because no actual weapons could be brought in, didn't mean you couldn't get killed. Some people were weapons. I threw enough punches to keep everyone else at bay, while letting the Brownian movements of the crowd carry me away from the centre and all the way back to the interior wall. I felt definitely relieved as I pressed my back against the solid stone, because it meant that was one direction no attack could come from now. And then, finally, I could take time out from defending myself, and allow the effects of the Armourer's potion to kick in. Finally, I could see the patterns in the crowd, and anticipate which attacks were coming my way, even before they happened. I ducked and dodged, and pulled other people in front of me to soak up the blows. I shoved people this way and that, so they would fight each other and not me. For the first time, I felt I was in some control of the situation.

Looking out across the heaving mob, it was quickly clear to me that the non-human fighters were targeting each other as the most dangerous players in the Game. Just as well, or we poor humans wouldn't have stood a chance.

A vampire sank its fangs into the shoulder of a werewolf, worrying blood from the wound. A group of ghouls dragged down an alien and ate it alive. There was a sudden stink of guts on the air near me, as a group of things with too many arms turned a werebear inside out. Fangs and claws, blood and gore, and above it all, the sacred wooden staff moving jerkily back and forth, snatched from hand to hand. And I couldn't help noticing . . . that the more dangerous players were actually cancelling each other out, by picking on each other. Until finally there were only humans left fighting for the prize. I stayed back by the wall and just let them get on with it. And they were all so taken up in their quest for the staff, and beating the hell out of anyone who got in their way, that they didn't even notice me. They slammed into each other, hitting and kicking, gouging and tearing, until finally, eventually, there was only one man left, standing surrounded by a pile of bodies, covered in blood that mostly wasn't his. Clutching at his gore-covered prize, and smiling. Last man standing—apart from me.

I coughed politely, to draw his attention. His head snapped round to stare at me. He glared at me with a cold, focused, murderous gaze. He really was very big, very muscular, and he'd soaked up a hell of a lot of punishment to get his hands on the staff. He kicked at a few of the bodies around him, moving them back to give him room to fight. One moaned, showing it was still alive. The big man stamped on the fallen man's head, and the sound stopped. The big man brandished the sacred staff at me, daring me to take it from him. I barely recognised the thing, it was so crusted in blood and gore.

"Come here," said the big man, the bloody man. "Come here, and I'll kill you. I've killed so many to win this Game, one more won't matter. Come here and let me kill you and I'll make it quick. Make me work for it, and I will make you scream and beg and bleed before I finish you." He smiled suddenly. "That is why I come to the Game, after all. Where else can you get to kill so many people, in the name of sport? I always have the best time here, every year!"

I reached into the pocket dimension at my hip, brought out my Colt Repeater, and shot him neatly between the eyes. His head snapped back, and he was dead before he hit the bodies piled up around him. The pocket dimension isn't actually in the pocket of my trousers, or I'd never be able to wear another pair. It just hovers at my hip, and goes everywhere with me. Most useful thing the Armourer ever made for me. I slipped the Colt back into the pocket dimension, and it disappeared again. I clambered carefully over the fallen competitors, heading for the man I'd killed. Some of them made feeble sounds of protest, which meant some of them were still alive. I was glad about that. I didn't want to think so many people had actually died for a stupid stick. I prised the sacred staff out of the dead man's hand, wiped some of the mess away on his body, and then turned and headed for the nearest open doorway.

It felt wonderfully cool, out in the open air again. The crowd went wild, laughing and cheering and applauding. They did love a good surprise ending. Some of them came rushing forward, wanting to shake my hand or clap me on the shoulder. I let them do it, though I drew the line at being embraced. At least until I was dressed again. Apparently a lot of people had won a lot of souls, betting on me. I wasn't sure how I felt about that. Molly pushed her way through the crowd, holding my clothes, and a towel she'd acquired from somewhere. She glared at everyone else until they fell back enough to give us room. And then she towelled me down carefully, removing as much of the caked-on blood as she could. I hadn't realised how much had ended up on me from other people. Molly bit her lip, as she saw the bruises under the blood, but said nothing. She helped me get dressed again.

A generic flunky approached me, and I looked him in the eye.

"Nothing in the rules against it," I said.

"You are allowed whatever you carry in with you, sir," said the flunky. "Though you did push it, a bit."

I looked around, as Frankie came rushing up. "Tell me I won big," I said. "Because I have had enough of these Games."

"Of course we won big!" said Frankie, beaming all over his flushed face. "You wouldn't believe how many souls we won!"

"We won?" I said.

"Oh, all right, you won," said Frankie. "The point is, you now possess more than enough souls to get yourself a place in the Big Game!"

"About time," said Molly. "Really don't like this place."

"Then let's get out of here," I said.

"Excuse me, sir," said the flunky, politely but firmly. "You have to hand back the sacred staff."

I looked at the soiled object I was still hanging on to. I honestly hadn't realised I still had the thing.

"I don't get to keep it?"

"No, sir."

"Then what did I win? What's the point of the Game?"

"The honour of playing, sir."

I handed him the sacred staff. "So, I don't get anything?"

"Of course you do, sir. You get your obol."

He pressed the small coin into my hand.

"And this represents . . . ?" I said.

"The soul of everyone who fell, living or dead, in the Game, sir. Please follow me now, and I will lead you back to your dimensional door."

"I will come back," I said to him. "I will come back here, to help you."

The generic flunky looked at me for a long moment. "Then I will look forward to seeing you again, sir."

He led us back across the purple-tinged grass, back to the door, and our world. Molly slipped her arm through mine.

"First you want to free all the faces in the corridor, now you want to free all the flunkies in this world. You just can't look away, can you?"

"The word *over-ambitious* does come to mind," said Frankie, behind us.

"That's my Shaman," said Molly. "Can't see a wrong without wanting to put it right." She smiled at me fondly. "Just remember, we still have a war to stop. And you promised me you'd help track down the Regent so I can get the truth out of him."

"I hadn't forgotten," I said.

"I'm actually beginning to believe it," said Frankie. "Maybe you really can break the bank at Casino Infernale, after all."

Molly looked at him. "If you didn't believe it before, why have you been helping us all this time?"

Frankie looked at her as though she was crazy. "For the money, of course!"

CHAPTER EIGHT

Decisions Are Made,
with Far-Reaching Consequences

I was bracing myself for another trip through the corridor of screaming faces, all those trapped souls I couldn't help, but when the generic flunky finally opened the dimensional door it opened directly onto our hotel suite. I stepped through automatically, with Molly and Frankie almost stepping on my heels, but when I turned back to question the flunky . . . the dimensional door had already closed, and disappeared. It did feel good to be back. The world of the Medium Games had just felt wrong, in too many small, telling ways. Mars had actually been easier to deal with, because it was so different. I sighed heavily, and sank down onto the bed. I hadn't realised how tired I was until I didn't have to be strong any more.

"It would seem the hotel's doors can drop us off wherever they want to," said Molly.

"Then why did they make us walk through the corridor of trapped souls in the first place?" I said.

"To make a point?" said Frankie. "Remind us where

the true power lies, at Casino Infernale? To put us in the right frame of mind for the Games? The Casino has been doing this for a long time, and it never misses a trick."

"I need to take another shower," I said, heaving myself back up onto my feet again. "I need to wash the Games off me."

"Sounds good," said Molly. "Think I'll join you."

"I think I'll go for another walk," said Frankie. "Maybe take a turn back into town, see if they've cleared up all those crashed Pteranodons yet. There's a future in fast food to be made there, by someone with ambition and the right connections. . . ."

"Hold it," I said. "I have a job for you, first. I want all the souls we won deposited somewhere safe, and secure."

"No problem," said Frankie. "I'll deposit them in the hotel safe. What are you both looking at me like that for? They'll be perfectly secure there. The Shadow Bank guarantees Casino Infernale's security. If they didn't, no one who mattered would gamble here. Why do you think they made such a fuss when you broke into Parris' office? People have to believe their winnings are safe here. You'd better give me your obols to deposit, too. They're the soul equivalent of cold cash."

Molly and I dug the small coins out of our pockets and handed them over to Frankie; but at the last moment I held back the first obol I'd won. I hefted the small coin in my hand. So light, it was hardly there.

"Think I'll hang on to this," I said, putting it back in my pocket. "As a reminder of how cheaply they value souls around here."

"He's getting sentimental," Molly said to Frankie. "That's always dangerous. Leave now. Quickly. Run, while you still have the chance!"

Frankie left, grinning. I took Molly by the hand and led her to the shower. The blood came off easily enough, but the memories still stuck.

Afterwards, we dressed in new clothes. A smart navy blue blazer and slacks for me, and a matching blue evening gown for Molly. She paraded up and down the room in it for me to admire, and smiled triumphantly at me.

"Now aren't you glad I packed so many clothes?"

"I trust you explicitly in such things," I said, carefully packing the Armourer's various secret weapons and devices about my person. "Except for when I don't."

"I knew you wouldn't stick with that shoulder holster," said Molly, as I slipped the Colt Repeater into my pocket dimension.

"Slowed me down too much. Stick with what works, that's what I say." I stood before the full-length looking glass to check out my appearance. Molly came and stood beside me, looking almost dazzlingly glamorous.

"We do make a good team," she said. "I'd back us against anyone, in this world or out of it."

I had to smile. "That is why we're here. . . ."

Frankie knocked loudly on the door, from outside in the corridor, but had the lock open and was inside with us before the echoes had died away.

"Good to see you both upright, and clothed," he said. "I have news!"

"What is so urgent?" said Molly. In a tone that implied that it had bloody well better be.

"We've been gone longer than you think," said Frankie. "I was just down in the lobby, when it occurred to me to check my watch against the lobby's clock. We've been away for half a day!"

I looked automatically at my watch. It had never occurred to me to check. We'd been away only an hour or so, maybe less. But the hands on my watch face showed ten past ten. Molly showed me her watch: 22:09. When I looked at the hotel clock on the bedside table, it said 1:14. And it was only then I thought to look out the window. It had been a dark evening when we left, now it was a bright sunny day. Midday, apparently.

"What was the point of that?" said Molly.

"To make another point, about how the Casino can control Time and Space through their dimensional doors?"

said Frankie. "Or, because they didn't want us hanging around the hotel with all its hangers-on, con men, and thieves, before the Big Game starts?"

"I hate time travel," I said. "It plays merry hell with your tenses."

"Casino Infernale is very nearly over," said Frankie. "When I was down in the lobby, it was almost empty. Most of the Players have gone, and all of the hangers-on. The few remaining Major Players are apparently sitting quietly in their rooms, behaving themselves, waiting to see if they've done well enough to be invited to attend the Big Game."

And even as he was saying that, there was a polite but firm knock on the door. Molly and I moved quickly to stand together, facing the door, while Frankie moved quickly to hide behind us. Before it even occurred to me to say *Come in!* the lock opened from the other side and the manager Jonathon Scott walked in. He smiled easily at me, polite and respectful, consideration itself.

"Allow me to present my compliments," he said, in his best professionally charming voice. "I am here to invite you to take your place in the Big Game, Mr. Bond. On the penthouse floor at precisely eight o'clock this evening."

Frankie punched the air. Molly beamed widely, and I nodded to Scott. He waited a moment, to see if there was to be any more exuberance, and then stepped forward and presented me with an engraved invitation. Nothing fancy, or fussy. Just a simple card with my name on it. Nice lettering. Shaman Bond had never looked better.

"Please don't lose the card," said Scott. "It has all kinds of security protocols built in. You won't be admitted without it."

"What if someone steals it?" said Molly, practical as ever.

"Heaven forefend that such a thing should happen in this hotel," said Scott. "But if you were to lose it . . . that would only prove that Mr. Bond is not worthy to attend the Big Game, after all. And we would give his place to whoever might turn up with the card. The Casino really is very blunt and practical about things like that."

"I'm sure you are," I said, slipping the invitation carefully into my pocket dimension.

Scott looked at me knowingly. "A very useful hiding place, Mr. Bond. You made very good use of it at Last Man Standing."

"You were watching?" said Molly.

"I watch everything," said Scott. "That's my job."

"Are there rules against using such things?" I said.

"Not as such," said Scott. "And the extremely powerful null zone operating at the Big Game will of course render it of no use to you. For the duration."

"Can't keep anything secret here!" Molly said brightly.

"No," said Scott. "You can't." He looked at me directly. "Eight p.m. sharp, Mr. Bond. Don't be late, or you won't be admitted. Card or no card. And Mr. Bond, the invitation to play is extended strictly to you, and you alone. You may of course bring Miss Molly Metcalf with you, as your plus one, should you so choose, but she will not be allowed to play, or wager, or interfere in any way." He glanced briefly at Frankie. "Leave your pet behind."

"Why is the invitation just for Shaman?" Molly said hotly. "I did my bit!"

"There can be only one," Scott said smoothly. "And Shaman won most of the souls through his efforts."

He then produced a heavy folder out of nowhere. Made me wonder whether he might have a pocket dimension of his own, and what else he might keep in it. The entire Jackson Fifty-five, for all I knew. Scott presented me with the folder, marked with the hotel crest in gold, and then looked at me expectantly. So I opened the folder. It contained several sheets of top-quality paper, also marked with the hotel crest, bearing row upon row of names. I leafed quickly through the pages, but it was all nothing but names. I looked at Scott.

"This is your receipt, Mr. Bond. For all the souls you won at the Games, and entrusted to our hotel safe. Every name is there, every soul that now belongs to you. The living and the dead. Again, sir, please don't lose this. It is your only proof of ownership. All lost souls revert to the Casino. Well, I think that's everything. Unless you have any questions?"

I would have liked to ask about the whereabouts of my own soul. Whose list it appeared on. But I couldn't, because the Casino only had a claim on Eddie Drood's soul, and I was Shaman Bond. The generic flunky at the Medium Games had seen the constraints on my soul, but he hadn't actually asked my name. Just as well, really. Could have been awkward. I decided to change the subject.

"Am I bringing the largest number of souls won to the Big Game?" I asked bluntly.

Scott couldn't hold back a small condescending smile. "Hardly, sir. But you did make a very good showing, for a first-time contender. I'm sure we're all very interested to see how you'll do at the Big Game, Mr. Bond."

He smiled again, nodded politely to one and all, and left. The door closed itself behind him. Molly made a rude gesture at the door.

"I should have been invited! A lot of those souls should be mine!"

"He won more than you," Frankie said impassively. "That's how it works here."

Molly sniffed loudly. I was still leafing through the pages in the hotel folder. So many names . . . I didn't like the idea of owning other people's souls. Too much like slavery.

"Stop looking," said Frankie, kindly enough. "You never know, you might recognise a name. It's better not to know."

"You can always set them free later," said Molly. "After we've broken the bank at Casino Infernale. In fact . . . if we break the bank really badly, and damage the Shadow Bank enough . . . then maybe their hold on their souls will be broken."

"Yes," I said. "I'd like that." I looked at Frankie. "Would that apply to all those faces in the corridor?"

"I don't know," Frankie said carefully. "I don't think the subject has ever come up before. I would have to say that we're treading in unknown and very theoretical territory here. Even if you do somehow manage to break the bank at Casino Infernale, a thing that has never ever been done before, that doesn't mean you'd in any way break the Shadow Bank's control over its many holdings. Economical and spiritual. The Casino's just a fund-raiser for the Bank, when all is said and done. The best you can realistically hope for is to weaken their position enough to stop this war you're so worried about over the Crow Lee Inheritance. Whatever that might turn out to be. But that's it! That's enough, isn't it?"

"That was before I got a good look at how the Shadow Bank operates," I said. "Before I saw the faces."

"Oh, God," said Molly. "He's gone all ambitious again. That's rarely good." She looked at Frankie. "I'd start running now, if I were you."

"That thought is never far from my mind," said Frankie. He looked at me thoughtfully. "You know, that is a whole bunch of souls you've got there, in your hands. Representing more money than you could ever hope to spend in one lifetime. I know you've been talking about releasing them all back into the wild, but I'm sure the family wouldn't miss a few. . . . I could get you a really good deal on the underground Soul Market. . . . No? All right, how about this? It occurs to me that the family might prefer you to hang on to certain bad guy souls. To give the Droods power and control over them."

"The family doesn't work like that," I said.

"Since when?" said Frankie.

I closed the folder, and put it away in my pocket dimension. Just in case.

"The important thing is to regain control of your own soul, Eddie," said Molly. "And those of your parents."

I looked at her. "What about all those claims on your soul? I'm going to have to do something about that."

"You're so sweet," said Molly. She came forward to

stand right in front of me, so we could stare into each other's eyes.

"Are you two going back into the shower again?" said Frankie. "Are you even listening to me? Oh, hell . . . can I have some money to go to the pictures?"

"Hold it," I said, tearing my gaze away from Molly to glare steadily at Frankie. "I still want to know exactly what's happened to my parents. I can't believe the hotel or the Casino would just let them leave, and escape, not when they had a claim on their souls. They must have some way of tracking them . . . so, just maybe, the Casino has my parents imprisoned somewhere here in the hotel. Ask around, Frankie. The Players may have left, but most of the staff are probably still here. Talk to them; see if anybody knows anything."

Frankie nodded quickly. "Got it, boss."

He left. Molly looked at me.

"We have to talk about your parents, Eddie. Even if we do break the bank here, we have to accept we might not be able to free their souls, or yours, from the Shadow Bank."

"Then I'll just have to do whatever it takes to bring down the Shadow Bank," I said. "Not just for my sake, but for everyone's."

"Whatever happened to better the devil you know, and all that?" said Molly.

"That was before I got a look at how they do things," I said. "I will not suffer this to continue, Molly. I can't. It's not just about me any more, or my parents. Or even stopping an inconvenient war. You saw the faces, Molly. Like Frankie said, they might as well be in Hell. If I turn my gaze away, it's like I'm saying *They knew what they were doing, they deserve it, it's none of my business.* And I can't do that."

"Of course you can't, sweetie," said Molly. "The Shadow Bank is going down! I'm with you all the way. But, how are we going to do it? We don't even know who or what might be running them. What can we do?"

"Haven't a clue," I said. "I'm working on it."

"Terrific . . ." said Molly. "Talk about getting a girl's hopes up . . . want to lie down on the bed for a while?"

Just as she was saying that, there was the sound of gunfire as the lock on our door was blown apart, the door was kicked in, and someone with a very familiar face stormed into our suite. The Little Lord looked very angry, even disturbed . . . and in pretty good shape, considering that the last time I'd seen her she was being carried unconscious from the Arena. She was back in a formal suit, complete with top hat and a monocle screwed firmly into one eye. She had a really large gun in one hand, and a piece of complicated-looking tech jammed under her other arm. She fixed me with a cold, dangerous look and pointed the gun right at me.

Molly moved quickly forward to stand between me and the Little Lord, and I let her. I thought about drawing the Colt Repeater from my pocket dimension, and then thought better of it. A drawn gun trumps a holstered gun, every time. I was better off letting Molly defend us both with her magics.

Until I recognised the tech under the Little Lord's arm; what it was, what it had to be. And I stepped forward, to put myself between Molly and the Little Lord. Her gun followed my every movement. It looked very steady; and the Little Lord looked very determined. Molly glared at me, as though I might have forgotten I didn't have my armour any more. I put out an arm to hold her where she was, and nodded to the Little Lord.

"Didn't expect to see you again so soon," I said calmly. "Nice gun. Is that tech thing . . . what I think it is?"

"What?" said Molly.

"It's a portable null zone generator," the Little Lord said grimly, glancing quickly at Molly. "So your magics won't work against me, witch."

"Where did you get such a thing?" I said quickly, to bring the Little Lord's attention back to me. And before Molly could say anything that might make the situation any more tense. "And how did you get back here from the Games world?"

"Pretended I was unconscious, until the flunkies weren't looking," said the Little Lord. "Then I slipped away, clubbed down a Player from behind, stole his obol and his identity, and a flunky escorted me back through the dimensional door. Seems they really can't tell us apart, after all. I stole this portable generator from one of the hotel staff, beat your location out of a Jackson, and stole his gun, and here I am."

"That's actually . . . pretty impressive," said Molly. "Sounds like something I might do."

"It's amazing how motivated you can get when you've just lost your soul," said the Little Lord. Her gun was still pointing straight at me. "And now, I want it back. Give me back my soul, right now! Because if you don't I will shoot you, Shaman Bond, and take my chances that with your death, all your bets will be declared null and void!"

"Sore loser," said Molly.

"Shut up!" said the Little Lord, her voice rising dangerously. "You don't understand! It's not just money I lost this time; it's my eternal soul! I thought I understood what I was risking, but I didn't. I'll do whatever I have to, to get my soul back!"

"All right," I said. "You can have it."

The Little Lord looked at me. "What?"

"It's just one soul," I said. "I've got loads—more than enough to get me into the Big Game." I looked at Molly. "I told you I wasn't comfortable owning souls."

"You expect me to believe you?" said the Little Lord. "You're really willing to just . . . give me my soul back?"

"Why not?" I said.

Moving slowly and carefully, I took the hotel ledger out of my pocket dimension, leafed through the pages to find the Little Lord's name, and then took out a pen and carefully crossed her name through. Then I put the ledger away again, took out the obol I'd kept, and handed it to her.

"This is your soul," I said. "Or at least what represents it. I revoke all claims to it."

And as I handed the small coin over to the Little Lord,

we both felt something pass between us. Like the handing over of a precious gift, or a heavy burden, or something of indescribable significance. We both breathed a little more easily. The Little Lord clutched her obol tightly in her fist, and looked at me with something like wonder.

"Thank you. . . . That was the most generous thing I've ever seen. I don't know what I'd expected would happen when I finally got here, but that wasn't it."

"He's a good man," said Molly. "I don't tell him nearly often enough, but he is."

"I'm Shaman Bond," I said. "If I was someone else, I might have responsibilities. I might feel it was my duty to hang on to the obol. But I'm not. I'm Shaman Bond, and a free man."

The Little Lord looked at Molly. "Am I supposed to understand any of that?"

"I'm right here, and I'm not sure I do," said Molly.

"I'd leave the Casino right now, if I were you," I said kindly to the Little Lord. "Hotel Security are probably already on their way here to investigate the shooting, and Casino Security will be hot on the trail of their stolen null generator. Besides, I don't think the Casino's a healthy place for you. Now you've got your soul back, there's always the chance you might be tempted to gamble it again."

"I didn't mean to," said the Little Lord. "I was just so desperate to get home again."

"Then you'd better have some money, too," I said. "To help you on your journey." I produced a thick wad of notes from my pocket, and offered them to her. The Little Lord put her gun away, and accepted the money almost shyly.

"Yes," she said. "Thank you. I . . . I'm out of here. I'm going home!"

She turned and left. I went over to the door and pushed it shut. I turned back to find Molly looking at me.

"You really think she can get out of this hotel, and evade Casino Security, on her own?"

"Why not?" I said. "She has a portable null generator and I'd like to see anyone stop her, the mood she's in. She's going home. Wherever that might be. Planet of the Aristocratic Imposters, perhaps."

"Oh, I can tell you where she comes from," said Molly. "The Nightside. She's an old friend of Razor Eddie, Punk God of the Straight Razor."

I sighed, quietly. "Tell me she's not the Little God of Transvestites, or something."

"No," said Molly. "Nothing so grand. She's from some other-dimensional city port called Haven, and the sooner she goes back there, the better. You know, you really are too good for your own good, sometimes. Come here."

Not long after that the door slammed open again, and Frankie came hurrying in.

"What the hell happened to the lock on your door? Did something happen while I was gone? Oh God, you're at it again. Don't you ever stop? Look, you have to listen to me! This is important! Really important!"

"All right," I said, stepping away from Molly. "I believe you. What is it, that's so very important?"

"It's your parents!" said Frankie. "I've found them! I got lucky first time out, talking to the right person. The Casino is holding your parents prisoner, and I know where!"

"Where?" I said, and something in my voice and in my gaze made Frankie stumble for a moment.

"Right here in the hotel," he said finally.

"Are you sure?" said Molly.

"Of course I'm sure!" said Frankie, regaining something of his usual assurance. "I told you—I can find out anything! The Casino has both of them locked up in a specially guarded holding cell, down in the hotel sub-basement. But you have to come with me, right now, because they're about to be moved!"

"Let's go," I said.

Frankie dithered impatiently, while I made sure I had all the Armourer's special weapons and devices stored away somewhere about my person. I wanted to be sure I was ready for anything. Molly stuck close to me, comforting me with her presence, making it clear that she was ready to back me up, in whatever I chose to do. Finally, I nodded to Frankie, and he led the way out of the room.

As we hurried down the deserted corridor towards the elevators, I rehearsed in my head all the things I intended to say to my parents when I finally caught up with them. To Patrick and Diana—or Charles and Emily. I hadn't spoken to them since my family home returned from the alien world it had been exiled to. We'd meant to sit down and talk, and catch up. But we'd all been so busy, and then Casino Infernale got in the way. There was so much I wanted to say to them, so many questions I needed answered. . . . I was still angry with them for abandoning me to the Droods to bring up. For not letting me know they were still alive. And, for betting my soul and losing it, without even asking my permission. But I was a field agent, just like they had been for so many years. I knew that sometimes you have to think on your feet in dangerous situations, and make sudden decisions for the good of the mission. I wasn't ready to judge or forgive them, just yet. I was ready to listen, and try to understand.

There just might be a lot of shouting involved, first.

We waited impatiently before the closed elevator doors, as the damned thing seemed to take forever to arrive. I kept looking up and down the empty corridor, but there was still no sign anywhere of any kind of Security. If I was Scott, I'd give them a real earful for their poor reaction times. But it was just as well, for the Security goons. I wasn't in the mood to be messed with. The elevator doors finally opened, and we all hurried inside. Frankie hit the button for the sub-basement, the doors closed, and the elevator started its descent.

It took a long time to pass all the way down through the dozens of floors, to the very bottom. I kept checking my pockets to make sure everything was where it should be. I was still dangerously tense; Molly was poised and ready for anything; and Frankie seemed to grow more and more nervous. I didn't blame him. He wasn't the fighting sort and he was about to see a Drood enraged. It was not going to be pretty. The elevator finally slowed to a halt, and we all braced ourselves as we waited for the doors to open. When they did, I was first out.

And then I stopped, and glared at Frankie.

"Wait a minute! I know this place! This isn't the sub-basement; it's the underground car park!"

"Same thing!" Frankie said quickly. "They don't have a call button marked for the car park, or anybody could get in! Now will you please keep your voice down! We're not supposed to be here, remember? There are still some staff around. . . ."

"I have to wonder," said Molly, looking carefully between the rows upon rows of parked cars, "when we were here before, did we perhaps pass right by the holding cell, and not even know it?"

"This hotel is full of secure locations," said Frankie, hurrying on ahead and glancing quickly about him. "They've got stuff holed away here you wouldn't believe. There are whole sections of Casino Infernale that don't even talk to each other. Now will you please hurry up and follow me!"

He quickly threaded his way through one particular set of parked cars, and I was right there behind him, with Molly bringing up the rear and shooting dangerous glances in all directions. The underground car park was exactly as I'd remembered it. A great stone cavern full of very old and very new cars, sitting silent and still in their orderly rows, and no sign of any staff anywhere. And then Molly stopped, abruptly. I sighed, and looked back.

"What is it, Molly?"

"Something's wrong," said Molly. "As in, something doesn't feel right."

And that was when the Casino Security people dropped their concealing illusion, and a whole army of very well-armed guards appeared all around us. We'd walked right into their midst, completely unaware. What looked like all of the remaining Jackson Fifty-five were in position around us, cutting off all the exits, pointing all kinds of guns at us. I stood very still and after I glared at her, so did Molly. From out among the parked cars, sauntering along, came the hotel manager himself, Jonathon Scott. Frankie looked at me, shrugged and smirked, and then moved over to stand with Scott. The Jacksons let him pass, unchallenged. Molly made a deep growling noise.

"So," said Scott, stopping a respectful distance away from me and Molly. He looked me up and down with more than common interest. "You aren't the shady and shifty Shaman Bond, after all. Instead, you're a Drood in disguise. And not just any Drood, but the almost legendary Eddie Drood. Your reputation very definitely precedes you. Though I always thought you'd be taller."

"I get that a lot," I said. And then I looked at Frankie, who flinched under my gaze, but quickly recovered.

"Sorry, boss. I really was with you all the way; right until you started that nonsense about bringing down the Shadow Bank. I was listening outside the door. Old habits. I am too old and too experienced to work with crazy people. So I went straight to Mr. Scott, explained my position, and struck a deal. He was most understanding. And it must be said, the Shadow Bank pays a hell of a lot better than the Droods."

"You really are a bastard," said Molly.

"One of the Grey Bastards," Frankie said proudly. "The clue is in the name."

"Don't try anything, witch," said Scott. "We have a full-strength portable null zone generator working down here." He indicated a large machine, standing to one side, guarded by half a dozen Jacksons. "Your infamous magics are being very thoroughly suppressed."

"I don't believe it," Molly said to me. "You're legendary, but I'm just infamous?"

"How about the machine?" I said.

"Oh, that. Yeah, scumbag here is right. I've got nothing. Getting really tired of that, I have to say."

"You don't have to say anything, witch," said Scott. "So shut up. Let the people who matter talk, or I'll have you gagged." He waited a moment, to make his point, and then gave me his full attention. "So, a Drood without his torc. No sign we can detect that you ever had one . . . I never thought to see such a thing."

"Giving it up wasn't easy," I said. "But bringing you down will make it all worthwhile."

"Typical Drood arrogance," said Scott, entirely unmoved. If anything, he seemed amused. "You have no idea how much money I'm going to make out of you. From auctioning you to the Major Players here. The secrets waiting to be dug out of your mind, and after that's gone, your body . . . What your new master will tear out of you will change the order of the world. . . . Drood secrets, for sale to the highest bidders." He stopped, and thought for a moment. "I suppose . . . I could always ransom you, back to your family. . . . They'd pay really big money to keep your secrets from getting out. But no. Too risky. Your family has a reputation for dealing harshly with anyone who wants a more equitable playing field. No, I think it best they don't know anything about this until it's all safely over, and it's too late for them to interfere."

He broke off to smile on the increasingly fuming Molly. "I'm sure we'll get a decent sum for you too, witch. And oh the things we'll do to you, before we let you go. I'm sure your new owner won't mind if we have some fun with you first. As long as your mind's intact, they won't care what we've done to your body."

I must have moved forward, because all the guns immediately moved to cover me, and Scott actually fell back a step. He glared at me.

"Stay right where you are, Drood! And don't try to run. I need you alive, not intact. Having the Jackson Fifty-five chase after you and drag you down would just be embarrassing for all concerned. Now, Eddie, please be so good as to remove that nasty gun of yours from your hidden pocket dimension, and drop it on the floor. And when you've done that, you can empty out all your pockets, and show us all the lovely toys the family Armourer gave you just for this mission. I'm sure my superiors will have such fun, working out what they do, and how best to use them against your family."

"Can I ask a question?" I said.

"What is it?" said Scott.

"Do you really have my father and mother imprisoned down here somewhere?"

"Of course not!" said Scott. "Haven't a clue where they are. Didn't know they were your parents, until Frankie volunteered the information."

"One more question," I said.

"It's no use trying to put it off, Drood," Scott said pityingly. "It's over! You lost. I never thought to see the legendary Eddie Drood beg and plead for just a little more time, before the inevitable awfulness."

"I just wanted to ask," I said, "whether you've informed your lord and master, Franklyn Parris, as to who I really am?"

"Not yet," said Scott. "That's going to be my little surprise at the end of Casino Infernale. My gift to him to ensure my promotion."

"That's all I needed to know," I said. "Lady! Now!"

And the Scarlet Lady came roaring forward, blasting out of her parking space just behind Jonathon Scott; sounding her horn loudly as she came charging to the rescue. She swept past Scott, who threw himself to one side, crying out, and ran right over the Jacksons defending the null zone generator. She smashed right through the machine, blowing it to pieces, and then spun around to run over the Jacksons she hadn't hit the first time. They opened fire on her, and their bullets ricocheted harmlessly from her chassis. They just had time to scream once, before she ran them down and chewed them up under her wheels.

I drew my Colt Repeater, and carefully shot Scott in the leg. So he couldn't run. I didn't want him dead, just yet. He screamed almost hysterically, as though he couldn't believe such a thing could happen to someone like him, and then he collapsed, clutching at his leg with both hands. He shouldn't have threatened my Molly. I turned my gun on the nearest Jacksons, and picked them off one by one.

Their bullets flew past me, but none of them even came close. They had their own problems.

With the machine destroyed, Molly had her magics back, and she was not in a good mood. She gestured sharply, and all the cars around us exploded. The Jacksons standing among them were caught completely off guard, terrorised by the sudden fiery explosions. Some were killed instantly, others caught fire. Those remaining tried to target Molly, but she was off and moving. Here, there, and everywhere. Popping up between the remaining cars, hitting the Jacksons with energy bolts, shaped curses, and really nasty hexes that made their flesh run away like water. Eventually, she got tired of playing with them, and summoned up a great storm wind that came howling through the underground car park. It ignored me, but picked up the Jacksons and slammed them into walls and ceilings and support pillars. With such force they all blew apart like rotten fruit under a hammer.

I lowered my gun. There was no one left to shoot at.

Frankie ran for his life. I ran after him. He really could run, but all the parked cars and blazing wrecks slowed him down. I used my pattern-spotting ability to work out where he was heading before he even knew himself, and then it was easy enough to get myself in just the right place to intercept him. I vaulted over a parked car, landed on him hard, and threw him to the ground.

We rolled back and forth on the concrete floor. Frankie tried to fight me, but he didn't really know how. And I've been trained. I knocked the breath out of him, and then slammed the back of his head against the hard floor. He stopped struggling. I hauled him back onto his feet, and he stood before me, holding his head with both hands, crying like a child.

"Where are my parents?" I said.

I had to slap his face a few times to stop him crying. Anyone else, I would have felt like a bully.

"Where are my parents?"

"I don't know!" said Frankie. "No one knows where they are! I only said they were here to get you to come with me! It was all Scott's idea!"

"You betrayed me," I said. "And Molly. And the family."

"They were never my family!" said Frankie. "Never. I'm a Grey Bastard, and I have to make my own way. Please don't hurt me. I can still be useful to you."

"You really think I'd trust you again, after this?" I said. "You'd sell my true identity in a moment. To Franklyn Parris, or the Major Players, or anyone at all, first chance you got. For money, or spite, or just to prove to yourself that you were still your own man."

"All right," said Frankie, drawing himself up with something like wounded dignity. "What are you going to do? Kill me in cold blood? That isn't you, and you know it."

"No," I said. "I'm going to kill you in hot blood. For what you would have let happen to me, and Molly."

I set the barrel of the Colt Repeater right between his eyes. I really did mean to kill him. I had to think only of what Scott had intended for Molly, and I got sick to my stomach. But in the end, Frankie was right. I couldn't do it. Couldn't just look into his pleading eyes and execute him. I stepped back, lowered the gun, turned my back on him, and walked away. Frankie laughed at me. And the Scarlet Lady went roaring past me and ran him over. I heard Frankie scream, and then go quiet. I didn't turn back to look. Just kept walking. After a while, the car came back to join me, idling along at my side.

"Some shit I just don't put up with," said the Scarlet Lady.

I nodded. I couldn't bring myself to thank her, but I think she understood.

I rejoined Molly, standing guard over Jonathon Scott. He had his back propped up against a support pillar, sitting in a pool of his own blood, trying to hold his shattered knee-cap together with both hands. Blood pumped between his fingers. His face was pale and beaded with sweat. His eyes were wide and shocked, but his mouth was set in a flat grim line. He was hurt, but not broken. He looked up to see me approaching but he didn't flinch.

"Frankie?" said Molly. I shook my head. She nodded, briefly. "Good. Now, what are we going to do with this vicious little shit?"

"I'm thinking," I said, staring down at him.

"You don't dare kill me," said Scott, forcing the words past his pain. "The Shadow Bank would declare war on the Droods for such an open insult."

"Over one failed mid-management type?" I said. "I don't think so. Your kind are always going to be expendable in such a big organisation. But you could still be useful to me."

He looked up at me then, the beginning of hope in his eyes. "I know things," he said. "I could tell you all kinds of things. . . ."

"Yes," I said. "You will."

I looked round at the Scarlet Lady, who'd parked just behind me.

"Do you know where the nearest Drood field agent is, Lady?"

"Oh, sure!" said the car.

"Good," I said. "Then take this gentleman for a ride. Hand him over to the family and tell them to tear every last secret he has out of him. By all necessary means. Be sure to tell them why . . . and then hurry back here. Our business isn't over yet."

"You got it!" said the Scarlet Lady. "Wouldn't miss it for the world! You two are so much fun to be around!"

She opened her back door, and Molly and I picked up Scott and threw him into the back seat. The door slammed shut and the car drove off, with Jonathon Scott screaming soundlessly through the rear window.

"The Big Game isn't till eight o'clock this evening," I said. "We have some time to kill. Fancy a lie-down?"

"Yeah," said Molly. "And afterwards, we can have a little nap."

"Wicked witch," I said.

She laughed. "You love it."

"I couldn't kill Frankie," I said.

"Never thought you would," said Molly. "But I would have. For what they would have done to you."

CHAPTER NINE

Poker: It's Not How You Play the Game; It's How You Play the Players

I hate being nervous.

It doesn't help, it doesn't get you anywhere, and it just gets in the way of thinking how to do things properly. As the elevator carried Molly and me up through the hotel to the penthouse floor, I felt more nervous than at any other time on this mission. Because everything I'd done so far, everything I'd been through and endured, had all been leading up to this. The Big Game. My one and only chance to break the bank at Casino Infernale. If I won, if I pulled this off against all the odds, then I could stop a war, save any number of innocent lives, and strike a blow against an organisation I was learning to despise more and more. And, I could win my soul back.

But if I lost, if I screwed it up in the final stretch . . . it didn't bear thinking about. So, of course I couldn't think about anything else.

I looked at myself in the mirrored steel wall of the elevator. I thought I looked pretty good in my tuxedo. (Magically restored by Molly to all its former glory.) I looked ready for anything. Because that's how my family trained me. To be a secret agent, to look just the way I needed to look for any situation. To show a mask and mirror to the world, and never let them see you're hurting. So I was Eddie Drood, or Shaman Bond, as the situation demanded. Only Molly ever got to see the real me with all my defences down. And even then, only occasionally. Because when you wear a mask long enough, it gets really hard to take it off. The mask becomes your face. I looked at my reflection in the elevator wall and Shaman Bond looked back—shifty and cocky, always looking for an edge. Just the man I needed to be, for the Big Game. So why was I so nervous?

Eddie, or Shaman, or me?

Molly stood beside me, up for anything, as always. She looked magnificent in her new ballgown and she knew it. I don't think she was nervous. I'm not sure Molly is ever nervous. I saw her scared, on Trammell Island, but then, she had reason to be. I knew how to deal with being scared—everything forward and go for your enemy's throat. Being nervous, being unsure, is different. When you can't plan your tactics because you don't know what you're getting into.

Luckily, my family's Sarjeant-at-Arms had a simple answer for nerves: *Shut the hell up and soldier.*

I breathed deeply a few times, and made myself concentrate on the matter at hand. I had a lot to think about. All the souls I'd won, that I never really wanted, just so I could take a seat at the table at the Big Game. I had to win, because if I didn't, everything I'd been through so far had all been for nothing. I glared at my reflection. I could do this. I could. I'd been through worse. But that was when there were just lives on the line, rather than souls. I had no armour this time, no backup, just me and Molly against the world. And I had to smile, despite myself. I'd bet on Molly and me, anytime. She squeezed my arm reassuringly, and I smiled at her. I might not have my armour, but I still had her.

"Do you think anyone knows what's happened down in the car park?" said Molly.

"I don't see how," I said. "No one in the Big Game should have heard anything. You disappeared all the bodies."

"And cleaned up all the bloodstains and stuff."

I grinned. "Always said you'd make a good housewife."

She punched me lightly in the arm. "I also performed a full mystic sweep, to keep any of the hotel psychics from picking up on what happened. You didn't even notice, did you? You don't appreciate me; you really don't."

"Unless the hotel's got a major league telepath stowed away somewhere," I said. "This is Casino Infernale, after all."

"Second-guessing never gets you anywhere," Molly said briskly. "Just makes you nervous."

"You were the one who was worried whether they were laying a trap for us at the Big Game."

"You see? Nerves, worrying, second-guessing. And stop frowning like that; you'll get lines."

"It just bothers me," I said, "that our standing at the most important Game depends on whether Jonathon Scott was telling the truth when he said he hadn't told Franklyn Parris who I really am."

"He wasn't lying," said Molly. "I would have known."

"You ready to bet your life on that?"

"We are, aren't we?" said Molly, brightly.

"I will never bet on anything else, ever again, after this," I said.

The elevator finally slowed to a halt at the penthouse floor. Hopefully, we'd have more luck than the last time we were here, to burgle Parris' office. The elevator doors slid smoothly open, revealing a corridor packed with heavily armed guards. Molly tensed, and I quickly put a hand on her arm to hold her still. I looked quickly around, but there were no Jackson Fifty-five anywhere. I very slowly and very carefully put my hand inside my jacket, brought out my invitation card, and held it up. Immediately all the guards lowered their guns, just a little. I stepped out of the elevator, doing my best to radiate confidence, and Molly was right there with me, glaring down her nose at everyone else. A small and svelte Japanese lady strode quickly down the corridor towards us, the guards falling swiftly back to get out of her way. She had long black hair, a calm and heavily made-up face, and wore a tight strapless little black dress. It was so still and quiet in the corridor, I could hear the soft tap-tapping of her shoes on the polished floor. She stopped right before us, and bowed to both of us, very politely.

"Hello and welcome to you both, Shaman Bond and Molly Metcalf," she said, in a soft breathy voice. "I am Eiko. Head of hotel Security. I am here to escort you to the Big Game."

"You know who we are?" I said carefully. "I don't think we've bumped into you before."

"I have studied both your files at length, Mr. Bond, Miss Metcalf," said Eiko. "To make sure I know everything I need to know about you, to protect you more efficiently."

"Of course," I said. "How very reassuring."

"Bet my file is bigger than his," said Molly.

"Bet mine was more interesting," I said.

"I think it best that all bets are saved for the Big Game," said Eiko, diplomatically.

She turned and strode quickly back down the corridor, leaving Molly and me to hurry after her. The guards stood well back to let us pass, lining both walls.

"How long do these affairs usually last?" I said, to the stylised dragon embroidered on the back of Eiko's dress.

"They take as long as they take," said Eiko, not looking round. "Hours . . . days . . . it all depends on the players."

"Why all the armed guards?" Molly said pointedly.

"All for your protection, of course," said Eiko. "We have had to tighten security recently."

"Why?" I said, because it would have seemed off if I hadn't.

"It would appear that we have lost contact with the Jackson Fifty-five," said Eiko, just a bit reluctantly.

"What? All of them?" said Molly, innocently.

"So it would appear," said Eiko, still stubbornly refusing to even look back at us. "Given that they are all clones, it is hard to be sure. Since they are gone, we cannot count them, and therefore we cannot be sure they are all missing. Still, for all of them to be out of contact for so long is . . . disturbing. But you must not worry, I have called in all of my own people to guard all of the players for the duration of the Big Game. And the hotel staff are searching the entire hotel, very thoroughly, from the top down."

"Best way," Molly said solemnly.

"We are now approaching the designated setting for the Big Game," said Eiko. "You will pardon me, but before you pass through the door and join your fellow players, you must be scanned."

She stopped abruptly, so we had to stop too, to avoid bumping into her. She turned and faced us, and summoned two of her people forward with a sharp wave of her hand. The guards were carrying hand scanners instead of guns, and came just a little closer to Molly and me than I was comfortable with. They didn't bother frisking us, which was just as well, but they did run their hand scanners over us with great thoroughness, from top to bottom and back again. I studied the scanners carefully, and then raised an inner eyebrow. Given their sheer complexity, and complete unfamiliarity, there was no way they were Earth tech. The scanner covering me made a series of low beeping noises, as though disappointed in me. Eiko smiled coldly.

"All weapons, and devices of any nature, must be handed over at this point, Mr. Bond. No matter how innocent they may be. We will start with the handgun you were seen using earlier at the hotel restaurant. Everything confiscated here will of course be returned to you, after the Big Game."

"Of course," I said.

I carefully removed my Colt Repeater from its pocket dimension, and handed it over to the guard standing by with an outstretched hand. The man with the scanner ran it over my hip again, and looked at Eiko again as the scanner beeped reprovingly.

"Pocket dimension," I said to Eiko. "It sort of floats around my hip. Afraid I can't remove it; don't know how."

"The room's mystical null will close it off, for the duration of the Game," said Eiko.

I had to empty out all my pockets, one by one. Eiko hesitated over the pack of cards the Armourer had given me. They did look very ordinary. The scanner didn't react to them at all. Eiko studied the cards carefully, and then raised a painted eyebrow at me.

"Sentimental value," I said smoothly. "Had my first big win with those cards. I carry them everywhere with me, for luck. I was told that such lucky charms are permitted. . . ."

"All gamblers have their superstitions," said Eiko. "If it was up to me . . . but apparently it isn't worth the fuss. So yes, Mr. Bond, you may keep your pack of cards. Though of course you will not be permitted to actually play with them."

"Oh, of course," I said, slipping the pack away in an inside jacket pocket.

The other guard was running his scanner all over Molly, and getting nothing. Eiko gave him a hard look. "Change settings, fool. She is a witch."

The guard hastily made corrections to his hand scanner, while I raised another inner eyebrow. It was very rare tech that could detect magical energies. Molly made a point of glaring down her nose at Eiko.

"I had to leave the tall pointy hat behind. It clashed with the gown. There are no toads in my pockets, no mandrakes or mushrooms, and I never was one for the whole broomstick-and-cat business."

"I used to love *Bewitched*," I said. "Especially when she used her magic to change her husband into an entirely different actor."

"Well?" said Eiko, glaring at the guard with the scanner.

He was down on his hands and knees now, having struck out everywhere else, and was banging the scanner on the floor, trying to make it work. It finally gave off a single beep.

"Oh, that!" said Molly. "Sorry, Shaman, I'd quite forgotten I was still wearing it."

She lifted up her gown to reveal a simple silver charm bracelet around her left ankle. She leaned over and undid the clasp, straightened up, and then dropped the bracelet onto Eiko's outstretched palm.

"It's safe enough," said Molly. "As long as you don't meddle with it. And whatever you do, don't drop it. Unless you're really good at running very quickly from a standing start."

"We will guard it most carefully," said Eiko.

"Do I get a receipt?" said Molly.

"Don't push it, witch," said Eiko. "It's all about trust."

"I'm really not the trusting type," said Molly.

"Me either," I said.

"Then you'll fit right in, Mr. Bond, at the Big Game," said Eiko.

She led the way down the corridor again, and the ranks of armed guards fell back to let us pass, forming two rows of something very like an honour guard. If they hadn't all still been covering us with their guns. Beyond the last few guards lay a single door, blocking off the end of the corridor. Molly's hand tightened on mine as we approached the door.

"That is another dimensional door," she murmured in my ear. "Just like the one that transported us to the world of the Medium Games. Which would suggest . . . the Big Game isn't actually being held on the hotel's penthouse floor."

"Of course not," said Eiko, in a perfectly normal tone, still not looking back at us. "The Big Game is being held somewhere far more private, and secure. For your protection."

"The more she says that, the more protected I feel," I said.

Molly nodded solemnly. "I could still kick her arse."

"She can hear you," I said.

"Good," said Molly.

Wisely, Eiko said nothing. She produced a special electronic key, apparently out of nowhere, opened the quite ordinary-looking door and led the way in. Molly and I braced ourselves, ready for anything, and strode through the dimensional door.

I didn't feel a thing, but we were suddenly standing in a really large open room, more than twice the size of our suite. At first glance it might have been just another hotel function room, bigger than most and far more luxurious. But most of the room was just . . . empty, a great carpeted wasteland, surrounding one long table, in the middle of all the open space. A bar took up one corner, with a handful of high bar-stools, but no other furniture. And the three huge windows in the far wall were all covered with heavy steel shutters. So no one could know exactly where the room was. The lighting was clear, and just a little on the dim side, to be comfortable on the eyes.

Several familiar faces were already seated around the long table, waiting impatiently. None of them looked at all pleased to see me, or Molly. A figure sitting at the bar slipped off his high stool and came forward to greet us. Eiko moved politely to one side to let him do it, which told me immediately who this had to be. The one person the head of hotel Security would still defer to. Franklyn Parris himself.

At first glance, he seemed disappointingly ordinary. Just another executive type in a good suit, with an expensive tie and flashy cuff links. Handsome enough, about my age, nattily turned out with a brightly patterned look-at-me waistcoat. He was smiling politely, but it didn't even come close to touching his eyes. Nothing showed in his face apart from what he allowed the world to see. He shook me firmly by the hand, and let go as soon as he politely could. He nodded briefly to Molly, so he could more quickly give me his full attention.

"Good to meet you at last, Mr. Bond," he said, in a dry dusty voice. "I am Franklyn Parris. Here to oversee the Big Game, and keep everyone honest. Normally that would be Jonathon Scott's job, but he seems to have disappeared."

"Along with the Jackson Fifty-five?" I said, innocently.

Out of the corner of my eye, I caught a stirring among the players seated at the table. They hadn't been told that.

"Indeed," said Parris. "Perhaps Mr. Scott has taken them all off somewhere to investigate a threat to the hotel. I am sure he, and they, will be back soon. No one should feel at all concerned. You are extremely safe and secure here, Mr. Bond. I feel I should point out that you and your companion were very nearly late. We were preparing to start without you."

"The elevator took forever to arrive," I said. "Do you want to see my invitation card?"

"That won't be necessary," said Parris. "If you hadn't had the card with you, the door wouldn't have brought you here. It has no further purpose. Feel free to keep it, though, as a souvenir."

"I still can't help noticing a large number of armed guards in this room," I said. "Are you expecting . . . trouble?"

I looked meaningfully around the room, at the twenty or so armed guards in formal suits, scattered around the perimeter, cradling their weapons. They were all ostensibly relaxed, with their guns pointing at the floor, but it didn't make them look any less professional, or menacing.

"A series of . . . unusual events have occurred during Casino Infernale this year," said Parris. "I felt it best to err on the side of caution, for the good of all. These gentlemen, and the formidable Miss Eiko herself, are here for everyone's protection."

"Oh, I feel very protected," I said to Molly. "Don't you feel protected?"

"Oh, lots," said Molly. "I feel so protected I can hardly stand. Think I'll have a little sit-down, and a drinkie."

"That would be best," said Parris, as Molly headed determinedly for the bar. "Only players can sit at the table. Come with me, Mr. Bond, and I'll introduce you to the other players."

I went with him. The guards all followed me with their eyes, if not actually their guns. Parris stood at the head of the long table, and smiled benevolently on the people seated before him.

"Mr. Shaman Bond, allow me to present to you . . . Leopold, the famous gambling priest. Jacqueline Hyde, famous for all sorts of unpleasant things. Earnest Schmidt, head of the reformed Brotherhood of the Vril, who wants very much to be famous one day. And a gentleman who prefers to be known by his old sobriquet, the Card Shark. Once, the most famous card player of them all."

We all nodded to each other, more or less politely. The only one I didn't already know was the fat old man called the Card Shark. His name meant something, but I couldn't quite put my finger on it. . . . He sat half slumped in his chair, bulging out of his suit as though he'd outgrown it, his stomach pushing out the bulging, food-spattered waistcoat. He had large fleshy hands, not quite as steady as they should have been, and a broad sweaty face with unhealthy grey skin. His eyes were flat and dark and suspicious. He didn't look at all well. He looked old and tired, as though he should have been in some retirement home, and that, at last, helped me to place him.

The Card Shark dismissed me with a glance, which was as it should be. He had no reason to know Shaman Bond. Wouldn't have lowered himself to move in such circles. But he'd have known my cousin, Matthew Drood, back when Matthew was the family's main field agent in London. He'd amassed quite a file on the infamous Card Shark—a man already well past his prime, but still a fearless and much feared card player in all the sleazier gambling houses in London. The Card Shark got his reputation from driving other card players to their deaths. The Shark liked to goad inexperienced young players into games and bets they weren't ready for, and then demand every penny he was owed, immediately. Many suicided when they couldn't pay.

I thought the nasty old scrote had retired. Was he back here for one last big game? And if so, how did he get this far? Last I heard, he was broke and vegetating in some nursing home. Could Casino Infernale have funded the Card Shark's return, so Parris could be sure of at least one celebrity name at his first Big Game?

I made a point of looking away from the table and the players, and gestured at the great steel-shuttered windows.

"What's out there?" I said to Parris. "Where are we, exactly? Why aren't we allowed to see?"

"Because you wouldn't like it," said Parris. "It would only distract you from the game. All you need to know is that this is home ground to the Shadow Bank. And we take our privacy very seriously."

I looked across at the bar, where Molly was perched on a high stool opposite Eiko. They were talking quietly to each other, not even bothering to hide their mutual hostility.

"Only the players are allowed to sit at table," said Eiko. "You are allowed to observe, Miss Metcalf, as long as you don't try to interfere."

"Well, whoopee," said Molly. She shot me a quick reassuring glance, and then glared at the bartender. "Give me a bottle of brandy and one glass. I would offer you a drink, Miss Eiko, but I've only got the one bottle."

Eiko ordered a single glass of saki.

"Am I the only guest here?" said Molly.

"No one else took advantage of their plus one," said Eiko. "Unless you count Jacqueline. But then, in my experience, I have found most gamblers to be solitary types."

"Are you sitting here to keep me company, or to keep an eye on me?" Molly said bluntly.

"Yes," said Eiko.

"If we could have your full attention, Mr. Bond?" said Parris.

I pulled out a chair, sat down at the table, and stared openly round at my fellow players. They looked me over just as openly. I supposed they weren't used to playing with people they didn't already know at this level of Casino Infernale. I smiled easily about me.

"So!" I said brightly. "Let's all get acquainted. Why are we all here? You first . . ."

"One last big game," said the Card Shark. His voice was harsh and breathy, as though he had trouble getting enough air. "To prove I've still got it. That I'm still the best."

It had to be said, no one else at the table looked particularly convinced. Most of them were looking at the Card Shark with barely disguised contempt.

"Go on, Shark," said Jacqueline. "Make yourself at home. Ruin someone's life and drive them to suicide."

"Why are you here?" Schmidt said to Jacqueline. He sounded politely interested.

"It's no secret," said Jacqueline. "I need to find a way to separate myself from Hyde, so we can exist separately. So we can be properly together, at last."

"But you're from the Nightside," said Leopold. "If you couldn't find an answer there . . ."

"Who says I didn't?" Jacqueline said harshly. "But miracles cost money, lots of money, even in the Nightside. Perhaps especially in the Nightside."

"I am here to fund the Vril," Earnest Schmidt said flatly. "The world is waiting for us, waiting for a Fourth Reich to bring Order out of Chaos. The world is waiting for the reformed Brotherhood of the Vril to return from the shadows and force the world to make sense again. Movements cost money. So here I am. Look on my cards, ye mighty, and despair."

"Molly and I were attacked on our way here," I said, "by big blonde Nazi girls, riding flying lizards. Pan's Panzerpeople."

"I know nothing of this," said Schmidt, not even looking at me.

A brandy bottle flew past his head, barely missing him, followed by raucous laughter from the bar. Schmidt went pale, and developed a twitch.

"I know," I said quickly to Parris. "She's my responsibility." I looked back at the bar. "Behave, Molly. Or they'll throw both of us out of here."

"Spoil-sports," said Molly. "You, bartender. Give me another bottle. And if you say I'm cut off, I'll start cutting bits off your anatomy."

"Girls just want to have fun," I said to Parris. I looked at Schmidt. "The Pan's Panzerpeople are all dead now. So are their Pteranodons. Hope you kept the receipt. Maybe you can get your money back."

"I am here to raise funds for Mother Church," said Leopold. Intervening graciously.

"What's the matter, priest?" said Jacqueline. "The Church doesn't own enough land, or cathedrals, or works of art?"

"I raise money for charity," said Leopold. "For orphanages and missionaries. Feed the hungry, and pass out Bibles to the lost."

"Ever think maybe you're part of the problem?" said Jacqueline.

"No," said Leopold.

I studied him thoughtfully. "How do you justify owning souls, priest? Doesn't it bother you?"

"I have been given a special dispensation by the Church," Leopold said calmly.

"And what happens?" I said. "To the souls you own?"

"Souls are currency, or ammunition, in the Great Game between Heaven and Hell," said Leopold. "You might say . . . the souls I win have been conscripted, to my side."

"Slavery is still slavery, however you justify it," I said.

"Then how do you justify owning souls, Mr. Bond?" said Leopold. He seemed genuinely interested in my answer.

"I don't," I said. "But then, I don't have to. I'm a bastard, not a priest."

"I work for the greater good," said Leopold. "The sacrifice of the few is sometimes necessary, if the many are to be saved."

"Even conscripts should have some say in what happens to them," I said.

"You are a far more thoughtful man than I expected," said Leopold. "We should talk, afterwards. I'm sure we'd find a lot in common. Why are you here, Mr. Bond?"

"I'm here to break the bank," I said, and everyone managed some kind of smile at that.

"Really," said Schmidt, smiling avuncularly, if a little coldly, "I think all of us would admit, if pressed, that we are all here for the thrill of the game. Even you, priest."

"Perhaps especially me," said Leopold, calmly.

"Before we start," said Jacqueline, "I want a bigger chair. Because this one will just break when I change into Hyde."

I think it was the way she said *when* rather than *if* that put the wind up everybody. Including the armed guards around the room, who immediately snapped to attention and aimed their guns at Jacqueline. Parris gestured to Eiko, who hopped down from her bar-stool and left the room through the dimensional door.

"I'm assuming there is a null zone generator in this room, somewhere," Molly said loudly. "To keep everyone honest. And to keep Jacqueline . . . Jacqueline. Can she really become Hyde, under these conditions?"

"I'm afraid she can," said Parris. "Hers is a pre-existing condition, a result of taking the Hyde potion long ago. So we must all therefore rely on Jacqueline's self-control."

I shot a look at Molly, who nodded briefly to me. We were both thinking of the potion the Armourer gave us, before we left Drood Hall. And then we all looked round sharply as the door banged open and Eiko strode in, leading two security guards carrying a really big chair between them. They set it down at the table, and backed quickly away. Jacqueline looked the chair over, and then tried it out for size. She looked small and lost in it. She nodded, briefly. Eiko went back to the bar, hopped up onto her bar-stool, and went back to glaring at Molly. The two security men left the room, at speed, closing the door firmly behind them. There then followed a certain amount of changing chairs and jockeying for position, because no one wanted to sit next to Jacqueline Hyde any more. In the end, Leopold sat down on one side of her, and not to be outdone, I sat down on her other side. Schmidt and the Card Shark immediately sat down on the other side of the table, facing us. Franklyn Parris sat at the head of the table, and produced a pack of playing cards. He smiled easily about him, shuffling the pack with calm, practised movements.

"I shall be dealer," he announced. "As the only truly impartial figure here. The game is, of course, poker. The traditional game, with no cards showing. None of the . . . amusing variations. Poker is the only game to have a real, almost mystical significance to all Major Players. A matter of chance and skill, and a test of character, poker has always been the Big Game, to decide the future of all souls won at Casino Infernale."

He set the pack of cards down carefully on the polished tabletop, and then produced, apparently from nowhere, a large red-lacquered box, to set down beside the cards. He waved his hand over the box, and the lid slowly opened. Parris then consulted a list, and counted out piles of obols for all of us. To serve as our gambling chips. I wasn't entirely surprised to find that everyone else had a much bigger pile than mine. The next largest pile belonged to the Card Shark, presumably courtesy of the Casino. I examined the obols I'd been given. Each small coin had been stamped with a stylised death's head, on both sides.

"Cool," I said. "Cool touch."

"We thought so," said Parris. And then he dealt five cards to each of us, round and round, while we all watched with avid eyes.

I picked up my cards, and took a look. A pair of eights, and three assorted hearts. Didn't mean a thing to me.

I hadn't played cards in general, and poker in particular, since I was a kid. And only then because all forms of gambling were strictly forbidden at Drood Hall. If it was against the rules, I was up for it, back then. But . . . it didn't take me long to discover that I had no gift, no skill, and no luck at all when it came to cards. So I gave it up, very quickly. Never once felt the urge to go back.

I looked at my cards again, with what I hoped was my best poker face, and hadn't a clue what to do for the best. I could discard as many cards as I wanted, and take more from the dealer, in the hope of improving my hand . . . but I had no idea what the relevant odds were. So I sat back, and allowed the others to make up their minds behind their various poker faces, and waited for the Armourer's potion to kick in. Only to quickly realise that the potion only helped with card counting and pattern recognition. Neither of which would be any use until a few hands of cards had been played. By which time . . . I could have lost all my carefully gathered souls.

Everybody anted up, throwing the bare minimum of coins onto the table, to show they were entering the game, and I had to go along. And then everyone discarded some cards in return for others, while I thought furiously. Finally, Parris looked at me and raised an eyebrow when I just smiled at him, placed my cards face down on the table, and shook my head.

"I'll play these," I said.

And while everyone else was still staring at me, I pushed forward every single coin I had, to start the next round.

"All of it," I said brightly. "Every damned obol. Anyone want to see me?"

I saw Molly sit bolt upright at the bar, out of the corner of my eye, but I didn't dare look at her directly. She was looking at me as though I'd gone mad, and to be fair, so was everybody else. But, because everyone else at the table was an experienced gambler, and knew what they were doing . . . they assumed I knew what I was doing. So they all folded, and threw their cards in. Rather than throw good obols after bad. I smiled again, and raked in all the coins already bet. With one single bluff, I'd just about dou-

bled the number of souls I had to bet with. Enough for me
to sit back for a few hands, watch the game develop, and
allow the Armourer's potion to kick in. I leaned back in
my chair, and felt my heartbeat slowly fall back to something like normal.

Parris reached for my cards, and Schmidt suddenly
leant forward.

"No!" he said. "I want to see the cards our callow young
friend thought so highly of."

"Sorry," I said, pushing the cards over to Parris, still face
down. "You didn't pay for the privilege of seeing them."

"Quite correct, Mr. Bond," said Parris, shuffling my
cards back into the pack.

"So," said Schmidt. "That's how this game is going to
be played."

My first big win had surprised, if not necessarily impressed, everyone else, and they were all very cautious in
their betting through the next few rounds. I anted up the
bare minimum, just enough to stay in the game, and
watched the other players as closely as the play. My card
counting skills eased in almost without me noticing, and I
was soon starting to recognise patterns in the play. Just
enough . . . to give me an edge. The cards went back and
forth, and I won a few hands here and there, while avoiding what might have been nasty losses. The other players
were taking me more seriously now, and genuinely seemed
to believe I knew what I was doing.

And then the Card Shark bet big, just as I had. He bet
all his obols, all his souls, on one hand of cards. And then
he sat back and glowered around the table. Only I knew he
couldn't have the kind of cards he needed to win that big.
I'd been counting. So I called him. It took pretty much
everything I had. The Card Shark glared at me, outraged
that a nobody like me should dare to call him. He wasn't
giving anything away; he'd looked angry and outraged at
pretty much everything and everyone since he sat down at
the table. There are, after all, all kinds of poker faces. He
turned to Parris, who was already shaking his head.

"No credit, Card Shark. You can only bet what you bring to the table. You have bet, and Mr. Bond has called. It's time to see the cards."

The Card Shark turned his over: a pair of kings. While I had three eights. And that was that. The Card Shark had bluffed, trying to intimidate the table with his old reputation, and he had lost. The others looked at him almost pityingly. The Card Shark lurched to his feet, and pointed a shaking finger at me.

"Cheat! I call cheat! There's no way you could have bet that much, on a hand like that, unless you knew what I had!"

"I suspected," I said.

"Enough," said Parris. "There is no room at this table for a sore loser. Perhaps you should have stayed retired, Mr. Fisk."

"No! No! Give me another chance, another stake!" The Card Shark looked wildly around him, as the nearest armed guards moved forward. He was still begging and pleading, without shame or pride, to be allowed to stay at the table, where he belonged, when he was dragged bodily out the dimensional door. He was crying when the door slammed shut after him, and the sound cut off abruptly. Parris smiled apologetically around the table.

"Some players just don't know when to quit."

And then the door slammed open again, and the Card Shark was back, brandishing a gun he'd somehow managed to take off one of the guards. We all sat very still as the Card Shark pointed the gun unsteadily at Parris.

"Give me another chance," he said harshly. "Just enough souls for a few more hands, enough to get back in the Game. I'm not being cheated out of my comeback!"

"It was never going to be a comeback," Parris said calmly. "Merely one last chance to play at the big table. Don't be a fool, Mr. Fisk. Give me the gun."

"I won't give up!" said the Card Shark. "I've got a gun, so you have to listen to me! I didn't come all this way just to be beaten by a nobody! You gave me the souls. Give me some more! You can afford it! I can do this!"

"So," said Schmidt, glaring at Parris. "The rumours are true. You did back a player of your own."

"You tried to fix the Big Game, Mr. Parris?" said Leopold. "I am shocked, I tell you, shocked."

"There has been no interference in the Game," Parris said carefully. "I merely wanted to be sure that there would be someone at the table that other people had heard of."

The Card Shark suddenly pointed his gun at me. "You couldn't have beaten me, you little shit. Not you!"

"You bluffed and you lost," said Leopold. "No one likes a bad loser. This is no way to end a long and distinguished career, Mr. Fisk. Please leave now, before things get out of hand."

"I've got a gun!" said the Card Shark, desperately.

"So you have," said Parris. "But I have an Evil Eye."

There was a pause as everyone looked at him. The Card Shark turned the gun back to Parris.

"I don't see any Evil Eye," he said.

"It isn't in my face," said Parris. "It's in my hand."

He held up his left hand, and there in his palm was an embedded metal eye. The lids crawled open, revealing a glowing eye, and the Card Shark couldn't look away. He looked into the Evil Eye, and was lost. All the expression went out of his face, and he just stood there, staring blankly. An empty shell. The metal eyelids closed, and Parris lowered his hand. He gestured to the two nearest guards, and they led the unresisting Card Shark away. The door closed behind him again, and this time they stayed closed. Parris looked round the table, at all of us.

"All his souls go to you, Mr. Bond. And his soul, as well. Because no one defies the rules of Casino Infernale." He turned and looked at Eiko, who nodded quickly, hopped down from her high stool, and hurried out the dimensional door. She left it standing open. After a moment there was the sound of a scream, stopped short by a single gunshot, and then Eiko came back through the door. She closed it, nodded briefly to Parris, and sat on her bar-stool again.

"That was the guard who was clumsy enough to allow

his gun to be stolen," said Parris. "I think you'll find the remaining guards will stay on their toes from now on."

He didn't look around. He didn't have to. Molly looked thoughtfully at Eiko.

Play continued. I bet small and played cautiously, counting cards and watching the play, waiting for another opening. Leopold seemed to be doing much the same. Perhaps he was waiting for God to whisper in his ear. Jacqueline studied her every hand carefully, glowering, thinking hard, as though everything depended on every hand. And perhaps for her, it did. She was winning steadily, playing conservatively, playing the odds. The pile of obols in front of her grew.

Schmidt seemed increasingly impatient. Things were not going well for him. He squirmed in his chair, rearranging his cards again and again, as though he could force them into a better combination. He scowled, almost sulkily, as he watched his pile of obols slowly diminish. No big losses or upsets, but he was running out of souls. He glared suddenly at Jacqueline.

"Come on! What's taking you so long! Make your bet; you're holding the Game up! We should never have allowed a woman to take part anyway!"

Jacqueline turned into Hyde so quickly none of us could follow it. There was no effort involved, no straining or crying out—one minute a small woman was sitting opposite Schmidt, and the next, there was Hyde. Huge and muscular, a great bear of a man. A big brutal engine of destruction. And before any of the armed guards could even react, Hyde reached across the table and tore Schmidt's head off. Just ripped it away, with shockingly casual ease. The body fell backwards from the table, still in its chair, blood spurting thickly from the ragged stump of neck. Hyde held up the severed head before him, smiling horribly into Schmidt's still-blinking eyes.

Some of the guards cried out, almost hysterically. They were trained to deal with men; Hyde was something else.

Something much worse. Leopold and I had both risen up out of our seats and stepped quickly back from the table, out of Hyde's reach. But he had eyes only for the head in his hands. He waited till Schmidt stopped blinking, and then he kissed the dead man on his dead mouth, and threw the head calmly to one side. It rolled away, stopping at the feet of one guard, who froze where he was, gazing down at the thing with appalled fascination. Hyde turned his great head slowly to look at Parris, who hadn't moved an inch.

"Clear up this mess," said Hyde.

Everyone in the room flinched at the sound of his voice. Parris gestured quickly for two guards to come forward and carry the headless body out. In the end, Eiko picked up the head and took it away, apparently entirely unmoved. The extra chair was removed from the table, and Leopold and I resumed our seats. Hyde turned back into Jacqueline. And once again, just for a moment, I thought I saw the two of them reaching out to each other in the only moment when they could meet. Reaching out, but never able to touch. This evil brute of a man, and this small delicate woman. Beauty and the Beast, or two sides of the same coin?

Jacqueline gathered the remains of her clothes around her. She didn't look at any of us.

"I'm just a woman in love with a man," she said. "I only want what any woman wants—to be able to hold her man in her arms. I only want to know what every other woman knows. I want to be together. And I will not suffer anything to get in my way. Do we have a problem, Mr. Parris?"

"I don't think so," Parris said carefully. "Mr. Schmidt broke the rules of the Game when he tried to intimidate you. I would have had my people remove him, anyway, if he'd continued."

"Then play on," said Jacqueline. And we did.

The cards went back and forth, to no productive end. Obols passed back and forth across the table, from pile to pile and back again, while I waited for my moment.

Leopold looked at me thoughtfully. "There's something about you, Shaman. Something I didn't expect. You're so much more than your reputation."

"The nail that stands up gets hammered down," I said easily. "I prefer to hide my light in the shadows."

"And I have to ask," said Leopold, quite casually, "what the infamous wild witch herself, Molly Metcalf, is doing here with you? According to Church files, she is quite definitely involved with a Drood, these days. The remarkable Eddie Drood, no less. I think I can safely say, none of us saw that one coming."

Molly snorted loudly at the bar. I carefully didn't look in her direction.

"She still is attached to her Drood," I said. "I just hired her to be my bodyguard. Dangerous place, this Casino Infernale."

"And how did someone like you, Shaman, acquire enough money to hire someone like her?" said Leopold.

"With a percentage of my winnings," I said.

"Of course," said Leopold. "I knew it would have to be something like that."

"How did you get to be the famous gambling priest?" I said.

"There's a lot of card playing goes on at Seminaries," Leopold said easily. "Almost the only vice we can indulge. Young men together—very competitive. . . . You know how it is. I discovered I had a gift for the cards, and the Church found a use for that gift."

"And you always win?" I said.

"God gave me a gift, not a miracle," said Leopold. "It's all about knowing which cards to back. Like these."

He placed his cards face down on the table, patted them almost fondly, and then pushed forward every obol in front of him. It was quite a large pile. Leopold smiled around the table.

"Would anyone care to call me? I assure you, God is on my side here."

I pushed forward my entire pile of souls, to match his.

"Do we really need to count them all?" I said to Parris. "It's every soul I have, against every soul he has."

"This is acceptable to me," said Parris. "If it is acceptable to you, Leopold?"

"Of course!" said the famous gambling priest.

Molly was all but bouncing up and down on her stool, trying to catch my eye. I didn't look at her. I knew what I was doing. I nodded to Leopold.

"You show me yours, and I'll show you mine."

He turned over a full house. Jacks over tens. Should have been a winning hand. Anywhen else, it would be. But I turned over four aces. And for a long moment, no one at the table said anything.

"God might be on your side, Leopold," I said. "But the cards are on mine."

Leopold stood up abruptly, staring at me with a shocked, ashen face. He looked genuinely upset. "I don't understand. . . . It's not possible! You are not who you appear to be, Shaman Bond! You are in the employ of dark forces! It's the only answer!"

I looked at Parris. "I'm not in the employ of dark forces. Really."

"No demonic possessions here," said Eiko, from the bar. "The mystical null is still operating."

Leopold's shoulders slumped, and the fire went out of his eyes. The guards escorted him out of the door, and he went quietly.

Jacqueline looked across the table at me. "Just the two of us now, Shaman."

"Shouldn't that be three?" I said.

"Funny man," said Jacqueline. "But don't try anything funny with my other half. You wouldn't like me when I'm funny."

"Lady and gentleman," said Parris. "Let's play cards. It's still all to play for."

He shuffled the cards, thoroughly, and play went on. It didn't take long before Jacqueline decided she had the perfect hand, and bet all her souls on it. You would have thought that she'd learned better by now, or at least spotted a pattern. But no, she bet every soul she had on her hand, and I pushed forward my pile to match hers. She slammed her cards down on the table, and glared at me defiantly.

"There! Four kings! Beat that!"

"No," I said, showing her my cards. "I have four kings. You have four queens."

Jacqueline looked down at her cards, and her jaw dropped. "No! That's not possible! I had the four kings! I did!"

"The cards in front of you are quite definitely queens," said Parris. And they were.

"You cheated!" roared Hyde, as he lunged across the table at me.

I was expecting the change, but even so it happened so suddenly it caught me by surprise. Only the width of the table kept Hyde's clutching hands from my throat. I threw myself backwards, rolling out of the chair and across the floor. Hyde threw himself across the table. I scrabbled backwards, and every guard in the room opened up on Hyde. He charged forward so fast he actually avoided most of the bullets, and the few wounds he did take healed almost immediately. He towered over me, massive and monstrous.

I could see Molly on her feet by the bar, frustrated because she couldn't use her magics to help me. I was feeling equally frustrated without my armour. I yelled to Parris to give me back my gun, but he just shook his head.

"You don't need a weapon," he said loudly. "I have my own weapon. Eiko!"

There was something in the way he said her name that made Hyde stop and look around. Just in time to see Eiko turn into a female Hyde. She didn't become big and bulky, like a female bodybuilder or wrestler. She was tall but slender, lithely muscular, full of a terrible burning energy. Like Jacqueline's Hyde, just looking at what Eiko had become made you want to kill her on sight. She was wrong, awful, an abomination. Everything a human being is not meant to be, brought to the surface and made material. Evil in the flesh. Eiko launched herself at Hyde, and the two monsters slammed together in a horrid form of violence that was almost sexual. They tore at each other with their bare hands, ripping flesh away in great bloody handfuls. The wounds healed quickly, and the fight went on.

Until Eiko, the better-trained fighter, got Hyde in a headlock, and held him there just long enough for Parris to shove the Evil Eye in his hand right into Hyde's face. He cried out as the metal eye looked into him, and then he changed back, into Jacqueline. Because that was the only way he could escape what the Eye was doing to him. The moment Jacqueline reappeared, Eiko punched her savagely in the side of the head, and let go. Jacqueline collapsed, weeping in pain and loss. The guards all looked at Parris, the same question in all their faces. *Should we shoot her now?*

Parris thought about it, and then shook his head. "Let her live. As she is. That's a far worse punishment."

Two guards hauled Jacqueline back onto her feet, dragged her to the dimensional door, and threw her out. Before the door closed, Jacqueline looked back at me and screamed *I'm glad I poisoned you at the restaurant!* Which solved one small mystery, at least.

Parris gave the transformed Eiko a hard look, and she changed back into her previous self. I thought I sensed a certain resistance in her, but apparently Eiko was smart enough not to argue with Parris while he still had his Evil Eye. Eiko went back to sit at the bar, and Molly looked at her thoughtfully.

"That dress didn't half stretch," she said.

Eiko ignored her.

I picked up my chair, pushed it back into place, and sat down at the table again. After a moment, so did Parris. He gathered all the obols on the table into one big pile, and pushed them over to me.

"All Jacqueline Hyde's souls are now yours, Mr. Bond. With the exception of her own, which she never bet. So, somewhat to my surprise, I must confess, you are now the winner of this year's Casino Infernale."

"The Game isn't over yet," I said. "You're still here, representing the Shadow Bank. So let's play on, you and me. What do you say, Mr. Parris?"

"I am tempted," he said slowly. "Though I'm not sure that's ever been done before."

"Come on," I said. "Don't you want a chance to win back all these souls I've accumulated?"

Eiko stood up at the bar. "This is not acceptable, Mr. Parris. You know it isn't. It is not in the traditions of the Big Game for the Shadow Bank to put the souls it owns at risk."

"Our game," I said to Parris. "We get to decide the rules."

"I am in charge here," said Parris, not even glancing back at Eiko. "I make the decisions." He looked at me for a long moment. "Why should I play, Mr. Bond?"

"Because I'm not much of a catch, am I?" I said. "Who's ever heard of Shaman Bond, that matters? You need a big name, a Major Player, someone important, to win this year's Big Game. On your first watch as the man in charge of Casino Infernale. You need a celebrity to win. That's why you brought in the Card Shark, just in case. But you won't get much credit off my name. Shaman Bond as the winner? You'd be a laughing stock. So I'm going to give you a chance to be the big winner yourself. What would that do to your prestige in the Shadow Bank organisation?"

"You're risking everything you've won," said Parris. "Why do you want to play on?"

"I told you," I said, smiling. "I want to break the bank at Casino Infernale."

"All right," said Parris. "Let's play."

"No!" said Eiko. "You can't do this! I won't allow it!" She strode forward, to glare at Parris. "I will become Hyde again if I have to, to stop you. To enforce the rules! The Shadow Bank will thank me for it, and give me your job!"

Parris nodded to the guard standing behind Eiko, and he shot her in the back of the head. The impact sent her stumbling forward, but she didn't die immediately. She'd already started the change, but it was too late. Too much damage had already been done. Her body lurched and twisted, muscles rising and falling, until she fell to her knees, cried out one last time, and died. She lay still, a horribly malformed shape that was neither one person nor the other. A single great eye bulged out of her face covered with blood from the great exit wound in her forehead. Parris gestured almost lazily to the two nearest guards, and they picked up the body and carried it out through the door. Parris looked round the room.

"I will not have my authority challenged." He looked at me, and smiled a horribly normal smile. "It is so much quieter in here, without her, isn't it? Now, what do you suggest, Mr. Bond? What game should we play? More poker?"

"I was thinking of something simpler," I said. "Why not bet it all, bet everything, on one turn of the cards? Man to man, luck to luck. I'll bet every soul I've won; you can match that with an equal number of souls owned by the Shadow Bank. You have the authority to do that, don't you?"

Parris looked down at the pack of cards on the table, the back stamped with the same stylised death's-head image as the obols. He looked back at me. "I do admire your style, Shaman! If not your sanity. Very well! Let's do it."

From the bar, Molly was looking at me as though I'd completely lost my mind, but she didn't interfere. *I hope you know what you're doing* was written clearly in her face. I shot her a quick reassuring grin. I knew what I was doing, but I was still so nervous my heart was all but jumping out of my chest. I had everything under control, nothing could go wrong, but this was Casino Infernale, after all.

Parris and I ended up standing at the head of the table, facing each other, the pack of cards between us. We both looked at each other, eyes steady and unyielding, the tension on the air so heavy you could have hammered in nails with it. Parris picked up the pack of cards, and shuffled them with professional thoroughness. He put them down again, breathed deeply a few times, and cut. His card was the jack of hearts. He smiled, pleased and relieved. A good card. A winning card, usually. I made my cut, and turned up the ace of spades.

Parris was so shocked he couldn't even make a sound; just stood there, looking at his card, and mine. I'd just doubled my already considerable number of souls. The surrounding guards made a whole bunch of impressed noises, despite themselves. They were all edging in closer for a better look, caught up in the thrill of the moment. Parris had gone grey in the face. He looked sick. I think he was genuinely shocked, to have lost so many souls that belonged to the Shadow Bank, so quickly. A wise man would have quit right there, got out while the going was good. So, of course I pressed the point.

"Double or quits?" I said brightly. "A chance to win back all the souls you lost."

He nodded quickly. He shuffled the cards again, not quite so steadily, and cut to his card. A ten of clubs. Not bad. I cut the king of clubs. And just like that, I owned four times the number of souls. Parris had lost, and lost big. Betting souls that weren't really his to bet.

"The Bank will have my balls for this," he said numbly. "They're watching, recording everything that happens here. They see everything, know everything, that happens at Casino Infernale. And they have to acknowledge my bets, my losses, made with the authority they granted me, or no one would ever wager at Casino Infernale again. . . ."

"You've still got a chance," I said. "One last cut of the cards. Everything you have, every soul you've acquired here at this year's Casino Infernale. Set against everything I've won here. One turn of the card from each of us; winner takes all."

"I have no choice, do I?" said Parris. "If I go back to the Shadow Bank with these losses, I'm a dead man. And even you can't fight odds this big, Shaman. You can't win three cuts in a row."

"I'm ready to risk it," I said. "It's all in the cards, after all."

Parris picked up the pack, and shuffled the cards slowly and steadily, taking his time, running his hands over the cards again and again, as though trying to remind them who they belonged to. He put the cards down, and looked at them for a while, breathing slowly, and then he cut the cards and turned up the king of hearts. He almost collapsed with relief. And then I made my cut, and showed him the ace of hearts.

Parris couldn't believe it. He just couldn't believe it. He stood there, staring in wide-eyed shock as I dropped the ace on the table before him. All the colour dropped out of his face. Even his lips went pale. He sat down suddenly. Molly let out a great whoop of joy, and ran forward to throw her arms around me. I grabbed her and spun her round and round, laughing aloud. We hugged the life out of each other. I grinned so hard my cheeks hurt. I'd just won every soul taken at Casino Infernale, and that had to include my own soul, and that of my parents.

"I did it!" I yelled, to the whole damned room. "I'm the man who broke the bank at Casino Infernale!"

And then Parris stood up suddenly to face me, with a strange, cold smile. "Wait. It isn't over yet."

I put Molly down, and we stood together, looking at Parris.

"What?" I said.

"He won, fair and square!" Molly said angrily. "The guards all saw it! The Bank saw it!"

"I still have one more thing left to bet," said Parris. His face was still horribly pale, but his voice was steady.

"You do?" I said.

"What might that be?" said Molly. "What could you possibly have to equal all the souls won at Casino Infernale?"

"The Crow Lee Inheritance," said Parris. "Yes . . . I see you've heard of it."

"Who hasn't?" I said carefully. "It's all everyone's talking about. A hoard of secrets, and treasure, and powerful things, left behind by The Most Evil Man In The

World. There are people out there who'd do anything to get their hands on it. How did you get it?"

"Crow Lee willed it to the Shadow Bank," said Parris. "Everything else . . . is just rumour and hearsay. Would you like to see it?"

"You've got it here?" I said, just a bit incredulously.

"Oh, yes," said Parris. His smile, his gaze, and his voice were all almost fey now. He reached into his jacket and brought out a simple silver key.

"That's it?" I said.

"Apparently," said Parris. "This key gives the owner access to the Inheritance."

"Okay," I said. "I can see how the Shadow Bank might end up with the Inheritance. Crow Lee probably did a lot of business with them, down the years. But, how did you end up with the key? And what's it doing here with you?"

"He didn't just leave it to the Bank," said Parris. "That would have been too easy. He left it to them, through me. Because I'm his bastard son."

"I thought . . . Crow Lee killed all his children," I said.

"All those he could reach," said Parris. "My mother was an executive at the Shadow Bank, so I grew up under their protection. Crow Lee didn't want to upset people he did regular business with. That's why I got to run Casino Infernale this year, because I brought the Crow Lee Inheritance to the Shadow Bank. I brought the key here, to put it on display . . . but when it became clear so many important groups and people were ready to go to war over it, I decided that was probably not a good idea, after all."

"But, it's just a key," said Molly. "What does it do? What does it open?"

"We don't know," said Parris. "Not yet. The Bank's best scientists have been studying it, very carefully, from a safe distance. Crow Lee always was so very fond of his little jokes, and nasty booby traps. Once Casino Infernale is over, I will return the key to them. But it was left to me, so I get to decide what's done with it. Come on, Shaman, you know you want it. Everyone does. One last bet—all your souls, against this key. What do you say?"

I looked at Molly. I didn't have to say what I was thinking. If I could win the Inheritance, right here, and walk away with it . . . that would be the end of the business. With the Inheritance safely in my family's hands, the fanatics would all back down. No more war. I looked steadily at Parris.

"How can I be sure that key really is the real thing?"

"If I were to cheat on a bet as a representative of the Shadow Bank our reputation would be worthless," said Parris. "They'd do far worse than kill me, for something like that."

"All right," I said. "Why not? Let's do it. One last turn of the cards . . ."

Parris looked at the cards on the table.

"They're your cards," I said. "I suppose I could call for a fresh deck, but this one's been good for me. Unless you . . ."

"No . . . no," said Parris. "I had these cards checked out very thoroughly, before the Games began."

He shuffled the pack one more time. Beads of sweat popped out on his grey face. He put the pack down on the table, and then cut to reveal the queen of spades. I made my cut, and showed Parris the ace of spades.

"The Crow Lee Inheritance is mine," I said. "Give me the key."

"What have I done?" said Parris. He wasn't talking to me, wasn't even looking at me.

"The key," I said.

"Of course," said Parris. "I'm a dead man now. What does anything else matter?"

He threw his card away, and handed me the silver key. The moment I took hold of it, Crow Lee appeared there in the room before me. Parris cried out at the sight of his dead father, and the guards all trained their guns on the huge, bald man in the long white Egyptian gown, with his bushy black eyebrows over dark hypnotic eyes.

Molly sniffed scornfully.

"It's just an image! A recording stored in the key, activated by Shaman's touch."

"Why did it never appear to me?" said Parris. "He was my father."

"Good question," I said. "Let's ask him. Assuming there is an interactive function . . . Crow Lee, what are you doing here?"

"Congratulations!" said Crow Lee, in a rich carrying voice. "Think of this as my living will. You have taken possession of my inheritance, my single greatest creation. A weapon big enough to destroy the world." Crow Lee stopped abruptly, and turned to look directly at me. "And you, my dear sir, must be a Drood, if you are hearing this. It pleases me that my greatest enemies should have taken control of the key. It opens a door, to a Singularity. An artificially created black hole. And by taking the key, Drood, you have activated it. The key will open the door, and the black hole will destroy everything! Because if I can't have the world, nobody can!"

He laughed loudly, triumphantly, as his image faded away. And then the key was jerked out of my hand by an unseen force. It thrust itself forward into the air, as though fitting into some invisible lock, and slowly began to turn. I grabbed on to it with both hands, but I couldn't stop it turning. I threw all my strength against it, but I couldn't even slow the steady remorseless movement. Molly ran forward, and put her hands on top of mine, but it didn't make any difference. Parris looked at me wildly.

"There was no Inheritance! Just another of my damned father's dirty tricks! And you—you're a Drood? All along, you've been a Drood? But . . . you don't have a torc! We checked you! We checked everyone!" He started to laugh, hysterically. "It's you! You activated the key, so whatever happens now, it isn't my fault!" He looked at his guards, standing around stunned by the sudden change in events. "Don't just stand there! Kill him! Kill them both!"

But they looked at the key, still turning in mid-air despite everything Molly and I could do, and every single one of them turned and bolted, fighting each other to get through the dimensional door to safety. Molly left me and ran back to the bar. I hung grimly on to the key. Molly vaulted over the bar, and threw everything back and forth as she searched desperately.

"Parris!" she yelled. "Where's the bloody null generator! I have to turn it off, so I can use my magics on the key!"

But Parris was still laughing wildly. He raised his left hand and looked into his Evil Eye, and just like that, he was gone. He'd escaped from a situation he found intolerable, and all it had cost him was his soul.

The key completed its full circle, and a door appeared in front of me. A flat black door, with the silver key set in a silver lock. The door began to open. I let go of the key, and put my shoulder to the door, trying to hold it closed, and it pushed me back with slow, contemptuous ease. A low whistling filled the room, as the air was sucked past the door's edges, to whatever lay beyond. I dug my heels into the carpet, and couldn't even slow the door. Given what it was, and what lay behind it, I probably couldn't have stopped it even if I'd had my armour.

Molly cried out triumphantly behind the bar, as something smashed loudly. She vaulted back over the bar, and came running back to join me, stray magics spitting and crackling around her. She'd found the null generator. She stood beside me, and hit the door with the full force of her returned magic, and couldn't even slow it. The air was rushing past the door's edges now. Crow Lee had put a lot of thought and effort into his last act of spite against the world. The heavy table was edging forward along the floor, pulled by the remorseless force. I looked at Molly.

"Can you teleport us out of here?"

"I don't know where we are!" said Molly. "Once we passed through that dimensional door, we could be anywhere! I can't teleport blind without coordinates."

The carpet was rolling up towards the door. The table was jerking forward. The air was rushing past me.

"Leave the door," said Molly. "We can't stop it. Let's just leave, through the dimensional door, before someone thinks to lock it from the other side."

"This is a black hole!" I said. "We can't just leave it! If this door opens all the way it'll suck in the whole world. Nowhere would be safe!"

"Isn't there anything the Armourer gave you that might help?" said Molly.

"I've already used everything!" I said.

And then I stopped, as a thought struck me. In the Martian Tombs, one of the machines had insisted on giving me something. What Molly called the *Get Out Of Jail Free* card. I never did figure out what it was, or what it was for, but clearly the machines thought I'd need it. . . . I dug into my pocket dimension, and pulled out the card. I glared at it.

"Do something!"

And just like that, I began to fade away, as a teleport field formed around me. But only me. Not Molly.

"No!" I said. "No! I won't go on my own! I won't leave her behind! Take both of us!"

But it wouldn't. The teleport field faded away. I thought hard.

"All right!" I said to the card. "Do something about the black hole!"

And I threw the card round the edge of the door, and into what lay beyond. Crow Lee magic, meet Martian tech. And just like that the door slammed shut again, and disappeared. The silver key fell to the floor. I picked it up, and put it carefully away, in my pocket dimension. The rushing air had stopped, and everything in the room was still and silent again.

"Deus ex Martiania," I said. "Get out of Hell free card. I think I may faint. Or puke."

"Puke first, then faint," Molly said wisely. She hugged me tightly. "You wouldn't leave without me. You could have saved yourself, but you wouldn't leave me. How did I ever find someone like you?"

"Just lucky, I guess," I said.

Molly pushed me away from her, and glared at me.

"What?" I said.

"Tell me the truth," said Molly. "How could you be so sure you would win every game, and every cut of the cards?"

"Easy," I said. "I cheated. Remember the pack of cards the Armourer gave me back at Drood Hall? With a built-in chameleon function, so it could look exactly like the pack it replaced? That would give me the winning hand or card, every time? I swapped it for the hotel's pack, during Hyde's first outburst. And no one noticed. Not even you. Parris trusted the pack, because he thought it was his."

"I think I like Shaman better than Eddie," said Molly. "He's so much . . . sneakier."

"And because neither of us could live without you," I said.

"I could have told you that," said Molly.

CHAPTER TEN

Fighting the Good Fight

"Al right," said Molly. "What do we do now?"

"I gave my word I'd do a great many things before I left this place," I said. "Free all the trapped souls in the hotel corridor; do something to help the generic people on the Medium Games world; and bring down the whole damned Shadow Bank to put a stop to the rotten way they do things."

"I've always admired your sense of ambition," said Molly. "Caution and common sense just get in the way of having a good time. But first, I have to ask . . . where exactly are we? Since we passed through that dimensional door we could be anywhere at all . . . and I can't help thinking there must be some really good reason why they covered these windows so we can't see out. . . ."

She looked thoughtfully at the heavy steel shutters covering the three great windows, and the metal shutters shook and shuddered under the impact of her gaze. She glared at them, and the heavy steel groaned out loud as it fought the locks holding it in place. And then, one after the other, the locks shattered and blew apart, and each steel shutter rolled upwards. I walked forward, with Molly smiling smugly at my side, to look out the nearest window. And there, outside, were the star-filled night skies of the Medium Games world, its wide grassy plains lit by the harsh moonlight of too many moons.

"What the hell are we doing back here?" said Molly.

"You heard Parris," I said. "This is the home world of the Shadow Bank. No wonder no one could ever find them. And no wonder they used this place to stage the more dangerous games of Casino Infernale. I think . . . there are a great many answers to be found in this other world. Think you can break this glass, Molly?"

"Of course," she said airily. She glared at the window before us. The glass vibrated, and then shuddered violently, but it wouldn't break. Molly jabbed an angry finger at the window, but although the glass bowed in and out, and shook desperately in its frame, it still wouldn't give. Molly spoke a Word of Power; and the wall around the window split and cracked and fell apart . . . while the window remained entirely intact.

"Ah . . ." said Molly. "I don't think this is glass, Shaman."

"Maybe we should ask Parris how to get out there," I said.

"Well," said Molly. "You can try . . ."

Parris was still sitting in his chair, but it took only one look at his face to convince me there was no one home. His eyes stared unseeingly, his mouth drooled, and nothing at all moved in his face.

"Stay away from the Evil Eye," said Molly, from a safe distance.

"I had already thought of that, thank you," I said, not looking round. "I do have enough sense to avoid something called an Evil Eye. . . ."

"News to me," sniffed Molly. "You know, we could take the Eye back with us. Your uncle Jack always complains you never bring him back a present. . . ."

"I am not dragging a mindless body around with me,

just so the Armourer can have a new toy to play with," I said firmly.

"We don't need all of Parris," said Molly. "Just his hand . . ."

"Oh, ick," I said. "Very definitely ick. I don't want the thing that badly."

"We could put it in a box. . . ."

"No!"

"Well, at least search Parris," said Molly. "See if he's got all the things he confiscated from us. I want my anklet back."

"Eiko took them, not Parris," I said. "But I suppose they might have ended up with him, as boss. . . . Worth a look."

Parris didn't react at all as I searched through his pockets, carefully and very gingerly. No sign of my Colt Repeater, or Molly's silver charm bracelet. I didn't really think there would be, but it's best to go along with Molly when she's in one of her moods. Unless you like being a frog.

"Look behind the bar," said Molly, remorselessly. "Eiko spent enough time there." I gave Molly a look, and she glared back. "I want my anklet!"

So I went and looked behind the bar. Nothing there of any interest, apart from a great deal of shattered high tech from where Molly blew up the null generator. Small things crunched noisily under my shoes as I investigated. I came back out from behind the bar, and gave Molly my best meaningful shrug.

"Not a thing," I said. "Chalk up more lost toys to the forces of experience. Uncle Jack will give me hell for losing yet another gun . . ."

"It doesn't matter," said Molly. "I can always make myself another charm bracelet."

I thought a great many things in response to that, but had enough sense to keep them to myself.

"I was hoping to use the Colt Repeater on the windows," I said. "How in hell are we going to get out there?"

"Forget the windows," said Molly. "We'll use the door."

I looked at the door, and then at Molly. "What?"

"It's a dimensional door, remember?" said Molly. She strolled over to consider the door in a *don't mess with me* kind of way. "Where you end up depends on setting the right coordinates. Like I do when I teleport."

"Then why don't you . . ."

"Because personal teleporting is very complicated, all right? And it takes a lot out of me. So we will use this door, once I've cracked the combination lock with my magic, and sorted out the right coordinates for the world outside those windows."

"Are you sure about this?" I said carefully. "Only, I can see a whole bunch of ways in which this could all go horribly wrong. . . ."

"Never met a dimensional door lock I couldn't have eating out of my hand, in no time at all," said Molly.

"What about booby traps?" I said.

"Do I tell you how to do your job?"

"Yes," I said. "All the time."

"I'm allowed," said Molly. "I'm a girl."

"I had noticed," I said.

We shared a quick smile.

Molly gave the door her entire concentration, and I could hear the built-in combination lock whirring through its variations as Molly sorted out the correct destination. It took her only a few moments and then the door opened, just a crack. Molly punched the air triumphantly, while I stayed where I was.

"Is there some way of checking first, before we go through?" I said. "All it takes is one digit out and we could end up . . . well, anywhere."

"This should be it," said Molly.

"Should?" I said, loudly. "I do not find that a reassuring word, in this context!"

"Don't be such a wimp," said Molly, kindly. "Think positive."

"I am positive. I am entirely positive I am not going

through that door until someone provides me with a written guarantee, and travel insurance."

"Don't give me those negative waves, Moriarty." Molly hauled the door wide open and waved a hand at what lay beyond. "There! See! Satisfied?"

I moved cautiously forward to stand beside her. A long grassy plain stretched away before me: dark green grass marked with the familiar purple tinge. A low murmuring wind came gusting through the door, carrying familiar subtle scents. It was still night in that other world, lit by the great swirl of stars and three bitter yellow moons. I made a point of going through the door first, and Molly made a point of brushing quickly past me. And just like that, we were in another world.

It was all very still, and very quiet. The night air seemed disturbingly cold this time, rather than cool. I felt a long way from home. I hadn't realised just how *alien* this other world felt, until there were no human games or gamers to distract me. There was no one around, no matter which direction I looked. The Medium Games were over, and the Players had departed. I couldn't see the Arena anywhere, or the stone Tower. And I had to wonder . . . just which part of this other world we'd arrived in.

"Relax," said Molly, anticipating my thoughts with the ease of long practice. "I checked the coordinates. We're within half a mile of where we arrived before. I do think these things through, you know."

"Then where is everyone?" I said.

"Right . . ." said Molly. "This whole place is deserted."

"Does rather raise the question," I said. "What do the generic people do when there aren't any Games to oversee? One of them did try to explain, in a vague sort of way, but I'm not sure I believe him, in retrospect."

"He lied to you?" said Molly.

"Shocking, I know," I said. "But it has been known to happen. What are the genetically created underclass coming to?"

"Good question," said Molly. "What does a race of people created to serve do when there's no one left to serve, and nothing to do?"

"I think we're about to find out," I said.

From every side they came, from in front and behind us and all around; rank upon rank, row upon row. The generic people. Thousands of them, all wearing the same formal clothes, and the same curiously unfinished, disturbingly characterless faces. They closed in on us, moving silently across the purple-tinged grass, saying nothing. They walked in perfect lockstep, with eerie synchronisation, all maintaining exactly the same space between them. Like flocking birds. The hairs on the back of my neck stood up. People aren't supposed to move like that. There was something openly menacing about the generic people now they didn't have to act like servants any more.

"I could be wrong," said Molly, "but they don't look like they want to be saved. . . ."

The generic people all slammed to a sudden halt, looking steadily at Molly and me from every direction. All standing perfectly, inhumanly, still. The same eyes, the same expression, on a thousand and more faces. I didn't need to look around me to know Molly and I were completely surrounded. Without making a big thing out of it, Molly and I moved closer together, ready to stand back to back, if need be. Though if this generic army wanted to overrun us, I didn't see how we could stop them. None of them were carrying any weapons, but then, they didn't need to.

One stepped forward, out of the crowd, and walked towards us. He didn't look any different from the others. He stopped a polite distance away, but didn't bow to me, or to Molly. His gaze was steady, and he didn't smile at all.

"Have we met before?" I said.

"In a sense," said the generic man. His voice was entirely characterless, like his blurred face. "I know you, Shaman Bond. I remember you. I remember everything you said, to every one of us. When you speak to one of us, you speak to all of us. What one of us knows, we all know. We see everything, we hear everything."

"Just like the Shadow Bank," I said. It was meant as a joke, but the moment the words left my mouth I was shaken by a sudden, awful insight. I could feel my jaw drop before I quickly took control of myself, and glared at the generic spokesman. "Oh my God . . . This is the home world of the Shadow Bank. And you live here . . . which means you are the Shadow Bank! You run the Shadow Bank!"

"What?" said Molly. "Oh come on, you have got to be kidding!"

"We were made to serve," said the generic spokesman. "So long ago, no one here now remembers by whom, or why, or what for. It doesn't matter. They are long gone. We were left alone here for a long time, just keeping the machinery going, replacing our numbers through the factory farms . . . but fading away through lack of purpose . . . until the original founders of the Shadow Bank came here and found us. Entirely by accident, as I understand. We needed someone to serve; we needed meaningful work to give our existence purpose; so we accepted them as our new masters. And they set us to work, to run their Games for them. Efficiently.

"Later, they brought us into the Shadow Bank, to run that efficiently. Because already the Bank was becoming too big and too complicated for its human managers to cope with. It didn't take us long to realise that the most efficient way to run the Shadow Bank was to remove the human element, which got in the way of true efficiency. So we removed them and took control. It was the logical solution."

"What did you do with all the bodies?" said Molly.

"Oh, we didn't kill them," said the generic spokesman. "We recycled them. We made them into us."

"How long ago did all this happen?" I said.

"Does it matter?" said the generic spokesman. "We run the Shadow Bank as it needs to be run. Successfully. For years. Many years. But no one else must ever know that. It is our belief that Humanity would not take well to discovering the truth about the inner workings of the Shadow Bank. They might want to change things, and we could not allow that. The proper running of the Shadow Bank gives us purpose, and reason for existence. We live to serve, and we serve the Shadow Bank. Therefore, Shaman Bond and Molly Metcalf, you cannot be allowed to tell anyone what you have learned."

"How are you proposing to stop us?" I said. "You really think you can kill us?"

"No," said the generic spokesman. "We propose to make you like us. And then you won't want to tell anyone anything."

"I'd rather die," said Molly.

"That is, of course, your other option," said the generic man.

I looked around. The generic army covered the grassy plains and hills for as far as I could see in any direction. Molly's hands had clenched into fists at her sides. I could feel her magics whispering on the air around us, waiting to be unleashed.

"Never fought an entire army before," I said. "Or at least, not without my armour, and my family to back me up."

"I think we should retreat," said Molly. "And come back with reinforcements. Heavily armed reinforcements."

"You can't leave," said the generic spokesman. "We control all entrances and exits to our world."

And sure enough, when I looked quickly behind me the dimensional door was gone. I looked quickly at Molly.

"Are you sure you can't teleport us out of here?"

"Very sure," said Molly. "We're on a whole different world, remember? Quite possibly a whole different level of reality. I can't trust my coordinates here. I mean, I'm good, Shaman, but reluctant as I am to admit it, I do have my limitations."

"Then I'll just have to bring the reinforcements to us," I said.

Molly gave me a look. "Really?"

"I've had an idea. . . ." I said.

"Go for it," Molly said immediately. "Whatever this idea is, I love it and want to have its babies. Because I've got nothing."

"I can't call on my family without my torc," I said. "But I believe there is someone who might still owe us a favour. So . . . Horse! Please, come to me! I need your help!"

There was a pause. Molly glared at me.

"That's it? That's your big idea? We're on a whole other world! What makes you think the Horse can hear us from here?"

"Because he's a living god," I said. "And I believe he can hear a prayer for help, wherever he is."

Every single member of the generic army suddenly tilted their heads right back, to stare up into the night sky. I looked up too, and grinned broadly. A massive White Horse filled the entire night sky, from one horizon to the next, blocking out the stars and shining bright as any moon. The generic people cried out as one—a terrible, awed cry. Because they'd never seen anything like the White Horse before. The Horse came riding down, out of the sky, shrinking rapidly in size without losing any of his grandeur and majesty, becoming finally a simple horse standing before Molly and me, regarding us with old, wise eyes. Molly threw her arms around his great white neck and hugged him fiercely. I bowed, respectfully. The Horse looked at me in a knowing way, and I couldn't help but grin.

"You may have noticed," I said to the Horse, "that Molly and I are currently surrounded by a whole bunch of enemies, who mean us harm. We need help. Reinforcements. If I were to give you the names of those I need, could you find them and bring them here? Really, very, very quickly?"

The Horse looked at me as though I'd just asked him whether he could gallop without tripping over his own hooves. For a horse, he did have a very expressive face. Comes with being a living god, I suppose.

Molly reluctantly let go of the Horse, after I'd cleared my throat meaningfully a few times, and turned to look at me.

"Who did you have in mind?" she said, just a bit suspiciously. "All the Drood field agents?"

"I don't think we should push our luck too much," I said. "The more people I ask for, the longer it might take the Horse to round them up and bring them here. And I don't know how long the shock and awe of the Horse will hold the generic army back. So, I thought, those who started this should be here at the finish. Horse, please locate and bring here, as fast as is godly possible: the Drood Armourer, from Drood Hall; Sir Parsifal of the London Knights; J. C. Chance of the Carnacki Institute; Dead Boy from the Nightside; and Natasha Chang from the Crowley Project. And, I suppose, Bruin Bear and the Sea Goat, from Shadows Fall. No reason why they should miss out on all the fun."

The Horse nodded his great white head, and disappeared. The generic people made a single, very disturbed, sound. Despite their characterless faces, they all gave every indication of being very upset. The generic spokesman looked at Molly and me.

"What . . . Who was that?"

Molly and I ignored him.

"Natasha Chang?" said Molly. "Are you sure? After the Sea Goat smashed a vodka bottle over her head at the Summit Meeting?"

"She'll have recovered by now," I said confidently. "Hard-headed creature like her . . . and I don't think she'll bear a grudge. She is Crowley Project, after all. She'll have done worse."

"You are clearly too dangerous to be allowed to live," said the generic spokesman. "You have to die. You have to die now."

"Too late," I said. "Listen, can you hear the sound of approaching hooves?"

The whole generic army raised their eyes to the sky again as the sound of pounding hoofbeats filled the night . . . and then they all fell back abruptly, pushed back by the godly pressure of a whole bunch of White Horses appearing out of nowhere, to stand in a great circle around Molly and me. It was the same Horse, appearing simultaneously in several places at once. You could tell. The Horse's presence slammed on the air, like a living thing, like an endless roll of silent thunder.

He was currently bearing several rather surprised-looking riders. The Horse turned his several heads to look at them, and they all dismounted quickly, in their various ways. After which all the Horses seemed to just . . . slide together, until there was only one—the living god of Horses, standing before Molly and me. He bowed his great white head to me, winked briefly, and was gone.

"Is that the end of our favours, do you think?" said Molly, practical as always.

"Who can tell with a living god?" I said. "Or a Horse."

My uncle Jack was the first to come forward and greet me. The others all seemed preoccupied with the surrounding army, which was only natural. The Armourer smiled easily at me, in a vague and confused sort of way. He was wearing his usual lab coat, with fresh chemical burns steaming all down one scorched and blackened sleeve. He looked at me reproachfully.

"I was just in the middle of something important, you know. But it is hard to say no to a Horse like that, particularly when it's just appeared right in the middle of the Drood Armoury, passing right through the Hall's defences as though they weren't even there, and without setting off a single alarm. . . ."

"He's the living god of all horses," I said. "I don't think they do defences or alarms. And I did sort of promise Ethel she could have the Horse as a companion."

"Oh, well," said the Armourer. "Someone for the dragon to play with. As soon as I've finished growing a body for his head. Hello, Eddie! Hello, Molly!" He looked about him. "Do I understand correctly that you're in some sort of trouble?"

"These are the generic flunkies," I said. "They want to kill me. And Molly."

"Ah," said the Armourer. "Can't have that, can we?" He fixed the generic spokesman with a hard look. "Any of you make even one move I don't like, and I'll let my lab assistants have you for experiments!"

"Trust me," I said to the somewhat bewildered generic spokesman. "That is probably the worst threat you have ever heard. So behave."

"When I agreed to attend the Summit Meeting on Mars, I had no idea I'd been conscripted into a war," said J. C. Chance, striding forward to join us in his bright ice-cream white suit. He glared about him with all his usual cockiness, apparently not bothered in the least by the sheer numbers surrounding us. "Not that I'm complaining, you understand. Always ready to do really horrible things to villains and scoundrels, but I do normally like a bit of warning. If only so I can stock up on really nasty weapons. I mean, there I was, just on my way home from the pub, when suddenly I am kidnapped by this really big horse! And before I know it, I'm riding through the dimensions without benefit of saddle or bridle."

"He doesn't like bridles," I said. "He got you here safely, didn't he?"

"Wherever here is," said J.C. "I take it from the sheer overwhelming numbers that those are the bad guys? Why have they all got the same face? Are we talking attack of the clones?"

"Something like that," I said.

"I don't even want to know how that Horse got into the toilets at Strangefellows," said Dead Boy, looming over everyone in his dark purple greatcoat, scowling at everyone with his dark fever-bright eyes.

"What were you doing in a toilet?" said Molly. "You're dead."

"I still eat and drink," said Dead Boy, reasonably. "It's got to go somewhere. Often suddenly and violently and all over the place. When I'm short of funds I bottle it, and sell it to the Little Sisters of the Immaculate Chainsaw for use in their emergency exorcisms."

Perhaps fortunately for all our tender sensibilities, Dead Boy was interrupted by the arrival of Sir Parsifal, clanking loudly in his plate steel armour, his plumed helmet stuffed under one arm. He frowned at the generic army, and the nearest rows actually fell backwards a few steps.

"We are used to horses in the London Knights," said Sir Parsifal. "They are our companions, our war chargers, our partners in the great cause. King Arthur recognised the White Horse the moment it appeared in our Court. I was honoured to be chosen, to be carried here to fight the good fight. Is this all of us?"

"Pretty much," I said.

"Good," said Sir Parsifal. "More deaths at our hands, more honour for us all."

"I don't know about the clones," said J.C., "but he scares the crap out of me. I may hide behind him, once the advance starts."

"That does sound like you," said Natasha Chang, striding elegantly forward to join us. "I am not even going to discuss what I was doing when the Horse appeared out of nowhere to carry me away . . . I just hope the cleaning lady will untie him in the morning, if I'm not back." She stopped, to glare at the Sea Goat as he came ambling forward with Bruin Bear.

"Living gods are two a penny in Shadows Fall," the Sea Goat said loudly. "And I hate riding horses. Makes me feel seasick."

"You stay away from me, you . . . animal," said Natasha.

The Sea Goat leered at her, showing large blocky teeth in his grey muzzle. "Come on, sweetie—in Crowley Project terms, what we did was practically foreplay."

Bruin Bear shook his head. "Can't take you anywhere. . . . Hello, everyone. Good to see you all again."

And the thing was, he meant it. You could tell. He was just that sort of Bear.

"It's good to see you again, Eddie," the Armourer said

gruffly. "I brought you a gift. From Ethel. I've been holding on to it ever since you left."

He held out a simple golden circlet, and I took it from him with an unsteady hand. Immediately the circlet opened, and shot forward to wrap itself around my neck. It was all I could do to keep from crying out. I had my torc again; I had my armour again. A Drood again, at last. I stood up straighter, and grinned savagely around me. I was back! I was Eddie Drood, and let everything and everyone in all the worlds beware! I threw my arms around Uncle Jack, and hugged him fiercely. He patted me awkwardly on the back, till I was finished. We've never been very good at the touchy-feely stuff in my family.

"All right," said J.C. "I am now officially confused. I was told Shaman Bond was infiltrating Casino Infernale."

"Shaman is my use name," I said. "My cover identity, when I'm out in the field. I hope you'll all keep this knowledge to yourselves, or I will have to track you down and kill you in inventive and highly distressing ways."

"Yeah," said Dead Boy. "He's a Drood."

Molly was looking at the generic spokesman, who'd retreated almost all the way back to the front row of his army. He actually flinched as she fixed him with her gaze.

"You're in trouble now, boys," Molly said loudly. "The gang's all here. Surrender now, and avoid the rush."

"We outnumber you," the generic spokesman said stubbornly. His face was pale and his eyes were wide, but his voice was still steady. "There are thousands of us, to your handful. You cannot win. You must all die so that the truth you know dies with you."

"Truth?" said the Armourer. "And what truth might that be? Have you been keeping something from us, Eddie? I think you need to bring us all up to speed, boy." He shot the generic spokesman a heavy glare, from under his bushy white eyebrows. "Anyone, and I mean any one of you, who makes the slightest aggressive move, or tries to interrupt us while Eddie's talking, will be made a horrible example of for the others."

"Yeah," said Dead Boy. "He's a Drood too. No one does a nasty threat like a Drood."

And he must have been right, because the generic army just stood there and did nothing, while I gave all the original members of the Summit Meeting a short, concise version of what had gone down at Casino Infernale, and what I had learned about the true nature of the Shadow Bank, and the Crow Lee Inheritance. I showed them the silver key, and they all expressed polite amazement over how such a small thing could be so dangerous. None of them interrupted while I talked. They were all good listeners. They were, after all, professionals. When I finally finished I liked to think they were all looking at me, and Molly, a little more respectfully. Even the London Knight.

"So," said Sir Parsifal. "The war over the Crow Lee Inheritance was finished before it began. A non-starter. Pity. I would have liked to get my hands bloody, punishing the various dirty factions. But"—and here he looked out over the standing rows of the generic army—"I suppose these will do." He picked out the generic spokesman with his cold fierce eyes, and raised his voice. "You, fellow, there! Do you still intend to kill us all?"

"Of course," said the generic man. "It is necessary. You cannot be allowed to stand in the way of efficiency."

Sir Parsifal looked at me. "You want us to kill them all?"

"I think that might be beyond even us," I said carefully. "No, I think we need to find their head-quarters, from where they actually run the Shadow Bank, and destroy it. Destroy their ability to support organised supernatural crime. Bring the whole thing down. It's all so clear, now . . . they run things in an inhuman way, because they are inhuman. No conscience, or compassion, in their day-to-day business, because they have none. This cannot be allowed to continue."

"That's my nephew," the Armourer said proudly. "More ambitious than a barrelful of Hollywood starlets. I'm sorry, I don't know where that image came from."

"But why should the rest of us fight for you, Drood?"

said Natasha. "A Summit Meeting is one thing; open warfare is quite another."

"Fair question," I said. "For justice. To stop further injustice. So we can all be free of the Shadow Bank and the evils it makes possible."

"So . . . I wouldn't have to pay off my loans?" said J.C. "Sounds good to me."

"Always did love a challenge," said Dead Boy, beaming happily around him at the generic army.

"You cannot win!" said the generic spokesman, almost desperately. "Why do you persist in this? The situation is clear. We are many; you are few."

"You never met anyone like us," said Sir Parsifal. He drew his great sword, and the long blade blazed a dazzling silver on the night. "This is the sword Ex Caliburn, soaked in the blood of evil men. I have fought Humanity's enemies on a thousand worlds, spilled alien blood in alien mud, brought down a thousand forces who thought they could prey on Humanity. I don't see why this should be any different."

He stood tall and proud in his gleaming medieval armour, and I believed every word he said.

J.C. stepped forward, and whipped off his sunglasses to glare at the generic army with his awful glowing eyes. "I have fought forces and beings from beyond the realms of death. Because I work for the Carnacki Institute, and we don't take any shit from the hereafter. We exist to make sure Humanity can sleep safely in its bed at night. You? You're just an annoyance that needs slapping down."

The Armourer activated his armour and the golden strange matter whipped itself around him in a moment, so that he stood there like a perfect golden statue, under the stars and the moons. "I represent Drood," he said flatly. "You know of us. You know what we can do. Stand down now. While you still can."

When it became clear that the generic army wasn't going to do that, Dead Boy sauntered forward, flashing his cold, dead smile. "Come on, then! Give me your best shot!

I can take you! Ah, there's nothing like a little vicious mayhem to warm the heart, once you're dead!"

Natasha Chang sighed quietly. "Testosterone—such a curse . . . I represent the Crowley Project. You've had dealings with us. You don't get to run Humanity; that's our job. And whilst normally I wouldn't be seen dead in present company, I will make common cause with them, against you. It has been a while since I helped commit genocide, and a girl does like to keep her hand in. . . ."

Molly looked at J.C. "Did you really go out with her for a while?"

J.C. shrugged, and smiled winningly. "You know how it is . . . it's always the bad girl who makes a good guy's heart beat that little bit faster. . . ."

"It was just sex," Natasha said crushingly. "And not very good sex, either."

Dead Boy shook his head. "Women always fight dirty."

I looked at Bruin Bear and the Sea Goat. "I don't know what I was thinking, bringing you guys here. You don't belong in a war. Just . . . sit this one out, till it's over."

"You brought us here to be your conscience," said Bruin Bear, fixing me steadily with his warm, wise eyes. "To make sure you wouldn't go too far. So the Goat and I will go with you. Don't worry; no one will harm us."

"He's quite right," said the Sea Goat. "No one will lay a hand on him. He's that sort of Bear."

"I will guard your back," said the Bear. "With the Goat's help."

The Sea Goat sniggered loudly. "Damn right. Because I'm not that sort of Bear." And suddenly he was holding a long ironwood shillelagh in one hand, thick and heavy and carved with nasty runes. A stick made for violence. "Ah, this takes me back! Been a while since I was an action hero."

"We were heroes and adventurers in the Golden Lands," the Bear said sternly. "Not thugs or bullies."

"Why are you here?" said Molly. "Really?"

"Because the Horse said we would be needed, later," said Bruin Bear.

"And we know better than to argue with a living god," said the Sea Goat. "Even if he is really just a stuck-up pony with delusions of grandeur."

Molly gave up on that one, and turned back to me. "We still have to locate the Shadow Bank's head-quarters. I don't see any suitable candidates. Hell, I don't see a single building anywhere! Could it be underground?"

"No," I said. "Isn't it obvious?"

"Clearly not, or I would be looking at the bloody thing!" said Molly.

"What did we say when we first saw the Casino Infernale hotel?" I said patiently. "That it looked like an alien starship. Frankie said it could travel to anywhere in the world, just popping out of nowhere and setting down into its next location. So where do you think such a thing came from, originally?"

"Right here!" said Molly. "Good thinking, Shaman! Or Eddie . . . Never mind that now. All I have to do is concentrate on the coordinates built into the dimensional door inside the hotel, and I can manipulate that with my magic and bring the hotel here!"

"That was my idea!" I said.

"You were taking too long," said Molly. "Now hush. I'm working."

She frowned hard, waved one hand in a certain way, and the hotel materialised on the hilltop opposite us. On the other side of the generic army. They all cried out together in a strange mixture of anger and loss. It made an eerie, almost plaintive sound on the night. Perhaps because they'd never lost control of the hotel before. Never lost control of the situation . . . Events were moving against them, and they could tell. For the first time, for all their blank characterless faces . . . it seemed to me that they looked uncertain.

"It's a big building," said Molly, scowling at the massive hotel dominating the horizon. "Where, inside all of that, would they hide their head-quarters? Could be anywhere!"

"I'm more concerned with the way the whole generic

army is gathering together to place themselves between us and the hotel," I said, just a bit reproachfully. "You couldn't have landed the thing right next to us, Molly? So we wouldn't have to fight our way through the whole generic population just to reach it?"

"Don't you criticise me, Eddie Drood!" Molly said fiercely. I always know I'm in trouble when Molly uses my full name. She stepped forward so she could glare right into my face. "I brought that hotel all the way here from another world, by remote control! Given how far the bloody thing's travelled, I think that is pretty damned close! Don't you?"

"Children, children," murmured the Armourer. "Not in front of the enemy. Or in front of the allies, for that matter."

"Argue about it after the war," said Sir Parsifal. "With those of us who survive. Now, come and present yourselves, all you forces for the Good. It's killing time."

"I will lead the way," I said. "I will take Molly with me into the hotel to search for the head-quarters, while the rest of you keep the generic army outside and off our backs. Think you can do that?"

"Piece of cake," said Dead Boy, cheerfully.

"I have Ex Caliburn," said Sir Parsifal. "And my duty, and my honour."

"I have a Hand of Glory, made out of a monkey's paw," said J.C. "And there was absolutely no need for all of you to look at me like that. Yes, I know such a thing is illegal under any number of internationally recognised pacts and conventions, and that you can be executed just for knowing such a thing is possible in a large number of countries, but in my defence, I don't give a damn. And, yes, of course I stole it, so can we please move on."

"I have my nasty piece of high tech," Natasha said demurely, "which I don't feel obliged to discuss. It isn't illegal, because you haven't heard of it. Yet."

Dead Boy sniffed loudly. "Weapons are for wimps. Just let me get my hands on them."

"I don't use weapons," said Bruin Bear. "In fact, I think if the time ever comes when it becomes necessary for me to take up a weapon, that will mean the end of the world is nigh."

"Trouble is, he's probably right," said the Sea Goat. "Don't worry, Bear. You stick with me, and my really big stick. I'll protect you. Just as I always have."

"Whether I approve of your methods or not," said the Bear.

The Sea Goat smiled down at the Bear, surprisingly tenderly. "That's what friends are for, old chum."

I stood beside my uncle Jack, subvocalised my activating Words, and armoured up. The strange matter flowed around and over me, surrounding and sealing me in, all in a moment. And immediately I felt stronger, faster, smarter. Like snapping fully awake after a long doze. A Drood in his armour, again and at last.

"This is how it should be," the Armourer said approvingly, looking out over the ranks and ranks of the generic army. "Fighting against impossible odds, for the ashes of his father and the temples of his gods."

I looked at him. "What?"

The Armourer sighed heavily behind his featureless golden mask. "It's a quotation! From Macaulay's 'Lays of Ancient Rome'! Don't they teach children the classics any more?"

Molly came forward to stand on my other side. Stray magics flared and discharged on the air around her. The generic spokesman stood at the front rank of his army, staring at us with his blurred, unfinished face.

"Please," I said to him, as earnestly as I knew how. "I don't want to have to do this. Stand down. Please."

"No," said the generic spokesman. "You must die. All of you. The Shadow Bank regulates Humanity. Keeps you under control. This is necessary. You cannot be allowed to run free. We know better than you what is good for you. We live to serve, to make you behave. Surrender. You cannot win."

"Lot you know," I said.

I started forward, and the others came with me. The generic army surged forward to meet us, like a great living wave. No weapons in their hands, just thousands of outstretched arms determined to drag us down and tear us apart. I raised my golden hands before me. Metal spikes rose up from the armoured knuckles of my left hand, while a long golden sword blade extended from my right hand.

Even then, at the end, I wanted to save them. But they weren't what I thought they were. So I went forward to kill as many of them as I had to, to get to the hotel and do the right thing.

One more time.

The generic army came rushing forward in an awful, focused silence, intent on violence and murder. Their outstretched hands clenched and unclenched convulsively, desperate to tear and rend our flesh. Their blurred, characterless faces never changed. The spokesman was quickly swallowed up in the crowd as they all moved forward with the same swift, eerie synchronisation. The first of them slammed into me, and their vicious hands broke against my golden armour. They tried to force me backwards, drag me down, overwhelm me by sheer force of numbers, but they'd never faced a Drood in his armour before. I stood firm, and would not fall, and would not retreat. I cut about me with my golden sword, thrusting and slashing, its impossibly sharp edge slicing through flesh and bone alike. I swept the blade back and forth like a golden scythe, and generic men fell dead and dying before me. Thick dark blood flew on the air, splashing against my armour. The blood ran quickly away, dribbling down onto the grass, and the earth. I moved steadily forward, step by step, striking about me with undiminished strength. Men with exactly the same face died before me, and not one of them cried out in pain or shock or fear.

I led the way and the others came with me, and together we committed slaughter under a starry sky with too many moons.

There were thousands in the generic army, swarming all around us, grabbing at our arms and legs, our necks and heads, fingers raking like claws, fists hitting us with savage force. But that was nothing to Drood armour. The strange matter soaked up the impact of their blows and deflected the rest, so I wouldn't be distracted from the messy business of killing. I struck fiercely about me with my golden sword, forcing my way forward, and a whole army wasn't enough to stop me.

The Armourer was right there on my right hand, striking about him with his golden fists with grim precision. He had never been a soldier, but he had been a field agent in the Cold War, one of the most quietly savage wars of recent times. He struck generic men down, and none of them ever rose again. He strode forward over their bodies, old man though he was, raised in an older time of relentless, remorseless duty. He would not be slowed or stopped or turned aside, because he was a Drood.

Molly jumped and danced and spun on my left hand, laughing out loud in sheer exhilaration as she let loose her magics. It was enough for her that she finally had a clear enemy, a chance to strike out at last, after so many frustrations. She threw fireballs with one hand, and lightning bolts with the other. When she tired of that she stabbed a pointing finger, and whoever she pointed at exploded into bloody gobbets. She laughed happily, but her face was never cruel. She just believed in doing everything to the best of her ability, and enjoying her accomplishments. The enemy came at her, determined to kill her horribly, and she laughed in their faces and killed them all. Molly always was a better fighter than me.

I caught glimpses of the others, as we went to war.

Sir Parsifal wielded Ex Caliburn with practised skill and silent fury. Cutting down every generic figure who came against him, moving always on to the next target. He fought for duty and honour and the protection of Humanity, as a London Knight should, and there was no room left in him after that, for small things like mercy or compassion. I don't think he cared who he was fighting, it was enough for him that they had been declared the enemy. He strode heavily forward in his armour, slamming the dead and the dying out of his way, singing a martial hymn behind his steel helm. Blood soaked his armour, falling away to be replaced by fresh. Sir Parsifal lived to fight the forces of evil. For him, this was a good day.

J. C. Chance thrust his Hand of Glory out before him— a wrinkled, withered thing whose sticklike fingers had been made into candles. The fingertips burned with a constant blue flame that never went out. And wherever J.C. pointed the monkey's paw, the generic men just froze up and fell paralysed to the ground. They fell in waves as he swept the nasty thing back and forth, and he strode easily over the unmoving bodies. Sometimes a generic man would get too close, and then J.C. would glare into the unfinished face with his glowing gaze, and they would scream and fall away, writhing in horror on the bloody grass. J.C. would laugh at them as they fell, and something in that sound made me shudder, just for a moment.

Natasha Chang waved her piece of secret tech around, almost aimlessly, as though wafting clouds of bug spray on the night air, but wherever she pointed the thing, generic men would just softly and silently vanish away. Gone, disappeared, banished out of existence. I had no idea whether they were dead or not, but given Natasha Chang's reputation, I had my suspicions. She laughed like a child as she stepped daintily over dead bodies, making men disappear forever.

Dead Boy just hit everyone who came within reach. He advanced happily into the ranks of the generic men, lashing out with the terrible strength of his dead arms. Flesh and bone broke under his blows, but he felt nothing, nothing at all. Hands grabbed at him from every side, fastening on to the deep purple greatcoat, but all their strength put together wasn't enough to stop him, or even slow him down. He punched heads and smashed faces, broke arms and backs and necks, striking everyone down who came at him, hammering generic men to the ground and then happily trampling them into the bloody dirt. They couldn't hurt him, and they couldn't frighten him, because the worst possible thing had already happened to him, years before.

Bruin Bear and the Sea Goat brought up the rear. And when the generic men would push past the rest of us, hoping to attack us from the rear, they came face to face with the Bear, and stopped dead in their tracks. Because they had never seen anything like him before. They bowed their heads and bent their knees to him, and adored him. Because he was that sort of Bear. And they had waited all their lives to meet someone like him, without ever knowing it. The Bear moved slowly, steadily forward, smiling on them all, patting them on their lowered heads with his fuzzy paw. The Sea Goat stuck close behind him, watching carefully, but his shillelagh was never needed.

Finally, I fought my way up a grassy slope to reach the Casino Infernale hotel. The generic men fought ever more desperately, but they couldn't stop me. I reached the front door to the lobby, and Molly was immediately there at my side. I kicked the door in, and the two of us burst into the deserted lobby. I spun around and locked the door, and my uncle Jack was right there to set his back against the locked door and defy anyone to get past him. To buy Molly and me time to find the Shadow Bank's head-quarters. Because they would have to kill him to get past him, and there weren't many good enough to take down Jack Drood.

But, it did rather put the pressure on me, to get a move on.

I armoured down, and Molly and I leaned on each other for a moment, to get our breath back. Killing is hard work, slaughter even more so.

"All right," Molly said finally. "What do we do now? That hopefully doesn't involve any actual effort, or even strenuous movement."

I looked around the lobby. The place was completely deserted, and eerily quiet. "Well," I said. "I was hoping to ask a member of the staff for directions, but . . ."

"They probably grabbed the petty cash and ran for their lives the moment it became clear everything was going tits up," said Molly. "I would have. I did check there weren't any people present, before I brought the hotel here. I do think these things through! Because I know you worry about things like that. . . . What are we looking for, exactly?"

"Computers," I said. "Records of financial transactions, details on all their clients. Everything the generic people need to run the Shadow Bank. They've got to be here somewhere. . . ."

"It's a hell of a big hotel," said Molly. "We haven't got time to search it top to bottom."

"Ah!" I said. "Where is the one place we went that drove the people in charge here absolutely batshit?"

"Parris' private office!" said Molly. "And since I've already been there, I have enough coordinates for a personal teleport!"

"Do you have enough magic left for that?" I said carefully. "Only I'd hate for only part of us to make it there. . . . Wouldn't it be easier to find a dimensional door and use that?"

Molly looked at me pityingly. "Would you trust one, right now? Or even the elevators?"

"Good point," I said. "Almost certainly booby-trapped. It's what I'd do. But, are you sure you've got enough magic. . . ."

"Shut up, and let me concentrate," said Molly. She scowled deeply. Beads of sweat popped out on her forehead. She snapped her fingers, and just like that, we were in Parris' private office.

We'd only just arrived when Molly cried out and grabbed on to me to stop herself from falling. I held her up, and glared about me, but there was no obvious threat anywhere.

"What is it, Molly?"

"A null!" said Molly. "There's a major null operating here! Ripped the last of the magic right out of me. Bastards!"

"Hold on, Molly," I said.

I subvocalised my activating Words, and my armour slammed into place around me. Because there isn't a null big enough anywhere to keep a Drood from his armour. I glared about me through my golden mask, with all its augmented vision, and it took me only a moment to track down the null generator. I could See it clearly, hidden behind a wall. I lowered Molly carefully onto the nearest chair, behind the desk, and hurried over to the wall. I ripped it apart with my golden hands, and wood and plaster flew in all directions. The generator stretched all along the wall, a thin layer of unfamiliar high tech, with moving parts and glittering lights. I plunged both hands into the exposed machinery and tore it apart, piece by piece, glancing back over my shoulder to see what effect I was having. Molly remained slumped in her chair, her face worryingly slack, until I finally found the right piece to destroy. And then all the lights in the wall went out and Molly sat bolt upright, smiling widely with relief.

"Oh, that is so much better!" she said loudly. "That's it. I'm back. I hadn't realised how low I was running till I didn't have anything left to keep me going." She grinned at me. "I knew there had to be a reason why I kept you around."

I armoured down, and went back to join her at the desk. Molly quickly used her magic to override the desk's security systems, and the built-in computer immediately showed her where the hidden switch was. She hit it, and the whole wall behind her slid smoothly to one side, revealing a huge open area beyond, packed full of computers and high-tech equipment.

"We were so close, all along, and never knew it," said Molly.

"We weren't completely ourselves then," I said consolingly.

"Bloody well are now," growled Molly. "Come on, let's go take a look around, and see what trouble we can cause."

"That's always worked for me," I said.

We moved cautiously forward into the computer room. A large, gleaming white hall, full of rows of massive machines, towering above us, falling away in every direction. We wandered between rows of machines I didn't even recognise, let alone understand, like children who had ventured into adult territory for the first time. It was hard not to be overawed by the sheer scale of things. . . . but, we had been to the Martian Tombs.

"I think . . . we are looking at the financial records and dealings of every suspect organisation in the world," I said. "Probably a lot of political stuff, too, the kind of things most of us are never supposed to know about. The Shadow Bank couldn't do what it needs to do if it didn't have political support . . . all the secret deals, the hidden agreements, all the bribes and blackmail of the private world. All here. Makes the actual Crow Lee Inheritance look small. . . ."

"Never thought I'd see the actual Shadow Bank's inner workings with my own eyes," said Molly. "Who owes what, who owns what . . . Look, Shaman, Eddie, whoever you are right now—we have to consider the possibilities. If we were to take control of this, just you and me, we'd have the power to put everything in the world right, at last. Make everyone place nicely with each other. We could put an end to all the bad guys, forever."

"Power corrupts," I said. "We couldn't do this on our own. We'd have to bring in my family. And the Droods are already far too powerful for their own good. I've had to pull them back from the brink once; this could push them right over the edge. If my family were to take control of the Shadow Bank, even for the noblest of reasons, we'd end up becoming the Shadow Bank. No. My family can't be trusted with this. No one can. That's the point. Better to destroy everything, and destroy the temptation that goes with it. Wipe all these records, and we financially cripple all the right people. And scare everyone else enough to give my family an advantage. I think that's the best we can realistically hope for. A fighting chance. Which is, of course, all my family has ever needed."

Molly sniffed loudly. "Sir Parsifal probably wouldn't agree with you."

"Just as well he's not here, then," I said. "Or any of the others."

"You're not tempted, even a little bit?" said Molly. "Isn't there anything you want?"

"Just you," I said.

"You always know the right thing to say," said Molly. "Do you have any idea how annoying that is?"

"Yes," I said.

We shared a smile, and then looked round again.

"Destroy it all," I said. "Wipe it clean, and put an end to the Shadow Bank, at last. What do you think, Molly—a series of fires or one really big explosion?"

"You know how to spoil a girl," said Molly. "Blow it all up!"

"And us, along with it?" said a quiet voice.

I looked round sharply, as a single generic man came out from between the huge machines. He was wearing a white lab coat that made me think immediately of my uncle Jack. He shuffled forward, almost tentatively, his hands held out before him to show they were empty. Molly brought up one hand, stray magics already spitting and crackling on the air around it, but I grabbed her arm, and made her stop. There was something about this one; he didn't look dangerous, or menacing.

"What are you doing here?" I said. "Why aren't you out fighting with the others?"

"One of us always has to be here," he said. "To keep an eye on things."

"You're really the only one here?" said Molly, glaring suspiciously about her. "Because I swear if I see anyone moving around in the shadows, I will turn them inside out and leave them that way."

"Just me," said the generic man. "But what one of us sees, we all see. You know the rest. There's always one of us here to see the machines run smoothly."

"So, you're the generic caretaker," I said. "Are you going to give us any trouble?"

"I can't stop you, whatever you decide to do here. I know that. But please, you must understand. Destroy the computers, and you destroy my people. We serve the Shadow Bank through these machines. We were made to serve. We will die without a purpose. We almost died out before the Shadow Bank's original owners found us. I don't believe we could survive another loss of purpose. Are you ready to commit genocide?"

"Hell yes," said Molly. "After all the evil the Shadow Bank's made possible? All the suffering and horror you people have been responsible for? And, you just tried to kill us!"

"After everything you're responsible for," I said to the generic caretaker. "Now there's a thought. . . . No, I won't be responsible for wiping you out. That's the difference, right there, between you and me. I've got a much better idea. What if I was to give your people another purpose?"

Molly leaned in close to me. "Are you sure about this?" she said quietly. "I mean, you know I love your ideas, but . . . can you rely on this lot to do whatever it is you're about to ask them to do?"

"Oh, I think so," I said quietly. "As long as my family is there, looking over their shoulders."

"Oh, hell," said Molly. "Go for it. Genocide always makes me feel queasy."

"Take what these machines know," I said to the generic caretaker, "and use it to set people free. Destroy the financial records of all the evil organisations and individuals, make them bankrupt . . . and then use that money to put right all the wrongs you people have made possible. And set free all the souls you own, so they can move on to wherever they belong. Then, use the knowledge the Shadow Bank has acquired down the years to expose the hidden deals and corrupt conspiracies, and help make the world a better place. I know, Molly, I'm being idealistic again. But we have to try. Because it's either that, or killing an entire people. And I'm just not in the mood. I'm an agent, not an assassin, remember? You, generic caretaker . . . do you accept the new purpose I give you?"

"Yes," he said. "We live to serve."

"Good," I said. "And by the time you've finished with everything I've just said, my family will have thought of something else that needs doing, to keep you occupied."

"Good," said the generic man. "It will help us to have masters again."

"Then tell your people," I said.

"They already know. The fighting has stopped. The killing is over. It is no longer necessary. We have a new purpose."

"Damn," said Molly. "You people are seriously creepy."

"And you people," said the generic man, "are seriously scary. Because you're always so certain."

We took the elevator back down to the lobby. Molly was almost completely out of magic. We walked out of the lobby, and found our friends and allies standing together outside the hotel. Looking around them in a confused sort of way. The generic army had moved back, and were standing still, awaiting new instructions from their new masters. The moment Molly and I appeared, the whole generic army bowed their heads to us. The Armourer armoured down.

"Eddie? Molly? What have you done?"

"We won," I said cheerfully. "The war is over, the Shadow Bank is no more, and the generic people work for the Droods now."

"Bloody typical," said J.C. He was breathing hard, and there was blood on his white suit. "We do all the hard work, and the Droods reap all the rewards. Don't the rest of us get anything out of this?"

"The satisfaction of a job well done," said Sir Parsifal.

Dead Boy looked at the London Knight. "You're weird. And I have to ask, why are some of those empty-faced people gathered around Bruin Bear, and worshipping him?"

"Because he's that sort of Bear," I said. I moved over to the nearest generic person. "Are you sure there won't be any bad feelings over all of your kind who died here?"

"We are one," said the generic man calmly. "What's a few bodies?"

"That," said Molly. "That, right there, is what's wrong."

"No wonder you ran the Shadow Bank the way you did," I said.

CHAPTER ELEVEN

Going Home

I stood at the end of a terribly long corridor deep within the hotel, with Molly at my side. Hundreds, maybe thousands, of faces lined both walls, staring out of simple wooden frames. Souls, lost souls; lost in games of chance at Casino Infernale. So many suffering faces, held in place behind polished glass, staring endlessly out with haunted eyes. Mouths moving silently, in pleas for help that the world never heard. Like insects trapped under glass, pinned in place, caught between Life and Death, for as long as Casino Infernale, or the Shadow Bank, had a use for them. I looked down the endless length of the corridor, at all the lost souls; and I don't think I'd ever felt so angry. Molly moved in close beside me, to comfort me with her presence.

"Some things just aren't right," I said. "Some crimes really are inhuman."

"I know," said Molly.

"I did ask my uncle Jack if he wanted to be here with me when I did this," I said. "He said thank you, but no. He wanted to make sure the others got home safely."

"He probably felt responsible for them," said Molly.

"He was the one who called them to the Summit Meeting in the first place."

"No," I said. "That wasn't the reason. I think he's not here because he knew about this and never did anything about it. He just followed the family's orders. Because they were afraid to do anything that might upset the apple cart. Because they were always ready to deal with the devil they knew . . . rather than risk something worse. And to hell with the cost. My uncle is a good man. A brave man. But he always was too ready to let other people make the big decisions for him."

"Good thing the family's got you, then," said Molly.

I looked up and down the corridor, taking my time, refusing to let myself avert my gaze, whenever trapped and suffering eyes met mine.

"Stop it," said Molly. "Stop punishing yourself."

"I have to wonder," I said. "Just how many souls aren't here to be saved because the Shadow Bank already traded them, to Heaven or to Hell."

"Never feel guilty about the ones you can't save," said Molly. "Be happy for the ones you can. And Eddie, never forget that everyone here . . . is here because they gambled, and lost. They knew the risks they were taking; they knew what they were getting into. They would have been quite happy to take other people's souls as their property, if they'd won."

"They didn't really understand," I said. "How could they? They were tempted; taken advantage of. I say that's wrong and I say the hell with it."

Bruin Bear and the Sea Goat came forward to join us. They stood very close together, staring about them with wide, shocked eyes. They held each other's furry paw, comfortingly. The Goat looked angry; the Bear looked sad. He looked accusingly at me.

"How could you let this go on for so long?"

"I didn't know," I said.

"Your family knew," the Sea Goat said harshly.

"Turns out there's a lot of things they didn't tell me," I said. "Even when I thought I was running things. But I know now. I promised these lost souls that I would set them free before I left, and I will."

"What can we do to help?" said Bruin Bear. "The Horse said we would be needed here, and I think this is why."

"That's why I asked you here," I said. "I can break open the prison gates, but you have to find somewhere for them to go."

"I can do that," said the Bear.

"Then stand ready," I said.

I held up the safe-cracking device the Armourer had given me. The simple black box that could open all locks. He found it for me, locked away in Parris' desk drawer. The Armourer could always find the things he'd made; he said they spoke to him, and I was inclined to believe him. The Armourer always did good work. I held the thing up, and then slammed it against the corridor wall. And the whole place exploded in a blast of almost unbearable light and sound. The walls cracked and flew apart, the glass in every frame broke and shattered, and thousands of trapped souls burst back into the world, free at last.

When the sound and fury died down, I was standing on top of a grassy hill under a night sky packed with stars and moons. There was no sign of the corridor anywhere, or any other part of the hotel. Molly stood to one side of me, Bruin Bear and the Sea Goat on the other. And we all looked up into the night sky with wide mouths and wondering eyes. Newly released souls flew back and forth, shooting this way and that like shimmering comets. They rose and fell, danced around each other, wheeled with unconcealed joy like shimmering Catherine wheels, flying free at last. The night sky was full of shining souls, blazing brighter than any moon. Molly clapped her hands, and jumped up and down on the spot. Bruin Bear and the Sea Goat danced together, stamping their feet down hard on the purple-tinged grass. And I stood very still, looking and looking. I hadn't realised just how many trapped souls there'd been, and I couldn't believe I'd waited one minute longer to free them than was absolutely necessary. I felt Molly's arm slip through mine as she hugged herself up against me.

"All right," she said. "Every now and again, you do something right. So right, even I can't find a way to knock it. Look at them go!"

"I promised them," I said.

"Of course you did," said Molly. "You're that sort of Drood."

In the end, Bruin Bear stepped forward and raised his voice to address the souls in the sky. And just like that, they heard him, and stopped. They came down to stand before him in shimmering rows of human forms—thousands of them, blazing in the dark, brighter than stars. Bruin Bear looked fondly on them and when he spoke, they listened.

"There is a town where dreams go to die," he said. "Where nightmares end, and hope itself can rest. Where all stories find their endings, and every lost soul finds its way home, at last. Come with me, my friends, to Shadows Fall. And I promise you, I will help you all find your way to whatever place is waiting for you."

"Or, we'll find a way for you to stay on, in Shadows Fall," said the Sea Goat. "In the place where legends go to die, when the world stops believing in them. It's a fun place to live . . . or die . . . or be something else. I'm an expert at being something else."

Bruin Bear waved a single small paw, and a great door opened in the night. A warm restful Light spilled through it, pushing back the dark. A Light that said *Come home. Come home.* The Bear and the Goat led the way through the door, and all the returned souls followed them through. And when the last glimmering figure had passed through, the door closed, and the Light shut off. The night was very still and very quiet and very empty. Molly and I were left alone, together, on top of the hill. And the lights in the sky were only stars.

After a while, I turned to look at Molly. "I promised I'd set them free. And I promised you . . . that I'd get you answers. About my grandfather the Regent, and the full truth about how your parents died. The truth, the whole truth, wherever it takes us."

"I know," said Molly. "I never doubted you, Eddie. You are the only thing in my life that I can always rely on."

"Really?" I said. "That's how I feel about you. Come on; let's get back to London and the Department of the Uncanny so we can start slamming people up against walls until they start telling us things we need to know."

"I thought . . . I wanted the truth more than anything," Molly said slowly. "But now I'm not so sure. I don't want to separate you from your grandfather, not after you just got him back again. I think that would be cruel. I can live without all the truth."

"No, you can't," I said. "And neither can I."

I took her in my arms and we held each other like we'd never let go. But eventually we did and we stood together, looking out into the empty night.

"I suppose my soul was in there, somewhere," I said. "Can't say I felt it return. Mind you, I didn't feel it go in the first place."

"I don't think they ever really had it, or your parents'," said Molly. "They just had a claim. All sorts have had a claim on my soul, for years."

I looked at her thoughtfully. "I'm going to have to do something about that. . . ."

"Sufficient unto the day are the trials thereof," said Molly. "Let's go home."

"You've seen me as Eddie," I said. "And as Shaman. So, who do you prefer?"

Molly kissed me unhurriedly. "I love you, you idiot. We're all . . . just who we have to be. Now, how are we getting home?"

"I arranged for someone to give us a lift," I said.

There was the sound of pounding hooves on the night, drawing near, and then a loud neigh. I looked around, with Molly, and there was the White Horse, shining in the night. Ready to take us home. It's good to have friends.

Shaman Bond
Will Return
in
PROPERTY OF
A LADY FAIRE

Want to connect with fellow science fiction and fantasy fans?

For news on all your favorite Ace and Roc authors, sneak peeks into the newest releases, book giveaways, and much more—

"Like" Ace and Roc Books on Facebook!

facebook.com/AceRocBooks